Arcane

The Arinthian Line: Book One

SEVER BRONNY

This book is a work of fiction. Names, characters, places and incidents either are the product of the author's imagination or are used fictitiously, and any similarity to actual persons, living or deceased, establishments of any kind, events, or locales is entirely coincidental.

Library and Archives Canada Cataloguing in Publication

Bronny, Sever, 1979-, author
      Arcane / Sever Bronny.

(The Arinthian line ; book 1)
Issued in print and electronic formats.
ISBN 978-0-9937676-0-9 (pbk.).--ISBN 978-0-9937676-1-6 (ebook)

      I. Title.

PS8603.R652A93 2014   jC813'.6

C2014-902405-3
C2014-902406-1

Version 1.3

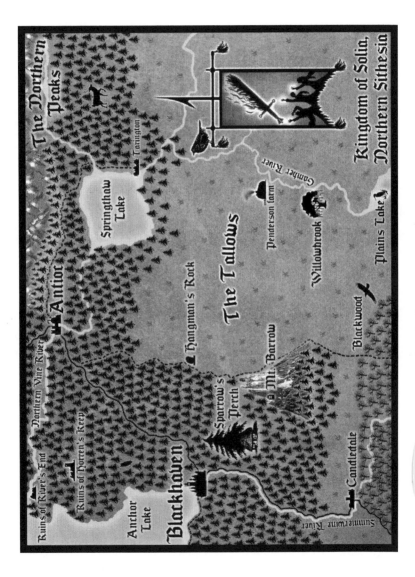

WILLOWBROOK

Augum picked up a wooden bucket and splashed the stallion. Its coarse chestnut hair gleamed in the afternoon sun as water dripped to the arid dirt. He imagined it hissing like kettle water spilling on a cook fire.

He grabbed the brush and began scrubbing, hands aching from splitting wood all day. That morning, Sir Westwood had bought two rough cords from a passing merchant, so while almost every Willowbrook youth swam the Gamber, Augum had spent his time hacking at dry oak.

It was late in the season and there should be snow everywhere. Instead, the horizon quivered and cicadas filled the air with a thick buzz, slowing his thoughts to the speed of molasses.

His eyes flicked to the unmoving waist-high grass beyond a cluster of huts with cracked earthen walls and thatched roofs. The grass stretched endlessly, a placid yellow ocean broken only by crooked fencing, tilled pastures, and the occasional willow tree. Sweaty men flogged teams of oxen, trying to squeeze in one more planting of quickroot before the snows buried their exertions. Horses milled near each other, heads low as they grazed. Fat hogs sat unmoving in the shade of a gray barn. A distant clanging rang out as the smith shaped iron.

There was a wooden creak. Augum turned to find Sir Tobias Westwood standing at the plank door of their home, mop of curly gray hair shining with sweat, wheat dangling from his mouth. His leathery face creased as he squinted against the blazing sun.

"Finished yet?"

"No Sir, not yet."

Sir Westwood scratched at his stubble and spat on the ground. "You can have a swim after. When you return, we shall study the written word."

"Yes, Sir." Augum wiped his brow as the old knight went back inside. He resumed washing the horse, hoping Sir Westwood would forego sword training tonight. By the time he finished, a wavering crimson sun kissed the horizon.

A voice fought its way through the hot air. "Hear ye, hear ye! Read the latest on the scourge known as the Legion! Two coppers for the Blackhaven Herald!"

Augum raised his wiry frame on tiptoes to glance over the horse's back. A gaggle of dirty children mobbed a dark-skinned boy of about fourteen—the same age as Augum. Women in aprons and men in muddy boots rushed forward. Voices called after the boy.

"What news already, herald?"

"Tell us the Lord of the Legion spares us common folk, we don't have none witches here!"

"We have not the money or the tongue, just speak it, boy!"

Augum groaned. He knew what this meant. They will all come over to have Sir Westwood read it aloud to them because he was one of only a handful in Willowbrook that could read.

One time the herald had come when Sir Westwood was away on a hunting trip, so the villagers made Augum do the reading instead, enjoying his nervous stuttering. Augum could read well, it was just having all those hostile and impatient eyes on him that made it difficult.

Sir Westwood approached Augum holding two coppers. He grimaced. "This I do not like. He comes too soon," and handed Augum the coins. Augum stepped before their hut and waited.

When the herald saw him, he rushed over with a crooked smile, exchanging the coins for a rolled parchment. He then strode off, continuing his entreaties, while the crowd remained behind.

A hunched man with one eye made an impatient gesture. "Well read it already, you daft boy!"

"Read it, gutterborn piglet!" Dap said. He was sixteen with a wide face and a neck as thick as the boars he butchered.

The crowd chuckled.

Sir Westwood stepped beside Augum, brows crossed like two swords. "Dap, if you do not want to feel the back of my hand, you will not repeat those words. I have told you many a time, we do not know where Augum was born."

"Yeah well, he *is* a bastard orphan then, ain't he? And ain't that mean he *is* gutterborn? I mean, look at him, he has that ugly gutterborn face, them gutterborn hands—heck, he ain't even have no friends—"

The part about friends had struck a nerve and Augum shot forward like a viper. After all, Dap had ensured he could not make any in Willowbrook, mostly by making up stories, like the one about him being raised by stray dogs.

Like many times before, Dap's beefy arms grabbed Augum and threw him to the ground like a sack of coal. His hammy fist immediately began ramming into Augum's face, until Sir Westwood pried the two apart.

"Go on home, Dap, else I take the proclamation and read it to myself."

The crowd, who seemed to have enjoyed the pounding Augum took, grumbled in disappointment.

"Best go on home to your pappy, boy," the one-eyed man said at last. "We needs to hear the news."

Dap scowled and gave Augum a pointed look. "I'll see *you* later."

Augum spat blood onto the dirt as he shrugged off help from Sir Westwood. "Can't wait." He knew he was in for it now. It was just a matter of time before Dap and his cronies found him and beat him raw. He was their entertainment. He fought them, sure, but there were always so many, and he could not exactly run to Sir Westwood every time he had a bruised face or a torn tunic. Sir Westwood knew of course, but the old knight said nothing, instead choosing to train Augum how to defend himself using a sword and the written word.

Unfortunately, knowing how to swing a sword was useless against a boy like Dap, who was a far better swordsman. Like most other boys in Willowbrook, Dap had held a blade before he could walk, whereas Augum first gripped the pommel of a wooden practice sword only after Sir Westwood took him in, and he hardly had a knack for it.

As for the written word, it was only good for more beatings. Showing even the tiniest bit of smarts led to calls of putting on airs or witchery, even from adults. Thus, he had learned to play dumb. It was better not to say too much.

All his life, someone had picked on him, and always because he was the odd one out, the stranger, the *gutterborn orphan*. No part of him ever accepted it though. He believed there was more to his destiny than serving as a whipping boy. At night, he dreamt of riding a stallion into battle with a great silver lance, a crowd of girls looking on with adoring eyes; and even though they may not be real, he dreamed of being a magician too—or witch, or whatever they called people that could fight with their mind. Regardless of who he was in his dreams, he always had plenty of courage, honor, wit and friends—especially friends, for he had yet to make even one.

Sir Westwood picked up the parchment from the ground and shoved it into Augum's hands. "Read it."

Augum wiped the blood from his nose with the sleeve of his red and yellow tunic, the royal colors of King Ridian, Sir Westwood's liege. He held up the parchment before him, trying to ignore his throbbing cheek, the one Dap had concentrated on smashing. Loopy characters slanted sharply, as if the scribe had been in a great hurry to pass on the news.

" 'Let it be known,' " Augum began reading aloud, " 'that the Blackhaven high council declares the rule of King Ridian the Third contrary to the interests of Solia—' "

The crowd gasped and exchanged anxious looks. Sir Westwood's face darkened.

" 'Therefore,' " Augum continued, " 'King Ridian is hereby stripped of all his titles and lands, as are those loyal to him still. With this proclamation, the council disbands itself and submits its will to Lord Sparkstone and his great army, the Legion. All hail the Lord of the Legion, our new master, savior and king.' "

There was silence.

"Is that all there is, boy?" the one-eyed man asked.

Augum turned the parchment so they could see. "Yes."

"Then we best prepare …"

The crowd dispersed, muttering amongst themselves. A few even ran.

Augum watched them go. "Prepare for what, Sir?"

Sir Westwood spat on the ground and took the proclamation from Augum. He stared at it. "For the inevitable." His eyes searched the horizon, stopping on a spot to the north.

"But they wouldn't come right this—" Augum's throat tightened as his eyes fell upon the same spot.

What was that?

He ran over to his favorite willow tree behind the hut and scrambled up its thick trunk. Men from the fields had already begun sounding the alert. Bells rang and pots banged all over Willowbrook. Barefoot children cried as their mothers scooped them up, running towards the Gamber.

He placed a hand over his eyes and squinted. It was a cloud … *a cloud of charging knights*—the herald's news was old!

"Climb down, Augum." Sir Westwood, bathed in the crimson light of dusk, was strapping on a battered breastplate. His sword dangled in its sheath on his hip. He held Augum's woolen coat under his arm.

Augum grabbed a handful of the willow's drooping branches and swung off like one of those tree-living beasts he had read about in Sir Westwood's books. The knight bent a knee and gripped him by the shoulders, looking up with stern yet kind eyes.

"Augum, if I were to choose a son, I would choose no other. You have been a faithful squire, but you cannot take part in that which comes."

Augum began to shake his head. "No, Sir, you can't leave me behind—"

"Look at me. It is my duty. Courage, Augum, courage. Now, the crowd will run east to the river. The soldiers will likely follow. That is why you shall travel west across the Tallows. I have thrown together a sack of journey bread, salted beef and two skins of water. Take it before you go. You are not to return, understand?"

Augum saw Sir Westwood's lips moving but the blood rushing through his head prevented him from understanding the words. "I'm going with you, Sir. Give me a sword and—"

"No. You are not ready, nor are you able. I shall not have you slaughtered in the field like so many before you. This is the Legion, Augum, *the Legion*. I have seen what they are capable of, and you are not to see that for yourself, not yet!"

Sir Westwood's gaze travelled beyond Augum. "I have been waiting for this a long time."

Augum opened his mouth to protest just as a fireball mushroomed into the sky from the far end of the village. He instinctively clutched at Sir Westwood, but the knight gently pried Augum's hands away, placing the coat around Augum's shoulders. Sir Westwood then mounted his horse and, with one last look, galloped off toward the flames.

Augum stood breathing rapidly, watching the back of the only person that had ever cared about him ride off to certain death.

Suddenly something huge smacked into his back, sending him flying through a wooden fence. A tiny piglet squealed and scampered through the hole, only to be kicked by Dap, his face contorting with victorious glee. The piglet landed near Augum and went still.

"Told you I'd get you—"

Augum barely had time to shield his head before the rain of punches began.

"And this one's for being smart—" Dap raised his fist just as a black-armored soldier in a pot helm careened through the fence, scattering chickens like a shark in a school of fish.

Dap, who was still sitting on Augum, raised his arms. "Wait, I'm one of you—"

The soldier did not break stride; a viciously large ball and chain flail whistled through the air, smashing into Dap's chest. Dap fell back with a sickening gurgle. The towering soldier placed an iron boot against Dap's hulking loaf of a body and yanked his weapon free.

Augum scrambled away as the spiked ball whistled by his ear, lodging into a fencepost with a smack. He ran around the corner of the house only to see a score of black-armored knights riding straight at him. He raced across to the other homes, listening as screams and shouts of attack filled the air.

The invaders were swarming through the village now. This was it; he had to either find Sir Westwood or flee.

The group of knights galloped past, giving him one last opportunity to escape to the Tallows. He swallowed hard and took another look.

There were too many, it was no use.

"I'm so sorry, Sir," he mumbled before making a run for it, not stopping until he was well outside the outer fence. There, hiding in the grass, Augum watched Willowbrook burn.

THE STORM

Augum headed westward when the soldiers began combing the fields with torches. He glanced back only once, and that was to engrave the image of the towering inferno into his mind. An occasional scream still punctured the night.

He walked on and on, eyes glazed, hands limp. The stars sparkled clearer than a still pond; he scarcely gave them any attention. Eventually, numb from exhaustion, he curled up among the tall grass, holding his legs close.

He barely slept.

Augum trudged that vast plain for three days and nights without food or water, having forgotten the sack of provisions Sir Westwood had thoughtfully prepared for him. He wore through his leather turnshoes, pushing his wiry frame to endure. Each night was cooler than the one before, as if winter itself hounded him along with those black-armored soldiers.

On the eve of the third day, black clouds raced overhead as a coarse wind pushed on his back, making waves in the ocean of waist-high grass. Lips cracked, mouth dry as parchment, he felt as if the sole purpose of his existence was to keep placing one foot before the other.

His thoughts drifted idly. Sometimes he pictured Sir Westwood alive and well. At other times, he envisioned him slumped over in a pool of his own blood, like fat Dap.

His heart panged. The old knight had been a strict but fair man, very different from the foster family Augum had previously lived with, the Pendersons.

The Pendersons … even thinking about them made his teeth clench. He glanced down at his cracked hands, remembering how blistered and bloody they would get as he toiled in their field. The longer he stared, the more he remembered, until a dirt farm and young corn stalks appeared before him. He looked up to find Meli, that old wretched mule, standing before him on wobbly legs. She was his only companion, occasionally sharing Mr. Penderson's lashing. He winced, recalling how that same whip would flash across his back, splitting open the skin like an overripe tomato.

Suddenly someone shoved him to the dirt.

"Hey Gutter—why you always falling down?" Garth Penderson asked.

Augum placed a hand between his eyes and the hot summer sun. "I need to get to pickin' cause—"

Garth burped loudly before Augum could explain how Mrs. Penderson would not let him eat until Meli's packs were full of corn. Garth's brother, Buck, and his sister, Wyza, cackled in support. All three shared the same muscular physique, flaming Penderson hair and identical ponytail. Garth was older than Augum by three years, Buck by two, and Wyza by one.

"Then why is you sitting there like some lazy dog?"

Augum stumbled to his feet. Meli glanced at him with tired red eyes. She was probably thirstier than he was. He needed to get to the well—

A blinding pain splashed across his face. His eyes immediately began to water from the slap.

Garth dusted off his hands. "You best answer when I talk, Gutter."

Buck's ruddy cheeks puffed out with a grin. "Dumber than a cow."

Wyza kicked the old mule. "Dumber than this here ass!"

Augum moved between Meli and the brats. "You leave Meli alone!"

Garth pushed him back down into the dirt with a lazy hand, a wicked smile playing across his lips. "Don't cry now, we is not going to do nothin' to this useless old mule." Suddenly he reared back and clobbered Meli with his fist. The animal fell to the ground, braying, as corn spilled into the dirt.

The brats roared with laughter as Augum dropped to help Meli. He tenderly smoothed her mangy hair before trying to help her stand, but she was too weak and kicked feebly at the air.

Mrs. Penderson's screeching voice floated over from the farmhouse. "Wyza? Buck? Garth? What you doing over there with that stupid boy!"

Garth rolled his eyes. "Nothing, Ma!"

"I need that corn picked, you hear?"

"Yes, Ma!"

"Tell that gutterborn trash to hustle up!"

Garth squatted down before Augum. His chin dropped as his neck bulged. A moment later, he belched a burp of rotten onion into Augum's face. Wyza and Buck laughed.

"You heard her, Gutter," Garth said, ignoring his siblings. "Get going, we needs you pickin'." His pig eyes swiveled to the spilled corn. "And by the looks of it, you ain't going to be eating for a while."

Augum's vision blurred. Suddenly the brats were gone and it was raining. Beside him, Mr. Penderson jerked at a leek, dropping it into one of Meli's pouches, muttering to himself all the while.

Augum somehow knew what was about to happen. The dread ate at his stomach. He reached out to her, wanting to tell her everything would be all right, that he would protect her—yet just before his hand touched her hide, Meli collapsed, leeks tumbling to the mud.

He scrambled to pick them up. "Mr. Penderson, I'll clean it right away, no need to get angry—"

"Don't be talking back to me, boy!"

The punch was harder than usual, doubling Augum over. With it came the stench of strong wine from the man's breath. Mr. Penderson loosened the whip hanging from his belt and wacked the animal across the snout. Meli only made a quiet whine.

"No, Mr. Penderson, please—!" but even when Augum lunged across the animal to protect her with his own body, Mr. Penderson did not stop, lashing boy and mule alike.

"You're killing her! Stop, Mr. Penderson, stop—!" Augum kept shouting between his own cries of pain.

Mr. Penderson did eventually stop, but only because he had winded himself. "You deserve each other," he spat, and weaved back to the house.

Augum lay with Meli, shoulders heaving. Her flank had long ceased rising.

Now there was nothing holding him there.

"I'm leaving, Meli," he whispered, lovingly stroking her neck. "Just like we've always said. I'm sorry you can't come with me." He gently closed her eyes, rose, and turned toward the Gamber, never looking back.

He had followed that winding river south until stumbling upon the village of Willowbrook, where an old knight by the name of Sir Tobias Westwood found him lying hungry and bloody by its banks. He took Augum in, fed and clothed him, and made him his squire.

Before long, life grew routine. Augum's hands browned from oiling and polishing Sir Westwood's armor. His tunic was constantly soaked from scrubbing the knight's stallion, the planks, the iron pots, the trestle table and benches. At night, he ached from the day's riding, straw prickling at his scalp. Splinters stung his hands from training with a wooden sword. He smelled like roast chicken, turkey, rabbit, boar or venison after learning how to cook. He sunburned tending to Sir Westwood's garden, chickens, geese and pigs. The wounds on his back slowly healed, leaving permanent ridged scars he would sometimes trace with a finger, scars that never stopped itching.

Sometimes Sir Westwood took him hunting, and Augum's elbow would be raw from constantly catching the sinew bowstring. The old knight made Augum taste bitter and sweet plants, pointing out which ones were edible; taught him how to locate north using tree moss; tired him out lecturing about chivalry, heraldry, and the basic etiquette required of a noble in court.

But Sir Westwood had been most particular about the written word, proclaiming that a knight who could not read or write was at the mercy of those who could. Thus, Augum often stayed up late, quill in hand, fingers stained with ink, copying dusty tomes. *Castle Stewardship, Arithmetic of the Treasury, On Horsemanship, The Joust,* and the like. Some had sunk in, most had not.

Sir Westwood also taught him how to speak properly. "Am not" instead of "Ain't." "We are not" instead of "We isn't." The Penderson drawl was patiently but methodically corrected at every turn. It was how the highborn city folk spoke. Sir Westwood was liberal when it came to more modern youthful contractions, however, as long as they were from the city.

Remembering those happy times with Sir Westwood warmed Augum's heart and made it easy to forget where he really was.

He stopped and glanced about. The tall yellow grass of the Tallows lashed at his hands as if possessed by the spirit of Mr. Penderson. The wind had increased during his reminiscence and he had not even noticed. Cold rain pelted his face, stinging his eyes. The clouds overhead were as dark as a Penderson heart.

Suddenly the grass flattened as a strong gust knocked him to the ground. His woolen coat shot over his head, choking and dragging him like a sail attached to his neck. He fumbled with the collar, only to discover he was too weak to undo it.

He gurgled what he thought was his last breath when there was an abrupt tearing sound. The coat ripped away, exposing his face to a torrent of icy needle rain. Gasping, he curled up into a ball, already shivering from the cold seeping through his clothes.

A mule hee-hawed. When he looked up, the Penderson brats had him surrounded, ponytails flapping in the wind, cruel grins on their ruddy faces.

"You is damn stupid, Gutter." Garth's wide fist reared back as Augum feebly rolled away, only to find Mr. Penderson standing before him, a giant bottle of wine in one hand, whip in the other.

The farmer took a long swig and wiped his mouth with an oily sleeve. "You done wrong, boy." The whip uncoiled like a viper.

"I ain't done nothin' …" Augum pulled on the grass, scrambling to get away, only to stumble across Dap's bloody body. A black-armored soldier stood just behind, wielding a spiked ball and chain flail, face obscured by a pot helm.

"No …" Augum tried to move back, but a great stallion blocked his path. It snorted and reared up, exposing a rotten ribcage, and bony thorns where there should have been hooves. The Penderson brats closed in from his left. Their father, whip snaking, from Augum's right. Behind Augum came the whistle of a flail. He raised his hands in defense and screamed, until exhaustion overcame all sense and he collapsed, succumbing to nightmares as turbulent as the rain.

It was pitch-dark when awareness returned. The grass whipped his numb face as the storm raged about him. His soaked tunic snagged on the dirt as the enemy dragged him along the ground.

"Please, sir, just leave me alone ..."

The wind moaned as Augum felt his body suddenly lighten. Had the soldier thrown him? His stomach lurched from the weightless sensation, yet the anticipated crash back to the ground did not come.

Lightning burst across the clouds, fanning out like a great spider web, making visible something Augum struggled to make sense of—yellow grass far below him. The ensuing crack of thunder rattled his innards and amplified the nausea.

It's only a nightmare, he thought frantically, it's only a nightmare ... yet every subsequent flash confirmed the unbelievable—that he was indeed flying.

Then, amidst the spearing flashes, he glimpsed an enormous mass of jagged rock, the top of which disappeared in cloud. The wind increased to a shriek as he hurtled towards the behemoth, slowly losing consciousness from tumbling end over end. With the tunnel of darkness closing in, Augum felt a final searing light illuminate his entire being. A warm glow settled over his heart, and as it faded away, so too did he.

MRS. STONE

Augum startled awake, forehead beaded with sweat. Feeling soft linen sheets beneath him, he sighed in relief, thinking what a vivid nightmare that had all been. He should probably get up and feed the horse …

He rubbed the sleep from his eyes, yet when his vision adjusted to the dim light, nothing looked familiar. He lay on an old bed in a cave-like room, dressed in a patched nightgown. Opposite was a heavy door with an iron handle. Beside it, a battered chest of drawers. Shelves stuffed with books and scrolls towered along the walls. Candles flickered from hollows in between. The scent of earth mingled with the smell of old books.

He searched his mind, trying to piece together where he was and what had happened. Like a moth, his eyes kept returning to the candles.

Fire …

Gods, no ... Willowbrook burning, the journey across the Tallows, the storm—it had all been real! Maybe the Unnameables took him and he was in some kind of afterlife. He pinched himself and felt pain; inspected for signs of trauma—no cuts, no bruises.

Augum went still. "Hello—?"

Other than his thundering heart, there was only silence. He nervously chewed on a finger, an old habit neither the Pendersons nor Sir Westwood had broken.

"Hello? Anybody there—?" A candle sputtered as if troubled by his voice.

Shuffling came from the other side of the door. He tensed as the handle turned with a squeak. A hunched woman in a sparkling white robe entered. One hand clutched a withered candle, the other a wooden staff capped with a crystal orb. Long silver hair fell around a face creased with a hundred years of time.

She stood examining him with bright blue eyes, grunted, and approached. Her robe shimmered with embroidered silver lions, birds, a castle, and lightning—*did the bolts just flash*?

Augum shrank away as she took a seat beside him on the straw-filled mattress.

"Well now, my child, I see you have awakened. How do you feel?" her voice sounded like wheezing bellows.

He eyed the door and gulped; he could make a run for it if he had to.

"Manners, child, manners. Surely you can speak."

"I ..."

Her silver brows rose. "Hmm?"

"I feel better, my lady ... I think. But where am I?"

"You are in my home, and I daresay you are one lucky boy. Or perhaps ... unlucky, as it were?" She leaned in a little and he caught the faint scent of rosemary. "And just what was a boy like you thinking, travelling in such unkind weather, hmm? Trying to get to the other side of death, were we?"

"The Legion burned my village, my lady, so I escaped across the Tallows. Then I was caught in a storm and ... and ..." His eyes unfocused trying to piece it all together. The memories were so ... unbelievable. He remembered soaring through the air, flashes of lightning, and something huge, darker than the night.

He should have died out there, he realized, if not from smashing into the ground, then from starvation or from the cold. He looked into her eyes, wondering if she was the reason he was alive.

"I'm ... I'm grateful. Thank you."

Her wrinkled face remained impassive.

He tugged at the frilly sleeve of his nightgown. "What happened to my tunic?"

"Burnt to a crisp and quite beyond repair, I daresay. But never you mind that—let us begin with names."

He blinked. Burnt? Why burnt?

She gazed at him expectantly.

"Augum, my lady. My name is Augum."

Her brows rose slightly. "Augum. Indeed. And what is your surname?"

"Orphans don't have last names, my lady. I was squire to Sir Westwood in Willowbrook—before it was razed that is." He scratched his head. "If that even happened, I'm not quite sure what's going on ..."

"I see. So you were training to become a knight."

"Yes, my lady."

"Enough of this 'my lady' business—Mrs. Stone will do just fine."

"Yes, my—err—Mrs. Stone."

The candle sputtered out. She glanced at it as a mother would at a misbehaving child and it immediately flared back to life. "And what do you know of the Legion?" she asked, still staring at the candle, perhaps daring it to disobey.

Augum recalled standing from afar, face hot from the heat of the blaze; the willows burning, their tendril branches flailing as if in agony; embers swirling like fireflies; black-armored men chasing screaming people. The smell of oil and thatch and animals ...

"They're butchers led by a man who calls himself Lord Sparkstone ..." a man rumored to be doing unspeakable things, ancient rituals testing the bounds of life and death; dark witchery the peasants feared and only whispered about.

"How old are you, child?"

"Fourteen.

"Two years from a man."

"One year and a couple of months."

She groaned, used her staff to stand, and padded to the door. There she stopped, face concealed in shadow. "Once again our brittle kingdom falls under the spell of ambition. King Ridian was old, perhaps unable to keep up with the many youthful intrigues that follow kings like flies follow lions. The royal court has always been a dangerous place."

She sighed and faced him. "You have been through much, child. I present you a choice—I can take you on to the next village, or—"

"Or—?"

"Or you can stay here with me, help around the home and, should you show the proper attitude ... become my apprentice."

What did she mean? Apprentice in what?

"It is rude to gape."

Augum closed his mouth, but the puzzled expression remained.

Mrs. Stone grunted and left. "No need to choose right away," she said from the corridor. "I find decisions are best made on a full stomach. Come. Breakfast."

"Breakfast? Is it morning—?"

LIGHTNING

Beyond Augum's room was a roughly hewn rocky corridor. The right led to another bedroom, the left a cavernous living room where Mrs. Stone shuffled past what appeared to be a mountain of books and scrolls. He entered to find her fussing over a kettle.

A small fire crackled in a rocky hearth to his left. Cookware and large copper ladles hung on the wall above. A rustic rocking chair sat in front, a thick book and pair of spectacles on its seat. Embedded into the far wall was an iron-fitted oaken door, flanked by a pair of round, leaded-glass windows.

In the middle of the room sat an old carved settee, pieces of parchment strewn on its faded rose cushions. Two armchairs sat opposite, along with a low tree-trunk table, inkbottle and peacock quill on top. Candles flickered in sunken hollows between shelves of all shapes and sizes. The shelves overflowed with hourglasses, stoppered vials, dry herbs, scrolls, books, and what appeared to be jars of multicolored drying sand.

He eyed the peacock quill and concluded she had to be a scribe.

Mrs. Stone pushed aside a pile of cloth and pulled open a small door, revealing a pantry filled with an abundance of carrots, onions, garlic, leeks, radishes and potatoes. Sacks of beans, lentils, and various grains sat lumped together. There were dried meats, hanging herbs, and jars of roots and spices he did not recognize. It was a rich stock; she had to be a wealthy scribe.

"As you have probably gathered," she said over her shoulder, "I have not received a guest in some time. Take a seat at the table."

He realized she meant the mountain of books and scrolls, and pushed some of it aside, uncovering a battered round table. As he fought the pile for a chair, something on the wall caught his attention.

"Mrs. Stone, what's that?" He pointed at a short sword and scabbard hanging by a window. It sparked occasionally, a most unusual thing for a sword to do.

"None of your concern, child," she said without turning around.

He marveled at the blade, imagining striking a black-armored villain with it, until his wandering eyes rested on a tome sitting high on a shelf. It was bound in vivid blue leather and ornately gilded, as if made for royalty—probably the most extravagant object he had ever laid eyes on. Sir Westwood had quite a few books, but nothing like this one.

Just as he was going to inquire about it, Mrs. Stone turned around with an armful of red radishes, carrots, apples and a loaf of bread.

"Perhaps you could stop being so curious and give me a hand."

He rushed to take them from her, placing the food on the table.

She gestured at a particularly grumpy-looking carrot. "These are from Antioc."

Augum was too hungry to care and began wolfing it down. He had always been a fast eater anyway, learning that the longer he sat with the Pendersons, the higher the chance of garnering their attention.

"Slow down, child, and you might taste something."

Augum made a show of patience, yet as soon as she turned her back, he gobbled down an apple and two chunks of bread. Midway through an eye-watering radish, a strong gust of wind rattled the windows. Shadows danced as candles flickered in response. A flash lit up the room, followed by the low rumble of thunder. It brought distant yellow grass to mind along with the stomach-churning sensation of falling.

He dropped the radish, no longer hungry.

Mrs. Stone glanced at the tempest through the leaded glass. "By all rights that storm should have killed you."

He stared at the table, unsure how to reply.

"Humph." She fetched the kettle from the hearth, fixed two mugs of lemon and honey tea, handed him one, and sat down in the rocker by the fire. The pelt of rain increased against the windows.

Augum took a sip, savoring the bittersweet taste. He glanced about; the place could feel like home, and a scribe's life *had* to be better than a wandering orphan's. Besides, where else was he to go?

"Mrs. Stone—?"

"Mmm?"

"I think I'd like to stay with you."

She rocked slowly. "So be it." Her gaze did not leave the fire, though he thought he saw the corner of her mouth briefly twitch upward in a smile.

"But Mrs. Stone, um, what did you mean when you said I could become your apprentice?"

"Mercy, needlessly daft," she muttered. "Have you not figured out why your clothes had burned, yet you yourself remain unharmed?"

Augum flinched as a bolt struck close by, illuminating the cavern. The crack of thunder rumbled through the room. He saw himself tumbling; a final bright flash …

"Can't be …"

"Oh, it can, my dear child. It is rare, but a person's talents can awaken like that. Few could be struck by lightning and still live, yet you do not have a mark on you." The rocker creaked as she turned to fix him with a piercing gaze. "You may be predisposed to a discipline, though it may not be knighthood as Sir Westwood had hoped. Tomorrow morning you will take the first of three tests. Should you pass them all, I shall consider your apprenticeship in the warlock element of *lightning*."

Augum felt the hairs on the back of his neck rise. "Lightning …" he whispered as thunder trailed distantly. He had always believed there was more to life than tilling the land, or wearing armor and swinging a sword—but was she talking about witchery? In the isolated places he had grown up—the Penderson farm and Willowbrook—people never saw witches, tricksters or magicians. They only accused others of the practice; or in Augum's case, used the term as an insult. The Pendersons said it was all parlor tricks, while Sir Westwood, a proud knight attached to the way of the sword, stayed quiet on the matter.

Although Sir Westwood held nothing but disdain for peasant superstition, he nonetheless alluded to other forces in his stories. When Augum asked him to elaborate, the knight answered with, "Some things are better left unsaid in small villages."

Augum heard other campfire tales too, from the children, from men when they had imbibed too much ale, or from village elders—but only when they thought he was not listening. There were whispers of men moving things with their minds and women controlling the skies. Yet despite the threats warning how any such activity would result in being burned alive at the stake, Augum's gut told him there was something authentic about Mrs. Stone.

He tensed, but the question had to be asked. "Mrs. Stone, are you a witch?"

She gave him a hard look. "Superstition is not welcome here, child."

"Yes, Mrs. Stone." He wrung his hands, secretly relieved. "So the stories were true …"

"Stories … humph." Mrs. Stone turned back to the fire to sip her tea. "Many years have passed since I had an apprentice, Augum. You will have to work very hard. I will not go easy on you."

"I understand, Mrs. Stone."

She raised a crooked finger. "No, you do not, not yet. Like many others, you may perish in training. The lightning element is the most dangerous of them all. You will have to be strong, determined and brave. You will have to withstand a lot of pain."

Augum felt a tingling as memories surfaced—Mr. Penderson caning him for being too tired and hungry to finish the day's plowing; Mrs. Penderson slapping him in a silent room while the rest of the family watched with smug faces; hiding in a tree like a coward while the brats called, "Here Gutter, here boy!"

Withstand a lot of pain …

He cupped the mug with both hands, feeling its warmth. "Is lightning your discipline too, Mrs. Stone?"

"Lightning is my *element* within the arcane *discipline*, but you shall understand all that later. Now, since you will be living here, you will assume duties. The first thing you will do is clean your bedroom."

"Clean my bedroom—?"

Mrs. Stone's eyes narrowed. "I will not stand for impudence, is that clear?"

He had not intended to be impudent, he was just surprised. "Yes …"

"*Yes, Mrs. Stone.*"

"Yes, Mrs. Stone."

She stood up, found her staff and leaned on it for support while ambling to her room.

Augum finished his tea, wondering where she lived. Was this cave-like place in a village? Were there other warlocks or apprentices near? The thought made him race to one of the windows, but it was too stormy to see anything.

The heavy oaken door rattled from a strong gust. He pondered opening it but changed his mind after realizing the wind would scatter all those scrolls, and he did not want to get in trouble so quickly into his stay. Instead, he headed to his room to begin cleaning.

He started with the shelves, studying the items as he went along. Most of the tomes were written in cryptic gibberish, the rest in the common tongue—*An Annotated History of the Academy of Arcane Arts*; *The Four Major Nodian Tribes*; *The Arinthian Chronicles*; *Historical Summations of the Necrotic Plague*, and others. All sounded interesting, and he could not wait to read them, though he wondered if she had any books about adventuring or treasure hunting too.

He carefully dusted each tome, sneaking a peek now and then but understanding little, before lining them up neatly on the shelves. Concentration was difficult; he was still coming to grips with what she had told him—a warlock, how exciting! Yet a part of him remained skeptical. After all, he had yet to see any real magic, and what if she had lied and it really was witchery? Would he be hung, burned at the stake, stoned to death? He had once witnessed a woman being dragged through the muddy streets of Willowbrook by an angry mob just for studying the stars. Sir Westwood had come to her defense, allowing her escape on bare foot. But the old knight could not save them all—Dap used to gloat about witnessing one boy caned to death for reading some "foreign" book.

The day dragged on. Mrs. Stone spent most of it snoozing away or reading in the living room. Sometimes Augum overheard her talking to herself, mumbling in some exotic tongue. In the evening, she appeared at the doorway and glanced about, giving the slightest nod.

"Come. Supper."

They spoke not a single word through the entire meal of cured ham, buttered potatoes, bread, onion soup and blackberries. Spectacles perched on the end of her nose, Mrs. Stone kept busy reading a dense scroll titled *Discussions on Uniting the Councils in Pre-scionic Times*.

Tired of the long silence, Augum decided to ask one of the countless questions on his mind. He cleared his throat in preparation. Mrs. Stone closed her eyes as if begging for patience.

All right, now was not the time, apparently. "Mrs. Stone, um, may I be excused?" he asked instead.

"Mmm."

He slouched off to bed, curious but sleepy. Lying there staring at the cavern ceiling, he wondered what a warlock life would be like. His thoughts turned to Mrs. Stone, eventually twisting into the rugged form of Sir Westwood, his favorite willow, clouds …

THE FIRST TEST

Augum woke to the rough prodding of Mrs. Stone's staff.

"Time to get up. The day must begin with energy—up, up!" She gave him another jab for good measure. "Your new robe is on the dresser. I have also mended your turnshoes. Dress and join me outside."

She departed while he clambered out of bed. He grimaced upon spying the robe, a hideous burgundy with mismatching patches, torn hood, and belt made of frayed rope. After putting it on, he discovered it one size too big, itchy and dusty. Nonetheless, he slipped on his shoes and hurried through the front door, only to gasp at what he saw.

Mrs. Stone's cave was high up on the side of a mountain!

Sharp morning sun shone from behind, casting a gargantuan pyramidal shadow westward. Occasional clouds broke up an azure sky, wispy remnants of the storm. It was windy and the air had the sharp smell of winter. Wet boulders peeked around the lip of the cave entrance. A tiny stream trickled nearby. Wild grasses, brush and scree dotted the mountain below. Near the bottom, the shrubbery graduated to a great forest extending west as far as the eye could see.

From where they stood, he noticed that the mountain straddled where the forest met the Tallows. Soon as he glimpsed that yellow grass, however, his stomach began churning and he had to look away.

Mrs. Stone inhaled deeply while scanning the horizon. "Quite the view is it not?" She seemed taller, younger, firmly holding her staff rather than leaning on it for support. Her long hair hung in a braided silver ponytail down to her waist. Her robe billowed in the wind, glittering even in the shadow of the mountain.

"No one can see this cave, not unless I give them *permission*." She placed her gaze upon him. "Are you ready for your first test?"

He braved a look north at the Tallows; thankfully, the nausea was gone.

"I am, Mrs. Stone." He was more than ready; he was excited!

"Very well." She raised a professorial finger. "Understand the following: spell-casting is like traversing through a thick forest. At first, there is no path and you have to make one. After, the more you tread on this path, the clearer it becomes. This is the first principle. Do you understand?"

"Um, I think so, Mrs. Stone."

"We shall see. Observe those two small stones on the ground there. Without touching them, bring them together."

He gave her a blank look.

"Do you think me a patient woman, child? Now stop wasting time."

He stared at the two stones near the lip of the cave, sitting about a foot apart. He scowled and imagined them hitting each other. Nothing happened. He glanced back at Mrs. Stone.

"Close your mind from distraction. Concentrate, Augum. Feel their attraction, their natural desire to come together."

He closed his eyes and concentrated like never before, groaning from the strain.

"Mercy, child, you will burst if you continue like that, and I said close your mind, not your eyes. Now, it must be natural yet assertive. Try again. Focus!"

He wanted to please her, but above all, yearned to believe moving objects with his mind was possible. He refocused on the stones with all his mental might, body quivering. Nothing happened.

Mrs. Stone sighed, nodded. "Let us leave it there, no sense in carrying on."

"Maybe if you could just show me—"

"No. The belief must come from *you*."

He stared at his feet like a chastened dog; he had failed the test. "I really did try …"

"Stop this nonsense at once, child. You cannot snivel your way to success; the arcane path is hewn with diligence and toil. One must build up strength of mind and character, yet you declare defeat without even having begun." She shook her head. "I expect better; I merely needed to see how developed you are, and my conclusion is we simply have to start from the beginning."

He felt his cheeks tingle.

"Now for your training. The rocks that have built up around the cave—you are to place them twenty paces downhill, and yes, you can use your hands. However, as you move them, notice their natural tendency to want to roll. Feel the attraction between them. Concentrate and build fortitude. Am I being understood?"

Augum gave a hesitant nod. "Yes, Mrs. Stone."

She grunted before disappearing inside.

He glanced at the countless rocks. Some of them looked very heavy, more like boulders. The task appeared extremely difficult, if not impossible. Sighing, he dragged himself over to the first cluster and picked up a large stone, carrying it twenty paces down the slope before trudging back up for another. It was difficult, even dangerous work, as some of the rocks nearly bowled him over in their eagerness to roll down the mountain.

He kept repeating this monotonous task until the door swung open. Mrs. Stone emerged carrying a small basket, setting it down by the lip of the cave before examining the slope. She fixed him with a reproachful look.

"You are struggling. Your attitude is as sour as the look on your face. Fortify your mind, Augum, the work is not physical—it is mental." She gestured impatiently at the basket. "Breakfast. Eat, work, concentrate." The door slammed.

Augum schlepped over to the basket and grabbed two hard-boiled eggs. After devouring them, he pulled out a piece of bread and skin of water. He sat there ripping chunks from the loaf, unable to enjoy the view because he could not make sense of Mrs. Stone's instructions.

After breakfast, he stood up and stretched, trying to re-focus. He set sights on a new boulder and began rolling it downhill. He observed how it tumbled a few feet at a time before he had to give it another push. He repeated this with the next bunch of stones, hoping to sense something, anything. After a while, he lost himself in the laborious rhythm of the work.

At noon, a baking sun shone directly overhead, making him grateful for every cool mountain breeze. Robe itching, he wiped his brow with his sleeve and sat down to admire his work thus far.

The door swung open and Mrs. Stone appeared, squinting. Augum quickly got up as she examined the area. Into the basket, she deposited dry salted meat, a pair of apples and another skin of water, before shuffling back inside.

He walked up to the cave, sat on the lip, and ate his lunch in silence, disappointed she was not impressed with his hard-won efforts. When he finished, he turned his attention to the next pile of rocks, vowing to concentrate even harder this time around.

However, after three more hours of grueling and frustrating toil, he plopped down, panting. What a stupid task …

He picked up a small stone and flung it at a large boulder. It clunked off. He picked up another one and threw it at the same boulder. This time the smaller rock smashed into smithereens. Finding it satisfying, he reached for a third rock when it slid toward his hand a bit.

Goosebumps rose on his arms.

Did that just happen? He reached for it again.

Nothing.

He reached and tried concentrating hard, straining from the effort.

Again, nothing.

"I order you to come to me, you stupid rock!" but the rock did not move.

Augum looked around to see if somebody was playing a trick on him.

Cool mountain winds stirred the shrubs. Probably just his imagination. Time to try something different.

Breathing deep, he took in the beautiful vista, the sound of the wind, and the trickle of the nearby stream. Relaxed, he calmly extended his hand to the rock and made the tiniest beckoning motion, envisioning it coming to him.

It slid forward.

He jumped up and down, whooping and hollering. He could not believe it—he had done the impossible, something straight out of a children's tale! He was so excited that he tripped on his robe and tumbled downhill, stopping in time to see Mrs. Stone watching from the lip of the cave.

"Mrs. Stone, I did it!" he shouted between coughs, "I made a rock move—!"

"Maybe you are not destined to carry rocks around the rest of your life after all. Are you certain you would not prefer tending to people's horses and scrubbing their boots? It is what happens to those that do not progress far in degree."

"No, Mrs. Stone, definitely not!" He stood up and brushed himself off, eager to try again.

"Then you ought to practice. I shall return in a few hours to test you—if I do not see movement, you will be doing this all day tomorrow."

He quickly began on a new pile of rocks and, although he still had to use his hands, was occasionally able to lighten the load with his mind. The amount of mental energy involved was enormous though and he almost preferred the physical labor. Nonetheless, by the end of the day he felt he was beginning to understand the essence of mentally pushing and pulling rocks.

At dusk, Mrs. Stone stepped outside. The dying sun bathed her in crimson light as she drew a shawl around her shoulders. It rippled in the cold wind. "Come up here, Augum."

Shivering, he did as he was told, hoping to pass the test before the first snow. As it was, he had a splitting headache and every muscle was sore.

"Do you feel you have made progress?"

"Yes."

"*Yes, Mrs. Stone.* Now let us see if you have indeed learned something today. Those two stones you failed moving this morning—try moving them again."

Augum gazed upon them with hawk eyes. Furrowing his brow in concentration, he willed them to move.

Nothing happened.

"I see. It appears you will be doing this again tomorrow." She turned to go back in.

"No, wait—! I mean … please wait, Mrs. Stone."

She stopped at the door, sighing.

Augum steeled himself. A moment of silence passed as he stared at the stones dispassionately, seeing them for what they were—two stones he could bend to his will. He calmly raised his arm and made a tiny gesture.

They smashed together, obliterating to smithereens.

He collapsed, head throbbing, a gigantic grin on his face.

Mrs. Stone's silver brows rose as she observed him. "Arcanery consumes energy through focus. The sharper and stronger your mind grows, the less energy you will expend. With practice, your ability to concentrate will improve, allowing you to cast spells of a more complex nature. This is the second principle. Do you understand?"

"Yes, Mrs. Stone."

"You are quick to embrace the path, Augum. Consider yourself lucky. You have passed your first test. I will test you two more times before I decide if you are worthy to be my apprentice." She turned to go.

"Mrs. Stone, wait—what's the name of the spell?"

"Telekinesis. Now, supper awaits." She padded back inside leaving the door slightly ajar.

Telekinesis. A strange word for a strange spell. Then a thrill ran up and down his spine; he actually moved something with his mind!

His stomach groaned as he caught the scent of roasted turkey. If not for his hunger and the biting cold, he would have gladly slept then and there.

He trudged inside, sat at the table and heartily ate spinach, boiled carrot and, of course, a succulent roasted turkey, washing it all down with freshly squeezed orange juice, something he only had once, and in summer. He wondered where Mrs. Stone managed to get fresh oranges, or for that matter, how she even brought food up the mountain. Seeing her immersed in a big book, he decided not to ask.

After another wordless meal, he cleaned up, bid Mrs. Stone good night ("Humph"), and went to bed early, sleeping like a bear in winter.

THE SECOND TEST

Mrs. Stone once again woke Augum by jabbing him with her staff. "Up, up!"

Bleary-eyed, he dressed and proceeded to the table. Mrs. Stone sat sipping spiced tea while reading a piece of parchment. Waiting at his place was a plate of bacon, eggs, salted onions, tomatoes, and a mug of steaming tea.

He took his seat. "Good morning, Mrs. Stone."

She grunted, turning over the parchment.

"Mrs. Stone, um, how do you think I did on my first test?"

She did not glance up. "Desperate for admiration, are we?"

"No, I just thought—"

"It took my last apprentice three days to move a pebble with his mind."

"Oh."

"Vion was successful in his studies, but in the end proved … a disappointment."

"Can I ask why he proved a disappointment, Mrs. Stone?"

She raised stern eyes. "Let us dispense with the prattling, child, there is much work to be done today. After breakfast, you are to clean and tidy the living room here. I will be making a trip to town for supplies and news. Upon my return, we shall conduct your second test."

"Yes, Mrs. Stone ..."

They finished eating in silence. After breakfast, she put on a thick white robe fringed with gray fur, grabbed her staff, and stepped out the door.

He wondered which town she referred to. Blackhaven had to be a three-day walk, Antioc five or more. He peered at the mess surrounding him before grabbing a dust cloth.

A few dull hours later, he rewarded himself with a break, opening the front door for some air. The year's first snow had come at last, obscuring the horizon. He stepped out and took a series of deep breaths, until a chill wind forced a retreat.

As he returned to cleaning, his eye fell upon the short sword and scabbard hanging on the wall. He reached for it under the pretense that it needed dusting. As his hand grasped the hilt, he remembered sparring with Sir Westwood. He could almost hear the thump of wooden swords crossing. He had always dreamed of owning a real blade; Sir Westwood had not let him touch his sword, not even to polish it.

Augum gingerly pulled Mrs. Stone's sword out of its scabbard, noting the fine balance. The steel blade was silvery-blue and looked extremely sharp. The crossguard was a tapered steel bar seamlessly joined to the blade, the grip tightly wrapped with links of chain.

He made a practice swing. The sword hissed as it sliced the air. Inspired, he sheathed the blade and attached it to his belt, where it hung awkwardly. He then marched to the end of the room, ready to face an imaginary opponent.

"Sir, you have offended my lady! I challenge you to a duel. Draw your sword, if you dare ..."

He then ceremoniously drew Mrs. Stone's sword and circled his pretend adversary.

"Defend yourself, Sir!" Augum made a wild slash, nearly slicing the settee, before dodging an imaginary blow. He parried a strike aimed at his head and countered with a swing that accidentally sliced through a fat candle. As a testament to the sword's sharpness, the candle remained standing.

"And now … It. Must. End—!" He plunged a final thrust. Suddenly the tip of the blade burst with a blue electric bolt that connected with the far wall, exploding a head-sized hole in the rock above the pantry. Electric fingers of lightning crept up his arm before disappearing with a sizzling crackle.

He dropped the sword and stared dumbstruck at the hole. It smoked and sizzled, filling the room with an acrid smell.

That is it. She is going to kill him, and if not, there goes his apprenticeship.

Unless …

He hurriedly sheathed the sword and hung it back on the wall. Knowing he needed to do something about the smell, he opened the door to let the air circulate. The snowfall was even thicker now, pushing its way inside with the wind.

The place cooled fast. Judging the smell gone, he closed the door and put more logs on the fire, glad Mrs. Stone was going to be a while.

He glanced at the gaping hole, breath fogging. A myriad of excuses came to mind; something in the hearth exploded, ricocheting off the wall; a brigand he fought off heroically; a comet—

The door suddenly swung open, blowing a fresh plume of snow inside. A hunched Mrs. Stone trundled in, carrying a wicker basket. She stamped her feet and closed the door, muttering about her old bones. She hung her winter robe and set the basket on the table, glancing idly about.

Augum, whose heart thundered in his chest, stood by the fire trying to appear as inconspicuous as possible.

"I expected you would have fini—" She stopped to sniff the air. "Merciful spirits, what is that smell!"

"I ... I ..."

She reared like a cobra. "In the name of all that is proper, why is there a hole in the wall?"

"I'm sorry, Mrs. Stone, I ... I played with the sword."

She only glared; he felt smaller than a dung beetle.

"It seems you have a hard time following instructions. That sword is extremely sharp; you could have cut your own head off and not even have known it."

Augum gave the candle a sidelong glance.

"It is not a toy, Augum. Look at me. Am I making myself clear?"

"Yes, Mrs. Stone."

"Humph." She turned her back on him and began to unpack the basket.

He swallowed. Was that all? Was he getting away with only a reprimand?

"Perhaps you have too much time on your hands. Well I assure you, *that* we can remedy. Make yourself useful and gather four armfuls of wood for the fire. You will find a coat, saw and gloves in the hall cupboard. There is a hidden door to a storage room outside the entrance."

Augum hurried to the cupboard where he found the items described. He left quietly, grateful to escape harsher punishment.

Outside, fat snowflakes swirled, curtaining off the sun and making it appear later than it was. The cold was intense; his breath steamed, hands numbing almost immediately.

The wind bullied him on the long descent, threatening to send him tumbling. He wondered what news she had brought back and what town she had visited. Above all, he wondered how she had made the journey so quickly ...

He finally reached the forest. Spotting a felled branch, he set to sawing it into manageable portions. The task complete, he bundled the wood in his arms and started back up the mountain.

The blizzard-like wind fought him every step of the way, blinding him and making breathing difficult. He stumbled many times, realizing this was no easy punishment after all. At last, he scrambled over the lip of the cave and searched for the hidden door, finding a camouflaged iron handle embedded into the cave wall. He pulled it and a portion of the rock swung open, revealing a spacious storage cavity filled with cords of wood. He added his wood to the pile and trekked back down for another armful, wondering how she could possibly have brought up all that wood herself.

Augum repeated this process three more times, descending further and further in search of wood. With each trip, the sky darkened and the blizzard thickened. By the time he gathered the last armful, he was shivering and wished he had a lantern.

Suddenly he became aware of just how dark and bare the forest was. He froze, peering past the trunks. "It's just a forest, keep going ..." he mumbled, and slowly began to walk again. With every step, however, shadows morphed into demons and branches shifted into snakes. His breath increased along with his pace; he forgot how cold and tired he was, all he wanted to do was get back.

At last, he spotted the mouth of the cave, scurried to the entrance, and peered back down the slope. A curtain of white obscured everything.

Fear creates enemies, Sir Westwood used to say. Fear creates enemies ...

Augum deposited the wood in the storage room and slunk through the oaken door, glad to be done with the task.

Mrs. Stone sat in the rocking chair by the fire covered with a blanket, a mug of steaming tea beside her and a large tome in her hands titled *Occulus: A Legacy of Mystery*.

"Finished, have we?" she asked without looking up.

"Yes, Mrs. Stone. May I join you by the fire?"

"You may."

He returned the coat, saw and gloves to the closet and pulled up a chair. The fire was a tremendous pleasure and he relaxed, enjoying the peace the moment afforded.

"Mrs. Stone—?"

"Mmm—?"

"What about the second test?"

Mrs. Stone glanced at the hole above the pantry. "There shan't be need," and resumed reading.

A tingle passed through him. Did she mean he had failed?

Mrs. Stone turned a page. "Tomorrow you will undertake your final test, the most important one. If you pass, you shall be my apprentice."

Augum breathed a sigh of relief; he still had a chance.

"And if I don't pass?"

She quietly closed her book, folding her hands over it. "I suppose there are plenty of other distractions in life. No sense in worrying though, just act your conscience and all will be fine."

He nodded, frowning. His thoughts drifted to her short trip today. "Mrs. Stone, is there any news from town?"

She placed the book aside. "Read for yourself," and handed him today's Blackhaven Herald.

Must have gotten it from a travelling herald, he thought. Then he wondered if this was her way of seeing if he could read. Just in case it was, he decided to read the parchment aloud.

" '… with pride we report the Academy of Arcane Arts has fully bent its will to the Legion's needs. Training of a new cabal of warlocks will begin immediately. Let it be hereby known that it is mandatory for all youths thirteen and older to report to the nearest Legion constabulary to determine if they have the skill to train at the academy.' "

He looked up. "They're *forcing* us?"

"That appears to be the case."

His eyes returned to the parchment. "What's the Academy of Arcane Arts?" The name sounded vaguely familiar.

The rocker creaked to a halt. "My word, you mean you know nothing of the most respected arcane institution in all of Sithesia?"

He shook his head slowly.

Mrs. Stone resumed rocking. "Sir Westwood was probably right to keep you ignorant. It seems certain knowledge could get one into trouble these days, especially in the villages." She sighed. "The Academy of Arcane Arts is an ancient school for warlocks, one all Solian warlocks aspire to attend. Perhaps if the Legion falls, you will have the opportunity."

"What happens to those that don't report to a Legion constabulary?"

She gave him a grave look that needed no explanation.

He grabbed a poker and stirred the coals, thinking about what she had said. "So what do they want?"

"They want what all conquering men want—power, glory, worship ..." She ceased rocking again. "Finish reading the parchment, Augum."

He returned to the scrawled page. " 'And let these names serve as warning for others thinking of taking up arms against the might of the Legion. The following have been put to death for the crime of treason:' " With a sinking feeling, he skipped down the list until he saw a familiar name.

" 'Tobias Westwood' ..." They had not even included his knightly title. He read on tonelessly. " 'Further, the following are to be commended on heroic actions taken on behalf of the Cause in the fierce battle of Willowbrook:' " another list of names, among them, " 'Commander Vion Rames' ..."

Mrs. Stone's voice was quiet. "It troubles me greatly that my former apprentice was the commander responsible for burning your village."

He could barely say the words. "It wasn't a battle, it was a slaughter ..."

She reached out a wrinkled hand and gently patted him on the arm. "I am sorry, child."

"Excuse me—" He shot out of the chair, hurried to his room and lunged into bed. He imagined Sir Westwood bleeding in the dirt, shadows dancing around his still form, willows burning in the background.

He lay in bed the rest of the evening, clenching his pillow, thoughts in turmoil. When sleep came at last, it did little to numb the stabbing pain in his heart.

COMPANIONS

Augum woke to a gentle shaking. "Breakfast is ready. Come, you have a big day ahead." Mrs. Stone shuffled off, leaving him to dress in his burgundy robe.

Breakfast was a quiet affair. The food would have tasted much better had it not been for the previous day's news. Mrs. Stone cast him a rare, sympathetic smile. Augum did not return it, dully pushing his eggs around the plate.

If she had only trained Vion better, Sir Westwood would still be alive and Willowbrook would not have burnt down!

He jabbed an already tormented potato.

After breakfast, Mrs. Stone retrieved a bulging rucksack and placed it on a chair.

"I packed a few things for your last test."

He took the rucksack and glumly pawed through the contents. There was a bedroll, blanket, flint, steel, and a lantern. A tightly rolled canvas tent lay strapped to the outside.

"You will also be taking enough provisions to last you three days, though I expect you back tomorrow." She unfolded a wrinkled map, pointing at a spot about a day's walk north of the mountain. "Hangman's Rock is your destination. You are to leave this package on top." She placed a tightly wrapped and heavy parcel on the table. "You are not to open it."

He just stared at it. Sir Westwood was dead. There was no point in anything.

"I know it is difficult, but you must find the strength to move on, Augum. In order for you to learn what I have to teach you, you will need strong character and a stronger mind. Use this as an opportunity to build on both."

He thought of Sir Westwood standing in the crimson sun, a straw of wheat in his mouth. Would the man have been proud of him? Would he have understood and given his blessing to this new path?

"If you leave now, you should reach the rock by nightfall," Mrs. Stone said.

He glanced at the map, noticing the mountain was named Mt. Barrow. His eyes wandered east to a drooping willow neatly inscribed *Willowbrook*. He ran a finger over the word, picturing the grizzled knight nodding his head as Augum practiced with the sword.

Yes, Sir Westwood would have been proud of him …

"I'll do my best, Mrs. Stone."

"I expect nothing less."

She began packing the provisions while he studied the map, deciding he would follow the tree line bordering the Tallows all the way to Hangman's Rock. He put on a fur-lined woolen coat, a pair of hide mitts and boots, and strapped on the rucksack, made much heavier by the parcel. He stopped at the door to look back at Mrs. Stone. She leaned on her staff, embroidered robe glittering, looking like a doting grandmother watching her grandson walk off to war.

"I will pass your test, Mrs. Stone, and return tomorrow evening."

* * *

Augum shivered in the wind and drew his hood. A crisp layer of ankle-deep snow blanketed everything in sight. Clouds stretched along the horizon, casting a pall over the beginning of his journey.

He descended the mountain and began following the boundary between the forest and the Tallows, keeping a respectful distance from the trees. He skimmed his hand over the chest-high grass rising above the snow, wishing he could fly like a bird. Occasionally, he would glance back at Mt. Barrow, its peak obscured by clouds, wondering how he had survived that fateful night.

It was past midday when he stopped for a bite to eat. He dug himself a little hole in the snow and hunkered down. Just as he finished lunch, a tiny chirping began nearby. Curious, he prowled toward the sound, finding a small bird nestled amongst the hardy yellow grass, its feathers ruffled.

"Now what happened to you?" He scooped the little bird up in his mitts. One of its wings appeared not to work. "You'll freeze out here in the cold, little fellow; I'll have to take you with me." He let it nibble on some sunflower seeds before nestling it in his rucksack. Then he set off again, the bird occasionally sounding a quiet chirp.

"I'm sure you'll love the cave. I just hope Mrs. Stone won't mind having another mouth to feed."

It was a tough slog, and he eventually gave up trying to keep his feet above the snow. After a few more hours of plodding, he spotted a black speck far ahead. Was that Hangman's Rock already?

Then the speck moved.

Augum ducked and watched. After a while, he was able to make out that it was an approaching group of men on horseback. He glanced at the towering line of trees, the light barely penetrating the first phalanx of trunks.

"Here we go, feathered friend." The bird chirped as he crawled to the forest to hide behind a massive pine, trying to ignore the creaking darkness.

Soon he was able to count them—twelve black-armored knights in single file armed with swords, axes, war hammers and spears. The lead rider carried a large black banner that waved in the wind. Augum's flesh prickled when he saw the emblem.

The burning sword of the Legion.

The knights had massive physiques and rough faces. Their breath escaped in powerful bursts of steam. Two riders at the back of the column were different though. One of these men wore a red robe, hood loosely draped over his head, obscuring his face. The other wore a sparkling black robe, heavily embroidered with what looked like silver tree branches, hood also drawn.

Augum cursed himself for not taking the trouble to hide his tracks. He could almost hear Sir Westwood say, "Did I not teach you better?"

He calmed down a little as the column trotted forward. The riders seemed to be absorbed in the journey, not paying much attention to what was on the ground. He was about to breathe a sigh of relief when the black-robed rider, the very last one in the column, yelled "HALT—!"

Augum's stomach lurched.

The Black Robe pointed in Augum's direction. "Tracks, you fools—"

Augum ducked just in time as heads turned his way.

Think, think—!

Yet his mind went completely blank. He stared at the woods listening to the sound of a horse approach. A small chirp escaped his rucksack as a scene unfolded in his brain ...

He was in a snow-covered forest on a hunting lesson with Sir Westwood, the pair wearing long rabbit-skin coats. It was the middle of winter and there was fresh snowfall underfoot.

"When you hunt, you must respect your prey," Sir Westwood whispered as they stalked a deer. "Your real enemy is your mind. Master your mind and you master your adversary."

Augum slunk around a large tree, spotting the deer no more than forty paces away. He raised his bow with trembling hands.

Sir Westwood crouched behind him. "Concentrate. Let loose when your breath has left your body. Be as still as the snow."

Augum tried hard to still his nerves. The deer looked right at him, but in its place, he saw Meli, standing on wobbly legs, eyes watery.

The arrow slipped away. It impaled into a tree just behind the deer, which bolted immediately.

Augum expelled a long breath. "It … it just stared at me."

Sir Westwood spat on the ground. "It is not the deer that froze, Augum …"

A horse's snort brought Augum back to the present moment. A muscled steed had stopped beside him, black robe dangling by his head. He noticed the embroidered branches were not those of a tree at all, but of *lightning*. Moreover, just like Mrs. Stone's robe, they appeared to flicker and flash.

He looked up at the rider. A pallid face stared back, framed by long night-black hair that fell down the man's chest—but it was the *eyes* that drew Augum's attention, crackling with miniature lightning.

"Why, it is just a boy!" The rider said back to his comrades. "What are you doing out in the middle of nowhere, boy? You an escaped prisoner? An insurgent?"

Augum heard the creak of leather as the man tightened his grip on the reins. "You better answer me, boy …"

"I'm neither—"

A twig snapped nearby. Augum and the Black Robe whipped their heads in the direction of the sound.

"You lie, boy. You behind the tree—show yourself!"

A very small boy with dimpled cheeks emerged. He wore a wolf pelt and held a miniature bow and arrow in his hands.

"Go away!" the boy said in a squeaky voice, aiming his little bow and arrow at the rider. "Or I'll shoot!"

The rider's horse neighed, but the Black Robe only laughed. "So brave for one so young. You shall make a fine commander one day."

The tiny boy tried to make his face hard but came off looking like a wolf cub.

"Perhaps if you brought that kind of bravery to the academy, you might earn an arm of stripes." The Black Robe made a show of flexing. The air crunched as his right arm flared with ten rings of crackling lightning. Augum felt an electric current pass through the area. The hair on his entire body stood on end; even the hair on the boy's wolf pelt stiffened towards the rider.

The boy stood with his mouth open, limply holding his miniature bow and arrow.

"Wow ... a lightning warlock! Those rings are amazing ..."

The Black Robe burst in a booming laugh and extinguished his rings. "You have spirit, boy. If you trained at the academy, I have no doubt you'd earn your own one day." He turned his attention back to Augum. "How old are you, son?"

Augum remembered the notice. "Twelve."

"Twelve? Too bad. Soon as you turn thirteen, you are to report to a constabulary for testing."

The red-robed rider cantered up. "Commander, everything all right—?"

"Perfectly fine, Lieutenant; we will be moving on now."

"But sir, should we not investigate the wood? There might be an insurgent village near."

48

The Black Robe eyed Augum and the boy. "No, Lieutenant, we do not have the time. They are too young anyway." He turned his horse and the pair trotted back to the column.

" 'Wow, a lightning warlock!' " mocked a second boy, emerging from behind a nearby tree. He had a pinched face, mottled sandy hair and wore a red robe. A rusty short sword dangled by his side. Accompanying him was a girl with long cinnamon hair wearing a patched emerald robe, clutching a simple wooden staff. Both looked to be Augum's age.

She swept her hair out of her eyes. "Oh shut it, Robin—he got them to go away, didn't he?"

"Yeah, but did he have to kiss up like that?"

"I did good, better than you would have!" the boy in the wolf pelt shouted.

Augum stood up and brushed snow off his bottom.

The little one's cheeks puffed out in a smile as he waved with his bow, almost dropping it. "Hi, my name is Leland Goss."

"Hi, uh ... I'm Augum." He tensed, not sure what to expect. All his interactions with other children had ended badly.

"I'm Bridget Burns," the cinnamon-haired girl said. She had a pert nose and hazel eyes that closely matched her hair. She nodded at the boy with the pinched face. "And that's Robin Scarson."

Robin folded his arms across his chest.

She tilted her head slightly. "We've been following you all day, you know."

Augum raised his brows. "You have?"

"Heh, wasn't that difficult either," Robin said. "A blind man could have followed you, walking in the open like that."

Bridget rolled her eyes. "Give it a break, Robin. Why always so cross?"

"Because I hate tending to the two of you babies!" He strode past them to watch the fading column of riders.

Bridget patted Leland on the head. "Don't worry, you did very well," adding in a whisper, "see how jealous you made Robin?"

Leland giggled and flashed a dimpled smile.

Bridget's gaze returned to Augum. "So, Augum, where are you going?"

He flushed, unable to remember the last time a girl actually addressed him by his real name. "Um, to Hangman's Rock." He cringed. Any moment now, she would make some comment that gave her true motive away. Yet when he met her eyes, he was surprised to see only concerned warmth.

Robin rejoined the group. "All alone? You on some kind of quest or something?"

"Kind of ... just delivering a parcel."

"Don't you know that place is haunted? Wait now, show your stripes—" Robin reached for Augum's wrist, but Bridget caught his arm.

"Robin Scarson, that is nothing short of rude."

Robin yanked his arm away. "What, going to tattletale to your older brother again?"

"Just ignore him, Augum. He's been foul ever since we were forced to leave the academy. You don't have to show your stripes to us." She flashed Robin a sharp look. "Besides, none of *us* have a stripe yet."

Augum only gaped.

Robin snorted a malignant laugh, the kind Dap or Garth Penderson unleashed when they thought Augum was being stupid. "He doesn't even know what we're talking about!"

Augum felt his skin go hot. "That's not—" he was about to deny it but stopped himself. Now that Sir Westwood was gone, there was no one left to teach him to be a better person, to prepare him for being a man. Sir Westwood once told him, "Learn to control your emotions, Augum, and you can control the outcome of a confrontation."

He gave a sidelong glance to Bridget and felt himself cool a little. "Um, I'm hoping to be accepted as an apprentice warlock. The parcel delivery is my last test."

"So *that's* what this is all about," Bridget said. "Then you simply *must* let us accompany you."

Leland began dancing and singing. "Yay, a quest, a quest ... we're going on a quest!"

Robin raised a hand. "Uh, excuse me, but you know we have to be back by nightfall."

"What, and leave Augum to do this alone, in this weather—? I think our parents would approve this time. Besides, *you* don't have to come; Leland and I will accompany him."

Augum blushed, completely unaccustomed to receiving kindness from someone his age, let alone a girl.

Robin thought about it for a moment before making a dismissive gesture. "Nah, I'll come. After all, somebody's got to keep you fools alive."

A tiny chirping began from Augum's rucksack. "Oh, I forgot—he must be hungry." He opened it up as the others leaned in for a closer look.

Bridget's face melted. "Aww ... it's a wittle birdie. It's so cute ..."

Leland reached out with a grubby paw. "Can I hold it?"

Augum gently enclosed the bird in his hands. "You'd better not; it's hurt. I'm going to bring it home with me and nurse it back to health."

Robin hissed, a putrid look on his face. "That bird is broken and all this lovey-dovey dung makes me sick. I'd have just let it be."

Bridget's brows crossed. "Of course *you* would have. You disgust me, Robin Scarson."

"Whatever, *Broken Bridget*." Robin went to grab his rucksack from behind a tree.

Bridget closed her eyes and sighed.

Augum gave her and Leland some seeds to feed the bird. "Why did he call you that?"

She gave a pained smile. "I once fell from an embankment after trying to reach a stranded baby goat. Broke my leg and collarbone, but I guess it could have been worse. Anyway, Robin and a bunch of his friends found me unconscious and seemed to think it was funny."

"I don't think that's funny at all."

She fed the bird a seed. "They took their time calling for the healers too. Robin made sure everyone saw first. Wasn't even him that brought them, but some stranger."

It was Augum's turn to give her a pained smile. "I'm sorry you went through that."

The little creature gave a contented chirp.

"Think he wants to go back inside," she said.

Augum scooped him up and gently placed him in the rucksack, minding his little wings.

They gathered their things and joined Robin on the Tallows.

"Take your time, no one is waiting," Robin said with a scowl.

Bridget gave Augum a *see what I have to put up with?* look.

They marched northward in single file, Augum leading the way. Bridget followed, prodding the snow with her staff, emerald robe fluttering in the wind. Leland crunched along after in his little wolf pelt, bow tucked behind his back. Robin ambled in the rear, rusty sword dangling, a sour expression on his face.

As the day wore on, the clouds darkened and a shrill wind picked up.

"We should arrive at the rock before nightfall," Bridget said. "My father and I passed through there just last month. We were on our way to Antioc for school supplies, but had to turn back when we spotted knights."

Augum adjusted his rucksack. "Was it the Legion?"

"We think so, they patrol the forest edge. Thankfully it was the Black Guard, if it had been the Red …"

"The Red—?"

"Yeah. Rumor has it you see one you're not going to live to tell about it. Easy to identify though seeing as they're named for the color of their armor."

Augum wondered if the last thing Sir Westwood saw was red armor. "So where do you all live then?"

"Just northwest of Mt. Barrow. We're a village of refugees from Blackhaven. The community is all parents and youths from the same class, with some relatives and friends of course."

"So you're all from the same school?"

"Our parents thought it best to escape together. We ran when the insurrection broke out and all the Legion supporters rallied in the streets. It was total chaos, an awful situation. So sad about the school too, and we just started there. Now it's in the hands of a bunch of hooligans." She sighed. "So what about you? Where are you from?"

"I'm kind of from Willowbrook, a village three days' walk east of here."

"Kind of—?"

"The Legion burnt it to the ground." Flames engulfing willows flashed across his mind.

"Is your family all right?"

"I'm an orphan." That was stupid; he shouldn't have exposed himself like that.

Bridget's voice was quiet. "I didn't mean to pry."

"It's fine, you couldn't have known." He felt the weight of his disclosure lighten a little. "I don't know much about warlocks …"

"It's all right, most people fear or ignore them. A lot of villages pretend they don't even exist, and some … well, some try to burn them at the stake."

"Yeah, I thought it was witchery at first …"

"That's common. So you're from one of *those* villages then?"

"Wish I wasn't. So, um, about stripes—why do you need them?" He kept his voice low, hoping these weren't stupid questions.

"Stripes have been around for thousands of years, dating back to the Founding. They're a major point of honor for warlocks. They not only serve as a warning, but tradition says it's proper to show them in battle. A high-degree warlock would generally not duel a low-degree one. That would be beneath her."

"How do you get them?"

"You have to be enrolled in an arcane school or become the apprentice of a warlock. You also have to choose an element, though many say the element chooses you. I suppose you can learn wild too—without ever meeting another warlock that is. It's rare but does happen."

Augum furrowed his brows. "Why's that? Is it too difficult or something?"

"That and wild warlocks tend to kill themselves off." Her voice quieted down. "Want me to explain how spells work and stuff?"

He felt his cheeks prickle. "Yes please."

She ran up beside him and smiled. Just the fact that she did that, like a real friend, was enough to send his heart soaring.

"All right," she began, still keeping her voice conspiratorially low, "most of the spells you learn are known as 'Standard Spells'. There are three in every degree plus one from your element. Once you learn all three Standard Spells *and* your elemental spell, you're tested on it. If you pass, you're awarded your degree—or as we like to say, your *ring*, or even *stripe*—because they look like stripes from afar."

He imagined his arm rippling with a full complement of lightning rings, just like the Black Robe.

"Traditionally, there's a whole formal ceremony," Bridget continued, "but the best part is really after, when a big celebration is held in your honor. Usually everyone you know—and even don't know—comes. Sometimes whole towns attend an advancement ceremony. Also, if you're part of an entire class that gets advanced, the party can last for days."

She paused. "Not everybody advances through. The more you study, the greater the chance of dropping out. It becomes harder and harder to attain the next degree, until you hit your ceiling, so to speak. Just by the number of drop-outs, everyone knows the arcane path is challenging."

Augum mulled over everything she had said. He had never attended school before, but secretly always wanted to. Willowbrook lacked one. Youths were expected to become farmers, millers, tanners, or blacksmiths, just like their parents, and everyone was home-schooled or apprenticed. Only the kids from richer families got to go to school in the city. As it was, Augum was grateful for Sir Westwood's teachings.

"So you really had no idea warlocks were real?" Bridget asked.

"I lived on a farm for a while, then in a small village. I heard about warlocks, but mostly in children's stories. Was always told they were demons, or witches and stuff. Didn't really think much of magic till I met—"

"—oh don't use the word 'magic'," she said. "It's considered, um … amateur."

"Oh, okay." He wondered what he should say instead, but she did not elaborate and he did not want to look even more stupid by asking.

A harsh wind forced her to walk behind him once again. They marched on in silence, plowing through fresh knee-high snow. All the while, Leland hummed to himself. After some time, Bridget pointed east across the plains.

"Looks like it's going to snow again."

Augum glanced at the dark clouds brewing on the horizon. He shivered thinking of the storm that nearly killed him. He could almost feel the tired aches return, the nauseous fear, the finger-biting cold. He loved storms, but that journey, after the harrowing events in Willowbrook ...

He pulled up his hood and tightened his coat.

"So what element are you hoping to specialize in?" Bridget asked.

"Lightning."

She stopped with a gasp, sending a drooling Leland bumping into her.

"Lightning—? Are you ... do you know how many kids get killed every year thinking they can tame *lightning*?"

"No, I—" but he was cut off by a derisive laugh from the back.

"Lightning? He knows squat about the arcane discipline and he wants to tame *lightning*?" Robin asked some mysterious force across the Tallows. "No. Chance. In fact, I give him a tenday before he blows himself up."

Augum contemplated going back and punching Robin in the face. After all, Robin was not built like Dap or the Pendersons, and he certainly did not have any cronies with him. But then, what would Bridget think of him? She would probably call him a base gutterborn animal like girls usually did.

He sighed and walked on.

Bridget caught up. "Wait—hey, sorry, don't run into many lightning students nowadays. Legion goes after them more than the others, and like I said, it's a more dangerous discipline."

Had a girl just *apologized* to him? He almost did not know what to say. "So, um ... what's your element?" he managed to blurt.

"Earth. Robin's is fire. Leland wants to train in ice but he isn't old enough yet. My best friend, Leera, is training in water."

" 'My best friend, Leera, is training in water'," Robin mimicked from the rear.

"Ugh, just ignore him," Bridget said. "He can't help himself."

Leland's voice was pouty. "I don't *want* to wait four more years ..."

" 'I don't *want* to wait four more years'," came the whiny echo.

Augum struggled to ignore Robin's taunting mimics. "How young can, uh, warlock talents appear?"

" '... talents appear.' "

"Rarely before thirteen," Bridget replied.

" '... thirteen.' "

She turned. "Ugh, *grow up*, Robin."

"*You* grow up. This is such a waste of time and all of you are insufferably boring."

"You don't even know what that word means." Bridget turned back, ignoring Robin's retort. She gestured for Augum to continue.

"So how many elements are there?" he asked.

"Loads. Let's see, the major seven are water, air, earth, fire, ice, lightning and healing. There's also summoning, illusion and alchemy—oh, and I forgot necromancy, which is mostly just evil stuff."

The wind increased significantly, making it hard to hear. They trudged on without speaking further. Every time Augum glanced east, the dark clouds drew closer. Definitely a storm. He took up a faster pace.

Finally, after what felt like hours, Leland spotted Hangman's Rock and wildly pointed with his tiny hand. "I think I see it, I think I see it! Laaaaand hooo!"

Augum and Bridget enjoyed a chuckle together. Night was almost upon them though and a distressed chirping began from Augum's rucksack.

"Almost there, little friend," he said through chattering teeth, but the storm descended quite suddenly, overtaking them three hundred paces from the rock. Leaning heavily into the wind, they had to claw through an icy gust that threatened to push them into the forest.

Augum shouted to have his voice heard above the din. "Let's make camp on the other side!"

They wordlessly followed him to the leeward side, which afforded a little shelter from the gale, but not much. The rock was tilted, the overhang just above, a plume of snow ceaselessly streaming off.

He unstrapped the tent from his rucksack while Bridget covered the little bird with her hands so it would not blow away.

Robin stood with his back against the rock. "It's getting worse, hurry up already!"

But every time they tried erecting the tent, despite having both sides staked down, a powerful gust would knock it over. They often had to jump on it to prevent it from blowing away.

"Maybe this will help!" Bridget dug out a coil of rope from her rucksack. "We can stop it from flying off by tying it to the rock!"

Augum quickly tied one end to the top of the tent and the other to a small outcrop from Hangman's Rock. It worked—they were able to concentrate on erecting the tent while the rope prevented it from flying away. Assembling it at last, they piled inside, collapsing from the effort.

Leland broke out with a wide grin. "Whee … real adventure!"

Nobody replied, still panting from the exertion.

Augum was just grateful to have shelter. After a period of well-earned rest, he opened his rucksack and removed the weakly chirping bird. He then dug out the flint, steel and lantern. After lighting the lamp, they arranged themselves in a circle around its flickering light. Augum bundled the bird close to the flame to warm it up, feeding sunflower seeds into its tiny beak. It warbled appreciatively.

The wind kept increasing in strength, blowing with such ferocity that they exchanged worried looks. The tent shook, threatening to blow away at any moment. Augum only hoped the two supporting poles would hold.

Bridget nervously swept aside a lock of hair. "Wow, this is something ..."

Robin snorted. "This is nothing—father and I were blown off our feet in a gale on the plains last year. Now *that* was a storm."

Bridget rolled her eyes at Augum.

Augum thought of his own recent adventure when a storm carried him off and struck him with lightning. "Will your folks worry about you?" he asked, taking out his bedroll. He wondered what it was like to have parents worry over you.

Bridget shrugged while rummaging through her rucksack. "Yeah, but they also know we can take care of ourselves ... for one night at least ... I hope." She pulled out a large piece of chocolate.

Robin helped himself to a generous portion. "Oh, I think they'll be angry, Bridget. But you're such a goody-good I'm sure you'll explain everything, won't you?"

She did not reply, passing the chocolate to Leland and Augum. Augum wanted to say something to Robin but did not know if it was his place, and so the four sat munching, watching their shadows dance on the flapping canvas walls.

Suddenly there was a loud snapping sound and the tent flattened, blowing out the lantern. Amongst the chaos came Bridget's muffled voice. "The rope—!"

"I'll get it!" Augum felt around for the entrance and scrambled outside, where his heart caught in his throat. He could barely breathe, let alone see anything; snow seemed to come from every direction, stinging his eyes. He felt the panic of drowning, like when Dap would hold him under water until Augum pretended to go still, then Dap would panic and raise him, playing it off as a joke.

His hands immediately froze in the cold; he cursed himself for forgetting his mitts. He wrapped his hood tightly around his head and stumbled blind, groping about for the rope, not daring to take one hand off the tent. He had heard enough stories of people taking a wrong step in a blizzard, getting lost and freezing to death.

As if the wind had been reading his thoughts, a strong gust bowled him over; and just like that, Augum lost touch with the tent. He lumbered in the direction he thought it was, but found nothing. His chest hammered as he eased off his hood in an effort to see. It was hopeless—the blizzard was just too thick, the wind too strong.

He was dead if he did not find the tent soon …

Suddenly he knew what he had to do. He took time clearing his mind, ignoring that the wind sounded like Death breathing. He ignored the burning tingling of frostbite. He visualized finding the rope, extended his arm, and made a beckoning gesture.

The rope smacked into his hand.

"Yes!" he shouted, the word lost to the roar.

Smiling broadly, he followed the rope on hands and knees, holding on with numb fingers. The wind punished him for his victory, clawing at him like a rabid beast. It took all of his remaining strength to find the rock and tie the tent back up, the task lengthened by painfully frozen hands. Finally, he tumbled back inside and collapsed on his bedroll, panting.

Bridget hurriedly tied up the door flap and relit the lantern. "Thank all that is good, we were starting to worry you got lost." When she spotted his hands, her eyes went wide. She immediately grabbed them between her own.

Robin opened his mouth to say something but Bridget scowled. "Don't you even dare—" She turned back to Augum. "Once they're warmed enough you can place them by the lantern."

He nodded. Her touch felt strange; he never had a girl *care* about him before.

Leland did not seem to think this was much fun anymore and stifled a sob.

"There now, Little Lee." Bridget gave him a hug, "It's just a storm, it'll pass ..."

Robin's eyes wandered over the madly vibrating canvas. "Hope you're better at rope tying than you are at covering your tracks."

Augum placed his hands over the lantern, hoping the same.

Robin gave Leland a dark look. "You know why they call it Hangman's Rock, don't you?"

Leland sat up. "No ... why?"

Robin's voice dropped to a whisper. "Well, legend has it that a long time ago, peasants would hang people they thought were witches from the top; and you know what? I think we're right under the spot they hung from."

Leland's lower lip trembled.

Bridget drew Leland in tighter. "Stop it, Robin, you're scaring him. That's just a silly old wives' tale, Little Lee, don't you pay any attention," but at that very moment the wind roared with increased fury. Leland began crying while Augum and Bridget exchanged nervous glances. The tent wall shook so violently and the wind screeched so loudly that Augum thought for sure it would rip the seams and scatter them like seeds.

Robin's face hovered above the lantern, the shadows playing on his features. "They say that everyone gets one wish at Hangman's Rock—in exchange for their soul."

Bridget sighed. "Oh, shut up already—"

Robin ignored her, making a show of closing his eyes for a time.

"Robbie, what did you wish for?" Leland asked quietly when Robin opened his eyes.

Robin's features twisted into a smile. He was about to respond when something behind Augum caught his attention and all the color drained from his face.

Augum whipped his head around to see the outline of five clawed fingers pawing the tent. As the vile hand reached the bottom, the lantern flickered and went out.

Everybody screamed.

Someone said an unfamiliar word and the tent flooded with green light. For a moment, Augum thought it was the monster's doing, until spotting what looked like glowing green ivy wrapped around Bridget's hand. Leland clung to her, shaking and whimpering.

She gestured them over. "To the middle, backs against each other!"

Robin scampered with his own arm outstretched, repeating the same strange word, except cursing in frustration because nothing was happening.

Augum placed his back against the group, wishing he had Mrs. Stone's sword with him. The claw soon reappeared, pressing directly before him, testing the canvas. He could barely hear above the blood rushing through his brain.

He needed to do something.

He thought of Bridget's lit hand; smashing those stones together with his mind; being struck by lightning; Mrs. Stone telling him to work on his fortitude. It all connected somehow.

Then something strange happened. Amidst all that chaos, his mind stilled. In fact, everything fell silent. Time slowed down to a crawl, things began to move in slow motion. He knew the others were screaming, but it sounded so far away …

Augum tilted his head and studied the claw, realizing he had plenty of time to think about what to do. It had long fingernails and moved at a snail's pace, as everything did at that moment—the vibrating canvas, the shadows, his companions. He felt the space around him warp as the hair on his arms, neck and head stood on end. An electric force began pulling. He decided that, instead of resisting, he would just go with it.

Then he watched himself do something that seemed perfectly natural—reach out to the claw. Upon contact, a monstrous surge of energy passed through him. The pain was excruciating, like being burned from within. Outside, he heard something shriek, echoed by screaming from within the tent.

Suddenly a gut-wrenching blue explosion tore the air and the world went black.

HANGMAN'S ROCK

Augum woke to a damp tent bathed in dull morning light. Wincing from a pounding headache, he sat up and glanced about. Stuff was everywhere, his coat sleeve was singed, and there was a scorch mark on the canvas wall. The others were slumped in sleep, their backs still against each other.

Suddenly remembering the bird, he scrambled for his rucksack, finding it scrunched in a corner. He took a deep breath before opening it, only to find the tiny creature snoozing away. Sighing with relief, he stuck his head outside the tent, digging through the partially buried entrance. Large flakes fell onto snow piled waist high, swirling about in a gentle breeze. It was chilly, the sun muted behind banks of gray cloud that stretched across the sky like a vast blanket.

Well, at least the storm had passed. Hearing someone stir within, he retreated.

Bridget moaned, head lolling.

"It's all right," he whispered. "It's morning now."

She shot up with a wild look. "What happened? Is … is it gone—?"

Augum reached beside her. "Yeah, it's gone. Here, have some chocolate."

She took it slowly, eyes unfocused. The others stirred and Augum broke off a piece for each of them. Robin snatched his piece, eyeing Augum distrustfully.

Leland looked about with a terrified expression. "Mama?"

Bridget put a finger to her lips. "Shh, it's okay, Little Lee, you're safe now."

Leland's voice was a whimper. "What happened?"

Bridget took a bite of chocolate. "Last I remember is seeing you move very strangely, Augum, as if you were sped up or something—"

"Yeah," Leland said, "you reached for the claw thingy—"

"—and then the air exploded," Robin finished, watching Augum closely.

Augum glanced at the burn mark on the canvas. "I … I don't know what happened exactly. Time seemed to slow down, and then I just …" He looked at them blankly. "I just went with it."

They stared at him. He looked away, feeling his forehead prickle. Was this how it would start? Was he a freak to be made fun of again? Then he remembered Bridget's glowing ivy. "That was a neat thing you did with your hand."

"I cast Shine. It's the first elemental spell you learn."

"I'm hungry," Leland said.

Bridget reached for her rucksack. "Me too."

Breakfast was a quiet affair of smoked beef sandwiches, hard-boiled eggs and a skin of water. Throughout, Augum felt their eyes on him. Maybe they were looking at him with a kind of pity, or maybe even fear. Regardless, he was happy to eat in silence, preferring not to talk about last night, mostly because he did not understand what had happened.

"I should place the package on top of the rock now," Augum said after feeding the bird.

Robin gave the parcel an ugly look. "What's in that stupid thing anyway?"

"No idea. I just have to place it on top to pass the test."

Leland's face lit up. "Maybe it's treasure!"

Bridget began tickling him. "Or maybe a treasure map—"

Robin gave the pair a disgusted look.

"In any case," Bridget said, fending off Leland's counter-attack, "it's not going to be easy climbing the rock with ice and snow on it."

"I'll just have to figure something out." Augum slapped on his mitts and made for the exit, hoping the monster was long gone.

Bridget grabbed her staff. "I'm coming too."

He was grateful to have company as the two lumbered out of the tent, pushing through the snow. They stared up at the black rock. It resembled a giant tilted egg plastered with frost. Their tent was directly underneath the overhang. He had a vision of a witch hanging there, legs dangling.

They searched the area for tracks but, if there were any, the blizzard had obscured them. However, they did find a bump in the snow a little ways from the rear of the tent, in the direction Augum had channeled that mysterious energy.

They stared at it, exchanged glances and scurried back to the rock.

"See any parts I can scale?" Augum asked after a time.

Bridget shielded her eyes as she pointed at a spot halfway up. "No, but you might be able to snag that small lip there with some rope. If you get that far you could probably climb the rest of the way."

The only rope they could spare was the tether Augum struggled with in last night's blizzard. He shuddered to think what might have happened if Telekinesis had failed, or for that matter, if he had bumped into the monster …

He untied the rope and formed a lasso, something he had learned at the farm. On his second throw, the loop tightened around the lip. He tugged on the line to make sure it was secure.

Bridget raised an eyebrow. "Neat trick."

"Oh, I forgot the package—" He headed back to the tent. After opening the flap, he saw Robin holding the parcel, except that it looked like a hungry dog had got at it.

Robin gave him an incredulous look. "Nothing inside but a bunch of stupid rocks—"

"Give me that!" Augum snatched the parcel from Robin's hands.

"I told him not to do it …" Leland said, stifling a sob.

Augum flashed Robin an angry look. "That wasn't yours to open," and began picking up rocks from the tent floor. Leland quietly helped, a troubled look on his face.

Robin shrugged. "Whatever … so yeah, thanks for almost getting us killed for a bunch of dumb rocks."

Augum rewrapped the parcel as best he could, cheeks burning. Was Robin right though? Were they almost killed for a bunch of stupid rocks? What kind of test was this?

"What was that all about?" Bridget asked when he exited the tent, Leland in tow.

He avoided her gaze. "Nothing." He tucked the package in his belt and tested the rope, heaving his weight onto it when he was sure it would hold. Underneath the snow, the rock had iced up. Leland and Bridget gasped each time they saw him slip. Eventually, he made it to the top.

Leland cupped his hands around his mouth. "Any treasure—?"

"No … nothing!" There was hardly any room for a parcel, let alone him. Steadying himself, he took a deep breath, retrieved the package, and carefully placed it on the rock.

Now to get back down …

Robin emerged from the tent, took one look, and guffawed. "What, stuck?"

"Don't listen to him, Augum, just take your time," Bridget said.

Robin folded his arms across his chest, "Yeah, because we have *all day*."

Augum recalled the Penderson brats discovering one of his hiding places in a tree, except they had thrown rocks at him until he fell.

Robin winked. "You be careful now."

"Hey, why don't you go and clean up the tent or something?" Bridget said, pointing. "Go!"

Robin snorted. "What, and miss this? Forget it, Broken Bridget—"

Augum hugged the rock and began edging his way down.

"Bet he's not going to make it," Robin said.

As if on cue, Augum lost his grip, yelped, and slid down the length of the stone, slamming the ground with his bottom and tumbling backwards.

Bridget's voice sounded like it was coming from a deep cave. "Augum, are you all right?"

He sat up, groaning. "Can't believe that happened."

Bridget offered a hand. "Well, it *was* icy. Anyway, what's important is you're all right and you accomplished your quest."

Robin laughed so hard he started coughing. "Did you see the way he slid down?" He mocked a face of surprise. Still hawing like a donkey, he went to clear the tent of their stuff.

Bridget watched him depart with narrowed eyes. "Forget him, Augum. You were very brave; there was no way I could have climbed that. Fear of heights and all …"

"Yeah!" Leland said. "And Robin's just jealous he didn't stop the monster."

Augum brushed himself off, giving a half-hearted chuckle. "Guess sliding down backwards *was* kind of funny." He retrieved the rope and they went off to pack, everyone ignoring Robin.

THE INVITATION

The added new snowfall made the return journey tedious, though at least the wind had eased off. The group trudged in single file, Augum again plowing in the lead, followed by Bridget, Leland and Robin.

Bridget caught up to him and smiled as they walked side-by-side. "You know, I've never seen someone our age use a power so beyond their degree—in any element. Even at the academy, kids only attempted one, maybe two degrees beyond their own; and some even died trying *that*."

Augum felt his face turn hot. A girl had never complimented him before. "I didn't have much control over it though."

"Sure, it *was* wild and uncontrolled, but it also showed real potential. If I were to guess, I'd say that was like a 4th degree spell or something. You just have to be careful, lightning is a dangerous element."

"That's what Mrs. Stone said."

"She your mentor?"

"If I pass the test, yes. After all, she told me *not* to open the package."

"But it wasn't you, it was Robin!"

"She won't care."

"Oh. So ... what do you think about coming to school with us?"

"School?" What would warlock school be like? Were the kids like Robin, or more like Bridget? "Um ... I don't know. I'd have to ask Mrs. Stone."

"Do you live with her?"

"She took me in after the Legion killed Sir Westwood."

"Oh ... I'm sorry. Who was Sir Westwood?"

"I was his squire. I was supposed to be a knight, even though I wasn't all that good with the sword. Didn't start early enough."

Bridget nearly fell tripping over a buried rock. She reached out to him for balance. Her touch made him blush fiercely.

"Sorry," she said. "Anyway, warlocks don't start training until they're at least thirteen, and sometimes older. So whereabouts do you live?"

"Mt. Barrow."

"That's so close to us! Wait—how do you live on a mountain?"

"Don't know if I should say. Mrs. Stone is a bit ... private."

"Ah, guess I understand." Bridget secured her staff to her bag and picked up some snow. "Is she a lightning sorceress then?"

Augum nodded as she began forming a snowball.

"What degree is she? How many stripes?"

He shrugged. "Never asked; doubt she'd show me if I did. She'd probably say something about pride, or that I'm being nosy."

"I wonder," Bridget said, tossing the snowball back and forth in her hands, "if she knows any Spells of Legend ..."

"Spells of Legend?"

"They're the most powerful tier of spells. The breakdown goes like this—the first five degrees are known as lesser spells, the next five are mid-range spells, the five after that are advanced spells, and the spells beyond the 15th degree are known as Spells of Legend."

She allowed herself to fall behind while Augum wondered what a Spell of Legend would do.

"So you ever seen someone cast a Spell of Legend?" he asked.

"Once, at the academy. I attended an advancement ceremony where a bunch of students were awarded a stripe with the Convey Degree spell."

Augum opened his mouth to reply when something cold slapped into the back of his head. Bridget laughed and ran off to re-arm. Glad it had not been Robin, he packed his own snowball, shouted for revenge, and returned fire. Soon, amongst giggles and shouts of attack, a full-on snowball battle erupted, ending with everybody splattered in snow—especially Leland, who had taken one right in the face from Robin.

Cold, tired and hungry, they decided to eat lunch and cleared a space in the snow.

"Can you tell me more about coming to your school?" Augum asked while feeding his bird, who chirped gratefully.

Robin, drinking from his waterskin, spit it out in a gush. "You want him to come to our school—? He'd fry the whole class!"

Leland's face lit up, cheeks dimpling. "You should really come, Augum!"

Bridget gave Robin an acid look. "Well, the village is still under construction, Augum. We're building a small school for general lessons and arcane studies. If you live nearby, I don't see any reason for you *not* to attend."

Mrs. Stone would probably find plenty of reasons, he thought. "How many students are there?"

"Twenty or so." Bridget tore pieces of journey bread for Augum and Leland. "Most of us are from the same class."

Robin raised his chin as he helped himself to a chunk from Bridget's loaf. "We're all from the *academy*, you know."

Bridget rolled her eyes. "Yes, I told him that already, Robin, thank you."

"I don't know if I'm cut out for school," Augum said.

"Oh, it's a lot of fun," Leland said, biting down on his bread, "id is agic kool ixed wid ormal kool!"

Bridget frowned. "Don't talk with your mouth full, Leland."

Leland swallowed the last of his bread. "I said, it's magic school mixed with normal school."

"Ugh. Leland, it's 'arcane', not 'magic'."

"Oh. Right." Leland gave her a cheerful smile.

Bridget ruffled his hair. "Little misfit. Anyway, Augum, lessons won't start for another few days, not until the school is finished and the proper supplies are in order. We'll have to talk to the Council of Elders about you though. They'll need to give their consent."

"Yeah, they *might* have a problem with a lightning student," Robin said, taking a big bite of bread.

"So I would be the only one studying lightning?"

"Yes," Bridget replied, "but the Council might think it beneficial for other students to train with you."

"Ah." He hoped that would indeed be the case.

"Doubt it!" Robin sang.

Bridget looked like she was going to say something to Robin, but scoffed instead as if he was not worth the effort. They finished lunch in silence, packed up, and continued south.

Bridget caught up beside Augum again. "Hey, tomorrow evening the village is going to have a naming ceremony.

There's going to be a feast and everything. Maybe you and Mrs. Stone would like to come?"

Augum felt a surge of excitement. "That'd be great, but I'll have to ask Mrs. Stone." He could practically see her disapproving expression. His hope of going dimmed.

"Oh, of course. How about we meet at the northwest base of Mt. Barrow then. Say … tomorrow at sunset?"

"All right." His insides tingled. Nobody had ever invited him to anything before.

Leland began to dance and sing in his squeaky voice. "I can't wait! I just can't wait! Wait wait wait! It's going to be so much fun! Fun fun fun!"

Bridget shook her head. "I swear he likes singing more than arcanery."

The day grew long as the group plodded on through the snow. Mt. Barrow loomed ahead, half obscured by low gray clouds dropping fat snowflakes. It was around sunset when Bridget finally spotted a familiar set of trees.

"This is where we should turn west. We can continue a bit further together—"

"—yup, this is the spot," Robin interrupted. "We don't need to keep walking together—anyway it'd be faster for him to walk straight south from here."

They looked at Augum.

"Um, yeah, I guess it would be faster—"

"—it's settled then." Robin turned to leave.

Leland, with his grubby wolf pelt and sleepy eyes, turned to Bridget. "Tomorrow can I come too—?"

"We'll see," though she used a tone that suggested it was not likely. "We have to deal with our parents first."

Leland's face fell.

Augum smiled at Bridget and Leland, his two travel companions and, dare he say it, friends? Like him, they were probably itching for a warm fire and a steaming mug of tea. A hollow feeling in his stomach developed that had nothing to do with appetite. Having never really needed to say goodbye before, he did not know what to say, so he just stood there.

"Well, see you then," Leland said, sticking out a dirty paw.

"Okay," Augum said, shaking Leland's hand, before abruptly turning to walk away, feeling stupid.

"Goodbye, Augum!" Bridget and Leland called after him as they caught up to Robin.

Okay? Is that all that he could have come up with—just *okay*? He had not even said goodbye to Bridget, let alone thanked them for helping him with his quest ...

Nonetheless, he felt a door had opened for him, one he had always hoped would appear—a door to friendship. For the rest of the trek home, he recounted his adventure.

Finally, with his extremities prickling from the cold and his stomach hollow with hunger, he stepped over the lip of Mrs. Stone's cave. Night had long descended by then, bringing with it a sharp mountain wind. The leaded-glass windows that flanked the door were lit with an inviting orange glow, a glow he suspected only he could see.

THE LITTLE BIRD

Augum stepped inside to find Mrs. Stone snoozing in her favorite rocking chair, a large book on her lap. Shadows generated by the hearth gave the room a gentle sway.

He closed the door quietly, took off his boots, coat and mitts, and cleared his throat.

Mrs. Stone snorted. The book fell from her lap, nearly landing in the fire. "Close the door, Livie, you are letting the cold in."

"It's me—Augum—the boy you sent to Hangman's Rock." He wondered who Livie was.

Mrs. Stone opened her eyes and blinked, wheezing, "My word ... Augum ... yes, of course."

He carefully opened his rucksack. A tired tweet sounded from within.

"I hope you don't mind, Mrs. Stone, but I brought a friend." He picked up the little bird and brought it to her. "Oh, and I left the package on top of Hangman's Rock."

When she saw the tiny creature, the faintest smile played across her lips. "Ah, yes, the package." She stood, leaving the chair to rock empty, and picked up the book, titled *The Wondrous Mountain City of Semadon: A Comprehensive History*. She placed it on a shelf and turned to Augum. "The package was unimportant."

Augum's mouth opened—Robin was right, it *was* just a bunch of stupid rocks!

Mrs. Stone's wrinkles deepened in the shadows cast by the fire. "The true test of your task was to see if you would bring this injured bird home—and you did." She paused as if to signify the importance of what he had done.

He blinked. "*That* was the test?"

"Indeed. Now, if I may—" She reached over with a veined hand and gave the bird the lightest tap, uttering something unintelligible. For a moment, a small light flared from the tip of her finger. The bird started flapping both wings, chirping joyfully. It flew from Augum's hands and paraded about the room.

Augum gaped. "But … how … what's going on?"

Mrs. Stone watched the bird flutter about before fetching the kettle. "You see, I shall never again teach someone the arcane art without knowing which way their moral compass points." She gave him a piercing look. "I shall not make *that* mistake again."

The little bird landed on the iron handle of the door and tweeted sharply.

Mrs. Stone filled the kettle with water and set it over the fire. "I think perhaps our friend would like to leave."

Augum carefully opened the door. The bird gave a grateful chirp and swooped outside.

"Goodbye, little one," he whispered, watching it disappear. He closed the door and took a seat by the fire, warming his hands.

"Mrs. Stone—?"

"Mmm?"

"So does this mean I can be your apprentice?"

"I daresay it does."

He tried not to grin too broadly even though his insides were doing back flips. He could not wait to share the news with Bridget. If only Sir Westwood were here! He imagined the grizzled knight clapping his back with a proud nod.

Mrs. Stone tended to the blaze with her wooden staff. Augum was afraid it would catch fire, but when she removed it from the flames, it was not even charred.

"The quest was a real adventure, Mrs. Stone."

"Was it now?"

"Oh—yes," and with no interruption, he spent the next while recounting the events of the previous day—the Legion; the black-robed rider and his lightning rings; meeting his new friends; the storm; the snowball fight; the invitation to go to school at his friends' village; and finally, the village naming ceremony tomorrow night. He omitted the whole bit about the claw though, fearing a lecture about the dangers of wild arcanery.

Meanwhile, Mrs. Stone had poured them chamomile tea and sat in her rocking chair to listen. She only raised a silver brow when he mentioned the black-robed rider.

"Indeed, and I know about the village in the forest," she said at the end of his retelling.

Augum waited, but she did not elaborate. "So ... about the ceremony ... can we please go?"

Mrs. Stone frowned just as he had imagined her doing. "I do suppose the time has come to return to the world again. Well, as long as you work hard in your training tomorrow, I see no reason why not."

Augum rubbed his hands together, vowing to work extra hard.

"As for you going to school there—we will have to see."

"Yes, Mrs. Stone." Then he remembered something. "Mrs. Stone, can I, um, ask you a personal question—?"

Her jaw firmed. "If you insist upon it."

"How …" He braced, trying to word the question as delicately as possible. "How many stripes do you have?"

Mrs. Stone stopped rocking and gave him a look that made him shrink in his chair.

"Be wary of power, Augum, for power corrupts."

He nodded quickly, cheeks burning, and took a sip of tea. Best to change the subject.

"So … if I went to school with my friends, how would apprenticing with you work?" It was strange to use the word "friends".

Mrs. Stone picked up her tea and resumed rocking. "If you studied only with me, I would assume full responsibility of all your arcane schooling. However, if you attended the village school, your apprenticeship with me would focus on the lightning element. Traditionally, a student would have a mentor outside of their regular schooling to guide them through the many subtle intricacies of their element. It has been that way since the Founding."

"What's the Founding?"

"Unnameables give me patience. Has Sir Westwood taught you nothing about arcaneology?"

He wrung his hands. "Um, well, Sir Westwood preferred to focus on combat and hunting. I've never seen a warlock visit the village, and magic was … not talked about except in children's stories …" He mumbled the last part.

Mrs. Stone's eyes narrowed. "We do not use that word, Augum. We use 'arcanery' or 'sorcery'. 'Magic' is for children and parlor tricks and other such nonsense."

"Yes, Mrs. Stone." He recalled Bridget mentioning something to that effect.

Mrs. Stone took a sip of tea, gaze returning to the fire. "I suppose now is as good a time as any for you to start learning.

The Founding was the most important event in all of recorded history. So important in fact, the calendar starts on that very date, the 1st day of the 1st month of the 1st year—3340 years ago. It was an illustrious affair; the greatest warlocks of the time from the seven primary elements came together and formalized the degrees, signified by arm rings. A degree is now three standard spells that every warlock learns plus—"

"—one spell from their element; Bridget told me."

"Do not interrupt, child." She glared at him before continuing. "Although anyone could learn spells beyond their degree level, it was deemed that learning them in this order was the most sensible and safe way to master the arcane discipline. It also gave a foundation to the study of sorcery, allowing schooling while simplifying advancement and apprenticeship. Before the Founding, arcanery was wild and volatile. Some southern faiths say the Founding was the moment the Unnameable gods descended on Sithesia to grant humans a portion of their powers. Other faiths have their own version of what happened."

She made to get up but he wanted to know more.

"So when was the Academy of Arcane Arts built?"

She sat back with a huff. "The academy, at least the one in Blackhaven, was founded about a thousand years ago. It is by no means the oldest, but it has achieved a level of respect few schools could match. Be that as it is, with the Legion in control … well, may the spirits have mercy on the place."

"There're other schools?"

"Gracious me, child, the capital of every kingdom has one."

Augum just stared at her.

"Oh, for goodness sake." She stood up with a groan and retrieved a rather large scroll from a shelf, handing it to him. "This is a map of all of the known lands of Sithesia."

He unfurled the crinkled parchment, finding a detailed plot of kingdoms and their capitals. He took note of Tiberra to the east, Nodia to the southeast, Canterra to the south, Sierra to the far south, Abrandia to the west, and Ohm to the north. Solia was in the top middle.

She fetched her staff. "I am an old woman who needs her rest. Tidy up before going to bed."

"Yes, Mrs. Stone."

She shuffled down the hall. "Tomorrow we begin your training. Be sure to get a good night's sleep."

Her door closed, leaving Augum with a dying fire but a brightly lit imagination. He rolled up the map, tidied the room, washed up in a basin, and headed off to bed.

As sore as he was from the journey, he was so excited to be an apprentice warlock that it was quite late before sleep finally took him.

FIRST TRAINING

The following morning, Mrs. Stone returned to prodding Augum with her staff. "Up, Augum, up! Your first day of training awaits."

He cursed the staff under his breath and imagined flinging it down the mountain.

After rolling out of bed, he dressed in his itchy burgundy robe and stumbled to the table, eyes puffy and hair askew. A steaming bowl of soup, an apple and tea awaited him. He ate slowly, trying to come to his senses. Even the windows were still dark. At the farm, he hated getting up before the sun.

"Mrs. Stone, do warlocks always rise so early?" It was an innocent question, but one he regretted immediately.

"I will not suffer impertinence, Augum. An apprentice does what he is told. This is not a game. Lightning is a serious element that takes concentration and discipline, and discipline is built on many foundations, not the least of which is waking early—"

He kept his bleary eyes low while she scolded. The way he felt, he would have gladly traded discipline for a few more hours of sleep.

"—nothing but good sense. Now clean off the table and join me outside." She strode through the front door.

Augum, recalling the village naming ceremony was that night, quickly did as she asked. When he stepped outside, a blast of cold wind almost sent him scurrying back in. He drew his hood and bounced on the balls of his feet, trying to stay warm.

The sky steadily brightened behind the mountain, casting a sword-like shadow that pierced the retreating night. Mrs. Stone gazed at the dark horizon, one hand gripping her billowing robe, the other her staff.

He was *her* apprentice, this dignified woman who seemed wiser than everyone at Willowbrook put together. The thought made him stand a little straighter.

"Thus far, Augum, you have shown that you have the interest and belief necessary to develop your talents in the arcane discipline. However, you must be wary of exercising the lightning element in an uncontrolled manner."

Augum recalled the incident with the claw.

Her eyes fixed upon him. "Therefore, we start your apprenticeship with a note of caution—you must always be careful of unleashing the maximum potential of your element, for it can spiral out of control. As you advance, your element may want to surge wildly like a river bursting its dam. Learn to control the river. Do I make myself clear?"

"Yes, Mrs. Stone."

"Take note—this warning applies to spells within the lightning element, not to standard spells. The energies are quite different."

"What would happen if I let go?"

"You may inadvertently kill not only yourself, but those around you. Even should you succeed, you may become infatuated with the power. Yes, your talent desires to express itself, but those warlocks that recklessly indulge, risk death and corruption. This brings us to the third principle— expanding on the natural tendencies of your element in a controlled manner is the path to mastery. Repeat it please."

He repeated the principle.

"And do you remember the first principle?"

"First principle … oh yeah, you create pathways in your mind when you cast spells. The more you cast them, the better you get at it."

"Close enough, but in the future, I expect you to know the exact wording. Now, the first elemental spell you will learn is called Shine. Allow me to demonstrate."

She held out her palm. Lightning crackled to life around it, snaking between her fingers. He recalled Bridget's version, a green vine that coiled around her hand.

"The arcane word is 'shyneo'. For some time to come, you will have to say the incantation aloud. This spell is a rudimentary beginning. It will teach you control, it can light your way, it can deliver a small shock and, as with all spells, it will grow in strength as you develop your arcane skill. Try it."

He held out his palm. "Sheeneo." Nothing happened.

"See it before you do it," she said, lightning reflecting in her eyes.

He drilled his focus into his palm. "See it before you do it, see it before you do it … Sheeneo."

Nothing happened.

Mrs. Stone's lightning briefly flared. "Work on your pronunciation. It is 'shyneo', not 'sheeneo'. Say it like you mean it and do not be afraid to shout; subtlety is something that comes much later with practice. Again."

Augum gritted his teeth; he did not want to disappoint her. He stretched out his fingers, shut his eyes, and vividly imagined lightning around his palm.

"SHYNEO!" A tiny bit of heat flashed on his hand. Relieved, he opened his eyes, beaming.

"A beginning, I daresay. Now I want you to practice until midday, and you ought to be patient as this is your first time casting in your element." She paced back inside.

Augum sat down on the lip of the cave and began practicing. It was tedious work—after hundreds of repetitions with different variations of thinking about it, he had only managed to make his palm actually shine twice, and both times the light had been feeble, vanishing quickly. He was surprised how much effort it took for what looked like a simple spell.

As the morning wore on, it grew harder and harder to concentrate and his thoughts began wandering. More than once, he caught himself mispronouncing the word or even blurting gibberish.

By midday, a bank of thick gray cloud obscured the sun, darkening the mountain. He was shivering, his voice was a frog croak, and his frozen fingers refused to bend. Still, he felt he had learned a great deal about the spell. Now all he needed was a rest.

When Mrs. Stone opened the door to inform him lunch was ready, he tried to impress her by holding the light for a count of three. It was barely visible; all she did was grunt before turning her back on him. Nonetheless, he took a deep breath of fresh mountain air, knowing he was a step closer to success and to going to the naming ceremony.

He was too tired to make conversation over lunch, which consisted of smoked cheese, leg of lamb, buttered spinach and aromatic pine needle tea. He ate slowly, savoring every morsel. It was some of the best food he had ever eaten, and he again wondered just how she had carted it up the mountain all on her own.

"You shall continue practicing until suppertime," Mrs. Stone said while reading a scroll titled *A Brief History of the*

Henawa, the Snow-skinned People. "And I most certainly expect results, otherwise you will practice through the night."

He understood well what that meant. Even the idea of missing the evening ceremony made him queasy. Needless to say, he took particular care clearing the table and washing the dishes.

He resumed his outdoor practicing with vigor, hoping to have results that would prove to Mrs. Stone he was a worthwhile apprentice. By suppertime, his head throbbed, hands ached, and his throat felt like sand, but at least he was routinely holding the light for a count of ten. When Mrs. Stone at last appeared to assess his progress, he gave a radiant smile, certain she would allow him to go to the naming ceremony.

"Yes, and hear how it has begun to crackle?" She steepled her fingers. "That means you are doing it correctly. As you progress in your training, you will be able to control the duration, brightness and strength of the spell; and that applies to your extension, which in this case is your ability to shock. Further, as you progress, you can expect to use less and less energy for casting. You may, with enough practice, diligence and skill, even be able to change its shape."

Augum kept nodding, hands behind his back, trying to appear as interested and obedient as possible, but his thoughts were already on the evening's event.

"All right, let us leave it there." She gave a stiff nod and went back inside.

He desperately wanted to ask if they were going to the ceremony but thought it best to wait; if he appeared too eager, she might not let him go.

Supper was delicious. Mrs. Stone surprised him with roast rabbit, country potatoes, red pepper hot sauce, and warm sweetened goats' milk. When he was done, he found himself rushing to clear the table a little too fast, smashing a mug on the floor. His heart sank—he was sure she would cancel going to the ceremony now.

Mrs. Stone knit her brows. "Please pick up all the pieces and lay them on the table."

He hurried to do as he was told.

"This is a Standard 1st degree spell." She held both hands over the mess. "Apreyo." The pieces rolled, jumped and flew together, a few tiny slivers he missed hopping up off the floor. The seams joined and disappeared and the mug soon stood as before. Augum's mouth hung open the entire time.

"The spell is called Repair. Although I need not have used the arcane word to perform it, I believe it best for you to hear the pronunciation. You shall learn it soon enough."

"Yes, Mrs. Stone." He carefully washed the mug in the basin before placing it on its shelf. "And I apologize for breaking it."

"Apologize for being careless and hasty. Patience is a skill that transcends, Augum. You will find it as useful in housework as in spellcraft."

"Yes, Mrs. Stone." Did she really have to correct every little thing?

She must have seen his expression. "Mind your thoughts, Apprentice. There are many lessons outside arcanery crucial for your instruction. Too often, mentors teach strictly within the confines of the arcane way. Thus, you have shallow, weak warlocks running about killing themselves in haste. No, I will teach you mastery." She padded to her room. "And you will learn, Augum. I daresay, you will learn …"

He plopped down in a chair. So that's it. He broke one stupid mug and now he could not go. Did she not understand how important going to the ceremony was to him?

He sat like this for some time, rubbing his temples and staring at the fire, until Mrs. Stone appeared, wearing a snow-white robe finely embroidered with silver lightning.

"Oh, for mercy's sake stop your sulking, child, are you wanting to go or not—?"

A LEGEND RETURNS

They departed at sunset. Mrs. Stone hiked with no trace of a hunch, using her staff as a walking stick, feet nimbly navigating obstacles. Augum wore the same patched burgundy robe with its frayed hemp belt. He felt like a bedraggled beggar next to her and wondered if there was a way to acquire a new robe. Nonetheless, he was grateful to be going at all.

He led the descent with extra bounce in his step, keeping a sharp watch on the forest for Leland or Bridget. He would run, but the thought of a reprimand in front of Bridget was enough to make him stop now and then for Mrs. Stone to catch up. She strode patiently along, in no apparent hurry.

At last, as they approached the snowy pines, he spotted two people waving. Soon he and Mrs. Stone stood before a smiling emerald-cloaked Bridget and a muscular man with a bushy mustache, bulbous nose, and hairy knuckles.

"Hello!" Bridget said, long hair shining. "Please let me introduce my father—"

"—Henry Burns, my lady," the man said with a stiff nod.

"You needn't play stern with me, Henry Burns. I distinctly remember catching you trying to melt the wall to the girls' dormitory when you were this one's size." Mrs. Stone gave a quick nod at Augum, who gaped with a puzzled expression.

Mr. Burns flushed a deep shade of crimson as his eyes grew. "Mrs. Stone—? How did—but surely this cannot be …! Forgive me but I thought you were—"

"—dead?" Mrs. Stone's silver brows rose. "Yes, well, although I may look it on certain mornings, I assure you, Henry Burns, I am quite alive."

Both father and daughter wore the same slack expression.

"Allow me to introduce my apprentice, Augum."

"Augum," Mr. Burns said absently, eyes fixed on Mrs. Stone. "Indeed … it's a pleasure."

Mrs. Stone waited a moment before turning to Bridget. "And who might you be, dear—?"

Bridget gave her father's sleeve a sharp tug.

Mr. Burns looked like he had swallowed a bug. "Oh, yes, forgive me, Headmistress—"

Augum's mouth opened in astonishment. Headmistress? What was going on here?

"—this is my daughter, Bridget. Bridget, this is Anna Atticus Stone, Headmistress of the Academy of Arcane Arts."

Augum now thought his jaw would hit the snow.

Mrs. Stone gave a grunt. "I have not been headmistress for some time." Her eyes fell upon Bridget. "And it is a pleasure to meet you, young lady."

Bridget curtsied, giving Augum a meaningful sidelong look, but he was still trying to come to terms with the news. Headmistress of the academy! So that is why she is so strict!

An awkward moment passed for everyone except, Augum was sure, Mrs. Stone, who stood patiently, robe glittering.

"I see nothing has changed with you, Henry Burns—still dawdling and making others wait on you."

"Yes—I mean no—I mean ... my apologies, Mrs. Stone, you are quite right; I forget myself still. Let us depart." A pink-cheeked Mr. Burns gestured for Bridget to lead the way. She grabbed Augum's sleeve and yanked him along, the pair walking side-by-side. For a while, the only sound was feet crunching on snow.

The evergreens drooped thick from winter, the forest barely lit by the fading light of a blood sun. Behind them, Mrs. Stone walked with purpose while Mr. Burns mutely brought up the rear.

Bridget marched ahead, forcing Augum to catch up. Then she spoke out of the side of her mouth. "Augum, why didn't you tell me—? Do you realize that your mentor is my mother and father's old headmistress from the academy? And that means she was headmistress to almost *all* the parents at our village—"

"I ... I didn't know. Seriously, she doesn't tell me anything about herself."

"Shh, not so loud." She checked over her shoulder before continuing in a whisper. "That's not all, your mentor is one of the most powerful lightning warlocks ever known, not to mention she's also supposed to be—"

"—dead. Yeah, I heard your father ... wait, why's she supposed to be dead?"

Bridget shook her head. "I can't believe you don't know; it's a legendary story. She was supposed to have died in the Narsinian War sixteen years ago. *She* was the one that vanquished Narsus the Necromancer in a duel. The final battle was in the dungeons below the academy, causing a collapse. When they excavated the ruins, they found his body, but not hers. Without their leader, Narsus' army fell to King Ridian's forces, and Solia was saved."

Augum's brows travelled up his forehead and lodged there.

Bridget threw up her hands. "I know, sounds like a fairytale, doesn't it? Well it's true. She's also known for her duels. Supposedly they use them as examples in Arcane Combat class, but you have to be 3rd degree or higher to attend."

He ran his fingers through his hair, realizing he knew precious little about Mrs. Stone ... and history.

"Augum, your mentor is a martyr, a real heroine among warlocks. She has a statue—a *statue!*—dedicated to her at the academy, right at the top of the stairs."

Augum ducked under a snowy branch. "I ... I don't know what to say, I can't believe she didn't mention any of this. I mean, I'm her apprentice!"

"I know, I can't believe it either. Then again, from what my parents said, she was a very private person. She hardly spoke to the teachers other than about school stuff, and she wasn't exactly the student favorite either; really strict and all that. Extremely good at her job though, that's why she was headmistress for so long—like thirty-five years or something." She paused. "Augum, do you realize what people will say when they see *the* Anna Atticus Stone again?"

He could barely comprehend all the news, let alone have any idea of what people will say.

Bridget gestured at an unremarkable bunch of trees. "Stop here, the village is just ahead,"

Augum did not hear anything other than the usual sounds of the forest. "Sure this is it?"

"Yes, but you have to be officially invited by my father; the elders enchanted it so that you can only see and hear it if invited by a sanctioned resident."

Augum was about to tell her that for once he understood, as the cave was like that too, when Mrs. Stone and Mr. Burns caught up. Mrs. Stone peered ahead while Mr. Burns cleared his throat, mustache twitching.

"Mrs. Stone, Augum—I'd like to formally invite you to our village."

Augum reflexively took a step back as the area flooded with the sound of many people talking at the same time. He heard the clinking of glassware, the chopping of wood, the crying of babies, and the bark of several dogs. Fire and torchlight glowed where there was none before.

Augum noticed a circular building, the roof of which was the branched portion of a massive spruce tree. "Is that a *house*—?"

Bridget grabbed his sleeve so he was not left behind. "That's where the Jones' live. The house doesn't go up though—it goes down."

"You mean ... *underground*?" He could not stop staring at the strange tree-topped homes, windows lit with an orange glow.

"Well obviously. Come on, let's go to the fire."

They soon entered a clearing with a large fire in the center surrounded by log benches. Groups of people in every skin tone, wearing all kinds of colorful cloaks, chatted amiably, clustering around twig tables hosting generous portions of fruits, vegetables, meats and drink. A roasted pig sat on a tray near a bunch of distinguished gray-haired people in ornamental robes. The scent of cooked meat mingled with the aroma of burning cedar, the acrid smell of torch oil, and incense. Younglings played in the snow while youths clustered in tight groups.

Mr. Burns raised an arm, voice booming. "If I can have everyone's attention here, please!"

Augum became painfully aware of every eye turning their way. The adults gawked at Mrs. Stone while everyone else stared at him.

Mr. Burns brought his two massive hands together. "Excellent. Now then, it brings me great pleasure to introduce a possible future student at our school by the name of Augum." He gestured Augum's way with an open palm. Scattered applause broke out. Some people even bid him welcome.

"And, to my great surprise, may I introduce his mentor—" Mr. Burns paused and turned to Mrs. Stone, who seemed annoyed, "—Headmistress Anna Atticus Stone!"

The crowd instantly went into an uproar. Younglings whooped and hollered while youths frantically whispered to each other behind their hands. A woman wearing a large purple hat with a peacock feather shrieked and promptly fainted. A tan-skinned man guzzled an entire bottle of wine before shouting, "Glory to the Unnameables, we're saved!" One particularly rotund man actually sat down in the snow to cry.

Some ran into a large tree home and brought even more people out. A new round of hysteria ensued. Everybody was trying to shake Mrs. Stone's hand and talk to her at the same time.

Augum, meanwhile, only had a moment to see the impatient look on Mrs. Stone's face before the crowd surged in on her. He scampered out of the way, trying to avoid being trampled, and jumped on top of a rock. He craned his neck looking for Bridget, finally spotting her animatedly talking to a girl with a blue cloak. He jumped off and found his way to her.

"Oh, hey Bridget," he said, trying to sound casual. "Kind of a crazy welcome, isn't it?"

"Warned you, didn't I? Mrs. Stone is a hero to warlocks, and everyone thought she had died. This is … this is huge. Maybe she can stop the Legion."

"Hey, yeah!" The blue-cloaked girl said, crinkling her nose. She had dark eyes, shoulder-length raven hair, and just the right smattering of freckles. Her arched brows accented her thoughts as she spoke them aloud. "Could you imagine if the people of Blackhaven found out? They might revolt!"

Bridget gave a wry grin as she gestured at the girl with both hands. "Augum, meet my very best friend, Leera Jones."

Augum's cheeks colored. "Hi."

Leera extended her hand. "Nice to meet you, Augum. Bridget told me all about your adventure together. I simply *have* to come along next time. Maybe we can explore the ruins of Horren's Keep, or even River's End!" She gave Bridget a quick look. "And I don't *care* if you think they're haunted—"

Augum accepted Leera's hand.

"Oh no no *no*—! That won't do at all. Shake my hand firmly, like this—" She seemed to put in extra effort to squeeze his hand while Bridget snickered. "See? Otherwise it shows a weakness in character, at least that's what Dad says."

"I thought you're not supposed to shake girls' hands hard," he said. "That's what Sir Westwood said."

She waved that idea aside. "We girls can take it."

Bridget elbowed Leera. "In the city, a man of honor kisses the hand of his lady."

The girls giggled while Augum felt his face glow so hot he thought it might melt the snow around him.

"Oh, and congratulations on passing that test," Bridget said.

Augum smiled sheepishly. "Right, thanks—and thanks for your help; don't think I could have done it alone."

"Sure you could have."

Leera raised a brow. "Bridget mentioned you might be attending school with us."

"Yeah, um, I might be, I guess. Kind of depends on your elders though. Don't know if they'll let me study with you," and he looked to Bridget for news on that front.

Bridget glanced back at the swarm around Mrs. Stone. "Oh, I imagine they'll let you in now. There *were* doubts though. Some of the elders—and even a couple of the teachers—didn't want to let you study with us, saying that lightning was too dangerous. They finally settled on seeing who your mentor was before making a decision, figuring if *he* was competent enough, they'd let you in."

"They certainly got more than they bargained for," Leera said, grinning. "We all did." The girls beamed at him. He smiled back, trying to stop his stomach from leaping around like that.

Something squeaked nearby. They turned to find Leland doing a celebratory dance, singing, "They have to let him in now, they have to let him in! His mentor's Anna Stone so they have … to … let … him … in! Hurrah!"

"Hello, Leland." Augum was glad for the distraction. "How are you? Get into trouble for coming home a day late with Bridget and Robin?"

Leland's cheeks dimpled as he smiled. "Mama and Papa were mad. They didn't let me come get you."

Bridget frowned. "I got in trouble … my parents were *so* angry. Said I was very lucky. Then my brothers joined in—the twerps—apparently their little sister can't take care of herself."

"I'm sorry. You helped me, got into trouble, and I didn't even say thanks."

Bridget snorted. "Forget it—it was heaps of fun."

"And next time, I'm definitely coming," Leera said, eyes widening at the prospect of adventure. "You have to promise, okay?"

Bridget pressed Leera's nose. "Okay, I promise."

" 'Okay, I promise,' " Robin mimicked in a whiny voice, emerging from behind a tree-home. Flanking him were a lanky boy with sunken eyes and a blue-eyed girl with blonde locks.

Leera's eyes narrowed. "Bored, Robin?"

Robin feigned surprise. "Hey now, Leering Leera found her first friend! Oh, wait—that's just Broken Bridget. She doesn't count."

His cohorts cackled.

"Still hanging out with the Leer, Bridgey-poo?" the blonde girl asked. She wore a pristine velvet blue cloak with embroidered silver snowflakes.

Bridget crossed her arms. "Yes, Haylee, and it's far better company than *you* keep."

"Yeah, because I hang out with six year olds."

Leland kicked muddy snow in Haylee's direction. "I'm nine and a half!"

"Hey, watch it, you little snot! Cloak's worth more than your parent's dung-filled hovel—"

"Probably more than all the gutterborn hovels put together," the lanky kid said.

"Don't you dare use that word," Bridget said. "If you had any decency at all—"

She went on chastising while Augum had a vision of the Penderson brats surrounding him, taunting and name-calling. His hands balled into fists. "Why don't you three choke on hog tails and get tangled in a fence!"

Both groups turned to him, mouths open.

That had been one of Dap's favorite insults. Apparently, they had not heard anything like it before.

"Certainly creative," Leera said out of the corner of her mouth.

Augum wanted to spit in the snow like Sir Westwood. Considering the company, he thought better of it.

Robin turned to Haylee. "Was that some kind of farm boy insult?"

The pair broke out laughing.

"What did that even mean?" the lanky kid added with a chuckle.

Augum took a step closer. "It means get lost."

Robin's eyes caught the firelight. "Why, just cause your mentor is Anna Stone?" He turned to Haylee. "Should have seen this kid cower before the Legion—" He made a frightened pose.

Haylee and the lanky kid cackled.

"No, because, because—" but Augum's brain froze. He wanted to say something about his fist meeting Robin's face, but the girls were looking at him and he did not want to come across as some baseborn brute like Dap.

Robin shook his head. "Listen to him stammer. Pathetic. You would have wet yourself if it wasn't for tiny Leland saving your hide. And fat good it'll do you having Anna Stone for a mentor, she's older than dirt."

"I wasn't stammering—you're just playing dumb, something that seems to come naturally to you—" Augum knew Robin's strategy all too well, and he was not having any of it, especially in front of his new friends.

Robin made his hand yap along while grinning with his cohorts.

"Hmm," Bridget said, looking skywards while placing a finger on her chin, "I seem to recall it was *you* that almost peed yourself in the tent with the claw, Robin. I also remember how *you* couldn't even cast Shine, pretty much the easiest spell there is. So, in the end, I guess we could say Augum here saved *your* hide, isn't that right?"

Robin stopped grinning. "You piece of gutterborn—"

Leera was quicker though, seizing a bristling Bridget and Augum each by the elbow and gracefully turning them away. "All right then," she said over her shoulder, "thanks for that wonderful chat, Robin, Haylee, Dilbur ... never cease to entertain. Think we'll go and have some chicken now."

Leland must have made some sort of rude gesture because Robin suddenly frothed with rage, asking the others if they saw, promising Leland would get his just-desserts later.

"Hey you little misfit, come here," Leera called to Leland with a roguish smile. "Just ignore them. You too, Augum— don't pay them any mind."

Augum was not at all afraid of Robin and almost regretted not going nose-to-nose with him, but a stunt like that would surely have jeopardized getting into the school. He could just imagine Robin exaggerating to the officials how wild and crazy Augum was.

Robin, Dilbur and Haylee continued shouting taunts, but Augum only smiled to himself; this was the first time he felt he was *in* with a group. He listened to Leera agree with Bridget about how stupid Robin looked, how bad Dilbur smelled, and how spoiled Haylee was. Leland, meanwhile, skipped off to play with a friend his age, the dust-up already forgotten.

"… and if it wasn't for Haylee's grandpa being Chief Elder and buying her all those things," Bridget said, "she'd probably have nothing to talk about."

Leera nodded along smartly. "She's about as shallow as a dry creek bed."

They stopped at one of the food tables. Augum helped himself to a candy apple on a stick.

"You know," Bridget said, waving a crispy chicken leg, "I think that Haylee might be a little jealous we snagged you for our side, Augum."

"Oh?"

Leera's fingers travelled over the sweets. "She wishes. Anyway, Robin and Haylee act like royalty, they even have a nasty little clique that fawns over them." She picked out some sugared ginger, licking her lips. "Robin is the favorite son in the Scarson family and Haylee's grandpa is Chief Elder. Both families know King Ridian, and Haylee and Robin claim to be friends with Prince Sydo."

"They were nobles back in Blackhaven," Bridget said with a tedious look, "so they see most of us as lowborn trash."

"Gutterborn is one of their favorite words," Leera added.

Bridget frowned. "Don't use that word."

"You get called that too?" Augum asked. "You don't even look like … well, whatever it is we're supposed to look like."

Leera smiled. "Exactly." She turned to Bridget. "You know, I think he'll fit right in."

Augum's palms tingled. That had to be one of the nicest things anyone had ever said about him.

Leera's voice dropped to a conspiratorial whisper. "Bridget told me you're an orphan."

"Hope you don't mind that I told her," Bridget said quickly, "she's my very best friend and completely trustworthy and loyal—"

"—and brave," Leera added with a grin, "and smart, and beautiful, and—"

"Oh shush already," Bridget said with a smile.

"Is everyone playing nice with the new boy?"

Augum turned to see a freckled woman with gray-streaked raven hair.

Leera rolled her eyes. "Yes, *Mother* ..."

"Good. I hope you won't get him into any trouble." Leera's mother extended a tray full of cups with a purplish mixture. "Now who would like to try my very special Naming Day concoction?"

Augum got a whiff of a most ripe odor, much like rotten meat mixed with rank onion.

"Please, Mum, we don't want to try anymore stinkroot experiments."

"That was only one time, Leera, this one is different, I promise."

"Ugh ..."

Augum felt bad for her just standing there. "I will try one, Mrs. Jones."

"You'll regret it," Leera said through a cough.

Her mother's arched brows crossed briefly at her daughter before she smiled encouragingly at Augum. They all watched as he took a sip.

Except for the time Garth Penderson shoved his face in cow dung, the concoction was the vilest thing Augum had ever tasted; he actually *heard* his stomach plead for pity before gurgling in surrender. It was hard not to grimace in revulsion.

"Very, uh, nice, Mrs. Jones ... thank you for that."

"See, I knew you'd like it! I wish Leera would take your example and try things her poor old mum labored over. One day, when her father and I are gone, she'll realize just how much she misses her mother's cooking." She moved along to offer the mixture to the crowd. Many seemed to have forgotten something in their homes as soon as they spotted her coming.

Leera groaned while rubbing her eyes. "Augum, please, take my parents—they're free."

"Her mother's an ale taster and a brewer," Bridget said. "She's really a very nice lady."

Leera gave an unfortunate nod. "And Dad's a saddler. Aren't we a fun family ..."

"Are they warlocks too?" Augum asked, wondering if Leera would take offense if he set the drink down somewhere. The smell was making him dizzy.

"Mum hit the ceiling at the 2nd degree and Dad at the 3rd." Leera reached across and snatched his drink. "And you can stop pretending to like this. That's right, I saw your face twitch." She discarded the contents under the table, handing him back the cup. "There, now you'll be loved for life when she sees you finished it."

"Mrs. Jones will just give you another one," said an approaching skinny boy with ebony skin. He had an oval face and wore a ruby-red cloak with fur-topped boots.

"Augum, meet Tyeon Sharpe," Bridget said. "He's with us."

Tyeon extended his hand with a polite smile. "Call me Tye."

"Augum."

"Bridge, Lee—how's it going?"

"We're recruiting," Bridget said.

Leera flashed a roguish grin. "Snagged one for our side."

"Ah, the war continues—Gutterborns versus Snobs."

"Tye, don't use—"

"I know, Bridge, sorry." He turned to Augum. "So the legendary Anna Atticus Stone is your mentor."

Augum put the empty mug near Leera, who promptly hid it behind a bowl of carrot sticks. "Yes, at least until she loses patience with me." He forced a smile, though truthfully he felt dumb; he had a lot of catching up to do.

"Are you kidding? If she was my mentor, I'd have taken the Lord of the Legion's place by now—"

"Tyeon Sharpe—"

Leera rolled her eyes. "He was *kidding*, Bridge."

"Correct, Leera, I was in fact kidding. Anyway, I can't believe she's alive even. It's big news. This is great for everyone."

"I'd love to be there when Lord Sparkstone finds out," Leera said, reaching past Augum to snag a branch of grapes the size of plums. "Just to see the look on his stupid face." Her eyes closed as she bit into a grape. "Mmm ..." She dangled the branch before Augum, singing, "I know you want one ..."

Augum plucked a fat grape. He bit into it and a spicy sweet and sour flavor exploded on his tongue. It immediately took away the nausea of that foul concoction.

"Wow ..." he said.

Leera's brows rose. "Wait, you've never tried Titan grapes? And I thought I was sheltered ..."

Augum swallowed and reached for another. They really were outstandingly good. "I grew up in a small village."

"You're not the only one," Tyeon said. "I was born in a hamlet in the Sierran deserts. About the only thing we had to do was chase sand snakes and beat each other up."

"Sounds familiar," Augum said, "except for the snakes part." He imagined running up a yellow dune, feet sinking into hot sand. "At least you got to travel, I haven't been anywhere yet. What brought your family this far north anyway?"

Tyeon gave up trying to swat the branch of grapes Leera kept dangling before his face and plucked one. "My family fled north during the Stormsand uprising when I was six."

"You remember it?" Bridget asked. "The uprising, that is?"

"The only thing I remember is seeing rain for the first time. Wagon got stuck in mud, but I got to play. Mother called me filthy. Come to think of it, she still does."

Leera scoffed. "There was a big war around you and *that's* all that you remember?"

"Mostly. Why, was I supposed to remember everything I saw at six years of age?"

Leera gaped a moment. "Well, *I* do. I mean, I remember crawling the streets of Blackhaven, visiting the Black castle with Mum and Dad—"

But Augum's attention snagged on a short woman with too much makeup, wearing a mustard cloak and saffron boots. She had been jumping up and down, saying "Yoo-hoo!" to Mrs. Stone, when she tripped over her own feet and fell face first into the muddy snow, nearly rolling into the fire. She hastily stood, swirled some of the mud onto her cheeks as if it was rouge, and resumed trying to capture Mrs. Stone's attention.

Augum nodded at her. "Um, who's that?"

Bridget snorted a laugh. "Oh, that's Ms. Drumworm. She's supposed to be one of our teachers."

"She's completely crazy," Leera said. "As in, eats-leaves-because-she-thinks-they're-good-for-aging kind of crazy. No idea how she got the job."

"Friends with my grandma," Bridget said, popping a honeyed almond in her mouth. "Nana thinks she's adorable."

"Both our grandmas are on the village council," Tyeon said to Augum. "I think they hired Ms. Drumworm just to get more of those anti-aging tips."

Leera tossed the remaining branch of Titan grapes back into the bowl. "Ms. Drumworm and your nanas also share similar tastes—knitting, drinking—"

"—and gossiping," the three of them chorused, chuckling.

Tyeon picked up a plate of goat cheese biscuits, offering everyone some. "So where are your folks, Augum?"

Augum caught a look of concern from Bridget as she took a sip of juice. He picked out a biscuit. "Actually I'm an orphan, but since I've never met my parents, I don't think about them much." He surprised himself with his candor, but had a good feeling about Tyeon. If Bridget trusted him, why shouldn't he?

Tyeon dropped his eyes. "I'm sorry, I shouldn't have assumed."

"It's okay, you couldn't have known."

"Being an orphan is nothing to be ashamed of," Bridget said.

"Maybe he's a forgotten war child," Leera said. "You know, a survivor from the Narsinian War."

Tyeon shook his head. "He can't be, the war ended when Mrs. Stone vanquished Narsus in 3324—sixteen years ago. Forgive me, but you don't look sixteen, Augum."

Leera turned to scavenge for more sweets, muttering, "Bookworm …"

Augum helped himself to a honeyed almond. "Fourteen, actually."

"Look at that, we're all the same age." Tyeon rubbed his forearm. "I should feed Warbeak soon."

"That's his hawk," Leera said. "I have a kitten named Skibbles. Bridget's family has like, fifty dogs—"

"—three," Bridget corrected.

Leera acted as if she had not heard. "Do you have any pets, Augum?"

Augum thought of Meli dying underneath him, feeling the sting of the lash as it came down again and again and—

"Augum?"

"Huh? What? Oh. No, no pets."

"Speaking of which, Bridget just got a puppy." Leera turned to her. "Name him yet?"

"Blinky," Bridget replied absently, curling a lock of hair around her finger.

"Copper for your thoughts?" Tyeon asked when she did not elaborate.

"I was just wondering how she did it ... how Mrs. Stone defeated Narsus and escaped alive. Father said everyone thought he was unstoppable."

"You should ask her, Augum," Leera said, plucking a cherry from a cheesecake.

"Doubt she'd tell me," he replied, watching the crowd buzz around Mrs. Stone. She looked like she regretted coming along; her lips were thinner than a needle, her answers short.

Soon a squat old man with massive overgrown eyebrows started shooing everyone away from her. He was balding and wore a regal robe with a fat golden sash that hung loosely across his chest. He flashed insincere smiles as he barked at people to move; they jumped out of his way as if bitten by a small angry dog.

The crowd slowly dispersed, most going to sit by the fire to talk with each other, some coming to the tables for refreshment, and some, like Ms. Drumworm, still feebly trying to get Mrs. Stone's attention. The old man finally bared his teeth at her and she scurried away with a yelp.

Leera elbowed Augum. "That shriveled parchment there, that's Lord Alexander Scott Tennyson, Chief Elder and Haylee's grandfather."

"He's a right old grouch," Bridget said under her breath. "Hates everyone except his precious granddaughter."

Tyeon nodded. "I heard that as a high-ranking noble in Blackhaven, he sold street kids to the mines."

"That's just a rumor, Tye," Bridget said. "Not even Lord Tennyson could be that cruel."

Leera and Tyeon exchanged a look saying otherwise.

Lord Tennyson raised his nose, placed his arms behind his back and loudly cleared his throat. "Everyone, if I might have your attention—"

A few people went quiet but most continued chatting on.

A sour look crossed Tennyson's face. He opened his palm and shot a bright ice-like sphere into the air. The globe kept expanding until it suddenly burst with a tremendous bang.

"Shut it, people!" he said, bulldog jowls quivering. The crowd instantly went silent.

"Right. Now then—" and he paused for effect, making sure all eyes were indeed on him. "I know how momentous the news is that Mrs. Stone is alive and well—"

People hooted, whistled and toasted to Mrs. Stone.

Tennyson raised a hand again. "And I daresay that we are most pleased that she decided to visit our humble little village."

More cheers, murmurs of approval. Mrs. Stone's lips thinned to the point of disappearing. Lord Tennyson grasped her elbow with claw-like fingers. "Now, I know many of you wish to have a word with Mrs. Stone—perhaps inquire about how she gloriously vanquished Narsus the Necromancer, or even ask where she has been all these years—" Tennyson gave her a greedy look as the crowd tittered appreciatively, "—but I am afraid I must insist that we give her ample space. Mrs. Stone is merely here to enjoy the ceremony as a friendly neighbor, and we should therefore not distress her with our niggling questions. After all, someone in such ... high esteem ... deserves nothing but our respect." Tennyson eyed Ms. Drumworm with a distasteful look.

"Now my dear Mrs. Stone," Tennyson continued, thick brows twitching, "I'd like to say, on behalf of the village and the elder council, that we most heartily accept your apprentice—Yogurt—as a pupil in our humble school."

A bunch of people started laughing, Robin's group loudest of all.

Augum sighed. Great …

Bridget's father ran up and whispered something into the old man's ear.

"What—? How do you say it again?"

"Aww—gum, rhymes with bottom."

More snickers.

"What kind of name is that? Oh, all right all right, buzz off, Mustache." Tennyson swatted Mr. Burns away before turning back to the crowd with a pandering smile. "My apologies, everyone. I'm an old man, hearing's not too good you see; apparently the boy's name is … Augum? Anyway, welcome to the school, uh, Augum."

There was much hooting, clapping and toasting, with some booing from the vicinity of Robin, Haylee and Dilbur.

Tyeon shook Augum's hand. "Congratulations."

"Yes, glad to have you with us," Bridget said, smiling heartily.

Leera lightly punched him on the shoulder. "Welcome."

Augum caught Robin's eye. "Nice job, Yogurt," Robin mouthed with a wink.

Augum ignored him. A warm sensation settled over his entire being—he had made friends and was going to an arcane school with them!

BETRAYED

Lord Tennyson held up his hands. "And now I would like the elder council to join me in commencing the village naming ceremony."

The crowd stirred as four other elderly people emerged, silver sashes strung across their chests. Mrs. Stone shuffled over to the food table where Augum and the others stood, helping herself to a branch of Titan grapes, a tired look on her face.

Bridget nodded at a large woman with pink cheeks and a pert nose. "That's my nana." She nodded at an ebony-skinned woman with curly gray hair. "And that one's Tye's." Two other elders, a squat man with double chins and a bald man with a pinched face, joined Bridget and Tyeon's grandmothers.

Augum focused on the man with the pinched face. "Is that—?"

"—Robin's grandpa, yes."

Lord Tennyson corralled the elders into a line. The group hooked hands and began a rumbling chant. Silver wisps emerged from between them and swirled around the crowd before circling the village. The chanting grew in intensity until Lord Tennyson broke his grip and held up a veined arm. The crowd gasped and went quiet.

"I now declare the name of this village to be ... Sparrow's Perch!"

Cheers and toasts erupted; Augum exchanged smiles with his new friends. The elders disbanded and the crowd moved in, buzzing with excitement. Augum happened to be looking at Lord Tennyson when he noticed him signal to the trees.

He turned to Bridget. "Did you see—" but before he could even finish, a tumultuous crashing came from the woods. Black-armored soldiers with massive physiques and rough faces emerged on horseback, brandishing swords, axes, maces and spears. Behind them came more riders—gargantuan crimson-armored warriors wielding burning swords and wearing flat helms pierced with two horizontal slits. They rode dead-looking horses with sharp teeth and bloody eyes.

Augum felt a chill as Bridget's words echoed in his brain—the Red Guard ... you see one, you're not going to live to tell about it.

The shouting and screaming began immediately.

"Save yourselves, it's the Legion!"

"Don't let anyone escape!"

"The children, grab the children!"

"Death to the insurgents!"

Tyeon ran for his family. Leera and Bridget were about to do the same when a Black Guardsman reared his steed before them. Augum instinctively shoved the girls aside as the horse came down, narrowly missing his head. He looked up to see the soldier release a spiked ball and chain.

Augum froze, skin prickling. The man swung the flail in a wide arc. Suddenly there was a bright flash and a sharp cracking sound. The rider landed with a dull thud beside him, armor smoking. The scent of burnt flesh filled Augum's nostrils, turning his stomach. He scrambled to his feet as Mrs. Stone stepped forward, arcs of lightning connecting with objects around her. She stood rigid, brows hawk-like, the space around her warping. She pointed at Augum and spoke an arcane phrase. A shimmering electric sphere appeared around him, Bridget and Leera, trapping them inside.

"Mum, Dad—run!" Leera screamed while Bridget shrieked for her family.

But there was nowhere to go; knights and soldiers surrounded them, circling like wolves. The villagers crowded around the fire, backs to each other. Tyeon shielded his blind grandfather, a stooped man with a cane who had to hold on to Tyeon's arm. A short balding man with dimpled cheeks held onto Leland, a bespectacled woman in a flowery dress by his side.

"Prepare for battle!" Bridget's grandmother said, green rings flaring to life just past her elbow. A colorful assortment of striped arms quickly joined the resistance. Nobody moved to attack, however. Only Mrs. Stone, a rippling field of electric blue, stood apart.

The throng of soldiers gave way. A massive horse with weeping bloody eyes and hanging skin emerged from behind the Red Guards. Tendrils hung like wet noodles from an exposed ribcage. Bleached skulls accented a spiked saddle. The man that rode this deathly stallion wore golden plate, chest marked with the burning sword emblem. A great crimson plume bobbed from his helm. His cloak, made from pure lightning, crackled. His gauntleted hands clutched the reins, prodding the horse forward until stopping beside the cluster of villagers. He ignored them as if they posed no threat, keeping his gaze fixed on Mrs. Stone, who calmly stood between him and the shimmering bubble.

"You know why I have come," the golden-armored man said. "I should have known better than to have taken your word."

Mrs. Stone extinguished the lightning that crackled around her body. "Oh, but he came to me, Lividius."

"I have a new name now, *Grandmother*," he said, voice full of spite. "Lord Sparkstone."

Quiet gasps and murmurs from the crowd.

"The nickname you adopted when we began your training."

"Most correct, great teacher. Now I am Lord of the Legion."

A hot prickle crawled up Augum's spine; Unnameable gods, Mrs. Stone's grandson was the *Lord of The Legion*!

"I have changed much since then, Grandmother."

"At the expense of many others, I daresay."

"You do not know me; you *never* knew me!"

"But I did know you, Lividius. A boy who spent hours before a mirror; a boy who used his friends like toys to be thrown away; a boy who lied, cheated, stole and m—"

"ENOUGH—!"

Horses whinnied; soldiers and villagers alike stirred. Only the Red Guard stood still, burning swords hissing.

Mrs. Stone's voice was heavy and laced with sorrow. "I am ashamed of you, Lividius."

Lord Sparkstone slowly raised his chin. "Show me my stolen heir. Show me the son of my beloved, you wretched old thief."

Mrs. Stone expelled a long breath and stepped aside.

Augum felt the hairs on his neck stand up as the Lord of the Legion's eyes found him, still trapped inside the bubble with Bridget and Leera.

"I reveal him to you only for his sake," Mrs. Stone said.

Augum took a step back, shaking his head. "No, it can't be … it just can't be …"

Mrs. Stone's voice was soft. "I fear it true, Augum. The Lord of the Legion is your father. He is my grandson, and you are my great-grandson ..."

Bridget and Leera's hands shot to their mouths. The crowd stood absolutely still, watching. Even the soldiers stood quiet.

Sparkstone, the Lord of the Legion—*his father!*—jumped off his horse and approached the electrified bubble, crouching before it. He removed his plumed helm.

Augum could hardly breathe. It was almost like a mirror image staring back at him, older but with the same wiry frame, strong chin, arched brows and umber hair, though longer and darker and streaked with gray. The face had a maniacal twist to it, however, like an evil twin that had grown up all wrong; *and the eyes* — they crackled lightning just like the Black Robe's.

Looking at that face, he knew it was true—this was his father, the man responsible for the burning of Willowbrook, for the death of Sir Westwood, for the death of so many others. Why had she not told him? *Why!* He fell to his knees, barely feeling Leera and Bridget each rest a hand on his shoulder, giving it a squeeze. He kept shaking his head. "No ... no ..."

The voice was quiet. "Yes. You are my son, and I have come to take you home."

Augum's lip quivered. "Home ...?"

"Yes, home, to the place of your birth—the Black Castle. I have so much to teach you. You are my rightful heir. You should be here by my side." Without averting his lightning gaze, Lord Sparkstone addressed Mrs. Stone. "Does he still carry the name, or did you change it in your arrogance?"

"Augum Stone, after his great, great, great-grandfather, bestowed upon him by you *and* your wife."

His father winced before his expression turned to granite. "You *dare* talk about her—"

"What is left of your conscience betrays you," Mrs. Stone said.

Lord Sparkstone continued as if he had not heard. "Same name ... good." His gaze softened as pain passed through his face like a wave. "You have your mother's eyes and nose. How I wish—"

"We cannot change the past, Lividius," Mrs. Stone said, pacing near.

The Lord of the Legion flexed his jaw. "I am speaking with my son."

"We must face our regrets. I can name a few—I regret training you despite reservations. I regret showing you the family inheritance. I regret not paying more attention to your ... *exploits*."

"First you stole my inheritance, and now I find out you stole my son!" Lord Sparkstone reached out to the bubble but Mrs. Stone caught his wrist. Both of their arms instantly lit up with electric blue rings. The Lord of the Legion's arm had a full complement right up to his shoulder, but Mrs. Stone's arm was a solid blue sleeve, as if all the rings had merged.

For a brief moment, the two of them locked eyes. Then Lord Sparkstone exploded backwards.

The crowd gasped as every single soldier surged forward.

Sparkstone threw up a hand, instantly staying his troops. He slowly got to his feet, picking up his plumed helm and brushing it off. "You will pay dearly for that, Grandmother. I will not be denied again."

Mrs. Stone's chin dropped a little as the space around her warped and crackled.

A commotion began behind the Lord of the Legion.

"My lord, this old bag of cabbage wants a word," said a man obscured from view.

"Bring him forth, Commander Rames."

Augum felt his blood run hot. Commander Vion Rames was Mrs. Stone's former apprentice and the man directly responsible for Sir Westwood's murder!

Rames stepped forward wearing a lightning-embroidered black robe. Augum instantly recognized him as the black-robed rider he had encountered on the way to Hangman's Rock. They had met face-to-face, and neither had known the other …

Rames' electric eyes briefly met Augum's before flicking over to Mrs. Stone; but if his presence affected her, she did not show it. He kicked Lord Tennyson forward. The old man landed face-first in the muddy snow.

"Grandpa—!" Haylee rushed forward, quickly caught by Robin. "Let me go—!"

"No, Hayles, wait, trust me—"

Tennyson coughed and raised a hand staying his granddaughter. "Great lord … our arrangement …"

"Yes, yes." Lord Sparkstone waved lazily. "The Legion is grateful for the information you have provided. You, your family and fellow loyalists may go. Consider your nobility and estates restored. Commander—pay the man."

Tennyson repeatedly bowed. "Oh, thank you, my lord, thank you …"

Rames removed a bag of coins from his belt and threw it at Lord Tennyson's feet. Tennyson picked it up and beckoned to his family and at the Scarson family, some of whom seemed genuinely surprised. Haylee's face contorted in confusion, Robin's in triumph. The crowd hissed as they passed.

Lord Sparkstone watched the group depart with a sneer before donning his helm and mounting his deathly stallion. His crackling eyes settled on Mrs. Stone. "You still have it, that which rightfully belongs to me?"

Mrs. Stone only straightened.

Lord Sparkstone nodded slowly. "So, since you do not want to return my son, nor that which belongs to me, you really do leave me no choice, Grandmother." He smugly reached into a pouch and removed a small crystal orb.

Mrs. Stone's face visibly fell. "A scion ... how did you get it?"

Lord Sparkstone smiled. "A most difficult acquisition, Grandmother." He held the orb for another moment, letting Mrs. Stone fully appreciate the situation, before releasing it to hover. The crowd took a step back, many looking about uncertainly.

The orb began glowing; in a ripple effect starting from its position, the villager's arms fell dark, one by one.

Pandemonium broke out.

The Red Guard reared up on their deathly horses and came crashing down on panicking people. Some villagers tried to cast spells that did not come, some tried to run, while others dropped to the ground trying to shield family members. The soldiers' burning blades found them, slashing men, women and children without mercy, setting some ablaze.

Tyeon jumped before his grandfather, taking a spear through the gut. He crumpled at the man's feet. His blind grandfather tried to scoop the boy up, but a blow to the head from a mace felled him. He fell onto his grandson.

While Mrs. Stone put a dozen black-armored soldiers to sleep at once, Sparkstone pointed his arms at the crowd, unleashing a ripping bolt of lightning. It spread from the first person to the next, linking them in a chain. They rose in the air en masse, convulsing, feet losing shoes and slippers. They began smoking before bursting into flames.

Bridget and Leera were beside themselves, frantically pounding the bubble with their fists, crying hysterically; but it was the screams from the villagers that made Augum's blood curdle.

Some of the riders stopped their butchery to watch, faces hidden behind steel helms. Meanwhile, the Red Guard, Rames, and his red-robed lieutenant raced towards Mrs. Stone.

She only had a moment, which she used to swing her staff at the bubble. Their eyes briefly met and Augum thought he saw fear there. Then her arm, sleeved in a mass of dense blue energy, went dark. That very instant, the crystal tip made contact with the bubble, shattering the wooden portion of the staff. Augum, Bridget and Leera smashed against the inner wall as the bubble soared into the air.

The last thing Augum saw was Mrs. Stone being overwhelmed.

ESCAPE

When Augum opened his eyes, he was laying face down in a thorny bush, the coppery tang of blood in his mouth. His head throbbed, as if somebody had slammed it against a stone wall. He was disoriented and nauseous.

Someone moaned nearby.

He began wrestling with the thorn bush. "Bridget, Leera—that you?"

Bridget's voice was shaky. "Augum ... I can't wake Leera up—"

Those words muted the pain and sharpened his senses. "I'm coming!" He struggled with the thorn bush, the branches raking his flesh and snagging his robe. The bush finally released him onto snowy ground. There he found Bridget sitting against a frosted boulder, face wet with tears, left arm limp by her side. Leera's head lay in her lap. Blood covered both girls.

"They're all gone …" Bridget whispered, rocking back and forth while absently sweeping raven hair from Leera's pale forehead.

Augum glanced around. The clouds had cleared, revealing a vast sky filled with brilliant stars, partially obscured by a gargantuan shape above them. "I think we're on Mt. Barrow."

Bridget only kept rocking. "They're all gone …"

"Come on, we'll take her to Mrs. Stone's cave." He nodded at the mountain. "It's up there. Can you walk?" He paused, gentling his voice. "Look at me, Bridget. Can you walk?"

Her eyes wandered over to him. She winced. "Yeah, but I think my arm is broken."

Horses whinnied in the distance. Bridget began to breathe rapidly. "We have to go—" She gritted her teeth as they hooked Leera's arms around their necks.

A general hollow feeling began as they climbed. Was this somehow all his fault? Were they all dead because his father, the Lord of the Legion, had come for him? Stomach-churning guilt and prickling shame gnawed at him until he stumbled, causing Bridget to cry out in pain. "I'm sorry," he said, hoisting Leera's weight onto himself while Bridget recovered. Thereafter he resolved to concentrate on the climb.

Bridget's face hardened with determination. "I'll be fine …"

Augum glanced back at the forest, spotting the occasional flicker of torchlight.

"They're looking for us, aren't they?" she asked.

He did not reply.

The ascent was grueling, magnifying every scratch and ache. They finally managed to slip over the lip of the cave, the sound of distant commands echoing through the crisp night.

Bridget peered around the hollow, panting. "There's … nothing … here."

Augum stared at the door and windows before grasping the problem. "Bridget Burns, Leera Jones—I formally invite you to my home."

Bridget exhaled. "I see it."

He wondered if the enchantment would protect them from his father and the Legion. Hadn't protected Sparrow's Perch though, had it?

They opened the door and shuffled in sideways, Leera flopping between them. Augum searched for any sign of Mrs. Stone. The coals hissed; otherwise, the place was silent. "Mrs. Stone—?"

No response.

They lay Leera on the old settee. Wincing, Bridget sat down beside her, nursing her arm.

He scanned the room for ideas. "We've got to revive her somehow."

"Boil some water," Bridget said through gritted teeth.

Augum quickly built up the fire, filled the kettle, and skewered it over the flames.

"Have any Stinkroot?" Bridget asked.

"What's that?"

"Check your stores; you're looking for brown and lumpy roots with small red welts all over."

He shot over to Mrs. Stone's pantry and started rummaging. At last, he found a jar of roots that seemed to fit the description.

"This it—?"

"Yes, grab one and grind it up."

Augum found Mrs. Stone's mortar and pestle and began grinding. He worked as fast as he could, expecting the door to be broken down any moment. The water was boiling when he finished.

"Okay, now what?"

Bridget's voice trembled with pain and sorrow. "Put the stinkroot in a mug, pour water in, and place it under Leera's nose."

He did as she asked, almost gagging when he poured the water. It smelled worse than rotten meat left out in the sun for days. He carefully walked over, holding it at arm's length. The instant he placed it near Leera's nose, she gasped and nearly vomited.

"Damn ... what is that!"

"Stinkroot," Bridget said, pinching her nose.

Leera collapsed back onto the settee. "Ugh ... disgusting ..."

Bridget gestured to the hearth. "Pour the rest in the fire."

He chucked the contents into the hearth; flames leapt as if the stuff was lamp oil.

"What happened? Where are we?" Leera asked.

"We're in Mrs. Stone's cave." Augum lit some candles and went back to make some mint tea.

Leera blinked. "Well, what are we doing—" Her hands suddenly shot to her mouth. Tears began rolling over her fingers. "Mum ... Dad ... we have to go back!"

"We can't," Bridget mumbled. "They're looking for us."

Leera covered her face and wept. Bridget cradled her close.

Augum felt a wave of nauseous guilt sweep over him. He slumped into Mrs. Stone's rocking chair. "I'm sorry," he mumbled. The words sounded weak and useless. In a single evening, he had gained a father, a great-grandmother, and an identity, while Bridget and Leera had lost everyone and everything in their lives—their parents, friends, family, homes, even pets; *they* were the orphans now. What were words in the face of all that?

He stared into the fire.

They sat like this for a while, the scent of stinkroot and mint mingling with burning pine. Augum's thoughts strayed to his great-grandmother. The last memory of Mrs. Stone was that look she gave him before being overwhelmed by a swarm of soldiers. She was dead and the only person in his family now was the Lord of the Legion, a murderer. A heavy, anxious feeling settled in his stomach.

Suddenly there was a sound at the door. Everyone froze. Augum glanced at the corridor, wondering if there was a secret escape passage back there. Then he saw something spark out of the corner of his eye.

The sword …

He snatched it off the wall and unsheathed it, placing the scabbard quietly on the table. The iron handle turned and the door creaked open.

Leaning against the frame was Mrs. Stone, breathing heavily, her once gleaming robe bloody and torn. Something small was in her hand.

The sword clanged to the floor as he ran to her. "Mrs. Stone, you're alive—!"

She took his elbow and allowed him to walk her to the rocking chair.

"Mrs. Stone—?" Leera said in between sobs, "any word of … of our families?"

"This is my friend, Leera Jones," Augum said. Suddenly the word friend seemed too strong. They would never be his friends now …

Mrs. Stone motioned for Augum to pour her some tea, which he did, grateful for something to do. She took the mug and peered softly at the girls, who watched her with desperate hope in their eyes.

Her words were quiet. "I am so sorry …"

Leera and Bridget cried out as if they had been struck, immediately hugging each other tight, shoulders heaving.

Mrs. Stone continued in a distant voice. "Lividius murdered them."

Augum went up to the girls. This time it was his turn to place a hand on each of their shoulders and squeeze. He thought of Bridget's father and his smiling bushy moustache. He thought of Leera's kindly mother and her quirky drink. He thought of Tyeon, Leland, their nanas, Ms. Drumworm—all those people ... and then he remembered Sir Westwood and flames devouring willow trees.

"Were there any survivors?" Leera finally asked between heaving sobs.

"There were three," Mrs. Stone replied, eyes upon the fire. "The mother, father and son of the Goss family. They were badly burned when I saw them to the forest. I stayed behind to give them a chance to escape. Beyond that, I am afraid I do not know."

Bridget sniffed. "Leland ..."

Leera's face darkened. "Everyone died, but the Scarsons and the Tennysons slithered away ..."

After a long silence, Augum wanted to ask the question that was eating at him—why had she not told him the Lord of the Legion was his father? But in consideration of the girls, he thought better of it.

Mrs. Stone set her mug down, eyeing Bridget. "You are wounded."

"Her arm is broken," Augum said.

Mrs. Stone groaned as she stood. She shuffled over, reached out with an open palm, closed her eyes, and said a soothing incantation. A dull glow spread over Bridget. When the light faded, Bridget's weeping ceased.

"Thank you," Bridget said in a meek voice, rubbing her arm. "I feel ... peaceful. I didn't know anyone could arcanely heal outside the healing element."

"The peace you feel is temporary. Your grief will return. As for healing, it is difficult but not impossible to learn. I have been fortunate in my long years to acquire a few select skills and spells beyond the scope of classical training." She then passed her palm over Leera and Augum in turn, healing their cuts and bruises, before finally doing the same to herself. Augum, suddenly calm and relaxed, thought it felt like taking a warm bath.

When she finished, Mrs. Stone padded back to her rocking chair, gesturing at her mug. Augum refilled it with tea and handed it to her.

"Mrs. Stone—" he began, unable to bring himself to call her Nana yet, "—when we were in that bubble, the last thing I remember was seeing you overcome. How … I mean, how did you escape?"

"With this." She revealed what was in her hand—the small blue sphere that once topped her staff. "I, too, have a scion."

Augum took a seat at the dining table to give Bridget and Leera space. "The same thing as my father?"

"Yes." Mrs. Stone let go of the sphere. It hung in the air, storming over with dark clouds, flashing noiseless lightning, and emitting a quiet hum.

The trio sat transfixed.

"When my staff shattered and my arm went dark, I became powerless. It was quite challenging retrieving the scion as it rolled between soldiers' boots."

"Is it some sort of ancient artifact?" he asked.

"Indeed it is—powerful and old." The orb returned to her veined hand, clouding over completely. "Scions were forged by a people many believe died off 1500 years ago."

"The Leyans …" Bridget said. "We talked about them in class a little bit …"

"Yes. The Leyans from the plane of Ley were an ancient sect of humans that had long life spans. They were a quiet and reclusive people, whose primary purpose was to safeguard ancient arcane knowledge. Not long before they disappeared, they faced a great genius who discovered and explored the arcane ways of death and rebirth, becoming a legendary necromancer."

Mrs. Stone paused to take a sip of tea. Augum could not stop staring at the scion. It suddenly appeared dangerous, as if it would attack at any moment; and the casualness she treated it with made him edgy.

"His name was Occulus and he became quite powerful, raising armies of undead that followed his every command. He equipped them with potent arcane weapons and armor, stolen from the Leyans." Her gaze went to the sparking sword on the ground. "His ambition was terrible; he coveted Leyan secrets, their artifacts and, above all, their lifespan, having failed to extend his own with necromancy. You see, the Leyans lived for hundreds of years, the oldest among them a millennium; but they also kept their numbers small, accepting members by invitation only, for they could not bear children. They were guardians of ancient arcanery, passing their knowledge from generation to generation in this manner for eons."

She paused, smoothing her bloody robe, eyes passing over the shelves of tomes and scrolls. "Legend has it the Leyans refused to share their knowledge with Occulus. Seething with bitterness, he unleashed a monstrous war that lasted for many years. In response, the Leyans forged seven scions, each empowered with ancient secrets of one of the primary elements. They then approached the strongest warlocks of the time, one from each of those elements—water, air, earth, fire, lightning, ice and healing, and bestowed upon them the appropriate scion. Occulus thus faced seven wielders of the scions, one by one. As a testament to his power, he vanquished six of them. Yet he met his match in the seventh warlock, the most gifted of them all. Sithesia's last hope was known as a true artist of the arcane, a gifted spellcrafter. An epic duel commenced that was said to go on for an entire day. In the end, the arcane artist emerged victorious—Occulus had been slain."

Mrs. Stone sipped her tea, peering at Augum over the mug's rim.

"What element did he belong to?" Augum asked, somehow already knowing the answer.

123

"Lightning. His name was Atrius Arinthian and he was a great man, passing his knowledge on to his children. He also gave his most worthy son the scion, who thereafter passed it down to his most deserving offspring; and so it went, from father to son, son to daughter, generation after generation, for 1500 years."

"But ... *you* have a scion ..."

"Yes, Augum, I have a scion, and yes, I inherited it from my father, many years ago."

He felt a prickle. "But doesn't that mean—"

"—indeed it does. I am Atrius' ancestor, and therefore, so are you."

Augum sat gaping while Leera and Bridget exchanged red-eyed looks.

"As per family tradition," Mrs. Stone went on, "I could not in good conscience bequeath the scion to one so unworthy as Lividius. I knew this the day your father failed an ancient test you have already passed."

"Do you mean the bird test?"

"Yes, your father left it to die. You can thus imagine my relief when you brought home the bird. It was then I knew you took after your mother. That is a fundamental difference between you and your father, Augum, never forget that. And when the right time comes, *you* shall inherit the scion."

A silence passed that amplified the crackling flames of the fire.

Augum frowned. "But my father also has a scion ..."

"Indeed he does, and it is a grave matter. Miscreants have ruthlessly coveted the scions ever since their creation, along the way destroying families, toppling kings, waging wars, and even extinguishing entire races of people—all in the pursuit of power. Only one scion has remained in the family that originally possessed it." Mrs. Stone held up the sphere before continuing. "The others have traversed Sithesia causing great envy in men, and therefore war; that is why, throughout the pages of history, mentions of scions go hand-in-hand with blood and suffering."

Augum could almost hear the echoes of old battles. The candles flickered as the wind picked up outside.

"You are wondering, perhaps, why I had not passed on the scion to my daughter, Thia. Thia died giving birth to Lividius at seventeen years of age, fifty-two years ago. I regret it now, but I was angry with her for carrying a child out of wedlock. She never revealed who the father was, nor did the man step forward to claim his son after the birth, leaving me to raise Lividius alone. He was the only heir to the scion—until you were born, that is."

Augum nodded slowly, his voice quiet. "What was he like …?"

"Now is not the best time as the story is somewhat long, though I suppose I can attempt to be brief, as I feel it is quite important for you to know who your father was. Even as a young child, he would look at me with scorn. I believe he blamed me for his mother's death, and perhaps, for his father's abandonment. He bored easily, lied and stole often, and seemed to have no remorse when caught.

"The first unambiguous warning sign showed itself when I happened upon a dismembered rabbit in his room. I confronted Lividius and he apologized in that particular way of his, making the gestures but having no remorse behind them. I ought to have had the good sense to keep a closer eye on him.

"Soon he attended youngling school, but circumstance was not kind. The other children picked on him at length. They called him by the usual names of his birth—bastard, gutterborn scum and beast of burden, among others. He became lonely and aloof. One day, in his tenth year, two of his most effective tormentors, a girl and a boy, fell ill and died. Poison, and not just any poison, but malignant nettle, resulting in days of writhing agony.

"I was concerned Lividius had something to do with it, but thought surely even he would not do such a terrible thing. When I brought the matter up, he denied any knowledge. Needless to say, the bullying ceased.

"At thirteen years of age, Lividius' ambition flowered. He studied arcanery late into the night. For the first time, he seemed to have a purpose. I believed him on his way to becoming a man of honor and decided to take a more direct hand in his studies by considering him for apprenticeship. He passed the tests with ease, all but the bird test, of course.

"It was then that I committed a grave error, foolishly ignoring the results of that ancient test. Although it told me Lividius was not fit for the scion, what I failed to grasp was it also told me he was not fit for the arcane discipline. To compound my error, I told him about the scion, hoping that by doing so, he would strive to earn it. You see, I still naively believed in his soul's reformation. Instead, he immediately demanded the ancient artifact as his rightful inheritance. From then on, our relationship fundamentally changed.

"It was a dark time. My hold on him steadily weakened as he resorted to ever more daring attempts to gain the scion. At one point, I even suspected him of trying to poison me." Mrs. Stone glanced to the girls, her countenance softening. "How many paid the ultimate price for my poor judgment? How many more will die?"

"You did what you thought best for your grandson, Mrs. Stone," Bridget said softly. "No one can fault you for that."

Leera suddenly got up and rushed to the window, the glass lit by a reddish glow. A shaking hand covered her mouth. "No …!"

Bridget and Augum scrambled over. Just as with Willowbrook, flames painted the sky orange.

Sparrow's Perch was burning.

"Time is against us," Mrs. Stone said. "I have left a false trail, but it will not be long until Lividius checks here. It is best we leave."

"But isn't this cave hidden by sorcery?" Augum asked, fixated on the distant inferno.

"It is, but Lividius' scion will allow him to see through that. Besides, he still has an open invitation here; I have always left the door open for him to come home, hoping beyond hope for some kind of change, for remorse. I now see how impossible that is, and just how foolish I have been."

Bridget's palms rested gently on the frame of the window. Tears dripped from her chin. Leera's face was also wet, her lips trembling.

"Where will we go?" Augum asked quietly.

Mrs. Stone tucked away the scion. "First we must pack provisions and supplies. Augum, grab your rucksack and fill it with as much food as you can from the pantry, and be sure to take the kettle, a pan, and flint. Bridget, grab one of the rucksacks from the closet and find the blankets—are you listening, child?"

Bridget tore herself from the window. "Yes, Mrs. Stone. Grab rucksack and blankets—"

"—and socks. Leera, find another rucksack and fill it with the scrolls on that particular shelf there, and that book—" Mrs. Stone pointed at the ornate blue tome. "Then fill all the waterskins you can find. It would be best to hurry."

They scampered to complete their tasks while Mrs. Stone rested in her rocking chair, occasionally calling out another item for them to bring. At last, the trio met in the center of the room, rucksacks bulging.

Mrs. Stone groaned as she stood. "Augum, grab the sword and scabbard, it is for you to use now."

For a moment, he thought he had not heard her right. Sir Westwood had not trusted him with a sharp blade, yet here she was giving him an arcane one to use.

He sheathed the sword and secured it to his waist, feeling brave like a knight, before realizing how useless it would be against his father.

Mrs. Stone gave the room a final long look, pausing at her favorite rocking chair, before striding down the hall, the trio right behind. Just before entering her bedroom, Mrs. Stone abruptly glanced back to the front door, eyes narrowing.

"They come. We must hurry."

Augum looked back at the old oaken door, which suddenly appeared threatening. "But how do you know, Mrs. Stone?"

Mrs. Stone paced to the center of her bedroom. "The enchantments I have placed on the mountain have been tripped. Now—prepare yourselves." She closed her eyes in concentration.

Just as Augum wondered how they were supposed to get out of there with no windows or doors, Mrs. Stone's arm flared to life, shining as one solid band of lightning. The room warped as she began invoking words in fluent arcane, tracing a large oval in the air with her finger.

Bridget gave Augum a look he understood as *Spell of Legend*.

When Mrs. Stone finished, there was a sharp ripping noise and a shimmering hole appeared where she had traced, its edges crackling with lightning. A strong wind began blowing from the portal, sending parchment flying and forcing Augum and the girls to grab a hold of each other.

Mrs. Stone turned to the empty hallway and raised her arm, robe flapping violently. A thunderous vibration began in the cave.

"Prepare to enter the portal!"

Augum, Bridget and Leera braced while Mrs. Stone wielded a thick rope of lightning like a whip. Whatever it struck it set ablaze in blue fire. The arcane flame spread in sheets, consuming everything in its path.

Leera grabbed the bed for support, raven hair flying about. "She's going to destroy the cave!"

Augum barely heard her above the screaming wind. Mrs. Stone's entire body suddenly ruptured with a pure white lightning that made his hair stand on end. The ceiling began to fracture and crumble; he witnessed the kitchen area collapse and caught a last glimpse of the dining table as it disappeared into a fissure. The fissure advanced toward them, swallowing everything in its path. Explosions boomed as larger chunks of rock tumbled from the ceiling.

Mrs. Stone glanced back, eyes flaring with lightning. "For mercy's sake, why are you still here—!"

Augum frantically gestured for the girls to go. They scrambled to the gaping hole just as large cracks began to open and close on the walls of the bedroom like hungry mouths. Bridget went first but the wind from the portal was too strong for her. Flailing, she was about to fall back when Augum shoved her into the portal—it swallowed her instantly. He pushed Leera through the same way.

The room grew very hot and the wind increased to a violent maelstrom. Augum looked for Mrs. Stone but was unable to see her through all the flying debris. He braced and lunged for the portal, but the wind threw him to the floor like a sack of potatoes. He found himself pinned against a shaking wall as the room crumbled around him. A huge chunk of the ceiling suddenly smashed onto Mrs. Stone's bed, pelting him with stone.

Realizing time was running out, Augum made one final attempt to fight through the roar. He reached for the portal but only grasped thin air—his exhaustion, the wind and the weight of the rucksack was too much, dumping him to the floor again. Around him, the room was a jumbling mass of rubble and lightning fire.

Just as it dawned on him he was not going to make it, an iron force gripped him and hurled him through the portal.

LONG ABANDONED

Going through the pitch-dark portal felt like being pulled apart in all directions while tumbling end over end. Thankfully, the trip was brief, discharging a dizzy Augum onto a blanket of pristine knee-high snow. Mrs. Stone landed on her feet beside him, wheezing, as the portal disappeared with a loud sucking sound.

"You all right?" Bridget asked as she and Leera helped him stand. "We thought you were a goner—"

"Me too," he said, trying to hold the contents of his stomach down.

They were in a clearing encircled by a needled forest blanketed with snow. Their breath fogged in the sharp frosty air.

Mrs. Stone studied a brilliant clear sky, nodding at a particular formation of stars. "This way, it is not far."

"What's not far, Mrs. Stone?" Leera asked, surveying the still trees.

Bridget hugged herself. "And is it warm there?"

"Not yet," Mrs. Stone said as she strode forth.

Augum exchanged perplexed looks with the girls. "Where are we, Mrs. Stone?"

"Ravenwood. I dare hope it far enough east to be out of your father's reach." She strode forth and they followed.

Ravenwood loomed thick around them, an evergreen forest of pines, cedars, spruces and firs. Sometimes the unbroken snow rose past their waists. At other times, when the canopy obscured the sparkling sky, only up to their knees.

Mrs. Stone made a small gesture with her right hand, out of which flew a pumpkin-sized globe shining with lightning. The floating lamp crackled gently, making shadows creep along with their plodding. She eventually stopped in a tiny glade to examine the stars again, while the trio watched the wood with wary eyes. Bridget's quiet voice broke the silence.

"Mrs. Stone, may I ask what spell you used to collapse the cave?"

"It is off-the-books, a Spell of Legend that took me years to find and proved quite difficult to learn." She nodded at the sky and renewed the trek, adding, "Narsus certainly failed to see it coming though."

Augum leaned near Bridget. "What does she mean by 'off-the-books'?"

"That the spell is unofficial; not taught in school. Off-the-book spells are usually dangerous for one reason or another, that's why they're responsible for a lot of self-inflicted warlock deaths. To find a lesser and mid-range off-the-book spell is uncommon enough, an advanced spell extremely rare, but a Spell of Legend—? Almost unheard of …"

He wondered how many off-the-book spells Mrs. Stone knew, or for that matter, the Lord of the Legion. Thinking about his father made his insides roil. He could not get those lightning eyes out of his mind.

They trooped onward, Augum noting the occasional set of rabbit or deer prints. He recalled once tracking a great brown bear with Sir Westwood, then making a giddy but hasty retreat when the bear noticed them. He felt a pang, missing those happy times.

They hiked for what felt like hours, the wood silent except for the gentle rustle of snow underfoot and the crackle of the floating lamp. Tired and shivering, Augum found himself fantasizing about a warm bed and a hot meal. He hoped to arrive soon, wherever it was they were going. Yet no matter how he felt, he knew his sufferings paled to Bridget and Leera's.

"Not far now …" Mrs. Stone said, waving the orb forward, but the march seemed to have worn Bridget down and she began weeping. Leera placed an arm around her, whispering soothing words.

The group trudged on, coming across the remains of an ancient stone wall.

"Yes, here it is." Mrs. Stone stepped over the rubble. They walked until something tall loomed ahead in the forest, blacker than night.

Mrs. Stone stopped, the shadows on her face moving with the floating light. "We have arrived."

"What is it?" Augum asked in a whisper, peering up at the dark structure.

"An ancient castle."

He noted how silent it was though. "Is it abandoned or something?"

"It certainly should be." Mrs. Stone flicked a finger and the globe dimmed. "It has not been used properly by a king in two hundred years, since then having been inhabited by thieves, brigands, travelers, and those with … darker natures. Let us be quiet now as we approach."

" 'Should be'—?" Augum mouthed to the girls. Nonetheless, he could not help but get a little excited; he always wanted to visit a castle. Sir Westwood had certainly told him plenty about them. He had pestered the knight about everything to do with castles, from what happened to the drawbridge during great sieges, to the routine life of its servants.

Augum surmised that the ruined stone they had passed was the perimeter wall and the entire area onwards the bailey, now long overgrown.

Mrs. Stone guided the way, following castle walls made of black stone and covered in frozen moss and dead vines. They soon came upon a large round structure—a battlement. The group fought the frozen overgrowth to circle it, continuing on to a new side of the castle. The stars provided enough light here for Mrs. Stone to extinguish her globe. There was a clearing with what looked like an ancient fountain in the center. In the distance, they could just make out another corner battlement.

Bridget pointed at a large pile of rubble in the center of the wall. "That must be where the doors were."

Leera gazed upwards. "Wonder if it's haunted …"

Bumps rose on Augum's arms as he followed her gaze. The castle's black silhouette pierced the sky with towers, tapering to a sharp point. The entire thing looked like a tomb.

Mrs. Stone turned and put a finger to her lips before creeping along the wall. To Augum, even the crinkling snow seemed too loud. The sound of an owl hooting in the forest made him think it was a guard alerting the castle. He pictured many dark eyes watching them, knowing, listening …

When they reached the rubble, Mrs. Stone signaled to wait before climbing the pile alone. At the top, she slipped into the castle through a hole in the wall.

The cold seemed to magnify with her absence, their breath freezing in quick bursts. Augum gripped the hilt of his sword as their heads swiveled to every rustle of the forest.

Finally, Mrs. Stone's quiet voice came from the top. "You can come in now."

The trio scampered up the pile, rucksacks swaying. They passed through the hole and clambered down onto a dusty stone floor strewn with debris, lit by Mrs. Stone's ethereal orb.

They were in a vestibule with a high vaulted ceiling. Faded murals decorated the walls depicting a king's court, servants catering to a prince and princess, a colorful crest, a jousting tournament, caped knights, and a line of warlocks in fine robes. Augum knew they were warlocks because their arms had stripes. Notably, every arm had a different color, as did every face.

Empty stone pedestals stood about, the kind that once held exquisite vases or marble busts. Ahead were two massive arched oaken doors with bronze fittings. Deep scratches gouged the ornately carved surface. He imagined some kind of large beast unsuccessfully trying to break in.

Mrs. Stone stood watching them, eyes reflecting blue light.

"Amazing ..." Bridget said, turning all about, voice echoing.

Augum pushed on the doors. They did not budge.

"Arcanely sealed," Mrs. Stone said.

Leera ran her fingers over the gouges. "How can you tell, Mrs. Stone?"

"Because I sealed them myself, child. I grew tired of hearing what transpired here. Something had to be done. This castle has ... history." She stepped before the doors, raised her arm and muttered something in the arcane tongue. Both doors shuddered and popped open with a click, releasing a plume of dust.

Mrs. Stone pushed on a door with one finger. It creaked as it swung inward. Augum winced; if something was inside the castle, it now knew it had company.

The crackling lamp hovered forward illuminating a central marble staircase flanked by two smaller curving staircases.

Massive stone globes stood sentry in the corners, two of which lay destroyed on the checkered floor. Sets of square oaken doors stood to the immediate left and right. An enormous tattered tapestry hung on the far wall above the landing, too shredded to reveal who or what it portrayed.

"This is the foyer. We will be going up to one of the bedrooms." Mrs. Stone began climbing the central staircase, the trio quickly following, gazing about. Embedded into the walls were perches and iron hooks that Augum guessed once held weapons, shields, armor and animal heads. There were more empty pedestals, as well as dark squares where paintings had hung. Everything had a thick layer of dust, yet there were no footsteps. Then again, he suspected ghosts left none.

Mrs. Stone stopped on the third floor. A pair of ornate doors stood before them, with more doors to the distant left and right. "Ah, yes," she said, turning one of the elaborate bronze handles.

It was the most beautiful room Augum had ever seen, and judging by the girls' quiet gasps, he was not the only one to feel that way. The ceiling was made of square wooden panels, each intricately carved with a different scene. An ornately carved ironwood canopy bedstead stood against the left wall. For a moment, he mistook the wispy drapery for giant spider webs. Opposite, six arched leaded-glass windows let in dim starlight. Tattered red velvet curtains hung stiff at the sides. In the center sat an elaborate double-pedestal desk covered with a layer of dust. Embedded into the right-hand wall was an enormous marble fireplace still cradling a pile of wood. To their immediate right stood a large three-door ironwood wardrobe, evidently, like the bed and desk, too large to steal.

Mrs. Stone ambled over to the fireplace. With a flick of her hand, the wood roared to life. The trio dropped their rucksacks and raced to warm up by the fire.

"Augum, please unroll the blankets, we are going to sleep by the fire tonight," Mrs. Stone said after they had warmed up a little.

"Yes, Mrs. Stone." He made the bedding as comfortable as possible while the girls stared into the flames. He knew what was on their minds.

"I know it has been a very trying day," Mrs. Stone said as the trio tucked in, "but I want you to know that you are safe now. Tomorrow is a new day and a new beginning for all of you. Goodnight."

"Goodnight, Mrs. Stone," they chorused.

Mrs. Stone stood watching the fire for some time before she too retired. As exhausted as he was, Augum had a hard time falling asleep. Judging by how much everyone rolled about, he guessed he was not the only one.

QUESTIONS

Augum awoke to a sharp ray of sunshine in his face. He sat up and looked around, yawning. Bridget and Leera were still asleep, Mrs. Stone notably absent. The fire had reduced to glowing embers, yet the room retained some warmth. He clambered out from under the blanket, stretched, and stumbled over to a window.

A sparkling ocean of snow blanketed everything, reflecting sunlight through the towering windows, painting the ceiling with prismatic patterns. Something else flashed below. He squinted through the brightness, finding Mrs. Stone hunched in the clearing, right arm ceremoniously waving about.

What was she up to?

He left as quietly as he could, the castle silent and frosty, freezing his breath. Sunlight reflected down from somewhere up high, dimly lighting the cold marble steps. Augum tiptoed through the dark foyer, pushed open the massive doors to the vestibule, and made his way outside, climbing over the rubble pile.

After carefully descending the other side, he got his first good look at the castle, glistening black in the sunlight. Arrow slits pierced the two battlements. The entire front face shot up four floors, the top two of which had windows. The six windows to their room sat on the third floor. The fourth floor had one enormous circular leaded-glass window, flanked by two pairs of arched windows. Above that was a terraced keep rising four more stories, each story smaller than the last, culminating in a sharp watchtower. Rooms, balconies and minarets jutted strategically from the facade.

Mrs. Stone stood near the snow-covered fountain, its top crowned by two warlocks frozen in an epic duel. She muttered while her hand made a complicated gesture. He crunched over and cleared his throat, hoping he was not disturbing an important spell.

"Mmm—?"

"Good morning, Mrs. Stone, I was just curious what you were up to."

She turned to face him, wrinkles catching the morning sun. "I have just concluded adding one last protective enchantment. Have the girls woken?"

"I thought it best to let them sleep."

She nodded. "Prudent. I expect you to continue to be sensitive; they lost their parents, friends, and almost everyone they knew—whereas you gained a great-grandmother and a father responsible for those deaths."

"Of course, Mrs. Stone." She needn't have even mentioned it.

"But you will need their friendship too, as they will need yours."

He nodded, wondering exactly what that meant. Did she expect them to stay? He shielded his eyes from the sun. "Mrs. Stone—?"

"Mmm?"

"I have a lot of questions."

"I expect so."

His words tumbled like logs over a waterfall. "Why didn't you tell me that I was your great-grandson? Why was I left with the Pendersons? Who is my mother—?"

She closed her eyes and turned to the sun, soaking in its warmth, hands behind her back. "Difficult questions, ones perhaps best answered if we continue the story about your father."

"My father ..." He still could not believe the Lord of the Legion was his father—*his father!*

"At fourteen years of age, Lividius began his first year at the academy and officially became my apprentice. I took a closer hand in the boy's upbringing, thinking a strong arcane focus was just what he needed.

"But Lividius hadn't changed. Instead, he learned to use charm to manipulate people. Dark rumors soon reached my ears, none of which I could prove, for he became secretive. He began to seethe with quiet jealousy. My famous pursuits and duels in the arcane community were intolerable for him. Further, his schoolmates held him to a higher standard simply because I, his guardian and mentor, was also headmistress. I only made matters worse by focusing my attentions on the problem of a young necromancer by the name of Narsus. Looking back, I think that was when it began."

Augum blinked. "What began?"

"Do you recall the horse your father sat on?"

"Yes, it was sort of ... dead."

She raised her index finger. "Or rather *undead*. I believe your father is, and has been for some time, learning necromancy in addition to the lightning element."

"But ... why?"

"A deeply rooted fascination with fear, death and power. I suspect that with his talent in the lightning element, he endeavored to surpass the most powerful necromancer known—Occulus. But I knew nothing of his exploits then—I still hoped for a change in his heart. At twenty-one years of age and in his seventh year at the academy, I thought that change had finally come in the form of a young lady."

"My mother …"

"Yes." Mrs. Stone gestured ahead. "Walk with me."

They began pacing around the yard, slowly circling the fountain. The sun shone brightly overhead, though the air remained sharply cold. Two small winter birds started a chortling conversation in the forest.

"Your mother was the opposite of your father in many ways—she was giving, trusting, caring and emotional, with a radiant smile she would eventually pass on to her only child."

Augum unconsciously touched his cheek.

"Somehow, she reached your father's soul. For the first time in what felt like years, I remember seeing him laugh without malice. She was a joy to be around and single-handedly restored my hopes in him."

"What was her name?"

"Terra Titan, of the Titans of Sierra, growers of Titan grape and makers of Titan wine."

Those grapes came from his mother's family? He could almost taste that sweet and sour flavor on his tongue.

"The Titan clan was a fierce tribe of lightning warlocks, whose blood flowed rich with talent. It was that talent, her beauty and vibrancy that drew Lividius like a moth to flame. One year later, in his eighth and what would be his last year at the academy, they married."

"Did she know about his necromancy?"

"I shall get to that. After they married, Lividius renewed quarreling with me about the scion, using the wedding as leverage. By then, Terra began to see her husband in a new light and spent many a night crying on my shoulder. This infuriated Lividius. At last, perhaps finally understanding he would not receive the scion from me, he cut me out of his life and disappeared with her. For nineteen years, I heard nothing other than rumors of his travels in distant lands, performing strange rituals. Think of that—*nineteen years*. What darkness had he been up to during all that time? What had poor Terra witnessed? One thing is certain, and that is that he continued his studies in necromancy, also achieving his 20th degree in the lightning element, a most difficult and rare feat."

"What did you do all that time, Mrs. Stone?"

"I tried to move on with my life. I occupied myself with the Narsinian war, took on new apprentices, managed the academy, and continued my own studies, striving for the most difficult and elusive goal in all of arcanery—mastery of my element. After defeating Narsus, I used the opportunity to retire from the world. I had no inclination to deal with the fame that I knew would come from my accomplishment. Besides, I was eighty-five years old, having spent thirty-five of those years as Headmistress of the Academy of Arcane Arts. I was simply exhausted.

"I spent the following years exploring Sithesia's more distant lands, finally achieving that life-long goal of mastery in the lightning element. I also built a cave into the side of Mt. Barrow, believing Solia would forever be my home. There I would spend most of my days, enjoying the crisp mountain air and quiet solitude. You are fourteen, therefore you were born soon after my withdrawal from the world, and since I still had not heard from Lividius, I knew nothing of you."

Augum imagined the famous landmark overseeing Blackhaven, the capital of Solia. "He said I was born in the Black Castle …"

"Yes, during Lividius' ascent to power. It was then, sometime after your birth, that I believe something terrible transpired."

"What do you think it was?"

Mrs. Stone stopped to peer at him, half her face in shadow and half in the sun. "I believe your father tried to involve your mother in the necromantic arts. Or, after twenty years of putting up with his possessive nature, she had simply had enough. After all, she had a toddler—you—to think of by then.

"Regardless of the reason, she took you and ran away. Your father, whose following had greatly grown by then, had your mother tracked down. They found her alone. When your father demanded your return, she told him you died as she fled. As you know, I recently went to Antioc to procure provisions. On a hunch, I stopped at the ancient library there and checked the archives. It turns out the Penderson family owed the Titan clan a debt that had been marked as paid sometime after your birth. I suspect that in exchange for that debt, they were to raise you as one of their own."

Augum scoffed. "One of their own …"

"Consider it a better fate than ending up by your father's side."

He sighed. "My father didn't believe my mother when she told him I had died, did he?"

"He did not. In fact, your father immediately suspected me of taking you, perhaps thinking I wanted an heir to pass the scion to other than him. In that last regard, he was quite correct, only it was an idle dream for me, for of course I did not yet know there was a new heir. Further, he never truly believed I died fighting Narsus—he thought I was too strong. In that, he was also correct. Your father sought me out and found me on Mt. Barrow, the only one to do so."

She continued pacing, the snow crunching underfoot. "Our meeting, however, was … unpleasant. He accused me of harboring you and once again demanded the scion. It was only then I discovered that he had a son and that I was a great-grandmother. So you see, I learned about you from him."

"I was born because he wanted the scion, wasn't I?"

"An astute observation, Augum, and one I agree with. Perhaps he thought I would bequeath it to him if he produced an heir. When he found out I did not have you in my possession, it nearly broke him. Only then did he truly think you were lost. The years that followed were supposedly his darkest. I, too, believed you gone forever, until eleven years later, when I found you on the mountain, clothes burnt to a crisp yet you yourself unharmed."

He recalled flying over fields of yellow grass ... a bright flash ...

"Perhaps it was fate," she continued, glancing skyward, "perhaps providence, or just sheer luck. In any case, there you were, safe and in my care."

"But how did you know it was me?"

"By your uncanny resemblance to your parents, but you confirmed it when you spoke your name. The fact you survived the strike of raw lightning was additional proof. Remember who you descend from, Augum. You have the same ancient blood I do."

He tried to think of the name of his ancestor. He knew it was someone important, but too much new information stuffed his mind; besides, he had other questions he wanted answered first.

"Why didn't you say anything right away? Why did I have to do those tests?"

She adjusted her long silver ponytail. "Knowledge can be dangerous, Augum. That is why, for your safety, I chose to withhold certain facts. As for the tests, I did not want you to study the lightning element just because it ran in your family, but rather that you had a passion for it—"

"—I do, Mrs. Stone, I really do—it's what I want!"

"After seeing how hard you worked on that mountain, I know that now. However, I also did not tell you because I needed to know the content of your character. I could not mentor someone—"

"—unworthy," he said slowly, remembering rescuing the injured little bird, a test his father had failed.

She said nothing as they walked, her finely embroidered robe glittering in the sun. The blood on it was dry and browning.

"So what happened to my mother? Where is she?" Just the idea of meeting her made his insides buzz.

Mrs. Stone stopped and sighed, turning her face to shadow. "I heard this from one of your father's followers as he lay dying—when Lividius recaptured your mother, not only did she swear you had died, but she also dared to say she was leaving your father forever. He flew into a rage, and ..." She trailed off.

Augum dropped his head and closed his eyes. Even though he did not have any memory of her, it was difficult to hear.

Murderer ...

In that moment, he truly hated his father.

"We must be free to make choices in life, Augum. Possessive attachment is a terrible thing. You would be wise to heed its lesson. Your mother knew your father's heart. She understood it was only a matter of time until he tracked her down. That was why she put you up with the Pendersons. She saved your life, perhaps even knowing hers was forfeit."

"So my father murdered my mother, and now he wants me just for the scion."

"That appears to be the case."

Augum was the one to resume walking this time. "Mrs. Stone, what did you mean when you said that I'll need my friends later?"

She placed her arms behind her back as she walked. He had a momentary glimpse of the headmistress she once was.

"There will come a day when I am not around to protect you. That is when you will need your friends most. Care for them. Learn with them. Respect them. All the while, be on your guard, for your father will do anything to take possession of the scion simply *because* it is the family heirloom. Further, his feelings of betrayal know no bounds, for he believes I stole you and the scion from him."

Augum shivered in a bitter wind and drew his burgundy robe closer. Mrs. Stone's robe rippled but she seemed impervious to the cold. They strolled in silence for a little while.

"So now that my father and his Legion took power, what do we do?"

"It is imperative we keep you and the scion away from him. In the meantime, you need to train very hard at your craft. You must be able to defend yourself."

"What will happen to Bridget and Leera?" He suddenly realized they will probably want to live with relatives. His heart dropped at the thought. Now that he knew friendship, he felt he could not bear to let it go.

"That is for them to decide."

He did not want to push it, but he had to know. "Would you train them if they wanted to stay here with us?"

Mrs. Stone raised a silver brow. "We shall see," and she smiled, a rare gift that almost made him want to call her Nana.

They walked for a short while longer around the yard, Augum noting the ruined outline of stone divisions. Perhaps, a long time ago, this used to be a garden, or even a training yard. Finally, they climbed over the pile of rubble and ventured inside, where he paused.

"Mrs. Stone—?"

She turned at the arched doors leading to the foyer. "Yes, child?"

"Do *you* think my father is the strongest the family has ever produced?"

She watched him a moment. "One of your father's weaknesses is his great arrogance."

"Do you think I will ever be stronger than him?"

She released a spirited laugh that came from deep within, something that sounded strange coming from her, almost as if she had not practiced it in years. "You will if you want to be, Augum. The real question is—will you need to be?"

And with that, she left him standing in the vestibule, a puzzled expression on his face.

BRIDGET AND LEERA'S
CHOICE

When Augum and Mrs. Stone arrived back in the room, the girls were sitting quietly by the fire. Their eyes were red when they looked up. Augum factfully averted his gaze.

"Come, it is time for breakfast," Mrs. Stone said. "Augum, grab the provisions, then everyone follow me."

She led them around the central staircase and down a hallway past a series of bedrooms, finally turning left through a pair of carved oaken doors. They entered a large rectangular room, in the center of which stood an enormous trestle dining table with over twenty high-backed chairs settled neatly underneath. A gilded throne chair sat on the far end carved with lion heads, a queen's chair on the near end. On the right-hand wall was a long row of arched stained-glass windows depicting a great battle—one side illustrated a dark warlock leading powerful-looking armored lions standing on hind legs;

the other portrayed a warlock champion surrounded by light and leading a bunch of armed peasants. A pair of massive gilt-accented marble fireplaces sat embedded into the left wall. Thankfully, wood remained in both. Mrs. Stone lit them with a flick of a finger, filling the room with the aroma of old cedar.

Augum strolled to the far end, hopping on the throne. The letter "A" was carved into the backrest. He swept some dust off the table, revealing intricate but shallow carvings.

"This is the grand dining room where the king and queen would have their meals." Mrs. Stone took a seat in the queen's chair, its arms and back carved with an evergreen forest. Bridget and Leera sat to her right and smiled weakly before dropping their eyes. Augum felt rather odd sitting so far away so decided to join them on their end, though he looked back at the throne longingly. When he turned to face the group, he noticed Mrs. Stone had been watching him.

"What do we have for breakfast, Augum?" she asked after he pulled up a chair to her left, across from Bridget and Leera.

He unceremoniously upended the rucksack onto the table. Stoppered jars of spices and roots rolled out, along with dry meat, limp carrots and stale journey bread. Their briefly quizzical expressions regarding the jars told him he probably should have thought his food selection through a little more.

"Now, as for plates and silverware—" Mrs. Stone pointed at each of their place settings, frowning in concentration. A full complement of simple but functional china and cutlery appeared in front of everyone, a sizzle sounding after each item popped into existence. Augum had never seen anything like it; did not even think it possible—arcane or not. He gawked at Mrs. Stone, mouth slack. Even Bridget and Leera forgot their sadness, staring at the objects with amazed looks.

"That spell," Mrs. Stone said, reaching for the bread, "you will master with your 13th degree. The items are temporary of course. Oh for mercy's sake, stop gaping and eat." She tore the bread, passing pieces around.

In an attempt to lighten the mood, Augum raised his nose and daintily poured the waterskin for the girls. "There you are, my ladies," he said in a snobbish tone.

The effort only drew half-hearted smiles, but even that did not last, as midway through the meal Bridget broke down and cried into her hands. Leera rubbed her back, sniffing. Mrs. Stone stopped eating and gave Bridget's hand a pat.

Bridget suddenly stood up, fork clanging on her plate, hands twisting the folds of her emerald cloak. She looked a mess—long cinnamon hair in tangles, robe torn and bloody. Tears streamed down her cheeks. "I would like to say …" she began in a choking voice, "that we are grateful that you saved our lives, Mrs. Stone." She gave Leera a sidelong glance.

Leera stood, smiling bitter-sweetly at her friend, freckles blurred by tears. "Yes, thank you, Mrs. Stone."

Mrs. Stone also stood, smoothing her robe. "Girls, please sit, if you will. I have something to say on the matter."

Bridget and Leera exchanged glances before sitting down, sniffing. Augum stared into his lap, feeling for them, missing them already. He knew they would want to live with relatives, and after what happened, who could blame them?

The fire crackled and sputtered as Mrs. Stone spoke.

"Bridget, Leera—I am so very sorry that I could not save your families or your friends. I do not deserve your thanks; I can only beg your forgiveness. I failed. It was my grandson that murdered those people." Her voice was distant, face ancient and frail as an autumn leaf.

Bridget shook her head. "Oh, no, Mrs. Stone, please—"

"—we were there, Mrs. Stone," Leera said. "We know you did your best—"

"That may be so, but I trained and reared my grandson. *I* am at fault."

Bridget shot up out of her chair. "No! We won't let you take their deaths on your shoulders, Mrs. Stone. You saved our lives. You saved Augum. You saved Leland and his parents. I know that if you could have, you would have saved everyone."

Leera also stood, cheeks wet, nodding along. Mrs. Stone scrutinized them both before sighing and sitting back down. "You three have witnessed an awful thing, a thing no one should witness. Later today we shall hold a memorial ceremony to honor the departed."

She motioned for them to sit but the girls remained standing. Bridget gave Leera a hesitant look. "Mrs. Stone—"

"We beg you, Mrs. Stone—" Leera interjected, eyes full of fresh tears, "please don't send us away—!"

Augum froze. What was going on? Did they mean they wanted to stay? His head whipped to Mrs. Stone, but her eyes were only for the girls. She furrowed her brow.

"Mmm ... have you thought this through? Are you absolutely certain?"

Both girls nodded.

"Yes, Mrs. Stone, we have," Bridget said. "We talked about it a lot this morning."

"We want to stay here with you," Leera said. "We would like ..." and she looked to Bridget for help.

"—we would like you to train us," Bridget finished.

Mrs. Stone grimaced; Augum's stomach tightened in a knot. Why won't she say yes? Please let her say yes—!

"I daresay you only had a morning to think about this. Do you not want more time perhaps? Maybe you would like to stay with relatives?"

"No—!" Leera's cheeks colored, maybe from the realization she had yelled the word.

Bridget's chin rose. "We don't need more time on this, Mrs. Stone. We'd like you to train us, and—" she looked at Augum, whose heart quickened, "—and we'd like to help Augum in the dark days ahead."

Augum stood up, chest buzzing. They really *were* his friends! Tears of joy and sorrow rolled down his cheeks, but for once, he did not care. The girls gave him bittersweet smiles.

Mrs. Stone studied them before standing and pacing to the fire, clasping her hands behind her back. "Mmm …"

Augum could barely stand still. Was she mad? What was there to think about? He shared an apprehensive look with the girls. Was this goodbye? Would she send them away immediately?

Mrs. Stone stopped pacing, rested a hand on a gilt lion and sighed. "Then let it be so …"

Augum, Bridget and Leera cried out in joy, hugging each other, before running to Mrs. Stone. She patted them on the back awkwardly. "That is quite enough now, let us not get too excited …"

THE FIRST QUEST

"So will the castle be our home now?" Leera asked, taking a bite of journey-bread.

Mrs. Stone leaned back in the queen's chair. "For the present, yes, although I hardly find it ideal.

Augum rubbed his hands together, thinking treasure hunting would be a great distraction for everyone.

Leera glanced about. "Can't wait to explore this place."

Mrs. Stone straightened. "I have something to say on that matter."

The trio stopped eating and tensed.

"I am now your guardian and mentor and you are my apprentices. At times you may find me strict, but I also believe in freedom of action and learning through one's mistakes. Therefore, you have my permission to explore the castle and its grounds, but no farther than the ruined perimeter walls."

The trio exchanged exuberant looks. If it were not for Mrs. Stone's serious gaze, Augum was sure they would have dashed out of there that moment.

She held up a stern finger. "However—" and glanced at each of them in turn, "you will always be ready in time for lessons, you will not falter in taking time for study, and you will obey me as your guardian and mentor. Lastly, you shall *always* be careful inside the castle and out. Do I make myself clear?"

"Yes, Mr. Stone," they chorused.

"Caution inside and out," she repeated.

Augum knew she was incredibly serious and did not think he would ever dare disobey. Bridget and Leera apparently thought along the same lines, nodding vigorously.

"Now," Mrs. Stone continued, tone shifting to one of politeness, "we begin your training tomorrow. In the meantime, until this evening's memorial ceremony, I charge you all with a small quest—heating the castle."

Augum almost groaned, remembering how much effort it took just to get four armfuls of wood up Mt. Barrow. How were they going to heat an entire castle?

A corner of Mrs. Stone's mouth curved upwards. "Do you really believe simple fire is all that warms this ancient castle—?"

He thought about this. "You mean we don't have to cut firewood for every room? It could be warmed arcanely?"

Mrs. Stone only stared back, a mysterious smile on her face that definitely signaled he was correct.

Bridget glanced to the ornate hearths. "But ... how?"

Mrs. Stone leaned forward as if telling a ghost story. "This is no ordinary castle. It was built a very long time ago with powerful sorcery. It has many secrets and powers, each of which has a key."

Leera crinkled her nose. "You mean ... like an ordinary iron key?"

Mrs. Stone steepled her fingers. "No, not an ordinary key. A spoken key—a *runeword*. Some runewords are written on walls, some on ancient scrolls, some are handed down from generation to generation by word of mouth, and some are simply lost to time, their powers never to awaken again. Also, only the king and queen, the Master of House, or a high-ranking member of the royal family can activate certain runewords. The rest, like some of the more common runewords, could be activated by even the lowliest servant."

She let the idea sink in before continuing. "The castle needs to be heated …" She leaned back, raising an eyebrow. "Think you can find the runeword?"

The trio began talking all at once, standing and making their way to the doors, before suddenly remembering themselves and turning to face Mrs. Stone.

Augum cleared his throat. "Um, sorry, Mrs. Stone, but may we be excused?"

"You may." Her brows corrugated sharply. "But now that I am your guardian and mentor, I expect only the best manners. Is that understood?"

"Yes, Mrs. Stone," they sang in unison.

She gave a curt nod. "Good. Find that runeword."

Augum, Bridget and Leera squeezed through the doors then made a giddy run for it, forgetting the tragedy of the night before and blaming each other for incurring Mrs. Stone's wrath. It was a moment Augum would remember for the rest of his life—the first quest together in the castle—how marvelous!

"So where should we begin?" he asked when they reached the stairs, panting.

Leera's face contorted in thought. "Well, if the castle needs heating, we need to find where you'd turn on the heat, like in the kitchen—"

"Exactly," Bridget said, eyes still red from crying, "or the servants' quarters."

"Or the cellar," he said, looking at them gravely. They fell silent; nobody wanted to venture down there even *with* Mrs. Stone's permission.

"Think this place is haunted?" he asked in a whisper, glancing about.

Leera smirked. "Aren't all castles haunted?"

"Oh, stop it, you two!" Bridget said. "You're going to make this impossible," though her eyes darted about. The castle suddenly seemed to darken as if a presence had entered. Goose bumps rose on Augum's arms. The trio stood still, listening intently, daring something to happen.

Bridget frowned. "Let's just concentrate on the task at hand."

"Agreed," Augum and Leera said in unison.

Leera raised a finger. "But let's stick together."

"Agreed," Bridget and Augum chorused, and they laughed at their silliness.

Bridget turned to the steps. "All right. Servants' quarters— let's start there."

They made their way downstairs, the sunlight that ricocheted from up high dimming as they descended.

Augum slid his hand along the cool marble banister. "Hope we find treasure."

"I'd love to find an arcane staff," Bridget said, gripping the air as if she already had one.

Leera made a slashing motion with her hand. "Or a blade. Dad bought me a short sword for my birthday. I named her Careena, because she kind of careened into things."

Bridget made a funny face. "What father buys his daughter a short sword?"

Leera stopped and her face fell. "One who loves his daughter very much …"

"Oh, I'm sorry, Lee, I'm such a mean—"

"It's all right," Leera said, sniffing hard. She took a deep breath. "We have a quest to attend to, and Dad wouldn't approve of me being a baby." She turned to Augum. "Don't you have a sword?"

"Yes, we should get it—" He shrugged. "You know, just in case …"

Leera and Bridget nodded immediately.

"Quickly then—!" Augum raced back up, the girls giving chase. He plowed into the room first, Leera just behind. Victorious, he strutted over to claim his prize, which sparked reassuringly by the mantel.

Leera gave him a blasting look. "Look at you preening; did Robin Scarson crawl into your skin?"

"Ouch!" Nonetheless, he smiled.

After securing the blade to his waist, they scampered back down to the foyer.

"All right, which way?" He glanced between the two pairs of doors opposite each other.

"Let's try this way." Bridget walked to the two doors on the west side, Leera and Augum following. She placed her hand on the ornate bronze handle and bit her lip. "Ready?"

They nodded. There was a click and she pushed the creaking doors open into pitch-darkness.

"Shyneo." Bridget's hand illuminated with green ivy that wound around her palm like a snake.

"Shyneo." Leera's palm trickled to life with glowing water, lapping quietly against her wrist.

Augum stared at Leera's in fascination. "Amazing."

Bridget placed her hand next to Leera's. "Hers is neat, isn't it? Brighter too."

Not to be outdone, he raised his own palm. "SHYNEO!" Weak lightning crackled to life, flitting between his fingers and around his palm. He grimaced. "Mine's weakest." He took mental note to practice controlling the volume of his incantations.

Bridget scoffed. "Yeah but you only started practicing what, a couple of days ago?"

"We've been practicing for two months now," Leera said, "besides, I like yours."

He felt his cheeks prickle. "Thanks."

They entered with outstretched palms, Augum's other hand on the pommel of his sword. Individually, their lights might have been too weak to get a good look through the darkness, but together they shone reasonably bright.

A chaotic room greeted them, its walls gouged and ruined, ceiling partly collapsed. On the right, a door stood slightly ajar.

"Whatever happened here happened a long time ago," Bridget whispered, examining a dusty rubble pile.

Augum peered through a gaping hole in the left wall, large enough to crawl through. Beyond he could make out two sets of narrow spiral staircases, one going up and the other down. "Take a look at this—"

Bridget and Leera peeked over his shoulder. He pointed at the one on the right. "That one there must go up the battlement."

Leera stuck her lit palm through the hole. "Wonder where the other one goes …"

They peered at the gloomy-looking staircase on the left. Augum knew everyone had a good idea of where it went, just nobody wanted to say it.

"Other way?" he asked.

Bridget quickly nodded. "Definitely …"

They headed to the door. Leera pulled at the handle and just managed to jump out of the way as the door detached from its frame, landing with a crash. They froze, listening to the sound bounce down the staircase behind them.

No one dared speak.

Augum expected a tremendous roar and fast thudding footsteps. He thought of the deep gouges in the foyer doors.

Leera made eye contact with both of them. "All right, nothing came to eat us. Let's keep going." She tiptoed to the next room, signaling for them to follow.

It appeared to be an ancient storeroom, filled to the ceiling with wrecked crates. The place had evidently been searched top to bottom. Hay lay strewn about along with the decayed remnants of grains. A thick layer of dust coated everything. At the far end was an open door, darkness beyond.

They crept forward, palms outstretched, eyes straining.

Leera suddenly whipped around. "What was that—?"

Bridget swiveled about, eyes darting. "What—what was what? I didn't hear anything—"

Now Augum was sure something was going to have them for lunch; he thought his heart would explode.

Leera grabbed Bridget's waist suddenly. "This!" and laughed while Bridget shrieked in terror.

"Leera Jones—!" Bridget said after calming down. "Ugh, I could just ... that wasn't funny." She turned to Augum to appeal for his support.

Augum quickly nodded. "Wasn't funny."

"Then you better stop smiling." Leera turned back towards the open maw of the door ahead.

Bridget frowned. "No more pranks, Lee."

Leera smirked. "Augum, you think Mrs. Stone can teach her a sense of humor?"

He could just see Mrs. Stone's stern face and tried not to laugh. He chose not to say anything though and shouldered past them into the other room.

On the left side was a tall row of cupboards, every door of which was open or hanging crookedly. Opposite stood a door with the top portion missing; on the right, a pair of large simple doors flanked by two more pantry cupboards. Broken glass, large cork stoppers and the remains of an ancient ladder littered the ground. Dust covered everything.

He picked up a stoppered glass jar with something green and slimy inside. "Anyone in the mood for two hundred-year-old pickled eggs?"

The girls both made the same face.

"You sure now—?" He tried giving the jar to Leera.

She squealed and jumped back. "Augum, if you want to live ..."

Bridget pressed her lips together, forcing off a smile.

He flashed a pretend hurt look. "Fine then, no one appreciates my cooking," and casually tossed it over his shoulder. It exploded on the floor with a nasty gurgle.

"Ugh. Boys ..." Bridget muttered.

Augum walked to the half-door, glass cracking underfoot, and extended his glowing hand into the room. "I think this is the kitchen—"

"—and I think we found the servants' quarters here," Bridget said. The girls had managed to push open one of the two doors on the right side.

He gave up on the half-door and quickly joined them—it was one thing to explore the castle together, quite another to do it alone.

The servants' quarter was a long room that had row after row of rotting beds, empty torch sconces, moldy strips of fabric, and other miscellaneous debris. There was a gaping hole in the far wall, as if something large had crashed through.

"There should be a room beside this one; one for women, one for men," Augum said.

"How do you know that?" Leera asked, picking up a torn sheet of cloth from the ground and inspecting it with a sour look. It fell apart in her hands.

"Just something Sir Westwood once said, that servants are segregated in most castles." He was happy to tell *them* something for a change.

Leera wiped her hands on her cloak. "Did he happen to mention where to find runewords?"

"Nope, never spoke about sorcery or warlocks—"

"Hey, come look at this—" Bridget interrupted. They joined her at the hole. "What do you think caused this?" She looked around the room as if expecting to spot the beast responsible.

"No idea," he said, "but whatever it was, I hope it's long gone ..."

Bridget peered in. "Judging by the dust, I suspect this happened many years ago. Here, lend me your palms."

He and Leera stuck their lit hands through the hole.

"I think you're right, Augum," Leera said. "Room's a mirror image of the other. Must be segregated."

Bridget gathered her green cloak. "This just gives me the creeps, let's get out of here."

They walked back, examining the floors and walls for anything unusual.

Augum spotted a small bronze plaque with two symbols, one of which was a torch. "Check this out. Looks like a runeword, doesn't it?"

Bridget wiped away the dust. "Yes, it does actually ..."

Leera pressed the torch insignia with her finger. Nothing happened. They tried to trigger it in various other ways, all to no avail.

"Bah, forget it, let's just continue on to the kitchen," he said. "I'm sure this isn't going to heat the whole castle anyway."

They returned to the pantry area and helped each other over the half-door, which seemed to be stuck.

Beyond was a massive rectangular room stretching across the back of the castle. The two back corners opened into opposite battlements, sheltering spiral staircases. In the center was a long trestle table, an echo of the royal one they had dined on earlier. Some ancient pots, pans and cookware still hung from iron hooks. Various counters and butcher's blocks stood covered with dust and debris.

"Smells gross," Leera said, inspecting a stone sink covered with black goo.

Augum picked up an old earthen mug. "The servants must have eaten here. Wonder how they got the food up to the third floor without it going cold though ..."

"*Magic*," Leera said, using a term he now knew was reserved for parlor tricks and children's fairy tales. He chuckled, happier to get the joke than anything else. She flashed a cheeky smile before examining one of three large ovens. "These are scary big, and hey—more of those plaques, except the symbols are different."

He placed the mug back onto its dust shadow and stepped over the ruins of an old bench. The ovens looked like massive stone jaws with iron teeth, starved for their next meal.

"Guess they're also used arcanely," he said. Leera gave him an *Obviously* look.

Bridget finished her examination of the area near the door and expelled a long breath, cheeks puffing. "Check the walls next."

"Stairs here!" he called from the other end of the room, voice echoing. Bridget and Leera appeared by his side, the trio staring at wide descending steps that disappeared in darkness.

"Cellar ..." Bridget whispered.

Leera's palm wavered. "If it was fiery and hot down there, I'd call it Hell."

Augum thought differently, feeling an ancient cemetery chill.

"The heating runeword might be down there though," Leera added with a shrug.

"Maybe we could take a quick peek," Augum said.

Bridget turned to him, searching his eyes. "Mrs. Stone wouldn't let us explore here if she didn't really think it was safe, would she—?"

"Of course not," he replied, before remembering his trek to Hangman's Rock and the dangers he faced along the way.

She gave a stiff nod. "Good. Well then … palms forward?"

He breathed deep and nodded, sliding his other hand over the pommel of his sword, gaining courage from the cold steel.

THE CELLAR

It was a long way down to the cellar. At the bottom, the trio encountered roughly hewn rock walls and dirt ground, the ceiling four times the height of a man. The air was cold and damp, smelling of earth and ancient stone. The chamber sounded vast, even the tiniest noise echoing distantly. Broken crates were stacked immediately to their left, in the northeast corner, partitioned by a rotten wall adjoining a massive pillar.

"Must be one of the castle supports," Augum whispered while approaching the pillar, palm outstretched with blue light. "Just look at the size of it."

Leera pointed her shiny watery hand at a low structure in the center of the chamber. "Look."

They approached, eyeing the darkness while listening for any sounds other than their own. Augum thought there was a very particular stillness down here, a kind of primordial silence long undisturbed. His entire body tingled knowing he was exploring something so ancient and mysterious.

Bridget tapped the rough stone lip. "It's a giant well …"

The well had two wooden overhangs once used to lower buckets into its depths. The rope had rotted away but the marks of use were still there.

She peeked over the edge, leaning forward just a little, before recoiling with a shriek as Leera pulled her hand away.

Bridget smacked her on the arm. "Now you're just begging to be thrown in—"

Leera put a finger to her lips. "Shh, there could be something down here."

"Ugh, you're impossible."

"Wonder how deep it goes …" Augum peered over the edge while keeping Leera in sight. He picked up a small rock and dropped it in before Bridget could stop him. The trio listened and waited … and waited … yet no sound came from that inky depth.

"Okay, so it's a little deep. I'm sure it has a bottom though." He picked up a second rock, but this time Bridget grabbed his wrist.

"Better not …" she said, suddenly teary-eyed. "We'll have to get our water elsewhere."

His cheeks flared with guilt. "I'm sorry, Bridget, I didn't mean—"

"—no it's not that." She wiped her face with the back of her sleeve. "It's just that my father used to tend to the village well."

"Aww, Bridge …" Leera hugged her gently and smoothed her hair. She gave her a moment. "So what do you think— where would the runeword be found in a place like this?"

Bridget straightened her cloak. "We should check the columns first; might be a servants' marker or something like that."

There were four gargantuan support columns spread evenly around the great room. The trio went back to the first and examined it carefully, finding nothing; but something else caught Augum's eye at the edge of their light.

"Is that a dungeon—?"

Bridget and Leera whipped around.

He stepped before two massive wrought-iron gates inset into the north wall. Iron-worked ivy leaves spiraled up the bars, their dull-green paint long faded and cracked. Flanked by two sentry booths, the arched gates towered to the ceiling, as if designed to hold some enormous beast. The black stonework around them was the same as the outside of the castle.

Bridget gazed past the bars into the darkness beyond. "What is this?"

Leera's head tilted back as she approached. "The gates to Hell …"

"I don't see a lock," Augum said, noticing how the entire central assembly came together to form the letter "A".

"Must open arcanely," Bridget whispered.

Leera held her palm close. "Wonder what 'A' stands for."

"Don't know," Bridget said, "but I've seen it around the castle; it was carved into the giant table we ate on."

"And the king's chair," Augum said.

Leera ran her fingers over the intricate letter. "Maybe it stands for the name of the royal bloodline the castle originally belonged to."

Augum extended his lit hand as far as it would go past the bars, hoping the light would reach something. All he managed to see was an extra few feet of the rough walls. He sensed great depth and wanted to shout to hear how the echo sounded, yet what if whatever made all those scratches was still here, trapped behind these bars, watching them from that seemingly eternal darkness?

Leera's voice was close to his ear. "Careful or you might lose it …"

He quickly withdrew his arm.

Bridget crouched. "Look at the dust. Dungeon must have stayed shut since the king ruled the castle two hundred years ago."

"Makes sense why it's locked then," Leera said. "The runeword that opens the gates must have been lost with the king. Imagine being the poor fool trapped behind these bars for all eternity—"

"—or beast," Augum added, nudging Leera.

The trio held their breath and listened a while.

"I don't like this, let's move on," Bridget whispered at last.

The trio quietly retreated, only turning their backs once the gates disappeared beyond their circle of light. Even though he could not see them anymore, Augum found himself looking back in their direction while inspecting the next column.

"Nothing on this side," he reported.

"Same here," Bridget said, having inspected the other sides with Leera. "You know, on second thought I doubt we're going to find the heating runeword on a pillar."

"Let's keep exploring then," Augum said, spying something at the edge of their light in the northwest corner. He led them to a gigantic pile of rubble. "Well, whatever had been here is totally destroyed now."

Leera kicked a stone. "I hope the runeword isn't buried underneath or it's going to be a cold winter."

Augum had a vision of spending half his time cutting wood. "It's got to be here somewhere." He glanced about with renewed resolve. "Come on."

They prowled the west wall until stumbling across a second set of massive iron gates identical to the first, minus the two sentry booths.

Leera grasped the bars, peering in. "What do you suppose is behind these, another dungeon?"

Augum reached beyond the bars with his lit palm. The way sound echoed within gave him the impression it was a vast room. There was something barely visible a distance away, like a stone slab. He squinted trying to make it out. "Wish my light was stronger."

Bridget took a few steps back and gazed up. "That will come with training …"

"You see something, Bridge—?" Leera asked.

"Can't tell, don't have enough light."

They assisted, raising their lit hands.

"There's writing there," Augum said, unable to quite make it out. The ceiling was so high the sign was just at the edge of their light.

"Think it starts with 'C'," Bridget said, blowing a lock of hair from her eyes.

"Think the next letter is 'R'," he said.

Leera frowned. "Think I need spectacles …"

Bridget abruptly covered her mouth and jumped back. "Crypt—!"

Augum and Leera recoiled away from the gates, as if the darkness beyond could come to life any moment. He felt the prickle of cold sweat, now sure he could discern the subtle scent of death. Mrs. Stone's words about how his father was learning the necromantic arts returned from that morning. He hadn't told the girls about that yet but intended to—now was definitely not the right time though.

"Well, we can be sure the runeword isn't in *there*," Bridget said.

Leera smirked. "Bet we could find out whose castle this was though—"

"Forget it, Lee. Not going in."

"Can't anyway," Augum said, stepping up to the bars and daringly giving them a rattle. "Locked." The iron sound reverberated deep into the crypt. They listened as it faded to silence.

"Think about it, if those gates can keep people from walking in …" Bridget moved on, leaving them to finish the thought, though Augum did not think "people" was the right word. He and Leera exchanged a look before scuttling to catch up, breath frosting in the chill air of the cellar. The cold was not as sharp as the rest of the castle, but the dampness certainly made it more uncomfortable.

He rubbed his hands. "Could do with a warm fire …"

"Isn't that the point of this little expedition?" Leera asked.

They next came upon the southwest corner, encountering the narrow spiral staircase first spotted through the hole in the wall a floor above. Beyond lay a myriad of rotten equipment.

"Looks like the poor weather training yard," Augum said, picking up the rusted hilt of a sword, the blade missing. He nodded at straw-stuffed circles. "And I think those are archery targets."

"Sir Westwood sure told you a lot about castles," Leera said. "What happened to him anyway?"

Augum tossed the broken hilt aside. It clanged loudly, drawing a stern look from Bridget. "The Legion killed him when he tried to defend the village. He sent me away just before they razed it to the ground. That's how I found Mrs. Stone."

Leera turned over a piece of rotten wood with her foot. "What a coincidence that she's your great-grandmother; and your father the Lord of the Legion—"

Bridget shot her a quelling look as Augum felt a creeping surge of guilt.

Leera rubbed her forehead. "Ugh, I'm horrible. Sorry, Augum …"

"But what you say is true," though his insides still prickled. "Mrs. Stone says it could be anything, from fate, to luck, to providence—whatever that means."

"Providence means the Unnameables had a hand in it," Bridget said,

"Oh." If there was one thing he barely understood, it was the gods. The common folk considered it a very bad omen to speak their names, not that anyone knew them. Only priests were allowed to utter them, and then only in church; and from what Sir Westwood had said, most churches resided in Canterra. Apparently, the Canterrans considered Solians heathens and Solia a godless kingdom. Anyway, why would the gods bother with an ant like him?

His voice darkened like the crypt. "And as for my father ... he's a murderer."

Leera suddenly hugged him. "I'm sorry, I know you're not your father." When she let go, there was a pained expression on her freckled face.

He nodded, eyes downcast. He wanted to say something about her loss, something meaningful, but could not think of anything. Words were just ... words.

"Think I found something—" Bridget said from the south wall.

Leera and Augum rushed over to what appeared to be a large bronze diagram.

He blew some dust off, revealing a complex network of symbols. "This must be it! Can anyone read it?"

Bridget bit her lip. "This is way beyond what I know."

Leera's face lit up. "Wait—the book!"

"What book?" Augum asked.

"The big blue book—you know, the one Mrs. Stone asked me to bring—? It was an encyclopedia on the arcane arts!"

"That's exactly what we need!" he said. "Let's get it. Come on—"

Cheered by their change in fortune, the trio rushed to the spiral staircase, raced up the steps, through the foyer, and up the grand marble stairs, finally shooting through the doors of the bedroom.

There was no sign of Mrs. Stone.

Leera rummaged through her rucksack, finding the large volume amidst a bunch of scrolls. She pulled it free and opened the cover. They read the title together with mounting enthusiasm.

" 'On Arcaneology: A Pupil's Encyclopedia of the Arcane Arts—!' "

"This is just the kind of book we would have used in school," Bridget said. "Except it's older and … far grander."

The trio's smiles faded as a life flashed before Augum's mind, a life of school, friends, family, an entire village learning together—all lost. He knew they were thinking the same thing. The three of them stared at the book with fallen faces.

Bridget abruptly placed her hand on the cover. "I solemnly swear, on the ghosts of my mother, father and brothers, that I will learn the arcane tongue. Their deaths will not have been in vain." She said it boldly, eyes closed, tears running down her cheeks.

Leera looked at her, sniffed, and placed her hand over Bridget's. "I swear, on the ghosts of beloved Mum and Dad, that I will master the arcane tongue. Their deaths will not have been in vain."

At last, Augum slowly placed his hand over theirs. "I solemnly swear, on the ghosts of my mother, Sir Westwood, and on those that my father has slain, that I will learn the arcane tongue. Their deaths will not have been in vain."

For a time they kept their hands in place, letting the meaning of the moment cement, binding them as friends forever.

Augum thought he was starting to understand what Mrs. Stone meant regarding the importance of their friendship. Together they will push each other to learn their craft. Together they will overcome their sorrows.

They solemnly picked up the book, looking at each other anew, now part of an alliance sworn to learn and grow strong against the Legion.

THE BLUE BOOK

The trio made their way back down, Leera reverently holding the arcaneology book in her hands, Augum and Bridget lighting the way with their palms. They soon faced the bronze diagram again.

"Let's see here," Leera said, opening the cover.

Bridget eyed the pages as Leera flipped them. "Must be over two thousand pages here; and the writing's so small ... Try the table of contents."

"How do they make copies of these books?" Augum asked.

Bridget waved absently. "Oh, it's done arcanely. They make lots of copies that way. It's still expensive though."

Leera riffled to the table of contents. It was enormous. There was a chapter devoted to every form of arcane use, from *Speaking the Arcane Tongue: A Syllabic and Semantic Introduction*, to *Final Applications and Theories of Advanced and Complex Arcane Use*.

Augum shook his head. "This thing's a lifetime study."

Leera snorted. "Whatever gave you that idea, Aug?"

His heart skipped a beat. Shortening each other's names was something friends did. No one had ever shortened his name before.

Aug ... he could get used to that.

"Wait, there it is—" Bridget said, shooting a finger to a line titled *Common Arcane Runes and Cantrips for Servant Use—page 341.*

They hurriedly flipped to the page, scanning the tiny scrawl for anything about heating.

Bridget read the headings. " 'Classic Cleaning Cantrips; Cleaning Large Areas Quickly; Dusting Cantrips; Finding Lost Cleaning Supplies; Food Preparation Cantrips; Gardening Cantrips' ... Nope, skip this part. See if there's a section on servant runes or something like that."

Leera riffled forward. "Here we go: 'Common Household Servant Runes.' " She then began reading the titles of paragraphs. " 'Bathwater Runes; Cleaning Fluid Runes; Door Runes; Escalator Runes; Garbage Runes; Hallway Runes ... *Heating Runes*!' This has to be it."

"What's it say?" Augum asked, leaning in with Bridget, the light from their two hands combining to give the words a blue-green glow.

Leera read aloud.

" 'An arcanely heated home is somewhat uncommon, mostly due to the initial expense of hiring a warlock who has mastered the 13th degree. Heating symbols are often found by doorways and can be invoked by all servants given they hold basic house permissions. The servant must speak the arcane word associated with the symbol followed by a number, also spoken in the arcane tongue.

" 'A home will typically have a plaque illustrating to the servant an allowable range of heating. A small domicile will have a fireplace or perhaps one symbol, but a larger domicile can have many symbols, one for each room. Additionally, it may have a control symbol for the entire home. In the latter case, the servant is instructed to search for the appropriate symbol in the servants' quarters—the kitchen (particularly near the ovens), or sometimes in the cellar. The heating symbol for a single room is typically a box within which there appears a single flame, followed by anywhere from a single dot (meaning a choice between basic heating or no heating), to ten dots (meaning the servant can speak arcanely the numbers one through ten for more precise variations in temperature). The heating symbol for an entire domicile is a box with three flames inside it.' "

Leera took an exasperated breath before continuing. " 'The runeword typically associated with the symbol for a single room is *net suo*. Care must be taken pronouncing the letters *U* and *O* shortly. The runeword typically associated with the symbol for an entire domicile is *net sukio*. Care must be taken pronouncing the letters *U*, *I* and *O* shortly.

" 'For arcane number pronunciation please see chapter 1. A note on servant etiquette: only the most lavish of estates can typically afford more than three dots.' "

Leera finished the last part rather fast and leaned back. "Well that was fun. Hope one of you got all that, because my job was to read it." She handed the heavy book over to Augum, who extinguished his palm to receive it. She then stretched and yawned while he and Bridget skimmed the long-winded passage over again.

"To think the entire book is like this," he mumbled.

"… 'and can be invoked by all servants given they hold basic house permissions,' " Bridget slowly reread. "I wonder about that. Will we have permission, and if not us … maybe Mrs. Stone—?"

He glanced upward. "Surely Mrs. Stone …"

"Look for a box with three flames inside, Lee."

Leera nodded, relit her palm, and started scanning the diagram. It was crammed with what looked like hundreds of runic symbols, from the very simple to the very complex. "Found it—!" She stabbed a finger at a square symbol near the bottom center of the diagram.

Augum strained to see. "How many dots beside it?"

She leaned closer and started counting. "… eight … nine … ten. Ten dots."

"*Ten*—?"

"Well, it *is* a castle," Bridget said.

Augum adjusted his grip on the book. "Now we just have to learn how to pronounce it. Netsookiu. No, that's not right. Netsokio …"

Leera soon joined in. It took them a while but they finally agreed on a pronunciation.

"All right, flip to chapter one," Bridget said. "We need to find out how to pronounce numbers."

"Fine, but I'm putting this monster down; arms are getting sore."

They sat on the floor, crowding around like eager schoolchildren. A short while later the trio was practicing how to say "lito", the arcane word for *five*, agreeing a number right in the middle was appropriate to start with. Soon they were trying to pronounce the two words together.

"Net sukio lito," Bridget said for the tenth time. "Ugh. Anything?"

Their breath still fogged.

"Don't think so." Leera returned to the diagram, scratching her head. "Maybe we're supposed to be in the foyer or something."

Augum would be glad to leave the dank cellar. "It's worth a try."

They ventured back upstairs and into the foyer, where they noticed Mrs. Stone slowly descending the steps, clutching the banister with a veined hand. Her eyes fell on the book. Augum tensed. Were they in for a rebuke?

"Mmm, sensible. I compliment you all on your initiative. How are you faring?"

Augum glanced at the girls. "Oh, uh … we're still working on it, Mrs. Stone."

"Net sukio lito," Leera blurted, but nothing seemed to happen. Mrs. Stone's brows rose ever slightly as the trio exchanged an awkward look.

"You try," Leera whispered out of the side of her mouth.

Augum and Bridget tried next, to no avail.

"Your pronunciation is perfect," Mrs. Stone said, descending the rest of the steps, "but that is not the problem." She stopped before them, the book once again open in their hands, the trio desperately re-reading the lengthy paragraph, absorbing nothing.

"Ah, the impatience of youth. Tell me—what are you thinking when you speak the words?"

The first thing that popped into Augum's head was the king's throne. "Lions—?"

"Flowers?" Bridget said, wincing.

"Cleaning?" Leera's face contorted in an *I know it's the wrong answer* look.

Bridget and Augum glanced at her.

" *'Cleaning —?'* " he mouthed.

Leera spoke through her teeth. "Well, it's what we were reading about, wasn't it?"

Mrs. Stone held her hands behind her back, the wrinkles on her face molding into a look of annoyance. The three of them stood at attention, quiet as mice.

"If you had the good sense not to rush, and if you had bothered to read the *introduction* to runes and runewords, you would have understood that in order for a runeword to be effective, one must visualize not only the symbol in one's mind, but also the *effect*."

An admonished silence fell over the hall after the echoes of her words died.

"Mmm." She turned her back on them and began shuffling up the marble steps. "I am going to take a nap. When I awake, I expect it to be to a warm castle."

"Kind of hard to impress her," Leera said when Mrs. Stone had gone.

Augum closed the book with a smack that echoed throughout the foyer. "Welcome to my world …"

"Well, she *was* Headmistress of the Academy of Arcane Arts for thirty-five years," Bridget said. "She had a reputation for being the strictest they ever had. We're getting off easy, I think."

"By the way, Leera—" Augum said, holding back a smirk, " *'Cleaning*—?' Trying to give her ideas?"

"No! I was just—I don't know …"

He chuckled and turned to Bridget. "Think Mrs. Stone could teach her a sense of humor?"

Bridget laughed.

"Oh, you're going to get it—" Leera began chasing him around the foyer.

"Mercy—!" he said between snorts of laughter.

Bridget finally put a finger to her giggling lips. "Quiet you two or we'll get in trouble again."

Leera stopped chasing him and returned to Bridget's side, watching him with narrowed eyes.

Panting, he clambered back down from the landing where he had taken shelter. "It was worth it."

Leera snapped around like an angry chipmunk. "What was that—?"

"Nothing—just saying we need to get back to work, that's all."

"Right …"

By her secret smile, he knew she was only pretending to be mad. He was happy to have diverted their attention and made them laugh, even if just for a little while.

"All right, seriously now—" Bridget said, putting on a scholarly expression and sitting down on the floor beside the book. "Let's try this again, all right?"

He and Leera joined her. Then, just when he thought he was safe, Leera punched him hard on the shoulder.

"OW—! Mercy already." He rubbed his sore arm.

Leera, a smug expression on her face, nodded that they could now begin. Yet after much recitation, she sprawled on the floor as if suffering defeat in swordplay. "This is hard ..."

"Maybe we should find a fireplace; getting a bit chilly ..." he said.

Bridget shoved aside a stray lock of hair. "And what, get comfortable? The cold will keep us motivated to *make* it warm."

He could not argue with her logic, but he was not about to let Leera off easily. "Get up, Lazy."

"Do I have to ...?"

"You have to," he and Bridget chorused.

Leera expelled a long breath before sitting up. "Fine."

At last, with only a sliver of sunlight left, Augum somehow managed to speak the runeword properly. They knew it was a success because there was an immediate click and a hissing sound. The castle soon began warming. They looked at each other and threw up a shout of victory, dancing in the middle of the foyer as if finding a large stash of treasure, then racing up the steps and bursting in to the bedroom, shouting "Mrs. Stone! We did it we did it we did it—!"

Mrs. Stone stirred in the canopy bed, the fire long extinguished but the room quickly warming from their efforts. They held their breath while awaiting her verdict. She took her time sitting up, grumbling something about the exuberance of youth, before falling into thoughtful silence. At last, she surrendered a nod. "You have completed the task."

They beamed with pride. Their first runeword successfully spoken—what an achievement!

Mrs. Stone stood, straightening her robe. "I suppose you have earned your supper."

THE MEMORIAL CEREMONY

Mrs. Stone surprised the trio at the table with fresh grapefruits, apples, buttered and salted chicken breast (still steaming), boiled broccoli, rosemary and pepper for spice, a flagon of fresh cider, and chunks of chocolate. Newly-arcaned cutlery and china sat spotless and immaculately positioned.

Augum gaped at the luxury. "Mrs. Stone ... where did all this food come from?"

She gestured for them to sit. "Teleportation is a highly rewarding spell. The warlock markets in Antioc use it to great effect, though the prices can be ... exorbitant."

Bridget claimed the chair beside her. "But Mrs. Stone, aren't you afraid of being recognized?"

"I use a particular spell to conceal my identity. Does anyone know which spell I am referring to, and what degree?" She swept them with a professorial eye.

Augum shook his head while Leera examined the table as if suddenly finding the carving interesting.

"Um, is it the 16th degree Spell of Legend *Metamorphosis*?" Bridget asked, cringing.

"Partially correct." Mrs. Stone made the motion for Augum to pour everyone cider. "That is the right spell, however Metamorphosis is of the 15th degree, and therefore *not* a Spell of Legend."

Bridget frowned.

That would make it an advanced spell, Augum thought, remembering the spell hierarchy.

Mrs. Stone picked up a fork. "Now let us put aside lessons for the day and eat."

For some time, the only sounds were the clank and clatter of cutlery as the trio devoured almost everything—except the boiled broccoli, which nobody wanted to touch. Mrs. Stone, meanwhile, conservatively picked away at the food.

After the meal, they munched on some chocolate and told Mrs. Stone all about their earlier adventure. She only nodded, toning out "Mmm" or "Is that so?" but not explaining anything about the castle—not the crypt nor the dungeon, as if expecting them to figure it out for themselves.

When conversation died, Augum found himself peering at the ornately carved letter "A" on the back of the throne. Just as he was going to ask what it stood for, Mrs. Stone broke the silence.

"Now then," she said, dabbing her lips with a napkin while leaning back. "I do believe it is time. Follow me, please." The trio exchanged curious looks as they stood. She gestured for them to leave the table as is and led them back to their room, where she opened the wardrobe revealing four black velvet robes. Additionally, there were three identical burgundy robes; new versions of the patched one Augum already wore, except with a new mustard leather belt instead of hemp rope.

"I was able to acquire these in town," Mrs. Stone said, removing one from the rack to show it off. "Burgundy is traditional for apprentices of the first few degrees."

Augum wondered what was more ancient—the castle or the style of those robes. Judging by the girls' faces, they must have been thinking along the same lines.

"—and these are traditional mourning robes," Mrs. Stone continued. "Please don the apprentice robes underneath. Augum, take your garments and excuse yourself from the room."

He did as he was told, re-entering when called, gladly putting aside his old rags. The new apprentice robe fit better and did not itch, whereas the black mourning robe was far too large; his arms disappeared and the hem dragged, though he realized this was probably by design.

"Let us go." Mrs. Stone departed the room, robe trailing, the trio close behind.

Augum had to be particularly careful not to trip. What he did not expect was suddenly getting choked as Leera accidentally stepped on the back of his robe.

"Ack—sorry!"

This pattern continued. Someone would yelp then receive a prompt apology.

At last, they stepped outside into a cloudy night. The Ravenwood stood sentinel around a fresh pile of wood in the center of the clearing, branches drooping with snow. Flakes blew about in a gentle breeze.

Mrs. Stone politely gestured at a spot on the other side of the woodpile. "Please stand facing west."

They did as she asked, snow crunching underfoot. Standing in the cold air, head bowed, Augum wondered what the ceremony did. It certainly could not bring back the dead, he thought. Then he realized that is exactly what his father was doing as a necromancer—bringing back the dead. Those lightning eyes, filled with hatred and covetousness, swam before his mind. He only hoped his deranged father would spare those murdered at Sparrow's Perch.

You have your mother's eyes and nose ...

Augum scowled. Murderer ...

"I call upon the spirits of the dead to listen to the cries of the living," Mrs. Stone began, "and to remember those they left behind, those that still breathe the air and walk above ground. Dearly departed, allow us a final goodbye as we mourn your passing from this life."

She held a hand before the woodpile until it burst with an unnaturally high fire, eventually settling to a guttering blue flame. She spoke once more into the night, head raised and eyes above the blaze. "Hear the cry," and began to sing.

It was the most beautiful melody Augum had ever heard, a wavering tune without words seeming to come from a very long time ago, a time when things were far simpler. As she sang this primitive song, he could not help but stare into those blue flames which blurred before him. Then, from the heart of the fire, form began to take shape.

He squinted, trying to make out what it was, unable to tell if it was in his mind or if it was real. The picture gradually widened until he was staring at a hazy image surrounded by a white light. A blurred shape stepped forward, edges sharpening as it approached. It was a woman holding a babe in her arms. She was delicate and lovely, with long locks of coffee-colored hair, light blue eyes and sharply arched brows. He did not recognize her. Nonetheless, something about her stung with familiarity.

She gave a radiant smile as a young man soon appeared by her side, cooing at the babe in her arms and giving her a peck on the cheek. He too seemed oddly familiar. The couple played with the babe, silently teasing it, until the man lost interest, staring beyond her at something unseen. She reached out to him but he shrugged her off, before abruptly walking off into the white, leaving the woman standing alone with the child. She watched his fading form, tears trickling down her cheeks. Then she slowly brought the babe to her lips, kissed it on the forehead, and began to whisper into its ear.

Augum strained to hear what she said, but it was too quiet. There was a stinging throb in his heart. "Mother—?" he asked softly.

The angelic woman raised her head and smiled through her tears. That smile … he numbly touched his face.

She slowly retreated, edges fading until she was gone. Distantly, the ancient song ascended an octave. He watched as a new figure emerged from the white, dressed in a worn steel breastplate, greaves and chainmail shirt, a mop of curly, unkempt gray hair on his head. A sword hung snugly in its scabbard by his side.

"Sir Westwood …"

Sir Tobias Westwood kneeled down to talk to someone beside him, the figure blurred until Augum focused on it. It was a boy—himself, but younger. Suddenly he remembered how Sir Westwood would often talk to him like that—on his level. It brought a pang to his heart.

When Sir Westwood finished speaking, the boy produced a wooden sword and made a slashing motion, the man approving with a nod. Augum remembered that sword well— Sir Westwood had carved it himself. The sword was well-balanced and fun to hold, the handle a perfect fit for Augum's hand.

Sir Westwood spoke again and pointed towards older Augum. An eager smile lit up young Augum's face; he hopped forward and waved with a skinny arm. Sir Westwood smiled softly from behind, raising a hand in salute. Augum could not help but feebly wave back.

Sir Westwood's attention drifted to young Augum, his face hardening. After a moment of watching the boy swinging the sword, he raised his firm gaze back to older Augum. With a final slow nod, he backed away into the white, disappearing in a smoky blur.

"Sir, wait—" Augum whispered, hoping he would return to counsel him, to finish the sword training …

Only the young Augum remained now, chewing on a finger while staring at older Augum. The boy glanced about and smiled uncertainly, rocking back and forth on his heels. Augum smiled at his younger self, who abruptly turned and skipped off, only to reappear guiding a whole group of people.

There was the ebony-skinned Sharpe family—Tyeon, grandmother, blind grandfather, father, mother and sister—all looking distinguished and peaceful; and there the Burns'—the tired-looking grandma that smiled nonetheless, the mother with the same long cinnamon hair and pert nose as Bridget, the burly father with the bushy mustache, and two grinning chestnut-haired brothers. Then a smiling couple with raven hair stepped forward, the mother freckled, father with protuberant eyes. Leera's parents … Augum recalled that pungent drink and the love that had come along with it.

There were others too, people he had not met personally but remembered from the village. Young Augum was at the front the entire time, smiling that innocent boyish smile.

Seeing the group together, it dawned on Augum what he and his friends had lost. Tears began flowing freely down his cheeks. "I'm sorry. I'm so sorry …" he whispered. "Goodbye to you all …"

They smiled at the older Augum. Then, one at a time, they departed, some waving goodbye, some nodding, and some simply smiling.

Augum slowly waved back, knowing he would never see them again, knowing this was indeed the final farewell. The group gradually blurred until disappearing into that blistering white haze, leaving him to watch an empty space, listening to a distant song, heart at peace.

He had had his chance to say goodbye.

The song abruptly ended and the white disappeared, the blue fire with it. It took a while for his eyes to adjust back to the night. He watched smoke tendrils curl skyward. Silence passed, the world appearing cold and sharp.

At last, Mrs. Stone quietly returned to the castle. He stood a long while before glancing at Bridget and Leera. Their cheeks were wet, hands folded in front. He departed with bowed head, feeling it was appropriate to leave them behind to mourn on their own.

Back inside the warmth of the castle, he clambered up dark steps. Finding it oddly comfortable, he did not light his palm, letting the cool marble banister guide the way. When he reached the room, he found the canopy bedstead fully repaired, draped with sheer netting, and made with a floral red velvet duvet. Laid out on top were three sets of nightwear—two gowns and a long nightshirt.

Mrs. Stone stood before the fireplace, gazing into the flames, hands behind her back. "Now that the castle is warm, Augum, you shall have your own room, as will the girls," she said in a weary voice, gesturing to the wall. "Yours is the next room over. Goodnight."

"Goodnight, Mrs. Stone." He picked up the nightshirt and left her staring at the fire. His new room had a single ornate oaken door that creaked upon opening. A low fire guttered in the hearth on the left side. Mrs. Stone stood just on the other side of that wall, staring into a fire just like it.

The room was about half the size of Mrs. Stone's. There was a small wardrobe, three windows as opposed to six, and a canopy bedstead with the same sheer curtain and red-velvet duvet.

He changed into the nightshirt, hung both his robes in the wardrobe, and jumped into the softest bed he had ever lain in. Getting comfortable, he once again wondered how Mrs. Stone managed to bring all those things home—the basket of food, the clothing, the sheets and duvet; until his thoughts drifted further—to a castle, a knight, a whiteness; and through-out, a lingering, bitter-sweet song …

TELEKINESIS

Augum woke from a deep sleep to a sharp knocking at the door.

"Get dressed and come to breakfast," Mrs. Stone said before shuffling off.

He was grateful she had not woken him as she used to—with the butt end of her staff. Then he remembered it had smashed while saving his life and he suddenly felt bad for wanting to throw it down Mt. Barrow.

Yawning and stretching, he stumbled out of bed and dressed in his new burgundy robe. Bright morning sun streamed in through the windows, the rays defined by slowly tumbling particles of dust. The fire in the hearth had gone out overnight, yet it had remained warm due to their runeword-finding adventure of the previous day. After securing his new yellow leather belt, he made his way to the grand dining room, stomach grumbling.

Mrs. Stone, Bridget and Leera already sat, chatting idly. Bacon, eggs, bread, apples, milk and honey sat on the table. The girls wore their new apprentice robes while Mrs. Stone was dressed in a plain off-white robe that had no embroidery or ornamentation of any kind.

Augum bid them good morning as he sat down in his usual chair. He noted how the circles under everyone's eyes had disappeared and the smiles came easily. They too must have slept well.

They ate mostly in silence, occasionally exchanging pleasantries and making light conversation. After breakfast, Mrs. Stone dabbed at her lips with a cloth and fixed them with a measured look.

"Let us begin the day's lessons. Who can tell me the qualifications for the 1st degree?"

Bridget spoke first. "One must show one has learned the three standard spells as well as the single spell of one's element."

"Correct. And the three standard spells are …?"

This time Leera spoke up. "Telekinesis, Repair and, um … Unconceal?"

"Correct again. Thus far I believe you have only practiced your elemental spell, Shine, is that accurate?"

"Yes, Mrs. Stone," they chorused.

"And I am aware I covered Telekinesis a bit with Augum, but how about you girls, have you had a chance to learn the spell yet?"

They shook their heads.

"A 'No, Mrs. Stone' or a 'Yes, Mrs. Stone' will do."

"No, Mrs. Stone," the girls said.

"Very well then, that is what we shall practice this morning." Mrs. Stone folded her cloth napkin. "Telekinesis is the movement of an item using your mind. It is the first standard spell because it is a most apt introduction to standard arcanery. Allow me to demonstrate."

She beckoned at Leera's fork; it flew into her hand.

"It is a non-verbal spell, meaning you cast it without an arcane word. When you excel with it, you may even be able to cast it without gesturing." Mrs. Stone placed her hands in her lap. Augum's fork suddenly moved over to Leera's side. Leera squealed in surprise, her chair tipping backwards. She clawed at the table like a frantic cat, just managing to hold on. Red-faced, she cleared her throat and settled in as if nothing had happened.

Mrs. Stone ignored her. "Should you remain studious in your craft and master this spell, you will be able to do it over ever larger distances and to ever larger things, eventually even being able to move people around."

He imagined throwing Robin from one end of the room to the other.

"Augum, you know how to perform the basics of this spell. I would like you to teach it to Bridget and Leera until midday. You can practice on the large pile of rocks at the entrance to the castle, which I want cleared by lunch. In the afternoon, we shall move on to the Repair spell. Am I making myself understood?"

"Yes, Mrs. Stone."

"So be it. Off with you now."

The trio excused themselves from the table, descended to the foyer and exited through the two massive entranceway doors, stopping at the foot of the rubble pile in the vestibule.

Leera scoffed. "She wants us to move this mountain when we hadn't even *cast* the spell before?"

"She doesn't fool around," Augum said, taking a deep breath. He was not feeling particularly confident about his ability to teach, seeing as he had never taught anyone anything before—and Telekinesis was a hard spell; he recalled how difficult it was just to move a small stone back on Mt. Barrow.

Bridget began climbing. "She has high expectations for us. All we have to do is work hard. Besides, we've seen our parents use this spell plenty of times; I'm sure we'll manage."

The three apprentice warlocks gathered at the bottom of the pile outside the castle, shielding their eyes with their hands. It was a bright yet cold day, the snow particularly brittle underfoot. The sky remained clear except for a distant haze of cloud that peeked over snow-encrusted evergreens. The occasional tweet of a winter bird sounded from the Ravenwood, which otherwise stood tall and silent. The pile of rubble glistened in the sunlight, the occasional boulder peeking through the snow.

Leera folded her arms and smirked. "All right, Teacher—teach."

Augum rubbed the back of his neck. "Um … okay, you have to, uh … to visualize, um … moving the uh, thing … and you use your hand to, um … to get it to … you know … to move … and stuff." He felt dumber than a toad, and for some reason his tongue was not working properly.

Bridget placed her hands on her hips. "So you mean we have to concentrate on moving the object while we gesture at it with our hand?"

"Yes exactly—couldn't have said it better myself."

"No, you certainly couldn't," Leera muttered.

Augum ignored the remark. "So yeah, focus on the object and think about it *moving*—" and he raised his arm and beckoned for a small rock to move.

Except the stupid thing did not obey.

"Um, hold on …" Red-faced, he beckoned again, yet the rock stubbornly refused to budge. He gestured frantically. "Dumb rock—move!"

Nothing happened.

The girls exchanged amused looks. He checked the six stained glass windows of Mrs. Stone's room and discovered her staring down at him, a sour look on her face.

Great …

He took a deep breath and closed his eyes, resolving to concentrate. *An enemy with a clear and focused mind is a fearsome one*, he heard Sir Westwood say. He then recalled successfully moving objects before, especially the lost rope at Hangman's Rock. He had to still his mind, that was all there was to it.

He slowly expelled his breath, let the thoughts slide away to emptiness, opened his eyes, and beckoned.

The stone flew into his hand. He expelled a breath in relief.

Leera uncrossed her arms. She took the rock from his hand and examined it, as if hoping to find a string attached. "All right, not bad …"

Augum stole a peek at the windows, but they were empty. "Clear your mind," he said. "That's the key—clear your mind."

Bridget nodded. "All right, what else do we need to know?"

Confidence regained, he repeated what Mrs. Stone taught him back on the mountain, explaining the three principles and how rocks had a tendency to want to roll downhill.

Leera's face scrunched skeptically. " 'Downhill'?"

"Yeah, like if I tried to move that rock up there at the top of the pile—" he pointed to a small boulder, "it helps to know which *way* the rock wants to go, making the spell easier. At least, I think that's what Mrs. Stone was getting at …"

"Makes sense," Bridget said.

Leera rolled her eyes. "Kind of obvious too."

Bridget gave her an elbow. "Stop being grumpy, *Robin*."

"Sorry, I'll play nice."

Augum raised his arm, focusing on the top of the pile. "All right, let's begin," and so they practiced for hours, Augum instructing as best he could, a new pile forming behind them. It was not long until Leera and Bridget were summoning small rocks. After pushing himself, he too progressed with the spell, now able to move slightly heavier stones.

The hours of casting took their toll on them, however—heads hurt, attention spans and tempers were short, and nausea prevailed.

Glancing at the sun, Augum noted it would soon be lunchtime, yet most of the pile sat untouched. An idea came to him. "This is taking too long, we have to work together. You two go for the small stones and I'll go for the larger ones. When rocks tumble from higher up we'll use their momentum and push them along with the spell—"

"—that way we can move stones that are far heavier than we otherwise could—brilliant, Augum!" Bridget said, beaming.

Leera only groaned, massaging her temples.

Augum blushed with pride and went to work. However, pushing falling rocks with Telekinesis proved difficult and took some getting used to. The snow certainly did not help and the rocks they missed on the way down were too heavy to begin moving anew—those they would have to manually push later. Nonetheless, stone by stone, they weeded the pile down. To make things easier, they separated the wood and iron.

By the time the sun shone directly overheard, the once small hole above the pile was now a giant maw. The trio was becoming quite practiced, Bridget and Leera even managing to move rocks closer in weight to Augum's. Unfortunately, the side effects forced them to take frequent breaks.

Augum, panting, gestured at a large rock. "All together on the big ones now." With Leera and Bridget's help, he managed to arcanely roll it to the new pile. Time was running out, yet there remained some large rocks in the hallway, not to mention a cluster of boulders outside that required brute strength to move. He glanced at the heap of wood. Well, at least they had completed that part of it …

They worked at a frantic pace now, expecting Mrs. Stone's arrival at any moment. There were a few narrow escapes as the stones came hurtling past, reminding them to remain alert.

When they could no longer move anything with Telekinesis, they put their backs into it and pushed the remaining boulders, yet even that was not enough for the last few, which required their combined strength *and* Telekinesis to move.

Finally, the entranceway cleared, the trio collapsed at the foot of the new rock pile, completely spent, heads splitting from the arcane effort—just in time too, for a shadow came between them and the sun.

"I see you have accomplished the task."

Augum wondered if that was surprise or disappointment in Mrs. Stone's voice.

"Lunch is ready." She walked off.

They were too exhausted to reply. Augum stood up, helping Leera.

Leera winced. "Feet … refusing … to budge …"

He and Bridget each took a hand and hoisted her to her feet. She pretended to fall back, tongue rolling out in defeat.

The trio eventually lumbered through the now gaping hole in the castle and staggered up the stairs to lunch.

REPAIR

Lunch consisted of leftover chicken, stale journey bread and boiled beans. Mrs. Stone chewed the bread and hacked at the chicken, oblivious to the trio mutely prodding their food. For Augum, every bite brought a new round of throbbing in his brain. Thankfully the side effects were subsiding, though he was not sure he could do another round of casting today.

"This afternoon you shall be learning the Repair spell," Mrs. Stone said once they had consumed everything but the beans. "Repair is verbal and a little more complex." She swept the room with her eyes. "The spirits know how much there is to fix around here."

Augum remembered her using the spell on a mug he had broken back in her cave. He hoped it was not as difficult as Telekinesis.

Mrs. Stone seemed to be waiting for some kind of response, yet the trio only stared at their plates.

"Mmm, yes, it is difficult, is it not? That is the way of it; the path you have chosen. I advise you to acclimatize yourselves to the pain, the nausea, the exhaustion. In order to advance in your studies you must learn the art of suffering. That is how you grow and develop fortitude. You must harden yourselves as it only gets more difficult."

She paused and leaned back in the queen's chair, letting the silence drive home the point, the frown lines on her face creasing sharply. "I shall allow one hour of rest this one time. Then I will expect you in the foyer where we will continue your training. You are excused."

"Yes, Mrs. Stone," the trio said without enthusiasm. They trudged off.

"I'm exhausted," Augum said in the dim hallway, almost tripping over a large tear in the faded carpet.

Leera managed a groan. "That food was so bland … at least compared to when Mrs. Stone teleported some in."

"I think it's part of the experience," Bridget said.

Leera made a face at her but said nothing.

They stopped before the girls' room.

"Your room the same as mine?" Augum asked.

"You tell us." Leera opened the door, revealing a room that was a mirror image of his own. "We share the bed."

Augum stepped inside. "Yup, it's the same."

Leera plopped down on the ironwood canopy bedstead curtained in the same sheer netting. "Can't wait to explore the rest of the castle," she said, glancing about as if hoping to find a secret door.

Bridget slumped onto the bed beside her. "Maybe tonight …"

Augum thought this would be a good time to talk about what he and Mrs. Stone discussed the day before. He paced to the windows, staring beyond the snow-covered Ravenwood. An angry bank of clouds approached, threatening to snuff the sunshine.

"There's something I've been meaning to tell you two about my father." He turned back to the girls and leaned against the windowsill. "Remember his horse?"

"Yeah, we remember," Bridget said.

"Mrs. Stone thinks he's practicing necromancy."

The girls exchanged looks.

Bridget's voice dropped to a whisper. "Come to think of it, remember the horses the Red Guard rode?"

Leera stood and began pacing. "Hmm. Mrs. Stone defeated a necromancer once …"

"That's right—Narsus," Augum said. "There's more. He … he murdered my mother."

After seeing the look on their faces, he turned back to the window. Even though he did not know his mother, he found it hard to talk about her. "He murdered her when she said she was leaving him …" He went on to recount much of what Mrs. Stone said about his mother and father. "… and I think I was only born because he thought it would force Mrs. Stone to give my father the scion," he concluded.

For once, the girls were at a loss for words.

"Think a storm's coming," he said after a while.

Bridget placed a delicate hand on his shoulder. "Are you okay, Augum?"

He shrugged. "I never knew my parents anyway. Besides, the memorial ceremony helped a lot."

"Helped us too," Leera said. "I'm sorry about your mother …"

He forced a smile.

Bridget drew her robe close, nodding at the angry bank of clouds. "Ominous."

"Yeah, hope we don't have to work outside." Leera fell back on the bed. Suddenly she sat up. "Wait, why would he *want* to become a necromancer? Why would anyone?"

"Mrs. Stone told me it's a fascination with fear, death and power."

Leera smirked. "Wonder how he felt when she snuffed Narsus …"

Augum grabbed the windowsill, which was as deep as the castle walls, and climbed on top.

"What are you doing?" Bridget asked.

"Resting my sore legs. Besides, I love watching storms." At the Penderson farm, a storm meant he could spend quiet time in the barn with Meli. In Willowbrook, he would curl up beside the fire with a book and listen to rain pound the thatch and tap on the windows. Even after one nearly killed him, that love of storms had not diminished.

"Rest … good idea." Bridget lay down beside Leera and the girls stole a quick nap.

Head leaning against the window, he watched the storm's steady approach for the rest of that peaceful hour, until Mrs. Stone walked by in the corridor.

"Time to go," she said.

They gathered themselves and descended to the foyer, dutifully lining up before her.

Mrs. Stone surveyed them a moment before speaking. "Following this lesson, I was planning on assigning you the task of repairing the entire entranceway, to be completed by evening."

There was a better chance of them all learning how to fly without wings than repairing that entranceway in this weather, Augum thought.

"But as you may have noticed, there is a storm heading our way. Therefore, I have decided to assist you."

The trio breathed a sigh of relief.

"Since we do not have much time, I will skip some of the details, but I expect you to study the spell from the book this evening when I am gone. Do I make myself clear?"

"Yes, Mrs. Stone," they chorused.

Augum wondered where she was going but knew better than to ask.

"The Repair spell is a bit more complicated," Mrs. Stone began, clasping her hands behind her back, "because it requires immense and unbroken concentration." She gazed at each of them in turn, as if to confirm they were paying attention.

"The spell will not work on living things, arcane objects, or anything incinerated. In the beginning, you will be unable to repair anything more complex than a teacup, or perhaps a plank of wood. However, I daresay you shall find no shortage of things to practice on in this castle. Now, does anyone know the arcane word for this spell?"

They gave her a blank look.

Mrs. Stone's brows sharpened. "The word is 'apreyo'. Say it with me."

"APREEO."

She made them repeat it a few more times until their pronunciation was perfect.

"Now, the gesture is important so pay careful attention— both of your hands must pass over the object just so," and she made her hands rigidly flat, guiding them over something imaginary, "and they must continue to pass over the object until the repair is complete, otherwise it will fail. As you concentrate on the repair at hand, see the cracks disappear in your mind. See two halves become one. Allow me to demonstrate."

She placed her hands over a fallen stone globe that once rested at the end of the marble staircase, and in a clear voice that echoed around the foyer, said, "Apreyo." It immediately began to reform. Even little pieces from the other end of the foyer slid along the floor to rejoin it. The sphere then lifted off the ground and secured itself back onto the banister. Lastly, the cracks contracted and disappeared.

"Amazing," Leera whispered, walking over to the globe. "But Mrs. Stone—there's a tiny piece missing here."

"That happens when the piece is stuck or not in range of the spell, which is approximately twenty paces." She padded over to another broken globe. "All right, let us see you practice on this sphere. One at a time now."

And so they began, Mrs. Stone instructing them on some of the many subtleties of the spell and the importance of concentration, especially with larger objects. On more than one occasion, they had to jump out of the way as the sphere crashed back to the floor, smashing anew. The learning was slow as they were still recovering from the morning's efforts. Thus, it came as no surprise that by the end of a grueling hour's work, not one of them had successfully repaired it.

Mrs. Stone's lips pursed as she once again demonstrated a proper repair on the globe, before herding them to the castle entranceway they had cleared earlier.

Leera groaned as she stared at the enormous piles of iron, wood and stone. Beyond, the sky quickly darkened. A biting wind swirled snow in miniature tornadoes.

Mrs. Stone raised her chin expectantly. "You may begin."

The trio tried to get the stones to reform into the entranceway while the wind kept increasing and the cold deepened. By the time the wind threatened to steal planks from the pile, not one of them had managed to get anything to reform with the five-foot thick wall.

"This is a vital lesson in concentration and belief!" Mrs. Stone's robe flapped in the wind, ponytail lashing like a snake. "Without absolute conviction and concentration, you will fail! One day, you may have to perform such a spell in the din of battle, with plenty to distract you. Cold, hunger, wind, pain, attack—these are all things that you must learn to ignore as you focus. Even a momentary loss of concentration can result in spell failure!"

Augum recalled using Telekinesis at Hangman's Rock and how, despite a brutal gale, he had to still his mind in order to find the rope. Staggering for balance, he tried to apply that lesson here. It was futile though—he was simply too tired, the spell too new.

Snow began blowing sideways, forcing them to avert their faces and draw their hoods. Augum wanted to keep going, to show Mrs. Stone they were capable, but his legs wanted to buckle; and now, glancing at the oncoming storm, he knew they had run out of time.

"Oh for mercy's sake—" Mrs. Stone marched over to the rock pile and, facing the wind, spread her hands. "APREYO!"

The rocks immediately began rolling, bouncing and vaulting back into the entranceway. The trio had to jump aside to avoid being bowled over. They watched in helplessness as the hole in the castle rapidly reformed into massive arched double doors. The rock pile consumed, Mrs. Stone strode over to the wood and iron piles and repeated the process, tackling both at once. Planks, splinters, hinges and nails flew back into the doorway, reforming like a floating puzzle. Her concentration was perfect, never wavering from the task. Upon completing the repair, she flicked her wrist at one of the doors. It flew open and she marched inside, leaving them lying in the snow, gaping.

Finally, they picked themselves up and shambled in, working together to close the heavy door against the gale. It clanged shut, locking with an ancient iron bolt that Augum slid in place. They exchanged looks. Nobody wanted to face what was surely going to be a very stern lecture. Steeling himself, Augum was the first to step into the dark warmth of the foyer.

As expected, Mrs. Stone stood waiting, hands behind her back, brows furrowed. Only after they lined up before her, barely able to see in the dim light, did she flick her wrist. Out popped the floating lightning sphere.

"Shyneo," everyone said, not advanced enough to do the spell wordlessly. Their hands barely lit up, glowing weakly.

Augum's flickered and extinguished almost immediately. He did not bother relighting it.

Mrs. Stone's face was hard as steel. "How eager you three are to surrender. I am disappointed. I daresay I expected greater ... fortitude."

The trio only stared at their feet as Leera's light flickered out. A moment later, so did Bridget's, leaving only the cold sheen from Mrs. Stone's orb. She merely watched them.

Augum felt the prickle of shame; the silence was worse than the lecture.

"I am leaving the castle for the evening," she finally said. "I expect you to make up for your lack of tenacity by working extra hard. You are to read up on the details of the Repair spell then spend at least two hours practicing it. Am I making myself perfectly clear?"

"Yes, Mrs. Stone."

She extinguished her light and marched through the foyer doors, arcanely slamming them behind her. The noise made them flinch. A moment later, one of the newly reformed outer doors opened and closed with a dull thud that reverberated through the castle.

When the echoes died out, all three collapsed in the near total darkness.

"I'm sorry, I should have tried harder," Augum said, staring up at the dim outline of the ceiling.

Bridget flopped to her side. "Me too ..."

Leera gasped like an old dying woman. "Not me, I was done for ..."

The wind roared distantly, muffled by thick walls. Suddenly Augum did not feel much like exploring.

Bridget sat up. "Shall we make a fire and study?"

Leera exhaled a tedious breath. "Might as well ..."

ENCOUNTER

The girl's fireplace was out of wood so the trio scrounged some from the other rooms. When it burned bright, Bridget brought out the ornate tome from under the bed and the three of them read up on the Repair spell, discussing its finer points. They then read the entire section titled *Concentration: Beginning Basics*, as well as *Introduction to Runes and Runewords*, as per Mrs. Stone's suppertime suggestion. After two solid hours of study and discussion, they felt they were ready to start practicing.

Bridget closed the book and slid it back under the bed. "Now the only question is on what ..."

Augum's brain had not fully recovered from earlier arcane efforts, and now with all this studying it felt like mush. His thoughts returned to Mrs. Stone. Where had she gone this time?

The windows shuddered from a particularly strong gust. Outside, the snow blew horizontally.

Leera gave the coals a stir with a fire-iron. "We could go upstairs and find something to repair, or explore the second floor, or even the rest of this floor; it'd be neat to find the throne room."

Bridget looked to Augum. "What do you think?"

"Well, if we go down, there's definitely lots to repair, but if we stay on this floor or go up, we can at least keep an eye on the storm while we practice."

"Good idea," Leera said. "Not quite in the mood for the lower castle anyway."

Bridget stood up and clapped her hands together. "Up it is then."

Leera's sharp brows rose. "Ooo, maybe we'll even find the king and queen's chambers."

"—or treasure," Augum added, imagination ablaze. "Let's get my sword and go." Together they retrieved his blade from his room, arcanely lit their palms, and began their way upstairs. Windows rattled as they crept up the dusty marble steps. Shadows played long and sharp to the sway of their hands, their lights weaker than usual due to arcane exhaustion.

Leera glanced at the rattling window between the third and fourth floor. "Storm's getting worse."

Augum grinned. "Looks like a blizzard."

"You're enjoying this too much."

Bridget picked up a small scrap of parchment from a stair. "Hey, think the repair spell works on paper?"

Leera found another scrap by Augum's foot. "Don't know, can't remember the book saying anything about it."

Augum also found a piece and handed it to Bridget. "Only one way to find out."

Leera frowned. "Don't see many pieces to work with here ..."

"So who wants to try first?" Bridget asked.

"You go ahead," Leera said, "it's your find."

"All right." Bridget extinguished her palm, darkening the landing. She squinted trying to make out what was on the paper. "Wish I knew how to chronocast ..."

" 'Chronocast'?" Augum asked.

"It's when you cast one spell and then another while the original spell is still in effect." She kneeled, piling the scraps on the marble floor. "It's something you learn as you go along."

"Oh. I thought it meant casting two spells at the same time."

"That's impossible—"

"No it's not," Leera said. "It's called simulcasting, and it's extremely difficult but *not* impossible. From what I understand, there are two rules—the first is you have to be extremely talented, and the second is that it can only be done using an elemental spell and a standard spell. You can't just cast two standard spells or two elemental spells at once."

Bridget's lips thinned. "Never heard of it—"

"Well it's real, Mrs. Stone can do it; my mum told me a story about it from when she was at the academy."

Bridget made a dismissive gesture. "She was just telling tales."

"Wasn't a tale, Bridge, I'm telling you, Mum *saw* it."

Augum leaned up against the cool marble banister. "What's the story?"

"It happened near the end of the Narsinian war," Leera began quietly, "when Narsus' armies marched on Blackhaven. His soldiers raided the academy, killing a bunch of teachers and students, even though Narsus promised to stay away from there. Well as you can imagine, Mrs. Stone—who was headmistress at the time—got very angry; Mum says you should have seen the look on her face—" Leera paused for dramatic effect.

Augum made an impatient motion with his hand. "Then what happened—?"

"Mrs. Stone told the students to hide while she made her way outside. Everyone took shelter in classrooms, but Mum managed to peek through the curtains. Well, along with a whole bunch of soldiers, there were these two powerful Narsinian warlocks there, one of whom graduated from the academy. Mrs. Stone just strode right up to them. What happened next is almost unbelievable, even Mum said so—and she saw it with her own eyes. Anyway, Mrs. Stone paralyzed *both* warlocks *and* simultaneously cast chain lightning on the soldiers. Those two sorcerers were forced to watch their troops sizzle like chicken, and there was nothing they could do."

"But that's crazy—" Bridget said. "Chain Lightning's like a 13th degree elemental spell and Paralyze Group—a what, 14th degree standard spell—?"

"That's not the end of it—after the soldiers were killed, she let the two warlocks go just to send Narsus a message. She must have known what she was doing because it wasn't long until Narsus himself came with a lot more soldiers, and we all know what happened next."

"She killed Narsus in the dungeons below the academy," Augum said.

"And now we know which spell she used," Leera said. "That off-the-books one she used to collapse her cave. I wonder if she simulcasted against him."

"Dare you to ask her," he said.

"Forget it, I like my head where it is."

Bridget contemplated the scraps of parchment at her feet. "Hmm, well if your mother saw it ... Maybe we can ask Mrs. Stone indirectly about what happened sometime."

"Indirectly—?"

"Yeah, by starting a conversation on chronocasting, then ask her if it's possible to simulcast. Maybe she'll tell us that way."

"She won't," Augum said with a shake of the head.

"How do you know?"

"It's Mrs. Stone—she *hates* talking about herself. But if you insist, *you* can be the one to ask."

Bridget's eyes flashed. "Maybe I *will* then—"

A silence passed as she fiddled with the scraps of parchment while Augum stood red-faced. What had just happened? Why was Bridget angry with him?

"You want to try repairing this then?" Leera asked in a delicate voice.

"Ugh, might as well—" Bridget arranged her hands just right and sat quiet, mustering her concentration.

Leera gave Augum a look that said *don't worry about it*.

"APREYO!" but nothing happened. Bridget sighed and rubbed her eyes. "I'm sorry for snapping at you, Augum."

"Don't even give it another thought."

"This whole thing is just so … trying and so new … and after everything that's happened …"

"I understand." He smiled.

Bridget smiled back, straightened her robe and splayed out her hands again. "Apreyo." The papers moved, turning this way and that, coming together to create some kind of picture. A few more pieces flew from above and below the landing, until the parchment appeared half-complete. Upon finishing, she plopped on the marble floor, pale from the effort.

Leera leaned forward. "It's a map!"

"Good job, Bridge," Augum said, genuinely impressed.

"Thanks." She picked up the map, stood and inspected it. "Looks like some kind of room, but I can't make out anything else; missing pieces must be out of range."

Leera's eyes brightened. "Could be a treasure room …!"

"We need to find the rest though," Augum said. "Let's try casting the spell in different places."

Bridget folded the map and tucked it away. "Good idea. We could take turns, it'd be great practice. Let's go."

They made their way up another flight of steps to the howl of a very strong gust; Augum swore the floor actually shook. He had a vision of something large stomping in the bowels of the castle. Suddenly he was glad they had chosen to go up instead of down—what if they had been in the cellar and lost their light? He thought of the crypt and shivered, imagining a bony hand on his shoulder.

The fourth floor appeared much like the third, but with refuse strewn about everywhere, from torn scraps of parchment to pieces of furniture.

"I bet that behind those doors is that room with the round window," Augum said, pointing at a pair of oaken doors that, if they were one floor below, would have opened into Mrs. Stone's room. He turned the handles; the doors creaked as they swung inwards. An enormous round stained-glass window greeted them, allowing them to look out into the blizzard.

"If the castle was a one-eyed giant, that would be its eye," Leera said.

"Sir Westwood used to say castles had a spirit, each with its own unique personality."

"Let's just hope this one isn't evil then."

They exchanged looks before inspecting the room.

On the ground was even more debris—broken furniture and bottles, torn spines of books, ripped scrolls, shattered glass, as well as copious amounts of loose or torn parchment. Bookshelves from floor to ceiling covered all wall space and a thick pile of dust coated everything.

Bridget shook her head. "Must have been quite the library. What a loss …"

"Look at all this," Leera said, picking up scrap after scrap of torn parchment. "This would take years to repair!"

"Imagine the secrets these books hold though," Augum said.

Bridget unfolded the map. "At least it's a great place to practice."

"Whose turn is it?" Leera asked.

Bridget put the map down onto a clearing she made with her foot. "Augum—want to try?"

"Guess so." He crouched, closed his eyes, and spent time envisioning the map repairing itself. Then he flattened his palms out over it. "Apreyo."

The map fluttered while a few more pieces flew from the pile, attaching to the parchment. Just when they thought that was the last of them, they heard rustling from underneath a broken desk. Bridget and Leera quickly pushed it aside, allowing one last piece to shoot out.

"It's almost complete," Leera said. "Nice work, Aug."

Augum slumped, dizzy. "I thought for sure I was going to lose concentration when you two moved the desk. That's a tough piece of arcanery."

"It sure is," Bridget absently replied, inspecting the map alongside Leera. "Where do you suppose this passageway starts?"

"Has to be somewhere in the castle," Leera said, "but we'll need this piece here to know exactly where."

Augum crowded close. "Think it's underground, the walls look rocky—but yeah, we need that piece. So, do we want to practice some more in here or move on?"

Bridget put away the map and glanced around. "It'll be difficult, but let's at least try to repair some of the furniture," and so they took turns casting Repair, advising each other on how to get it just right. They also took turns casting Shine to conserve arcane energy. Meanwhile, the blizzard raged on, caking the giant window with snow.

After two hours, they had managed to repair the desk, two library tables and eight chairs. They had even cleared the debris off to one side.

"That should make the room a bit more livable," Augum said, wincing from an arcane-induced headache.

Leera collapsed into a chair, dusting her hands. "Now all it needs are some books ... who wants to spend the next hundred years repairing a shelf's worth?"

Augum snorted.

Bridget approached the window. "Must have been a great place to study, especially with the view." She recoiled as a sudden gust rattled the glass.

Augum eyed the frame, wondering if it would hold in this storm. He imagined it abruptly crumpling and all of them getting sucked out into the night. "Let's move on, my concentration's shot anyway; don't know if I can repair another thing tonight."

Leera massaged her temple. "I second that."

Bridget moved to the door. "We did get a lot accomplished already; I think we're getting the hang of the spell."

"We'll see if that's enough for Mrs. Stone," Leera added as they left.

They explored the rooms flanking the library—more broken bookshelves, desks, chairs, glass and torn paper. Bridget pronounced them study rooms. Too tired to do anymore repairing, they left everything as is, though they did find a few more examples of the letter "A" carved into the furniture.

Then, as they passed the staircase, there came a metal shuffling sound from within the southwest battlement.

The trio froze. Something moved at the far edge of their light, deep inside the battlement.

"Who's there?" Augum asked, feeling the hairs on the back of his neck stand up. He unsheathed his sword.

"Wouldst thou fancy a duel, mine lord?" asked a nasal voice from the darkness.

Bridget shrieked, Leera covered her mouth and Augum nearly dropped his sword. They scurried back to the staircase.

"A duel—?" Augum asked.

"Indeed, mine lord. What setting dost mine lord beseech of me—defender, beginner, intermediate, advanced, or expert?"

Augum exchanged mystified looks with Bridget and Leera.

A gust of wind sent windows clattering and the trio instinctively took a step downstairs.

"Come forward so we can see you!" Augum said in the most menacing tone he could muster.

Something advanced, clanking and clattering. The trio took another step downstairs. A suit of dented child-sized armor limped to a stop just at the edge of their light. It held a wooden practice sword in a gauntleted hand.

"Thou hath besought, thus hither I come," it said in that nasal voice.

Leera snorted a laugh before slamming a hand over her mouth. She took a few steps closer, lit palm held forward. "Who are you?"

The suit of armor rattled as it bowed. "Fentwick at thine service, mine lady—trainer, defender and sparring partner to thee young princes and princesses of ye castle."

Augum could hardly believe what he was seeing. "Are you a ghost?"

"Nae, mine lord, merely an arcane suit of armor. Dost mine lord care to duel?"

Augum sheathed his sword, noticing he had been able to keep his hand lit throughout the ordeal, and the same went for Leera and Bridget. They were getting better at Shine.

He took a cautious step forward. "How long have you been here?"

"Long, mine lord?"

"Yes, how—long—have—you—been—in—this—castle?"

"He's not stupid, Augum," Bridget said. "It's probably just not the kind of question he could answer. Interesting how he speaks in the old tongue though."

Fentwick rattled to life again. "Mayhaps mine lord or mine lady wouldst care to duel? I canst set mine self to defender, beginner, intermediate, advanced, or expert rank as befits thou needs."

Leera strode up to Fentwick and examined him from all sides. Augum advanced with her, hand on the pommel of his sword. She blew at Fentwick's helmet. A cloud of dust billowed, yet Fentwick stood as still as a statue.

Bridget hesitantly approached. "Is he safe?"

Leera peered in through the visor. "Whoa, there's nothing inside the helmet!"

"Lee, that's kind of rude."

"It's only a hunk of armor, Bridge."

Bridget sighed. "I suppose you're right. You know what though? It's kind of cute."

Leera gave Bridget a repulsed look.

"Anyway," Bridget continued, "it's an *animated* suit of armor, so it must be ancient arcane."

"Well it certainly *talks* ancient."

Augum tapped it on the shoulder. "Um, Fentwick—?"

Fentwick abruptly turned toward him, throwing off a fresh cloud of dust. "Mine lord, wouldst thou care to duel?"

Augum swatted the plume away, coughing. "Um ... maybe later, but you wouldn't happen to know what the letter 'A' stands for that's carved into everything around here, would you?"

"Thee letter 'A', mine lord? Mayhaps mine lord or mine lady would care—"

"No thanks, Fentwick." Augum shrugged and turned to the girls. "Was worth a try anyway. So should we bring him with us?"

Bridget scrunched up her face in thought. "He might be too loud and slow. Let's leave him here for now—no offense, Fentwick."

The armor made no reply.

Augum leaned in close. "Fentwick—stay—here—okay?"

"Ugh, Augum—"

Fentwick bowed. "As ye say, mine lord," before stiffening like a statue.

The trio moved on down the corridor, checking over their shoulders.

"He's certainly a treasure," Leera said upon entering a debris-filled room on the west side of the castle, one of many like it in the corridor.

Augum examined the rubble before them. "Wonder what other oddities this castle has."

"Or once had." Bridget withdrew the unfinished map and grimaced. "I'm just surprised someone hasn't made off with little Fentwick."

Augum imagined that dented suit of armor struggling in the arms of a bandit.

"There's a good reason for that," Leera said.

"What, that stick of a sword?" Bridget asked.

"No—he'd annoy you to death. We'll probably find bodies of bandits who've committed suicide in that battlement."

"Maybe that's what drove the people out from the castle," Augum said. "Fentwick's high-pitched nattering."

Bridget placed a finger to her lips. "Shh—he'll hear you. You'll hurt his feelings."

Leera snorted. "He's got about as many feelings as a door knob …"

Bridget rolled her eyes and turned her attention to the room. "This one's a mess, let's keep exploring."

They made their way to the opposite side of the corridor where a plain black door awaited. Augum wrestled it open and a burst of hot, humid air greeted them.

The girls gasped. Before them was a room overgrown with ancient-looking ferns, gnarled ropes of ivy, rainbow mosses, thorny rose bushes, blue palms, and a vast array of bizarre tropical plants in every shape and color. All it needed were sounds of insects and animals and they would be in the jungle, as other than the door, there was no sign of castle structure anywhere.

Bridget poked a huge blue leaf. "Why is there a garden in the center of the castle?"

Augum had heard stories of exotic plants of the south from Sir Westwood, who himself heard them from people who ventured down there on trade missions; but this—

"—this is impossible," Bridget said.

"We just spoke with a talking suit of child-sized armor named Fentwick," Leera said. "Nothing's impossible."

"Fair point." Bridget raised a hand for them to be still. "Anyone else hear water trickling ahead?"

"I can hear it too," Augum said, spotting an overgrown trail. "There's a path here."

Leera strode past, grinning. "Come on then, there's exploring to be had!"

The path wound snake-like. Each of their steps squished into soggy aqua grass or crusty purple moss. Their hands cast chameleon-like shadows into thick foliage.

"Spooky," Bridget whispered.

Soon they arrived at an ancient stone fountain of a bald man with a serene look on his face, hands spread in a gesture of welcome. Clear water spouted from his palms into a shallow basin, before overflowing into the earth. Small colorful flowers grew around the base.

Augum reached for the water but Bridget caught his arm.

"Don't," she said. "Could be poison."

He doubted it but withdrew his arm nonetheless.

Leera looked up into the canopy. "How do these plants survive without the light of day?"

"Must be an arcane room," Bridget said.

"Probably as ancient as Fentwick too."

They stood silent for a time simply enjoying the peace of the room. The plant growth was near impenetrable, so thick a small cat would have a hard time slinking through.

Bridget seemed to recognize a particularly odd-looking plant with black shoots and blue leaves near the fountain. "This place would be an herbalist's dream …"

Augum studied the fountain. Who was this serene man? Had the royal family used this strange room as a peaceful retreat, or was it something more?

"Shall we see where the path ends?" Leera asked.

They travelled on to the other end of the room, exiting through another black door and emerging into a hallway on the eastern side of the castle.

Augum grimaced. "I was hoping the path led somewhere more—"

"—exotic?" Leera said. "Me too."

The distant sound of wind rattling windows emphasized the difference between the dark castle and the peace of the forest room. It almost made Augum want to go back.

The trio explored the rooms in this hallway, which turned out to be empty or ruined like the ones on the other side. They walked on towards the north room, which sat directly above the grand dining room where they had eaten.

Bridget was the first to open the heavily scratched oaken door. As soon as she laid eyes on what was inside, however, she shrieked and recoiled.

Beyond the door, extending far into the room, stood an iron maiden, a head vice, a chair with a spiked seat, a guillotine, and a great many other dusty torture devices that seemed perfectly heinous.

They backed away as if from a crumbling cliff. Then the door started to close on its own, creaking as if in agony, finally slamming shut. The trio screamed and bolted back down the hall, the quickly moving light from their hands throwing claw-like shadows.

"Fentwick—help!" Bridget called as they rounded the staircase.

The trio did not wait for an acknowledgment, careening down the stairs and piling into the girls' room, slamming the door behind them. Panting quietly, they stood frozen, listening. It was not long before shuffling was heard.

Bridget paled; Leera and Augum put their ears to the door, eyes wide.

The sound steadily came closer, echoing off the walls.

"Fentwick?" Leera whispered, freckles glistening.

"Don't know," Augum replied.

The sound only grew louder. They backed away to the end of the room. Augum drew his sword.

The sound screeched to a halt right on the other side of the door.

Then silence.

The trio watched the crack underneath, but it was pitch-black on the other side. Whatever it was, it could see in the dark. They held their breath. Behind them, the windows rattled from the wind.

Finally, Bridget took a cagey step forward, robe rustling. "Fentwick—?"

"Mine lady—" began the muted nasal voice, "wouldst thou care to duel? I canst set mine self to defender, beginner—"

They breathed sighs of relief and chuckled at each other while Fentwick prattled on.

"You were scared—"

"No, *you* were—"

Augum sheathed his sword and extinguished his palm. Then an idea struck him. "Fentwick, will you stand guard outside the room?"

"As ye wish, mine lord," and they heard him turn around.

Leera collapsed onto the bed. "Wow—can we also get him to clean the castle?" Then she propped herself up on her elbows. "Wait, why is there a torture chamber on the fourth floor?"

Bridget sat on the bed beside her. "Didn't Mrs. Stone say that the castle was used for dark purposes for a while?"

"Yes, she did, when we first came here," Augum said, remembering that initial freezing late-night walk.

Leera teased her raven hair. "Wonder who by ..."

They sat pondering that question. To Augum, the castle no longer seemed as welcoming, with gouges on doors, holes in the walls, a dark dungeon, a crypt, and now a torture chamber. Nonetheless, he found himself yawning. It had been a long day. "Think I'm going to turn in, I'm tired."

"We did get a lot accomplished tonight," Bridget said, catching the yawn.

"Practiced loads," Leera added, preparing the bed. "Even found a map. Let's continue tomorrow."

He nodded and made his way to the door. "And we've got Fentwick now too. Can't wait to have him meet Mrs. Stone. Goodnight then."

"Night, Augum!"

"Shyneo," and he went through the door.

"Mine lord, wouldst though—"

"Goodnight, Fentwick."

"May thee stars brighten thy dreams, mine lord." The words echoed gently in the cool dark of the castle.

As he entered his room, Augum imagined Fentwick saying that line to princes and princesses of old. He dressed in his nightgown and jumped into bed, bundling the covers close. For a time, he listened to the howl of the wind and the way it rattled the windows. He wished he had a second Fentwick outside his door. Would that forgotten suit of arcane armor protect him too should something come in the night? He tried not to think about the cold darkness of the castle, its ancient secrets and ancient ghosts, its eternally silent crypt and dungeon. When sleep took him at last, his thoughts had drifted to Fentwick watching life from a thousand years ago; a forest behind a black door; and a dark room ...

THE HUNT

"Where is it? Tell me or I will squeeze the life out of you," the shadowy figure said in a growling voice, its hands wrapped tightly around Augum's neck. Augum did not know where this mysterious "it" was though, and tried to communicate that with horror-struck eyes. Around him, he heard the sound of torture devices screeching and clanking away. Fire blazed in two massive hearths somewhere behind; dark figures moved nearby. The sound of girls screaming in pain came from out of view.

Let me go, you fiend, he thought, struggling in the vice-like grip. The figure above him laughed and started squeezing. Augum kicked and gasped, feeling his life slither away.

His heart started to bang thunderously in his chest. The noise persisted, growing louder and consuming his entire being, until he bolted up in bed, soaked in cold sweat.

"—sake, Augum, breakfast!"

He wiped his brow, breathing heavy. It was just a nightmare, a horrible, horrible nightmare …

The door banged again. "Augum—!"

"Coming, Mrs. Stone!"

She grunted and shuffled off, grumbling.

Augum rubbed the sleep from his eyes, frustrated that he was unable to recall what the figure had been after, as if the answer was around a corner just beyond reach.

He slid out of bed and tread to the window, feeling out of sorts. It was sunny but windy outside, and the blizzard had covered everything in a silky blanket of fresh snow. The trees swayed in the breeze, releasing milky plumes.

He donned his burgundy apprentice robe and made his way to the dining room, greeting everyone through a bleary haze. The anxious feelings from the nightmare were still with him as he ate his breakfast of buttered bread, salted spinach and peppered beans.

Bridget and Leera sat in their usual places, immersed in an energetic retelling of last night. When they told Mrs. Stone about the torture room, she merely said, "Indeed now."

The girls blathered on, describing the library and the strange garden and Fentwick and how he simply had to be ancient arcane …

Augum did not pay much attention, the combination of a bad dream and beans making his stomach feel like it was filled with acid. He pushed his food away unfinished and eyed the two massive fireplaces with suspicion, unconsciously touching his throat.

"—have to know, Mrs. Stone," Bridget continued, curling long strands of cinnamon hair behind her ears, "has there always been a torture room in the castle?"

Augum glanced to the ceiling; it was just above them.

Mrs. Stone dabbed at her lip with a cloth and sat back in the queen's chair, taking a long breath before replying. "No, Bridget, I daresay there was not. The previous tenants had an appetite for torment, however, and thus thought to ... redecorate."

Bridget mulled this over, an unsatisfied look on her face. "But ... why, Mrs. Stone, to what purpose?" She tried to buy an answer with the most endearing look she could muster. Augum knew what was coming—Bridget had simply forgotten that Mrs. Stone had been a headmistress for thirty-five years and knew all the tricks.

Sure enough, Mrs. Stone's eyes flashed. "Mercy, girl, you are going to send me to my grave with all that prattling."

Bridget hid her face behind her hair. "Sorry, Mrs. Stone."

Mrs. Stone expelled a weary breath. "I brought the Blackhaven Herald."

Augum and Leera perked up.

Mrs. Stone reached into her robe and withdrew a curled parchment. She handed it to a red-faced Bridget. "Read it aloud, child. I believe it shall speak for itself."

"Yes, Mrs. Stone." Bridget unrolled it and began. " 'All take notice of the following proclamations. Proclamation one: Let it be known the uprisings in Blackhaven and Antioc have been crushed. All insurgents guilty of treason are hereby sentenced to death. Let all the kingdoms in Sithesia hear that the Kingdom of Solia is under the rule of Lord Sparkstone. Foreign dignitaries are invited to pay the standard courtesies.' "

Bridget looked up uncertainly.

Mrs. Stone's lips thinned. "Continue please."

" 'Proclamation two: Those that plead undying allegiance to the Legion shall stand to gain greatly, for Lord Sparkstone's benevolence shall express itself in the form of eternal life bestowed upon his loyal subjects.' "

Augum and Leera shared a look. His father had gone crazy.

" 'Proclamation three: In order for Lord Sparkstone to bestow the gift of eternal life, he requires the possession of seven ancient spheres known as "scions". All peoples from all kingdoms take heed! Eternal life, great wealth, power and fame await those who bring Lord Sparkstone a scion. The name his eminence chose for this enterprise is "The Great Quest". Once Lord Sparkstone possesses all seven scions, he shall use them to take back the secrets of eternal life from those that have jealously guarded them for eons. Lord Sparkstone believes all loyal followers deserve eternal life.' "

Bridget shook her head disbelievingly before reading on.

" 'Proclamation four: Let it be known that a previously presumed dead fugitive by the name of Anna Atticus Stone, former Headmistress of the Academy of Arcane Arts, has committed treason of the highest order. She has stolen a scion and kidnapped Lord Sparkstone's very own son, Augum Stone. Lord Sparkstone's gratitude for the capture of this vile witch, the return of his son, and the retrieval of the scion would be immeasurable.' " Bridget paused before numbly reading the last line. " 'A new era of pride and glory begins. Those that swear fealty to Lord Sparkstone shall reap the rewards. Those that will not are enemies to be butchered like pigs.' "

A marked silence fell over the room.

"All of Solia will be hunting us," Leera said quietly.

Augum rubbed his face. "This is insane. So my father's plan is to get all seven scions and then give his loyal followers eternal life with them?"

"Or so he claims," Mrs. Stone said. "One thing we can be sure of—Lividius, by subjugating the Leyans, intends on succeeding where Occulus had failed. Whether he shares Leyan secrets with his subjects will remain to be seen."

"He's too selfish for that," Augum blurted.

Mrs. Stone looked his way. "This I believe as well."

Bridget placed the parchment on the table. "So that's how he's gotten so many to follow him!"

"Indeed, you can imagine how enchanted people are by the idea of eternal life. Already they erect statues in his honor. In the towns that survived burning, word is spreading like wildfire; ordinary folks are taking up the search for the seven scions, the so-called 'Great Quest'."

Augum absently bit at his fingernails. "How many scions does he have now?"

"He has one, but there is word he knows of the location of another."

"Does he know about this castle?"

"He does, but not that we are in it. Nonetheless, we should certainly be on our guard."

They sat in silence a while, each contemplating their own thoughts.

"On to other matters," Mrs. Stone said. "In my absence I chanced upon a precious few still loyal to King Ridian's crown. As per the dictates of conscience and duty, I offered them shelter here with us."

"When will they come?" Augum asked, unsure how he felt about this.

"I expect them today. You are to show the highest courtesy to our new guests."

"Yes, Mrs. Stone," they chorused.

"Good." She slapped her knees and straightened. "Now let us continue your training. Thus far, you have practiced Shine, the first spell in your element, as well as the standard spells Telekinesis and Repair. Today, we study the final standard spell required to complete the 1st degree—Unconceal. It allows the caster to find nearby hidden objects."

Leera caught Augum's eye. He was sure both were thinking the same thing—using the spell to search for treasure.

"Now can anyone tell me the arcane word for Unconceal?" Mrs. Stone glanced around at them all. "Am I to presume that you have not had the good sense to read up on the spell?"

They stared into their laps, avoiding her gaze. Augum wanted to say they had been too busy practicing the repair spell and exploring the castle, but the truth was, it simply had not occurred to them to study ahead.

"The lot of you could do with a dose of forethought. I can only hope that one day it will dawn on you just how important your training is. Time is precious. Accelerate your learning and strive to stall your youthful tendencies. I do not presume it easy, but I expect a greater measure of discipline." She sighed. "Now, the word is—"

"Un vun deo!" Leera blurted. When she noticed Bridget and Augum gawking at her, she quickly added, "Mum used to use the spell to find sweets I hid around the house."

Mrs. Stone's brows rose slightly as she studied Leera. "That is correct, and your pronunciation is perfect."

Leera flushed as if having never been complimented before.

"Unconceal is about detecting intent," Mrs. Stone went on. "You cannot find something that has been accidentally misplaced or lost, nor something arcanely hidden—*that* you will only be able to do with the 11th degree spell Reveal."

"Are there any gestures involved, Mrs. Stone?" Bridget asked.

"The gesture is simple but important. Hold your hand out with an open palm and fingers spread, like so." She demonstrated, the trio awkwardly mimicking.

"What you will be looking for is a very subtle emanation, or pull. As usual, concentration is the key, but you will also need to still your mind. You must quiet the chatter and pay attention to faint reverberations of the ether."

" 'Ether'—?" Augum said before he could stop himself.

"How long does the spell last?" Leera quickly asked, diverting Mrs. Stone's attention just as she was going to reproach him.

"Thanks," he mouthed to Leera. She winked.

"That depends on your ability to concentrate," Mrs. Stone replied.

"So … not very long then," Leera said under her breath.

"Have any of you heard of the Mountain Monks of the North?"

They shook their heads.

"A 'No, Mrs. Stone' or 'Yes, Mrs. Stone' will suffice."

"No, Mrs. Stone," they said tonelessly.

"The monks say only a dead man expends all his energy climbing to the top of a mountain whilst saving none for the descent." She let that thought simmer a bit before standing with a grunt. "Now then, let us learn the fundamentals of the Unconceal spell. I have hidden half a dozen eggs in this room and the hallway. Find them with Unconceal."

They practiced for two hours, but in that entire time, only one egg was found, and it did not really count since Augum had stepped on it by accident. Upon spotting the flattened egg, Mrs. Stone shook her head and mumbled something about what a dreadful waste it was, before making him clean it up.

She even caught Augum and Leera trying to look for eggs when it was evident they were not using the spell at all. That brought a harsh reprimand and then a lecture about honesty, hard work and concentration.

After those two difficult hours, Mrs. Stone departed, giving them the rest of the morning and early afternoon to finish finding the eggs. At the door, she turned, adding, "It is your lunch you search for, so unless you want to go hungry, I suggest you concentrate."

It did not have the desired effect. They did not do as well with this spell as with the others. Bridget kept second-guessing herself and Leera jumped at everything she saw, while Augum kept confusing the ether with drafts.

It hardly helped that Augum's thoughts clouded over with his father's Great Quest and the coming visitors. By noon, to his great frustration, he still had not found a single egg. Bridget and Leera fared marginally better—each found one egg, though Leera confessed she might have found hers by accident.

When he caught himself staring at an empty picture frame for who knew how long, Augum plopped down where he stood, which at that moment happened to be on the marble staircase.

"Brain feels like mush …" He pinched the bridge of his nose and closed his eyes.

Leera slumped down beside him. "Mine too." She fixed her gaze on the child-sized suit of armor standing guard outside the girls' room. "Maybe we should get Fentwick to help."

Bridget leaned over the banister. "Uh, that would be cheating. Besides, he probably couldn't anyway; it's too complex a task."

Leera cast her eyes skywards. "I was only *kidding* …"

"Maybe we can train him to hunt rabbit," Augum muttered. His stomach croaked like an old frog, reminding him he had left his breakfast half-finished that morning.

"You two give up too easily, we still have an hour or so before lunch. Come on, let's keep going." Bridget disappeared behind the railing.

He sighed and stood up, thinking it pointless; the spell simply was not his strong suit. It required him to connect with his inner feelings, which was like trying to find a squirrel's stash of nuts.

Bridget's voice floated from nearby. "Let's try the hallway again."

Augum and Leera exchanged a weary look and gathered themselves. The two combed over the hallway like tired miners going over the same bit of earth, now and then mumbling the arcane word.

Suddenly Bridget's head popped out of one of the rooms. "I think I've got something—!"

"But I thought Mrs. Stone said she hid the eggs in the hallway and the dining room," Leera whined, blatantly using her hands to search around a hall table.

Bridget scoffed and disappeared back inside. Augum shrugged and followed, deciding he might as well see what she was up to, especially since his attempts at the spell were leading him nowhere.

The room was like others in the hall—simply decorated with two carved wooden chairs, a small bedstead, a hearth, two empty bookshelves, and a chest of drawers Bridget kneeled before.

"I felt a pull; might be something hidden inside …"

"Let's take out the drawers then." He helped her get five of the six drawers out, finding nothing. The last and lowest one refused to cooperate.

Bridget strained with the handle. "It's stuck—"

"Let me try—" but he too had no luck.

Bridget gave him a questioning look. "Telekinesis?"

He nodded. They stood back and held their palms forward, concentrating. The drawer rattled but did not open.

"Leera—give us a hand?" Augum called over his shoulder.

She strode in wearing a scowl, probably disappointed she had not found another egg.

"Telekinesis on the last drawer," Bridget said, raising her palm. Leera nodded and joined in. With the three of them casting the spell, the drawer shook violently and then suddenly flew loose, smacking Augum square in the shin.

"OW—!" He fell, grabbing his leg.

"You all right, Aug?" Leera asked, giving him a hand while trying not to snicker.

"Fine … thanks," he said through his teeth, rubbing his leg. "Check inside the chest."

Bridget did just that, finding nothing.

"Well that was fun." Leera turned to leave.

"Wait—there might be something *underneath* the chest. Give me a hand."

They helped Bridget push the chest from the wall. Again, they found nothing, neither behind nor underneath.

"It was a good effort, Bridge," he said. "Might as well try to find more eggs …"

She sighed, staring at the chest as if being denied the answer to an ancient riddle. They began to leave the room, Bridget trailing reluctantly.

"I don't get it, I was sure I felt something there," she said, still eyeing the empty chest of drawers.

Augum turned at the doorway. "Let it go …"

"Ugh—" She kicked the drawer that hit his foot, sending it tumbling end over end.

"Look!" She kneeled and pried something off. "Stuck to the bottom of the drawer!"

"What is it—?" Leera asked, craning her neck.

Their eyes widened as Bridget held up an ornate dagger and sheath. The hilt was ebony, pommel bejeweled with onyx, blade decorated with woven designs. The sheath was made of leather, studded with cut hematite and black diamond.

"It's beautiful," Bridget whispered, handling it like a priceless artifact.

Leera gave an approving nod. "Beats finding an egg."

"Now *that's* treasure," Augum said. "Wonder how old it is."

Bridget passed it to him. "Should we show it to Mrs. Stone?"

He felt its cool steel before passing it to Leera. "She might not let you keep it."

Leera unsheathed it and examined the blade like some old expert, even weighing it in her hand. "It's super neat, might even be arcane." Her eyes twinkled. "I agree—she won't let you keep it if you show it to her."

"Except if I show it to her and she lets me keep it I'd be able to wear it openly—not to mention it's the honest thing to do."

Leera gave the dagger back. "It's your decision, Bridge, you know what I'd do—"

"I'll think on it. Back to the egg hunt?"

They scoured the corridors for the next hour, though Bridget was the only one to find another egg, which she promptly gifted to Augum.

"There—now we each have one."

"Thanks, Bridge." He wanted to turn it down but his stomach would have openly revolted.

Leera's chin rose. "I would have given you one too, Aug—if I'd found another one that is."

His cheeks reddened. "I know."

Mrs. Stone appeared soon after holding a frying pan and a skin of water. When they each showed her an egg, she eyed their acquisitions with a placid face. Any triumphant expressions quickly vanished.

She gestured at the fireplace. "Well, get on with it," and began gathering the remainder of the eggs, which seemed hidden in plain sight.

Augum and Leera wordlessly watched Bridget cook their precious finds on the hot pan.

When Mrs. Stone finished, she set the extra eggs in the middle of the table so they could see what they would not be eating. Augum knew she was only trying to teach them a lesson, but it still felt harsh.

Bridget doled out the fried eggs. "Aren't you going to eat, Mrs. Stone?"

She sat back, hands in her lap. "Sometimes there are unintended consequences for doing just enough."

Augum realized what she meant—she was not going to eat because they had not found enough eggs. He and the girls were about to offer a portion when Mrs. Stone forestalled them by holding up a veined hand. The trio dropped their eyes, finishing the eggs quickly and in silence. They tasted bitter with defeat.

After lunch, Bridget gave Augum and Leera a meaningful look and cleared her throat. "Mrs. Stone, I ... I found this in a chest of drawers today." She placed the sheathed dagger on the table. Firelight glinted off the onyx pommel.

Leera's shoulders sagged at the sight of it.

Mrs. Stone raised an eyebrow and picked it up.

"Is it arcane—?" Bridget asked.

Mrs. Stone placed the dagger back on the table and suspended an open palm above. "I daresay it is."

Bridget leaned in close but did not touch it. "What does it do?"

"I have not the faintest idea; you would need to consult an arcaneologist."

Bridget's face fell. "Oh …"

"What's an arcaneologist—?" Augum asked, hoping it was not a stupid question.

"Somebody who studies the arcane arts in detail and identifies arcane properties in objects," Bridget replied glumly.

Leera frowned. "They're expensive to hire."

Mrs. Stone fixed her gaze on Bridget. "You wish to know if you can keep it."

Bridget put on a bracing expression. "Um … can we?"

"You were wise to bring it to me. It may be cursed, or an instrument for necromantic work. However, if you accept the risks, you may keep it."

Augum and Leera's mouths fell open; he thought for sure she would confiscate it immediately.

Bridget reached for the dagger then hesitated. "But what if it *is* cursed?"

"Then you will suffer the consequences, will you not?"

Bridget glanced between Leera and Augum. Leera mouthed, "Keep it," while he made a non-committed gesture, though he thought it would be neat to discover its powers together.

Mrs. Stone leaned forward and watched Bridget over steepled fingers, dagger resting between them all.

Bridget's shoulders slumped. "I think I … I think I better give it to you for safe keeping, Mrs. Stone. Until we know what it does."

"A wise decision, young lady." Mrs. Stone removed the dagger, hiding it in her robe. Bridget nodded, avoiding Leera's exasperated expression. Just then, a muffled banging sounded below.

"My word, I do believe our guests have arrived."

GUESTS

"I can't believe you gave it up—" Leera whispered as the trio followed Mrs. Stone downstairs.

"You're not helping," Bridget said through her teeth.

Augum gave her a friendly elbow. "Don't worry, Bridge, better safe than sorry, eh?" though part of him still wished she had kept the dagger.

Bridget only grunted. The banging at the door came again, louder this time.

"Yes yes—" Mrs. Stone said, opening the chunky foyer doors with a wave of her hand. The gesture simultaneously produced a globe of blue light that lit their way.

Augum exchanged a quick look with Leera. Had they just witnessed an example of simulcasting?

After entering the vestibule, Mrs. Stone made a rising motion with her hand. The latch rose on the newly repaired outer doors, one of which opened. A gust of biting wind sent a pile of snowdrift cascading into the hall.

Three figures stood against the bright snowy landscape. The first was a tall armored man with gray hair, bushy eyebrows and steel-gray eyes. A shield hung on his back, longsword by his side. The second man was short, balding and fat, with an anxious look on his face. The third was a sullen-looking boy of about Augum's age with neatly combed red hair. He wore a bearskin coat, reminding Augum a little of Leland.

"Mrs. Stone—what a great honor and pleasure," the armored man said with a deep bow, fog billowing from his breath. "I am so very glad you came to our aid in such a manner. Please, allow me to—"

"Sir Eldric Gallows," Mrs. Stone said with a somewhat weary voice. "Perhaps introductions ought to be made indoors, lest the boy freezes."

Sir Gallows looked like he was going to protest but entered instead, followed by the fat man and the boy in the bearskin, both panting. Once inside, they proceeded to brush the snow off themselves while Mrs. Stone arcanely closed the massive door with a subtle gesture. It clanged shut with a thud that reverberated through the castle.

Sir Gallows gestured ceremoniously. "If I may introduce the heir to the Kingdom of Solia, His Royal Highness Prince Sydo Ridian the Fourth—and his minder, Lord Boron."

Lord Boron gave a slight bow.

The prince gawked at Mrs. Stone's lightning orb. His face contorted in a scowl. "How is it that you cannot produce such an effect, Lord Moron?"

Augum wondered if he had misheard the prince.

Lord Boron flushed. "Heh heh … now, Your Highness, I—"

"—so this is the benevolent heir to our great kingdom," Mrs. Stone said, "the son of Wise King Ridian."

Prince Sydo gave her a withering look. He opened his mouth to say something when Sir Gallows hastily interjected.

"Your Highness, may I introduce Mrs. Anna Atticus Stone."

"*The* Anna Atticus Stone that all of Sithesia searches for, the one with the scion?" The prince whipped around on Lord Boron. "Ignorant fool, why did you not inform me? You have made me appear daft!"

Lord Boron sputtered while fiddling with his fingers.

"Mrs. Stone is in need of discretion, young prince," Sir Gallows said. "For good measure, I made the decision to inform you only upon arrival."

Sydo glowered at the knight before turning to Mrs. Stone. "Show it to me!"

The trio exchanged looks—Sydo was about to get the dressing down of his life.

"Your Highness," Sir Gallows began, "that is most unbecoming—"

"I do not care, I want to see it! Show me the scion; show me what everyone searches for!"

Sir Gallows stiffened. "Mrs. Stone will certainly *not* show you the scion. You will stop asking for it immediately!"

Prince Sydo turned purple shaking with rage, but said no more.

Mrs. Stone made a tactful gesture at the trio. "May I present Leera Jones, Bridget Burns, and my great-grandson, Augum Stone."

They bowed at the call of their names, as expected when in royal company.

Sydo smoothed his hair. He looked them over as if just noticing them. "I thought they were the help."

The trio stirred, but under Mrs. Stone's watchful gaze did not dare reply.

"Interesting choice of robes," Sydo continued, making a face like there was a terrible stink in the air. He then proceeded to remove his bearskin, revealing a finely embroidered red doublet over a pristine white silk shirt and black velvet pants. "I find it so ... *barbarian* ... to wear this thing." He threw the bearskin at Lord Boron, who barely caught it, a look of exasperation on his round face.

"It was for your own protection, Your Highness," Sir Gallows said. He stepped past the prince toward Augum, snow falling from his shoulders with each stride. The tall knight bent a knee, fixing him with those steel-gray eyes, bushy brows crimping. "So you are the Lord of the Legion's true son."

Augum felt his spine tingle. "Not by choice, Sir."

Prince Sydo suddenly appeared beside the knight, red hair quivering. "Your father murdered my father! He is a villainous traitor and I shall have his head on a spike! A branch *never* falls far from its tree—"

"Augum isn't a traitor!" Leera said from Augum's left.

"He certainly isn't," Bridget added from his right, "and Sparkstone murdered Augum's mother."

Augum looked to Leera and Bridget in surprise then back to Sydo. He crossed his arms. "Well, you got the villainous part right."

"How *dare* you speak to me without deference, peasant scum—"

Bridget gasped.

"That is quite enough, Your Highness," Sir Gallows said in a patient voice, as if this kind of thing happened all the time. He raised a thick gray eyebrow and turned his gaze to Mrs. Stone. "Is it true they are that different?"

"It is true, Eldric. Lividius seeks his son, but the two are as different as a puddle is from an ocean."

"Lividius?"

"Lord Sparkstone as you know him."

Sydo looked mutinous but said nothing. Sir Gallows gave a curt nod and stood. "Please do forgive our rudeness, Mrs. Stone. The journey has been long and fraught with peril. We are grateful for the hospitality and thus in your debt. If you hadn't chanced upon us in our distress—"

Mrs. Stone made a dismissive gesture. "I hardly think it worth mentioning, Eldric. We must work together for the good of all. Perhaps now would be the time to tell the young prince what we have discussed."

"Indeed, Mrs. Stone." Gallows turned to Prince Sydo and Lord Boron. The prince's fists clenched; Augum surmised he was not accustomed to being kept in the dark.

"It is my duty, as the Royal Guardian to the Crown, to secure shelter and safety for the heir to the throne. We will henceforth take shelter in this castle."

The prince's shoulders slumped as he peered at the barren walls. "You cannot mean what you say—this rotten shack? I hardly think it fit for royal blood!"

Lord Boron made a nervous chuckle. "Heh heh … I'm sure Your Royal Highness will find it amply adequate upon seeing the accommodations."

Sydo smoothed his hair and flexed his jaw. "Oh, stuff it, Lord Moron."

Augum exchanged looks with Bridget and Leera—the prince was a spoiled ass!

"Perhaps it would be best I see to the entourage," Sir Gallows said. "We have horses, the royal wagon, four servants and another six men."

"I recall last we met you had many more, Eldric."

"That is true, Mrs. Stone, however the Legion surprised us; cut twenty of our men down before we could organize. We even lost our healer, though I count us lucky it had been the Black Guard and not the Red; I fear we would have been much the worse for it. There was one who was particularly dangerous though, a sorcerer with a black robe of lightning who slew most of our men, including Sir Matthew Silvers, the Havensword."

Augum felt himself stiffen.

Mrs. Stone frowned. "From your description I would guess him to be Commander Vion Rames."

"You know of him?"

"Indeed, he was once my apprentice, before joining Lividius."

"She trains our enemies too?" Sydo asked.

"Manners, young prince," Sir Gallows said. "Mrs. Stone, are there stables where we can see to the horses? I fear we also have injured that need attending to."

"Behind the castle, but they are buried in snow and damaged from the years. I will come with you to repair them and see to your injured." She pulled the hood of her robe over her head, tucking her long ponytail in before turning to the trio. "Can I trust the three of you to show our guests to the great dining room?"

"Yes, Mrs. Stone."

Sydo snorted.

For a moment, Augum thought Mrs. Stone was going to deliver a most withering reproach, but she only pursed her lips.

"Is there a place to leave the wagon?" Sir Gallows asked.

Mrs. Stone arcanely swatted one of the outer doors aside. "Yes. Allow me to show you where," and she departed with Sir Gallows. The door clanged shut behind them, drenching the vestibule in darkness.

"Got away with one there," Leera muttered.

"I beg your pardon—"

"You'll see. Shyneo." Her hand rippled to life. Augum and Bridget lit their palms as well, lighting the vestibule with blue-green light.

"Shyneo," Prince Sydo and Lord Boron chorused, their right hands lighting up with fire. The prince's light was the weakest of everybody's, flickering like a candle. Lord Boron's fire was brightest of all, but only mildly so. The prince scowled when he spotted Augum's lightning palm.

"This way, um, Your Highness," Augum said. He led them to the marble steps.

The prince kept making snide remarks as they ascended. "And there, Lord Moron," he would say, pointing at the giant shredded tapestry behind the landing. "Look at what they did to the tapestry—!"

Augum had to keep from saying something rude; yeah, as if he and the girls were the jackals that had torn it up.

Lord Boron mopped his brow, each step a wheezing trial. "Heh heh … I believe the castle has been abandoned for some time, Your Highness."

Sydo dragged a finger across the banister and held it before his eyes. "Disgusting. This is what happens when you leave a castle in the hands of gutterborn—"

The girls gasped.

"Your Highness," Lord Boron whispered, "that is a most base and uncouth word for a royal to use."

Sydo shrugged. "What is the name of this so-called castle anyway?"

Augum extinguished his palm, the others doing the same. "We don't know actually."

"Then I shall title it. It shall henceforth be known as … Castle Dirtclod!"

"Heh heh, a most intriguing name, Your Highness."

Leera turned her head so quickly her hair whipped Augum's face. "That's the stupidest name ever—"

"*Exactly.*" The prince flashed a triumphant grin.

Leera was going to say something else when Bridget elbowed her.

Upon reaching the third floor, the prince abruptly stopped, pointing at the child-sized suit of dented armor standing by the girls' door. "I say, what is that—?"

Bridget waved a nonchalant hand. "Oh, that's just Fentwick. He's an animated suit of armor."

"You jest with me!" Sydo marched up to Fentwick, who immediately sprang to life.

"Wouldst thou fancy a duel, mine lord?"

Sydo recoiled. "Gods, it speaks! But how can it be so?"

Fentwick bowed, joints squeaking. "I art nothing more than an arcane suit of armor, mine lord. Mine sole purpose is to train and defend thy young princes and princesses of ye castle. Wouldst thou care to duel, mine lord?"

"You shall call me Prince, you sorry gathering of rust!"

"What setting dost mine lord beseech of me?"

"I said *prince*!"

"It's no use, Your Highness," Bridget said, sauntering around Fentwick. "He doesn't understand. We don't know much about him, but we're sure he's ancient arcane—probably been with the castle a long time; quite harmless anyway."

Prince Sydo smoothed his red hair and began examining Fentwick, poking at the helmet and even giving him a cagey push.

"So it only wishes to duel with me—?"

Fentwick rattled to life again. "Indeed, mine lord, wouldst thou care to duel? What setting dost mine lord beseech of me—"

"And you say he trains the princes of the castle?"

Bridget shrugged. "I think he spars with whoever wants to spar. We actually haven't tried yet."

"Lord Moron! Fetch me my sword."

Lord Boron took a nervous glance at the stairs and mopped his forehead. "Heh heh … but Your Highness, your sword is all the way in the royal wagon. Perhaps His Highness would care to spar with the, uh, armor another time?"

"NO! NOW, Lord Moron."

Lord Boron resigned a bow. "As His Highness commands …"

"Wait—" Augum said, feeling sorry for the man. "You can use my sword, Your Highness. It's just in my room here."

Lord Boron froze, face lighting with hope.

The prince weighed the choice a little while. "Since I do not care to wait for your snail-like stride, Lord Moron …" His eyes fell disdainfully upon Augum. "You may fetch your sword, my subject."

"I'll get it, but I'm not your subject; you aren't king yet." Augum retrieved his blade from his room and presented it hilt first. Unnoticed by the prince, the blade stopped sparking the moment he took it.

Nose in the air, the prince took a few practice swings. "It will have to do, I suppose." He turned to Fentwick. "All right, you ragged collection of scrap—let us spar."

Fentwick bowed. "As ye wish, mine lord," and limped to stand across from the prince. "What setting dost mine lord beseech of me—defender, beginner, intermediate, advanced, or expert?"

Sydo let out an involuntary snort. "Expert, of course." He raised the sword in a battle stance.

"Your Highness … heh heh … is this wise?"

The prince silenced Lord Boron with a look.

"This should be good," Leera muttered as the trio stood back to watch.

Fentwick backed away a few steps then became as agile and fluid as a cat, limp disappearing. He raised his wooden sword and deftly spun it in his hands.

Sydo hesitated before the two circled each other. Suddenly the prince lunged at Fentwick, who dodged and wacked him hard on the shins. Sydo howled like a wounded dog. "How dare you—!"

Leera snickered. "Had enough there, *Your Highness*?"

The prince gave her an unsure sidelong glance. "Of course not! I was merely testing his stance. On guard!" and he leapt at Fentwick again, but the animated armor was too nimble, evading the strike and giving Sydo another hard thwack. The blow landed on the side of his head and sent the prince sprawling to the ground, sword flying from his hands.

"Gods, how it hurts …" Sydo said, tears in his eyes, hair askew.

Fentwick lowered his wooden sword. "I beseech thee; mine lord is naer skilled enough to duel at this rank. Mighteth I suggest beginner difficulty."

Leera began to crack up but Bridget gave her a quelling look and she composed herself, but not before the prince saw. He picked himself up, holding the side of his head, a malicious look on his face.

"First I shall have you locked away for impertinence, and then I will have this hunk of rust melted and made into a helmet …"

Leera ballooned, about to unleash a scathing response, when Bridget stepped between them. "Perhaps we should move on to the great dining room," she said with a diplomatic smile.

"Heh heh … yes, let us sit and be merry, Your Highness."

Augum picked up his sword and returned it to his room. When he came back, Sydo and Leera were avoiding each other's gaze.

Bridget beckoned. "This way, Your Highness."

Sydo scowled but followed, the side of his face as red as his hair, doublet slightly askew. The group entered the great dining room. Sydo gave it a bored look and plopped down into the throne-like chair. Lord Boron placed himself to his left. Bridget, Leera and Augum sat in their usual seats, putting a wide gulf between the two groups.

They waited in silence. The tension rose steadily until horses nickered outside. The trio rushed to the windows.

Sydo leaned closer to Lord Boron. "Have the peasants never seen a horse before?"

"We have, but Mrs. Stone is about to repair the stables," Bridget said, nose against the glass.

The prince shot from his throne and ran over to a window, Lord Boron laboring behind. Ruined outlines of buildings traced lines in the snowy bailey. Eleven horses and seven armored men—the tallest of which Augum recognized as Sir Gallows—congregated by one particular ruin. Mrs. Stone shuffled beside four women, each wearing black winter cloaks and white servant hats. After a bit of discussion the men and women stepped back and Mrs. Stone raised her arms. Suddenly the horses neighed and rose up, fighting their handlers. A moment later, giant blocks of stone silently began to emerge from the snow, reforming into a structure.

Augum glanced at the prince, who stared at the scene with wide eyes.

"That is most … most …" The prince seemed to struggle finding the words to downplay Mrs. Stone's formidable talent.

"Your Highness," Lord Boron said, "Mrs. Anna Atticus Stone was the headmistress of the Academy of Arcane Arts for thirty-five years, even personally instructing your father for a brief period."

"Is that true?"

"Quite true, heh heh; but I'm afraid your father—if you forgive me for saying so, Your Highness—had no head for sorcery. His Highness was gracious about it though, bless his old soul." Lord Boron's eyes misted over.

Sydo gave him a furious look.

"B-b-but I do believe Sir Gallows did attend the academy, Your Highness, reaching the 4th degree in fire before being called into service for your father." Lord Boron's head bobbed with a wide smile.

Sydo spoke through his teeth. "I am well aware of how many *degrees* he has, Lord Moron. He taught me the Shine spell, remember? Something *you* were unable to accomplish."

"Of course, Your Highness, my apologies."

They watched Mrs. Stone rebuild the stable. Upon its completion, the servants and knights clapped. Then the men led the horses inside while the servants walked back with Mrs. Stone.

"Where are *your* servants?" Prince Sydo asked as everyone took their seat.

"We don't use any," Bridget replied. "The four of us just recently arrived. We're exploring the castle."

The Prince scoffed. "No fire, no servants, no food—welcome to the legendary Castle Dirtclod!" and he broke apart laughing at his own joke, stopping suddenly. "Well, Lord Moron—? Do you not find the jest amusing?"

"Heh heh ... yes, Your Highness, very amusing." Lord Boron flashed a fawning smile.

"Really now, Lord Moron, you bore me to no end ..."

Leera turned to Augum and gestured as if she wanted to be hung, before whispering in an undertone, "You think we'll get to explore the top of the castle tonight?"

Augum leaned in a little. "That'd be great, though it'll depend on how much work we have to do."

The prince craned his neck.

Bridget also leaned in, pretending to scratch her cheek. "I'd really like to find that one crucial piece of the map."

"I say—what are you lot whispering about over there? You are not to keep secrets from your prince!"

Leera flashed a cheery smile. "Nothing important, *Your Highness*."

Sydo jumped up from his throne chair. "Insolent peasant girl! If you speak ill of me, I will have you flayed and—"

"You will do no such thing," said a deep voice from the doorway. Sir Gallows strode into the room followed by four servant women with bowed heads. The prince scowled and slid back onto the throne. The servants lined up. Each wore a white hat over hair spiraled in a bun, as well as a white apron over a plain black dress.

After his eyes swept the prince, Gallows did a double take. "Your Highness—what happened to your face?"

Sydo turned his cheek. "Nothing at all. I am quite fine."

Gallows grunted, directing his steely-eyed gaze to Augum, Bridget and Leera. "Allow me to introduce our servants. We once had many more, but alas …" He left what happened to them unsaid. Augum remembered crimson-armored warriors hacking away at defenseless villagers in Sparrow's Perch. Is that what they had suffered through?

"The youngest here is Mandy," the tall knight said, standing behind a plump girl with reddish-brown hair.

She curtsied, keeping her eyes on the floor.

"I believe her to be fourteen. Is that not so?"

Mandy's hands writhed. She curtsied quickly. "Yes, m'lord."

"The next oldest here is Rafinda." A girl with blonde hair curtsied. She looked to be around sixteen, skinny and with a small nose. She too did not raise her eyes.

"This one here is Mya." He stepped behind a tall girl that looked about nineteen years old. She had porcelain skin, rosy cheeks, a well-proportioned body, and shiny hair blacker than Leera's. Mya raised almond-shaped emerald eyes and gave a radiant smile, before lowering them when the older woman scowled.

"She's so pretty …" Leera whispered.

The butterflies in Augum's stomach agreed. In fact, she was the most beautiful girl he had ever seen.

"And the last is our illustrious head maid, Ms. Gertrude Grinds."

A woman in her sixties frowned in disgust as she curtsied, before Augum realized it was some kind of smile. She had a prudish face with a hawk nose.

"The servants will not interfere in your business," Gallows continued, pacing back and forth before the staff. "They are here to serve and work." He turned to the women. "Because of the danger we find ourselves in, you will not be permitted to venture beyond the perimeter walls of the castle grounds."

Augum felt bad for the servants. Was this their life? It seemed harsher than in the books.

Ms. Grinds gave a stiff curtsy. "Begging your pardon, m'lord, but where will we get provisions?"

"I have discussed the matter with Mrs. Stone and we have come upon an arrangement. She will retrieve food using arcane means and we will pay for it from the royal coffer."

The prince made a hissing noise.

"Perhaps His Royal Highness would prefer to hunt his own food?" Gallows asked without taking his eyes off the servants. Sydo crossed his arms and muttered something under his breath.

"Now, will that be all, Ms. Grinds?" Gallows asked.

"Not quite, m'lord, there is the small matter of the accommodations."

"The accommodations?"

"Indeed, m'lord." She cleared her throat in a delicate fashion. "Well, you see, they are rather ..." Her voice dropped to a whisper. "Substandard, m'lord."

"Ah, I see. Perhaps I have been unclear in our predicament. We are only alive and have shelter by the grace of Mrs. Stone. If this displeases you, perhaps you would care to report to the closest Legion constabulary and ask for a new royal station. I am sure they would be more than willing to place your head on a spike." He glared at her. "Now leave my presence."

Ms. Grinds swallowed. "Yes, m'lord."

The servants quickly curtsied and exited. From the hallway, Augum overheard Ms. Grinds doling out duties in angry bursts. He wondered if the women will be sleeping in the servants' quarters, in that dreary-looking room with the hole in the wall.

Gallows paced to one of the giant marble hearths and began preparing a pipe. "Mrs. Stone is the most gifted sorceress I have ever seen," he said to no one in particular, tapping the pipe and filling it with tobacco. "She repaired an entire stable before mine own eyes—work that would have kept ten men busy for days in weather like this. She has also healed all our minor injuries. Only Sir Dollard Canes suffers still." He lit his pipe and shook his head. "I did not know it possible for a sorceress to learn more than one element …"

"Heh heh … she is indeed most gifted, Sir."

Prince Sydo gave Lord Boron a disapproving look. "She is also the grandmother of the Lord of the Legion. Do not forget that, Lord Moron."

"Your Highness—" Lord Boron whispered, giving the slightest nod at the doorway.

The prince looked over and seemed to pale a little as Mrs. Stone shuffled into the room.

"Mrs. Stone—please allow me to help you to a chair," Gallows said.

She swatted him away. "I am no infant, Eldric." She sat down in the queen's chair with a groan. When she spotted Sydo in the throne, she turned to Gallows with a sigh. "Please inform your men they are welcome to dine with us this evening. They may occupy quarters on the second floor, though I daresay the rooms are in dire need of a thorough cleaning."

"The men would welcome a warm meal, Mrs. Stone, and I shall have the servants attend to the rooms."

Mrs. Stone nodded. "There are also rooms on the east side of the first floor for the servants to use. I fear those shall require more extensive repairs, however."

"I can set the men to it right away—"

"—I was rather thinking my trio of apprentices could do it, seeing as they need the practice." Her eyes swept over Augum, Bridget and Leera.

"Those clods are her apprentices?" Augum heard Sydo say in an undertone to Lord Boron, who immediately covered up with a cough.

"Oh yes, we can do it—" Augum said, the girls nodding along vigorously. He was hungry and would have almost preferred to stay and eat a second lunch with them, but the east side was the only part of the first floor they had not explored.

"Then it is settled." Gallows took a seat to Augum's left. "Now, let us discuss the finer details with regards to the defense of the castle and the tasks needing completion in the days ahead."

"May we be excused, Mrs. Stone—?" Augum asked. The last thing he wanted to hear was boring talk about maintenance and work when there was adventure to be had.

"You may, but before you go, know that I expect the three of you to practice all four of the spells you have thus learned. Is that clear?"

"Yes, Mrs. Stone."

"They know *four* spells already?" Sydo whispered to Lord Boron.

"Apparently so, Your Highness."

Sydo promptly stood up. "What about me? I demand to come along!"

"Surely repair work is below the prince's station," Mrs. Stone said.

"Heh heh, it most certainly is," Lord Boron said. "We need to discuss the prince's accommodations, as well as other particulars of note."

"Yes, there is much to discuss, Your Highness," Gallows added, biting his pipe.

Sydo gave the trio an envious look before plopping back down in defeat.

"Now, as far as castle provisions are concerned ..." Gallows began, but Augum, Bridget and Leera were already out the door and rushing down the hall.

A SECRET MESSAGE

"Ugh, what a brat," Leera said as they descended the steps.

Augum nodded as he pawed the banister. "Imagine if he'd come along ..."

Bridget trailed last. "I think he should have been allowed to come."

Leera stopped suddenly on the landing between the first and second floor. "Are you crazy?"

"I just ... I kind of feel sorry for him, that's all."

"You feel sorry for him? He called us *gutterborn*, Bridge."

Bridget winced at the word. "I know, but he can't help himself. He wasn't brought up right, that's all. I'm sure he's a good person inside."

Leera gave Augum a look as if Bridget had completely lost her mind. "I ... I don't even know what to say, Bridge."

Bridget exhaled a long breath. "Just forget it. Here, let me try this—" She withdrew the map, placed it on the ground, and held her hands over it. "Apreyo." For a moment, nothing happened. Then a wrinkled piece of parchment fluttered out from under a covering of dust, re-attaching itself to the map.

"And just like that she's partly redeemed!" Leera said with a sly smile. "But how did you know?"

Bridget shrugged. "Just guessed." She examined the map and frowned. "It's not the piece we need though; we're still missing this one near the wall which should tell us where the passage starts."

"Good idea anyway, Bridge, let's keep it up," Augum said. "Let me try next."

They traded the map and practiced the spell as they descended. When they reached the foyer, they lit their palms and passed through the east doors for the first time.

Pieces of broken furniture, straw, mud, shards of glass, parchment, and other refuse littered the corridor.

Leera kicked a scorched wooden crate out of their way. "We've certainly got our work cut out for us. Some of this stuff's burned, so we can't even repair it."

"It's almost like something went on a rampage here," Bridget said.

Leera pointed upward. "Maybe it was the prince when they refused him sweets."

"If there's anyone who can't get enough sweets, it's you."

"I make no apologies."

The trio did a bit of exploring before setting to work. There were seven small rooms and one larger room, each windowless and with a thin door. Augum guessed the larger room was for the head maid.

They began with the obvious—furniture and walls. They had little trouble using telekinesis on small objects; it was the larger ones that required all their concentration. More often than not, they had to tackle them together, as with the castle entranceway. Repairing steadily became easier with practice, especially once they found their rhythm. Someone would occasionally have a go at the map as well, though to no avail.

At other times, they would try their hand with the Unconceal spell, which still gave them the most difficulty. They chatted as they worked, about Prince Sydo and the formal way he spoke; about Sir Gallows and his pipe; and about the servants and what kind of lives they led.

Augum recalled Mya's almond green eyes and that radiant smile. He wondered which room would be hers.

"They're just lucky Mrs. Stone gave them these rooms instead of the big communal one," Bridget said, inspecting a repair they had just performed on a door. "Otherwise they'd have to sleep beside each other."

Leera made a face. "I'd rather sleep in the crypt than beside Gertrude Grinds."

Augum deposited an armful of broken furniture parts. "Mrs. Stone once said that if I don't progress in degree, I could always push rocks around or become a servant. Is that what warlocks do when they hit the ceiling?"

"Not at all," Bridget said. "Every occupation you can think of has warlocks in it. They're not very common, of course, so are always in demand. Apprentice warlocks can even earn a wage working in a regular profession. But high degrees are extremely rare and very expensive."

"So imagine a potter shaping pots with the earth element," Leera said.

"Or a cook warming bread with the fire element—"

"A shoemaker—"

"—I get it, thanks."

"Right." Leera tapped her lips. "I wonder how far the servants got with their degrees …"

"Or if they even had the chance to study," Bridget said. "Most people grow up like you, Augum, hardly knowing much about the arcane path." She held her hands over the wood he had brought. "Apreyo." Wooden spindles began attaching themselves to a seat; soon a chair stood before them.

Leera sat on it. "And most of those that do study don't even get beyond the first few degrees."

"I think everyone should have the chance to try," Bridget said. "All those villages where they don't even believe in arcanery ... how many more kids could be going to academies?"

Leera shrugged. "Chair's fine—next item."

While the girls bantered on, Augum cast Unconceal for at least the tenth time that morning. He held his palm before him like a sensing rod. Settling into the spell, he suddenly felt a peculiar tug he never felt before. He slowly followed it, careful to keep focused. The source was a burned-out bed in the corner of the room. He slid underneath its charred frame.

Leera broke off what had turned into a heated conversation over the point of a warlock ox herder. "Find something, Aug?"

His focus shifted only a moment, yet that was all it took for the subtle pull to disappear. "Think so, hold on. Shyneo." His palm lit up electric blue, making the bottom of the bed visible. He pawed around until his fingers closed over a burnt piece of parchment stuck between the slats. He removed it and sprang to his feet, beaming.

"I'm impressed," Bridget said. "Well open it up, let's see what it says—"

Leera crowded close, one hand on his shoulder, other on Bridget's. "Might be another treasure map ..."

"That's the first time the spell has worked for me," he said, carefully opening up the charred parchment while Leera and Bridget leaned in.

It was a letter. The portion that stuck out from the slats had burned off, but the rest was still readable. They read in silence.

... and in all haste. We have been unable to breach the castle's secrets. We tried everything known on the fountain, yet still it refused to yield. As for the scion, we conclude it does not reside within these walls. Unfortunately, we ran out of time. She came and

the castle opened for her like a flower. Its defenses are fearsome to behold and as sinister as your justice.

Alas, she comes! I now must attend to my final duty.

I sign with the hopes of incurring a swift death rather than suffering eternal damnation in undeath for having failed you, Lord Narsus.

The signature was burned away, but that did not matter.

"Darkest damnation," Leera said. "Narsus …"

The trio glanced at each other.

"Think the woman it's talking about is Mrs. Stone—?" Bridget asked, re-reading the parchment.

"Don't know," Augum replied. "I'm curious about the fountain part—entry to what?"

"Oh, the map!" Bridget retrieved it from her robe. They crowded around her. "You think the passage starts from the fountain?"

Leera shook her head. "The only thing is that the walls are a bit rocky; and that high up in the castle—? Seems kind of unlikely, don't you think?"

Bridget frowned. "I don't know …"

"Guess the only way to know for sure is to find the last piece of the puzzle," he said.

Bridget swept a lock of hair with an ivy-laced palm. "I agree—let's redouble our efforts."

"At least now we know why there's a torture room," he muttered.

"They must have tormented people in the hope of learning about the scion and the fountain," Leera said.

"—and it didn't work," Bridget added. "I wonder why a scion was supposed to be here though."

They examined the letter again.

"Well whatever secret that fountain is hiding must be very important," he said, pocketing the letter. "Can't wait to find out what it is."

Leera flashed a competitive grin. "Golden find, Aug—my turn to find something next!"

They continued with the repairs. After much toil, Bridget and Leera extinguished their hands and plopped down on a repaired bench.

Augum slumped against a wall, head throbbing and stomach churning from the arcane effort. Nonetheless, he kept his hand lit for them. He glanced about and smiled. Not only had they repaired every salvageable piece of furniture in the rooms and hallway, but all the doors and walls too. The only thing left to do was remove the burnt wood.

"Wish we had an hourglass," Bridget said with closed eyes. "Think supper is almost ready?"

Leera rested her head on her knees. "Hope so."

Bridget turned to Augum. "You know, this is far more practice than you'd get in school."

"Really?"

"Absolutely, arcane school is much more about theory than practice."

"Oh, didn't realize. Hey, mind if I extinguish too?"

Bridget shook her head while Leera only moaned. He doused his palm and the three of them rested in pitch-dark silence until someone knocked on the foyer doors. The trio dragged themselves up, lit their palms, and went to see who it was.

When Augum opened the door, he saw two almond emerald eyes staring at him. Surprised, he just stood there gaping. Leera finally nudged him and he reddened, stepping aside to let Mya slip through the door.

"Thank you," she said, holding a candle that allowed the trio to snuff out their palms.

Leera made a grand gesture at the hallway. "Welcome, Mya. Come to inspect our work?"

"Indeed yes."

Augum felt his stomach flutter as she smiled. All he wanted to do was spend time with her and ask her questions about herself. What kind of person was she? Where did she come from?

"Ms. Grinds would like to know if the rooms are ready." Mya's rosy cheeks shone against her porcelain skin and jet hair.

"They are," Bridget said. "Only the burnt wood needs to be removed."

Mya waved a delicate hand. "Please don't concern yourselves with that. I've come to tell you supper will be served shortly."

Leera licked her lips. "Good, cause we're starved."

"Ah, here comes the inspection," Mya whispered, gracefully turning to the sound of footsteps from the stairs.

Ms. Grinds glided down the stairs pinching her dress. "Well, girl, how does it look?"

Mya curtsied and dropped her eyes. "Begging your pardon, m'lady, I haven't had the chance to look, however the children report the work is complete."

Children? It was like a kick to his stomach.

"We shall see then, won't we?" Ms. Grinds, wearing a perpetual frown of disgust, stopped a short way down the hall and snapped her fingers. "Come along now."

The trio and Mya hastily followed.

Augum thought the flickering candle too dim. "Shyneo." His hand crackled to life.

Ms. Grinds briefly stopped and gave him a disapproving look before gathering her dress and moving on in rapid step.

Mya gave him a roguish smile. His heart tripled its pace and he felt his cheeks grow hot.

Ms. Grinds inspected each room as if her life depended on it, testing some of the furniture and re-arranging it into a more "adequate countenance."

"But what of the charred remains?" she asked, frowning. "Did you not feel it necessary to remove the detritus?"

"We didn't have the time, Ms. Grinds," Bridget said in a strained yet polite voice.

"It's nothing we can't handle, m'lady," Mya quickly said. "I don't mind getting my hands dirty with soot."

"Nor should you, girl. Very well then, you can do it this evening with the others after we set the kitchen right, just be sure to find out where the torches are." She glanced about, shaking her head. "I have yet to see a single sconce or brazier. What sort of castle is this?"

"It's an arcane castle," Augum said. "There's a servant diagram with instructions in the cellar."

Ms. Grinds turned to him, face paler than usual in the blue light of his palm. "A diagram, you say?"

"Yes, in the cellar. It has loads of symbols and stuff. We can take you there if you like."

"That will not be necessary. You three are excused. Mya, come with me, girl."

Mya curtsied and followed Ms. Grinds, giving them a disconsolate backwards glance.

"Down to the cellar with only one candle ... how brave," Bridget said with a concerned look. "Should we follow them to make sure they find it all right?"

Leera crinkled her nose, swatting the idea aside. "Bah, they'll be fine. Let's eat."

Augum badly wanted to follow and be useful, to light Mya's way, to show them exactly where the plaque was—instead he found himself mutely following the girls.

"I'd hate to be her servant," Leera said while climbing the marble steps.

"We do have Mrs. Stone," Bridget said.

"True. Who do you think is stricter though?"

Bridget skipped the top step to the landing. "Mrs. Stone for sure—"

Augum extinguished his palm. "Mrs. Stone—she's got more experience with it."

THE PRINCE

The trio entered the great dining room only to find it empty—except for a large bowl of hard winter apples in the middle of the table. Leera reached for one the moment they sat down.

"Leera Jones—" Bridget whispered in a scandalized voice, "what if that's for the knights—or the prince?"

"Nonsense, I'm hungry." She took a greedy bite. "Mmm … so tasty." She shook the bitten apple under Bridget's nose. "Bite?"

Bridget scoffed, crossed her arms and looked away.

Augum hesitated then caved to his hollow stomach. Having skipped breakfast, all he had eaten today was a single egg. He reached into the bowl and fished out the largest apple.

"Really now—" Bridget shook her head, but her eyes lingered on the bowl.

The skinny blonde servant girl Augum recognized as Rafinda walked in with a basket of sliced bread. Feeling guilty, he snuck bites when she was not looking.

"Wow, where's all this coming from?" Leera asked, eyeing the bread like a predator sizing up prey.

Rafinda placed the basket at the far end of the table and curtsied. "My lady, some is from the prince's supply, the rest is thanks to Mrs. Stone's … magic." An anxious look crossed her face upon spotting Leera biting an apple; she quickly curtsied and trundled off.

"*Arcanewy*, you mean," Leera absently said while chewing.

"See, I *told* you it isn't for us," Bridget said.

Leera shrugged. "Off with my head, I suppose …"

"Maybe we should put them back," Augum said with a crooked grin.

"Ugh, don't be silly."

He was deliberating on how to deliver the core to the prince's seat when Mandy, the youngest and shortest servant girl, quietly walked in holding a tray of cheeses and meats.

The trio gaped, salivating. Mandy placed the tray beside the bread and gave a shy curtsy. Just as she left, Rafinda waltzed back in with an armful of fine porcelain plates, each engraved with King Ridian's royal emblem—a wise-looking owl perched on two crossed swords above a gilded crown.

The servants traded off like this, each bringing food, cutlery or fine china. With every trip, Augum's stomach growled louder. Before long, the table overflowed with exquisite porcelain, silverware, cut crystal goblets, and plenty of food, including roasted pheasant; seasoned parsnip; steamed carrots and peas; buttered potatoes and chives; candied yam; and pumpkin pie with honeyed almond. This would be the most luxurious meal he had ever attended, and by the looks on Bridget and Leera's faces, he suspected the same was true for them.

Conversation echoed from the hall as he realized he still had the apple core in his hand. Disposing of the evidence would simply have to wait.

"... your help with the wall would be greatly appreciated, Mrs. Stone. We can start this evening."

"I am afraid that is out of the question, Eldric; I will be departing the castle for the night."

"We shall begin the work nonetheless, Your Ladyship—"

"—Mrs. Stone will do."

"Mrs. Stone—of course." Sir Gallows sounded like a chided pupil. Augum pictured the shaggy-browed, distinguished knight sitting in a school desk at the academy, and stifled a laugh.

Five more knights entered the room still wearing their fur-padded armor, though helmless.

"Please sit, Sirs," Mrs. Stone said, extending her hands in invitation. The knights sat in the middle, three on each side of the table.

"Allow me to introduce my great-grandson Augum Stone, and his friends Leera Jones and Bridget Burns."

The knights immediately stood back up and nodded their acquaintance. Augum, Bridget and Leera hastily stood as well, acknowledging with nods of their own. To Augum it all felt so formal. He squished the apple core in his fist, hoping he would not have to shake anyone's hand. Meanwhile, Gallows made the introductions on behalf of the knights.

"This is Sir Fostian Red—"

A knight with bushy red hair and a big red nose bowed.

"And here we have Sir Edrian Castor—"

A skinny knight with sallow skin, hollow cheeks and a bald head bowed stiffly.

"Over here is Sir Wilbur Brack and his brother, Sir Wilfred Brack—"

The brother knights bowed with smiles. Each had short brown hair, brown eyes, and complexions ladies surely swooned for.

"And lastly, we have Sir Jayson Quick, also known as the Nightsword—"

A powerful-looking knight with dead eyes and a grizzled appearance brushed his mustache with his thumb. He stared at Augum without blinking.

"Alas, Sir Dollard Canes is lying wounded in his room. Therefore, his introduction will have to wait."

Augum, tired of holding the core, quietly placed it on the edge of his plate. It was rude to start eating before everyone sat, even ruder to do it to royalty. The evidence was far from inconspicuous too. Luckily, the servants ignored the infraction. Bridget merely pursed her lips while Leera rubbed her nose to hide her smile.

Prince Sydo sauntered in followed by Lord Boron. Everyone remained standing until he sat on the throne, a sour expression on his face. The servants, now including Mya and Ms. Grinds, quietly walked back and forth retrieving hot food from who knew where. Augum thought there had to be some arcane way for them to get it so fast from the kitchen.

Sydo eyed the core on Augum's plate and turned to Lord Boron. "I see courtesy is unknown to the peasants. I suppose we must be patient with their ... low breeding."

Lord Boron cleared his throat nervously whilst looking around the table. "Heh heh, my, the food looks delicious today!"

"Hear hear!" said Sir Gallows, raising a glass of ale and standing. Chairs creaked as everyone immediately joined him. "A toast to our distinguished host, Mrs. Anna Atticus Stone. Thank you for giving shelter."

"Hear hear!" said the crowd.

Mrs. Stone surrendered a small bow as everyone took their places once again.

"Do we get to eat now?" Leera mouthed to Augum.

Sydo was the first to dig in, sending the signal the trio had been eagerly waiting for. The knights, Mrs. Stone, Augum, Bridget and Leera then began helping themselves, while Lord

Boron and the prince had the servants fill their plates for them. Each time Mya passed near, Augum felt his body tingle.

"Ms. Grinds reported your repair work satisfactory," Mrs. Stone said amongst the measured scraping of cutlery on china. The trio smiled sheepishly but did not reply. Augum thought "satisfactory" was likely high praise coming from Grinds.

"I have a new task for the three of you this evening," she continued while herding peas onto her fork with her knife. "You are to help the prince repair his room on the fifth floor."

Bridget smiled, Leera grimaced, while Augum felt his curiosity stir, as they had yet to explore the fifth floor.

"Can't he do it himself—?" Leera said a little too loudly. A hush came over the table as she turned beet red.

"What did the little peasant rat say?" Sydo asked. "Lord Moron—?"

Lord Boron cleared his throat. "Heh heh … I believe something to the effect that His Royal Highness has yet to learn the Repair spell so he could fix—"

"What—? How dare that gutter—"

Mrs. Stone sighed and stood. With much scraping of chairs and clanking of silverware, the knights and Lord Boron immediately rose as well, followed by a begrudging prince and a pensive trio.

She gestured in irritation for everyone to sit. Exchanging looks, they reluctantly did as she asked. A thick silence befell the room as she directed her gaze at the prince. "I had the privilege of briefly knowing your late father, the king."

Augum, wondering where she was going with this, stiffened in his chair.

"He was wise in many things, though when it came to his children, I daresay he was a mighty fool."

No one moved. Sydo looked like he had just been run over by an ox cart.

"He never could find time for them, choosing to hear the complaints of his people over the complaints of his children.

Thus, when his first three sons died fighting Narsus—nobly, and with courage—he did not weep, for he did not know them. When his daughter died by Lividius' hand, still King Ridian did not weep, for he barely knew the child. Anger and revenge carried his heart in those dark times. It is said only when my grandson was about to put King Ridian himself to death, that he finally wept, saying that neglecting his children was his greatest regret."

Augum wished she had used *Sparkstone* in place of *grandson*; he wanted to distance himself from his father and his deeds.

"You, Prince Sydo Ridian," Mrs. Stone continued, "are the last of his line; the last son and heir to the throne. Your father heeded life's lesson with his dying breath, yet he left a son with a cold heart, a short temper, and little wisdom, wisdom that his wise father—the Lord of Owls and Protector of the Realm—had been known for. And so the question then becomes—will his son, the heir to the Kingdom of Solia, learn to love before it is too late?"

Her wrinkled face softened as she sat back down. Everyone turned to watch the prince. A few nodded in agreement, notably Sir Gallows, the brother knights, and Lord Boron, who lowered his eyes when Sydo looked upon him. The prince slumped in the throne. Suddenly he stifled a sob and bolted from the room. Lord Boron stood and made to follow but Gallows raised a hand.

"Let him go." Gallows then turned to Mrs. Stone. "The young prince is not used to hearing such naked truths, Mrs. Stone."

"Perhaps the boy would be better served if he heard it more often, especially from his council." Her eyes flicked to Lord Boron, who mopped his brow. "If he ever hopes to sit the throne and lead, he will need to learn compassion, love, wisdom, and the ability to listen—all traits his father had in abundance."

Many of the knights nodded.

Lord Boron adjusted his great body in his chair. "The boy does lack discipline, but the truth of the matter is that I do not have the skill to teach him the arcane arts, as his father desired. Perhaps … heh heh … perhaps Your Ladyship, the most esteemed sorceress of our age, would take on this task? For the kingdom, of course."

Augum shared a look with Leera. The last thing he wanted was to train alongside Sydo.

"Lord Boron, we cannot possibly ask Mrs. Stone to undertake such a burden," Gallows said, though there was a note of disappointment in his voice.

"I am honored by the request." Mrs. Stone took a moment to organize her plate. "However, if I were to take on the training of the prince, it would have to be on my terms, and I fear them impossible for the child."

Lord Boron leaned forward with a gleeful smile. "What kind of terms do we speak of … heh heh … gold?" The remark drew titters from some of the knights.

"I am afraid the price is substantially higher than gold; he would have to completely and utterly forsake his dress, his titles, and any pretense of the throne." Mrs. Stone gave Boron a hard look. "If I were to train him, he would be treated as nothing more than a common boy."

Lord Boron looked about for support. "Why, I am afraid that is quite impossible."

The burly Sir Fostian Red cleared his throat. "Although the prince would benefit greatly from Mrs. Stone's training, I cannot condone the stripping of His Grace's title."

"Hear, hear," said the others.

Gallows thought it over. "Perhaps the prince should decide on the matter."

"I will be sure to pass on the issue in private then," Lord Boron said in a manner that suggested there was no chance of the prince accepting the idea. Augum and Leera relaxed with audible sighs while Bridget frowned. Too late, Augum noticed Mrs. Stone watching him, and instantly knew he was in trouble.

"Any word from our brothers in Antioc?" asked the bald Sir Edrian Castor.

"None I daresay; I shall make an enquiry tonight," Mrs. Stone replied, still frowning at Augum. To his immense relief, the servants interrupted by clearing the plates for a second course. The prince did not return however, and conversation did not resume.

Augum tried to catch Mya's attention by flashing an excessively grateful smile for the peppered stew she set before him, only to be disappointed when she missed it.

The servants stood near the door, ready to serve their fancies, though neither Augum, Bridget, Leera, nor Mrs. Stone called on them. The knights and Lord Boron, on the other hand, regularly summoned them with a look or idle flick of the finger.

As Augum finished his meal in the usual quick fashion, he only hoped Mrs. Stone would not lecture him in front of Mya.

LESSONS

After supper, Mrs. Stone excused the trio from the table to repair the prince's room. They scurried off, grateful for being spared a public reprimand, and gathered at the marble steps.

"So the prince has a tragic tale of his own," Bridget said with a dramatic sigh. "He suffered from a lack of love ..."

Leera scowled. "So did Augum; he seems a decent enough fellow though."

Augum flushed.

"I'm just saying—oh never mind." Bridget began marching up the steps.

With a wicked grin, Leera turned to Augum. "You know, I think she has a crush on the prince."

Bridget whipped around, face purple. "I do not! I merely feel *sorry* for him, is that *okay* with you—?"

Leera took a step back. "Bridge ... you know I was just kidding. No need to get upset ..."

Bridget turned away, sniffing and raising a hand. "I'm sorry, it's just that the prince reminds me of … of my brother, Oswald." Then she crumpled and began sobbing into her hands.

Leera glanced at Augum guiltily before hugging her. "I'm sorry too, Bridge."

Augum just stood there until he realized all Bridget needed was for him to be her friend. Her wet face emerged from behind a curtain of tangled hair. He sat down beside her and gave a pained smile.

"He was the meanest brother, truly wicked," Bridget said between sobs, wiping her eyes. "He used to make fun of me, calling me 'Icky Bridgey'. He'd trip me and throw me to the mud. He'd even throw food at me. Sometimes, though, he'd do secret things to help me that he didn't think I'd notice, like feeding my puppy, or cleaning my muddy shoes so the other girls wouldn't make fun of me …" She sniffled, the hair sticking to her face. Leera brushed it away.

"… and he once said … he said I was the only one that listened to him … and now he's … now he's gone …"

"I'm sorry, Bridge, truly," Leera said. "We'll give the prince a chance, right Aug?"

"Right."

Bridget nodded between sniffs, smoothing her burgundy robe in an effort to compose herself. "I suppose we should go up and see about this room of his then, eh?"

Leera wiped Bridget's tears like a big sister. After another hug, the trio made their way to the fifth floor.

It was smaller than the other floors due to a terrace that circumvented the exterior of the castle. Gilded hawks, lions and wolves supported where the ceiling met the walls, guarding faded grandiose tapestries, most torn, one missing altogether. Gilt wall pockets held ornate candelabras, a few of them cracked. Plant pots, at least the ones not destroyed, sat empty in the corners. The remnants of a finely carved settle lay strewn against the base of a wall. The flooring was a checkered marble pattern of black and white squares, freshly swept. A hallway with double doors at the end opened on to the balcony. There were four rooms, two on each side of the stairs. Each room had an intricately carved black oaken door.

But the grandest were the two massive arched windows that let in the majority of the light to the lower floors. The leaded stained glass depicted a hairless man in a plain robe meditating in a desert. It reminded Augum of the fountain in the forest room.

Bridget strode up to the settle, kneeled before it and splayed her hands out. "Apreyo." The pieces slowly reformed. Augum, meanwhile, fixed the pots, Leera the candelabras.

"There, good as new," Bridget said once they finished.

"Shh—I hear something," Leera whispered, freezing. Sure enough, the sound of muffled voices came from the southwest room. They crept to the door and listened.

"—I do not want to stay in this miserable hovel!" the prince shouted. "That old hag is uncouth and her tongue is too spirited. I want her head!"

"Your Highness, please …" said a voice they recognized as Ms. Grinds'. "Sir Gallows deems the castle suitable. Your father put all his trust in him, as should you. He is your regent and captain of your royal guard. Surely you must know he has your best interests at heart—"

"—Castle Dirtclod is not fit for a prince! I want to go home, and I want them flayed for their insolence."

"Your Highness—you know we cannot go home, and this is no way to talk about those that took us in, especially of Anna Atticus Stone."

"I am not a child—I am a prince, and heir to my father's throne! Do not forget it, or I will have *your* head when I turn of age and take the crown—"

"Begging forgiveness, Your Highness—I meant no disrespect."

"And when are you going to fix this place? Look at this, the bed is hardly fit to sleep in!"

"Your Highness, I believe Mrs. Stone's three apprentices are coming up to repair it this very moment."

"I do not want those peasant rats in here! Send them away, I can repair it myself!"

"But Your Highness, you have already tried—"

"Do as I command, Grinds!"

"Yes, Your Highness," Ms. Grinds said in a stiff voice. The trio barely had time enough to jump back and pretend as if they just arrived when the door opened.

"Oh—!" Ms. Grinds hastily closed the door behind her. She was pale and a few hairs poked out of her usually perfect bun.

"Um, we're here to repair the prince's room," Augum said, keeping his voice light.

Ms. Grinds herded them towards the stairs, adjusting her hat. "The prince is … indisposed at this time. You will simply have to find something else to do—"

The sound of feet running up the stairs echoed from below.

"Ms. Grinds—!" called a breathless young girl's voice. "Ms. Grinds, come quick—!"

"What is it, child, what happened?"

"It's Sir Dollard Canes, m'lady," huffed a red-faced Mandy. "His wound … it's much worse … come right away."

"Right—off you go to boil a pot of water. And summon Mya."

"She's already there, m'lady."

"Then tell Rafinda to fetch clean towels. Well, what are you waiting for, wretched child—go!"

Mandy curtsied and ran back downstairs, Ms. Grinds hurrying after. Augum, Bridget and Leera took one look at each other and followed Grinds to the second floor, somewhere they had not visited yet. It looked identical to the third where they slept, except without windows. To compensate, the servants had installed torches and candles for light. Augum wondered if they had missed an arcane solution to the problem; after all, they now knew where the servant plaque was. Then he realized it had to be because none of them knew arcanery, not even Ms. Grinds.

Sir Gallows was quietly speaking with two other knights on the east side when Mya's tall figure emerged from a room behind them.

The trio gasped—Mya's porcelain hands and apron glistened with blood. For a moment, Augum was terrified something had happened to her.

Mya pointed a bloody finger at them. "The children … they mustn't see such a thing—"

Ms. Grinds turned and started shouting and making shooing motions, but Augum did not register a word, he just kept staring at Mya's bloody hands. Finally, Ms. Grinds took him by the scruff and yanked him upstairs, herding Leera and Bridget with her other hand. She only let go when they reached the third floor, giving a stern warning to stay there, before marching back downstairs, muttering to herself.

"Sir Canes must be in dire straits," Bridget said, gripping the marble banister and looking down.

Leera gave Augum a nudge. "You look as pale as Grinds. You all right?"

"Fine …" he croaked.

It was not the blood that bothered him, however; he had seen his share of it hunting with Sir Westwood. What really bothered him was seeing *her* covered in blood—and the fact that she called them children. He was fourteen, two years from becoming a man, though he desperately wanted to be older.

Mrs. Stone soon strode by without a word, followed by a perspiring Lord Boron. Upon spotting her, Ms. Grinds, patrolling below so the trio would not sneak back down, advanced up the steps.

"Mrs. Stone, Your Ladyship—he is at death's door, do come quick."

"Mrs. Stone will do, Ms. Grinds." She turned to the trio. "I want you three to come and watch."

Ms. Grinds visibly shook. "But, Mrs. Stone, surely it is no sight for—"

"This is part of their training, Ms. Grinds. I am afraid I must insist."

"But—there's blood!" Grinds' already pale face went one shade paler. Augum worried that she might faint if this continued.

"Indeed," Mrs. Stone said, marching past her. Lord Boron and the trio followed, careful to avoid eye contact with an exasperated Grinds.

"I say, what is happening? I want to see!" shouted an indignant voice from above.

"Absolutely not, Your Highness," and Grinds stormed upstairs while holding her skirt, declaring the scene quite inappropriate for a prince.

Meanwhile, the group made their way to the room. Three knights stood out front, silhouetted by torchlight.

"This will not be pleasant to watch" Mrs. Stone said as they walked, "I want you three to stay quiet and learn, is that understood?"

"Yes, Mrs. Stone." They exchanged uneasy looks.

She padded past the knights and into the room. Augum saw grim faces as he passed. Lord Boron engaged in hushed conversation with Sir Gallows and one of the brother knights, Augum could not tell which one. Sir Jayson Quick, the Nightsword, stroked his mustache while staring at a torch. Mandy hurried out of the room carrying a bloodstained towel and a bowl of crimson water. Augum paid her little attention, focusing on the flickering shadows within the room.

Soon as they entered, they froze. Blood was everywhere— on the walls, on the floor, on the people, and all over the bed. Mya was busy doing something with a wound that Sir Dollard Canes had sustained in his stomach. The curly-haired knight with a bulbous nose squirmed, a fearful and agonized look on his face. Mrs. Stone stood with her hand over him, speaking soft arcane words. When she finished, his eyes closed and he went still.

Bridget took a hesitant step forward. "Is he … is he—"

"Merely asleep," Mrs. Stone said, "so Mya may work."

"Almost … have … it …" Mya said through clenched teeth as she tugged at something, brow beaded with sweat. Her hand shot loose. It glistened with blood and held a jagged piece of metal. She gave it to Rafinda, receiving a bottle of white wine in its place, and proceeded to clean the wound with it. "Cautery, please," she said after wiping the area with a cloth.

Rafinda scurried forward with a glowing hot iron she had been holding over a torch. Mya took it and pressed it to the wound. The trio looked away as it sizzled. The smell of burnt flesh filled the room.

"Now we can dress the wound." It was then that Mya noticed the trio. Her delicate face registered surprise.

"I insisted they attend, Mya," Mrs. Stone said, turning to the trio. "Come closer. Watch and learn. Mya knows the ancient art of non-arcane healing. There may come a day when a healer is not present; it would be prudent to know how to care for an injury yourselves."

Augum, Bridget and Leera edged forward, wincing upon seeing the wound.

"Will he live—?" Augum asked quietly, staring at the knight's swollen pale face.

"I don't know," Mya said, bandaging the wound. "We must keep it clean. Should you face an arrow strike, pull it out if possible, clean the wound with boiled water or white wine, cauterize it with hot iron, then wrap it with a bandage; and make sure to change the cloth frequently. An herbal poultice helps, as well as a diet of garlic, lemon, fruit, fresh vegetables and red wine. For the pain you can use whiskey or the bark of a white willow."

Augum had not registered what she said, instead admiring her soft lips and the confident way she spoke. Strangely, he wanted to be the one injured, cared for by her, the center of her attention.

"How did you learn this skill?" Leera asked, taking a bowl of hot water from Mandy and placing it near Mya.

"The knowledge has been passed down from mother to daughter in my family for generations. I learned it from my mother, who learned it from her mother. One day, when I have a daughter, I shall pass it to her too. My mother was a traditional battlefield healer who served King Ridian in the Narsinian war. Arcane healers were very expensive and hard to come by. The king made do with the people he had."

"But why are you a servant then?" Augum asked, before realizing it was a rude question. Instead of reproach, Mya only smiled, rosy-cheeks blossoming. His stomach fluttered.

"By the urging of the wise king. He knew of my mother's talents and wanted me near his son in case he became wounded with no arcane healer present. As it turns out, our healer was slain when the Legion last attacked us." Mya finished dressing the wound. "Now I am afraid I have to ask everyone to leave as Sir Canes needs rest."

The group obeyed her wishes and trooped from the room.

"I think it best I leave for Antioc immediately," Mrs. Stone said to Gallows as she passed by.

"I will continue the work on the wall, Your Ladyship."

"Mrs. Stone will do, Eldric."

"Begging your pardon, Mrs. Stone. Old habits die hard."

"So they do indeed," she muttered.

The trio followed Mrs. Stone to the stairs, where she turned to address them. "Ms. Grinds reports the prince is indisposed. Very well. I wish for you to help the knights repair the perimeter wall, after which one of them is to impart a sword lesson. Then in late evening, you are to read up on the Unconceal spell from the blue book."

"Yes, Mrs. Stone," they said together tonelessly.

Her blue eyes flicked over them one last time before she slowly descended to the foyer.

Augum wondered what had they done to deserve such a thing. He had barely slept last night from that nightmare; this morning they had to train with Unconceal to find their lunch, each only having one egg; they repaired the servant rooms, in itself an incredibly exhausting task; and now she expected them to repair the wall, take a sword lesson, then do some studying?

"Ugh, that's a lot of work," Leera said when Mrs. Stone disappeared from sight.

"She's pushing us hard for a reason," Bridget said.

"That's for sure." Augum's thoughts drifted to Mya. "I didn't know she was a healer …"

"Hmm—? Oh, you mean Mya." Leera smirked, studying Augum. "You like her, don't you?"

His face reddened. He shrugged. "She's pretty, I guess …"

"Yes, and she's also like five years your elder; don't let her beauty torment you."

That took him aback. It was not something he expected to hear from Leera.

"Oh, Sir Gallows—" Leera said as the knight made his way past them. "We wish to help you with the wall."

Sir Gallows' bushy brows twitched. "You wish or you have been ordered?"

Leera deflated. "Ordered …"

Gallows looked past them and smiled. "I recall my first year at the academy, particularly when Mrs. Stone had me repair a statue I broke. To teach me a lesson, she made me break it twenty times more, repairing it again and again. I thought I would surely expire from exhaustion."

Augum noticed the knight looked to be around the same age as his father. "Sir Gallows, were you by chance at the academy at the same time as my father?"

His expression soured. "I was not. Your father attended after I had already departed."

"What about my mother?"

"The same, though I can see why you wish to know more about them." Gallows brought his hands together. "Now let us go outside. I am sure we could all use some fresh air."

DEATH AND
PERSEVERANCE

The group assembled outside the castle at dusk, the air blisteringly cold, fogging their breath.

"… and here is the section we started on earlier," finished the hollow-cheeked Castor, nodding at a crudely reassembled portion of the wall. "We shall work southward. Why don't you three magic your way north?"

Some of the knights chuckled.

Augum wanted to correct the smug knight—*arcane*, not magic. "We will, Sir," he said instead.

Castor and company began looking for stones, laying them onto the wall where the grim-faced Nightsword stood by a small vat of mortar warmed by a brazier. Without arcanery, they were slow, which was interesting to Augum because Gallows had his 4th degree and could easily use Telekinesis and Repair. As it was, the work would take forever at the pace the knights were going. Had to be a point of honor, he concluded, observing the ruined wall. It stretched distantly, circumventing the castle in a great oval. But what if …

"Sirs—!" he called. "Sirs, hear me please—"

"What is it, Augum?" Gallows asked, lifting a large snow-covered stone.

Say it gently and with respect. He cleared his throat. "We could do this, save you a lot of trouble. Perhaps Sirs would be better served repairing the ovens—"

Gallows dropped the stone amidst roars of laughter. The Nightsword merely raised an eyebrow.

Castor glanced at his colleagues as if Augum was nothing but a silly child. "Better served—? You mock us!"

"No, no—I only mean … that is …" but the words got all jumbled in his head under the knights' challenging glares.

"He meant we can do this ten times faster than the lot of you!" Leera said from behind. The knights laughed anew and slapped each other's backs.

"Not a chance—"

"On my word—brave little scamps, aren't they?"

"They jest—"

Only the Nightsword did not share their amusement, face unexpressive.

Gallows picked up the stone again and dropped it on the wall with a loud crunch. "Is that what you mean to say, Augum—that you three can do this ten times faster than the six of us *grown men*—?"

Augum rubbed his neck. "Well … yes."

Gallows leaned against the wall. "All right, young one—prove it."

"Yes, do prove it!" one of the Brack brothers said. The others soon took up the call.

Sir Fostian Red shook his head while retrieving a stone. "Comrades, there is work to be done. Let us stop making a mock of these children."

Augum felt a hot flush. There is that word again. He marched to the wall, the girls following.

Castor elbowed Gallows. "Fostian's right. Look there—already they give up."

One by one, the knights went back to work.

"Let's show them a thing or two," Bridget said with a determined gleam in her eye.

"They asked for it," Leera added.

Augum splayed out his palms over the ruins. "Ready?"

The girls nodded, extending their hands. After a brief moment of concentration, the three yelled, "Apreyo!"

Chips, pebbles, rocks and even small boulders began to appear from the snow, some rolling, some dragging, some flying. Augum dimly heard the knights stir but resolved to keep his focus on the wall.

See the cracks disappear; see two stones become one.

The snow whipped around them as they kept increasing their pace, as if racing each other to see who could repair more. At last, after reaching a furious speed, Augum cracked a smile. He immediately lost his concentration and fell to the snow. Bridget and Leera followed, giggling. He sat up and saw they had repaired ten feet of the wall.

The knights quibbled and laughed amongst each other while Gallows approached, hands spread in conciliation.

"If we get the stoves ready, perhaps we can sup a second time tonight, but with some roast chicken. I of all people should have known what kind of mentor Mrs. Stone is." Then he turned to his companions. "Come, gentle Sirs, let us be gracious in defeat—the warmth of the kitchens awaits!"

"Mmm, chicken is my favorite ..." Augum mumbled. Spiced roast chicken was the first dish Sir Westwood had served him after finding him on the edge of the Gamber. To this day, it was the most delicious single dish he had ever eaten—though perhaps it was the taste of freedom that made it so special.

"Mine too," Leera said. "Creamed chicken …"

Bridget quieted down. "Mine is Mother's pumpkin pie …"

The knights picked up the vat and brazier and left, muttering about the youth these days. The Nightsword's cold gaze lingered on the trio before he turned to walk away with his companions.

Bridget stood and brushed the snow off. "I don't like the look of that one."

"Same here," Leera said. "We should keep an eye on him."

Together they continued work but at a far slower pace, stamping their feet and rubbing their arms to ward off the bitter cold. They plopped down after dusk, numb from exhaustion, heads throbbing. While catching their breath, they admired their work—one hundred feet of newly repaired wall, barely visible in the occasional patch of starlight that shone through the clouds.

It was then a peculiar noise came from the woods beyond the wall. They stood up, faces tight with apprehension.

"Who's there—?" Leera called out. When there was no response, she took a step forward.

Bridget caught her arm. "Remember what Mrs. Stone said—we're not to go beyond the wall. Besides, it's probably only a rabbit or something."

"Or a wolf," Augum said, wishing he had his sword with him.

There was a rustling followed by what sounded like a child's sob.

"Shyneo," Bridget said. "Who's there—? Show yourself!"

Pine branches parted revealing a dirty young boy in ragged cloth, sniffing and rubbing his eyes. He looked to be five years old and reminded Augum of Leland.

"Mommy—?"

Bridget surged forward. "A child—! Come here, little boy, come out from under those branches—"

"Wait—!" Leera said, but it was too late. The boy flashed a greedy smile and crawled over the ruined wall, where he suddenly began transforming—the skin rapidly grew hair, a snout formed from the nose, and his hands took the shape of paws.

Bridget screamed as Leera and Augum snatched her away from the wolf-like creature. Its eyes shone the color of blood, its body twice the size.

The moment the transformation stopped, the beast pounced, snapping its black-toothed jaws. Bridget barely got her hands up in time as it clamped down on her right forearm. She raised a bloodcurdling shriek as the wolf-thing started thrashing, tossing her around like a rag doll, knocking Augum and Leera aside.

Spitting snow, Augum remembered something about the Shine spell, something he had yet to try.

"Shyneo!"

His palm ruptured with lightning. He lunged at the thing and grabbed a chunk of its squishy flesh, concentrating on giving it a shock. Yet the moment he touched it, he knew he had lost arcane control; his body stiffened, the space around him warped, and time slowed.

He found himself sitting on Mt. Barrow, extending his hand towards a stone. A moment later, he was back in the tent at Hangman's Rock, reaching for a claw. Suddenly he was flying over the Tallows, lightning blazing at rapid intervals, a looming mass ahead. He sensed what was coming before it happened—a ripping flash and a surging heat. As his world blackened, something sizzled and yelped.

When he opened his eyes, he had no idea how much time had passed, or where he was. His body shivered and he appeared to be lying in snow. He saw a freckled girl's head framed in starlight, eyes tearful and frightened. She started shaking him.

"Get up, Augum, get up!"

He gave her a lost look. Who was she and what did she want?

"Get up—Bridge needs our help—!"

Upon hearing Bridget's name, it all rushed back—along with a wave of nausea that made him wobble. He scrambled to his feet, trying to keep from throwing up. "Where's the thing—is it gone?"

"It ran towards the castle after you shocked it. Bridget's hurt! We need to take her inside."

He rushed to Bridget. She gave him a wild look that raised bumps on his arms. Hair stuck in clumps to her shiny forehead. The robe on her right arm was shredded and stained with blood.

"There's snow in my eyes," she gurgled.

He and Leera exchanged looks before hoisting her up. Leera grabbed Bridget by the waist while he wrapped her good arm around his neck.

Bridget cried out in pain. "When Father returns, we're going on a journey …"

"She's delirious," Leera said. "Bite must have been poisonous."

They stumbled toward the castle. Along the way, Augum spotted the creature's footprints in the snow. His heart nearly stopped when he saw they led straight to the castle doors—*and they were open.*

Bridget's skin now burned through her robe. "It's so pretty outside. I don't feel well, Mommy."

"Hang in there, Bridge—" Leera said, voice infused with panic.

They made it through the repaired outer doors. Augum felt his body stiffen as he braced for an attack.

Bridget was now slurring her words like a drunk. "Water … thirsty … tell Father … I'll return," then her eyes rolled back into her head and her body slumped.

They carried her through the inner doors, which were also open.

Augum scanned the foyer. "Mya, Sir Gallows, anyone—we need help here—!" His words echoed up the castle stairs as Bridget's head lolled about between them.

From somewhere above came the sound of frantic shouting.

"Let's take her to Sir Dollard Canes' room," he said, hoping Mya was there attending to the injured knight.

They trundled along as fast as they dared to the second floor, where Canes was recovering; but upon entering, they discovered Mya absent and Canes asleep, forehead beaded with sweat, bandage soaked through with fresh blood.

"Next room over—" Leera said. They rushed Bridget next door to a dark room with a dirty bed. Lighting their palms, they laid her down, carefully placing her injured arm on her stomach. She stirred, moving her lips.

Leera placed her ear close. "Did you say something, Bridge—?"

"Oxy ..."

For Augum, the word brought back memories of identifying herbs in the forest with Sir Westwood, though he could not quite remember what oxy looked like.

"I think it's some kind of herb," he said. "I need to get my sword and find Mya, maybe she could help."

Bridget's head shifted from side to side. "The man ... no hair ... oxy ..."

"She's trying to tell us something," Leera said.

"Bald ... arms ... water ..." and she passed out.

Augum locked eyes with Leera. "The fountain—!" they chorused.

"She must mean oxy is near the fountain," he said. "You stay here and keep the door shut. I'm going to get my sword and make a run for it."

Leera nodded and started tearing pieces of cloth from the feather-filled mattress. He guessed she was going to start binding the wound like Mya would have, though he knew blood loss was not the concern here.

"Aug—!" she called as he was closing the door, freckled face glistening in the watery light of her palm. "Good luck."

"Thanks."

He closed the door and ran as fast as he could up the steps, screeching to a halt on the landing between the second and third level where he found two people sprawled on the floor.

"Shyneo." His stomach plunged when he recognized Mya. Her almond-shaped eyes were closed, long jet hair splayed out around her head. She had a bite on her arm, but thankfully still breathed.

He palmed her forehead; skin was fire hot. He needed to find that herb immediately.

He glanced at the other body. Amongst the armor was a big red bush of hair—Sir Fostian Red. The knight was pale, bloody, and completely still.

Augum continued racing up the stairs and into his room, where the blade stood in the corner. He tore it from its sheath then grabbed his waterskin, fumbling to tie it to his waist. Water would help flush the poison …

Hurry, hurry, hurry!

He bolted from the room, halting at the foot of the steps to listen, breath escaping in short bursts. Shouts echoed from somewhere above. He glanced over his shoulder and happened to spot Fentwick standing before Bridget and Leera's door.

"Fentwick, we have an intruder! Go down to the second floor and guard the room Bridget and Leera are in. It's the one across the way with the closed door."

"As mine lord commands." Fentwick limped off, screeching, "Hark, knaves, villains and foes! Hark, for thou shalt lament thy deceitful ways!"

Augum wished the clumsy thing would go faster. Sword in hand, he sprinted up toward the fourth floor. As he drew close, he heard a loud growl and then Gallows' voice.

"Edrian—get behind it!"

"I'm trying, I'm trying—!" Castor said, before suddenly screaming.

Augum raced up the rest of the steps to find the beast tumbling with Castor. Blood sprayed as Gallows tried to pry them apart. Nearby, two more bodies lay on the floor—Sir Wilbur Brack and his brother, Sir Wilfred Brack. The Nightsword held a battle stance before the library doors, blade drawn. He gave Augum a cold look. Muffled cries came from behind him; everyone else had to have barricaded themselves in the library.

"It's too damn strong!" Gallows said through gritted teeth.

The Nightsword took a step toward them.

"No, Sir Quick—stay and guard the door in case the other one comes back—"

Other one? What other—something slammed into Augum from behind, sending him sprawling. The sword flew from his hand and clanged down the stairs. He did not even have time to get up before the thing was on him, jaws snapping. He twisted and flailed, trying to punch and kick it off, all to no avail—the beast was far too strong.

His left arm exploded with white-hot pain. For a moment, he thought someone was branding him. He screamed as the searing pain drove deeper, one jarring movement at a time. He chanced a look and saw black jagged teeth sunken into his flesh. Malevolent red eyes stared at him. They reflected the end of his life; all his aspirations, his dreams, everyone he cared about—all of it would end soon. They made him think of his father.

Murderer ... damn you!

He stared back, determined not to show fear. Another hot surge of agony shot through his arm and a warm feeling began to course through his body, helped along with every beat of his heart.

The poison …

The thought crystallized his focus. Existence became just him and the beast, eye-to-eye, tooth-to-flesh. Pain subsided to a dull thud as he felt the familiar sensation of time slowing to a crawl. Clarity returned and the space around him warped, as if he was peering through a glass globe. The thing gradually growled—a low-pitched, stretched guttering. He watched it carefully, waiting for the precise moment. The energy within him ebbed and flowed, desperate to go wild. When the moment came, he steeled himself and slammed his open palm into the side of the beast's head.

"SHYNEO!"

The time dilation allowed him to see the lightning emerge from his palm and spider around the thing's head. Lightning fingers crept through every one of its rigid hairs, circling its crimson eyes and tearing the pupils apart.

As the last of this energy expelled, the beast exploded backwards in a percussive burst of light. It slammed into the far wall, leaving a bloody splat stain. As it fell, time rapidly sped back up, so much so that Augum vomited from the onrushing nausea, acid burning his throat and mouth.

He slipped around as he fought to stand in blood and vomit. The smell was almost enough to make him pass out.

He blearily took in the scene—Castor lay in a bloody heap, Gallows wrestled with the other wolf-thing, and the Nightsword still had not intervened, even though Gallows looked to be losing the fight.

"Help him—!" Augum gurgled.

"No!" Gallows said. "Guard … library!"

The Nightsword gave Augum a cold look—and did not move.

Augum's arm stung as if it had been plunged into a molten vat. Just don't look at it, he told himself.

His vision tunneled, shrinking down to the size of a grapefruit. He descended a few steps, stumbled, and fell down the rest. He felt around the landing before becoming dimly aware he was gripping his sword.

Standing up was difficult. The black tunnel widened and closed as if breathing. He could barely feel his body as he staggered to where Gallows rolled with the beast. He raised his sword over what he judged to be rotten fur and thrust downwards with all his strength. The sword plunged deep into flesh. He placed all his weight on the pommel. It pressed against his stomach. Something strong flailed underneath and promptly tossed him aside as if he was made of straw. There was a long moaning shriek and then quiet.

"Is … it … dead …?" Augum slurred.

Gallows rolled away from the furry mass, covered in blood.

"Unnameable gods … it bit me. The vile thing bit me! Where's the other one—?"

Augum, too tired to inform him the other one was dead, simply shuffled off holding his left arm, leaving the sword embedded in the beast. Gallows called after him but he just kept going. There was no time; he had to find the fountain.

He careened through the black door of the forest room. "Shyneo," but his palm did not light up. "SHYNEO!" Still his palm refused to light. He was vaguely aware that what had actually come out of his mouth was probably gibberish. He stumbled forward in the dark, determined to find the fountain anyway, but tripped and fell face-first into the foliage. He knew he needed to stand but it just felt so good to rest, like curling up beside a warm fire after trekking all day in the snow.

He did not know how much time had passed, but when he became conscious that he was not doing anything, he fought to stand. Then something fantastic happened—he could see the path! Ever so dimly, the moss on the trail glowed, lighting his way.

He barely felt his feet squish into the moss. He passed through waves of hot, cold and nausea. Shakes came and went like the light of a teetering lantern in a storm.

Sir Westwood's face swam before him. "When you do not have a torch, use the light of the moon. When there is no moon, use the stars. When there are no stars, use the moss. When there is no moss, disappear …"

His vision narrowed down to the size of a plum as he stumbled through the bush, grabbing branches for support with his good arm, the injured one dangling uselessly.

Suddenly there was the fountain, right before him. He wavered, trying to recall why he had come, when his vision closed completely and he fell. He did not feel the impact with the ground however, only a cold sensation as his head plunged into the shallow pool of water. Thirsty and delirious, he took a large gulp. Water had never tasted so fresh. The cool liquid invigorated him instantly. His senses roared.

He sat up, dripping. "Shyneo." His palm fluttered to life. The light and pain faintly pulsed to the beat of his heart.

He had come here for something, but it was like trying to think through a fog. The water's clarifying effects already began to wear off. From some distant place came the thought he was dying.

He glanced at the fountain. He could rest here, just a little nap …

The stone statue of the bald man peered at him, serene and calm. Did it just smile—?

He thought goose bumps rose on his skin. He lifted his arm to check if it was so, only to see torn flesh and oozing blood. Bile rose up his throat as a wave of nausea blackened his vision. Before complete unconsciousness overtook him, he plunged the arm into the basin of water. There was a prickly sensation, as if a thousand ants began nibbling. It was strangely soothing. When the sensation went away, he removed his arm. The bleeding had stopped and the wound seemed to be slowly closing. He gawked at it, unsure if he could trust his eyes.

Although the wound became less of a worry, flushes of heat and cold surged. His entire body ached. There was still the poison, and it was winning. Vision once again narrowed as a distant field of yellow grass flickered below. All he wanted to do was go to sleep.

Must … stay … awake …

He loosened the waterskin and with a shaking hand filled it in the pool.

"So how are things coming along, Augum?" Sir Tobias Westwood asked, a straw of wheat in his mouth, curly gray hair unkempt as usual. He sat cross-legged on the ground across from him, dressed in a brown leather jerkin, mustard hose, steel gauntlets and field boots.

"Not so well, Sir …" The voice in his head somehow did not match what came out of his mouth.

Sir Westwood spat on the ground. "Oh? Why is that?"

"I can't seem to get my thoughts together …" The dark closed in.

The old knight squinted up at the sun, sweat glistening on his brow. "It is rather hot out. Maybe you should have a drink of water."

Birds chirped, grass rustled softly. Augum put a hand between his eyes and the bright sun, thinking it indeed was hot out. "All right … one drink … don't let anyone know …"

Sir Westwood crunched the straw in his teeth. "Focus, Augum."

Augum let his head fall into the fountain and this time, like a man lost in the desert, drank as much as he could. When he raised his head, cool water dribbled down his chest. The black tunnel retreated, but not completely. His arm tingled.

"Ah, that's better. Sir, do you think we could rest now?"

Sir Westwood picked at dirty fingernails. "Of course not, we are in the middle of training. Now tell me, Augum, what did you come here for?"

"What did I come here for …" The question seemed deep and profound. Indeed, why was he here? What purpose did his life serve? *Who* was he really? It was such a good question; Sir Westwood always asked good questions …

Suddenly it hit him.

"I came here for … I came here for an herb! You showed it to me once …"

"I did indeed. You remember—it was a grassy knoll and there was a large spruce bent at an awkward angle."

"I remember … it was a grassy knoll … there was a large spruce bent at an awkward angle … and you showed me a plant … black shoots and blue leaves."

"Black shoots and blue leaves."

The tunnel tightened.

"Was it … was it oxy, Sir?"

"Oxy." Sir Westwood spat on the ground.

Augum followed to where he spat and saw black shoots and blue leaves everywhere. "Oxy …" He began scooping it with his good hand. After he grabbed all he could carry, he turned to Sir Westwood.

"Thank you, Sir."

The old knight smiled.

Augum crammed an oxy shoot in his mouth and chewed. It had a milky, acidic tang. His heart immediately quickened and Sir Westwood disappeared, briefly leaving an afterglow. Had that all been real? How had he found his way without his palm being lit—?

"Shyneo." His palm sputtered to life, weak and still tied to the beating of his heart. He examined his injured arm. It had almost completely healed. There was no time to gawk at the miracle of it though; he had to save the others.

He raced through the wild growth, through the black door, and on down the hall, skidding to a halt as he spotted a bloody Nightsword slumped against the library doors.

"Hello—? Anyone here?"

From behind the door came the muffled voice of Gertrude Grinds. "One of them is still alive! Seek shelter, Augum. Seek. Shelter!" It was followed by muted cries from the servant girls.

The bodies of Sir Gallows, Sir Castor, the Nightsword, and the brother knights lay motionless around one of the wolf-things, still pierced with Augum's blade. He wondered if he had killed it or someone else had; his memories of what had happened were murky.

He ran up to each of the knights and stuffed an oxy shoot into their mouths, followed by a splash of fountain water from his waterskin. With his hands firmly around their jaws, he made each of them chew the herb. The entire time he could hear Ms. Grinds' cries of warning, but he worked on, hoping the thing would not attack in the meantime.

Sir Gallows was the first to stir when Augum heard rabid growling from somewhere below.

The girls!

He did not wait for the rest to come around. He stuffed the remaining oxy shoots into his belt, ripped his sword free from the dead beast, and scrambled downstairs, almost completely lucid now.

When he reached the landing where Mya and Sir Fostian Red lay, he stopped to help them too. After administering to the burly knight, whose skin was cold to the touch, he cradled Mya's head. He placed the oxy into her mouth and gently made her chew it, feeling a tingling flush in his cheeks. Then he poured the fountain water. He wished he could stay and hold her until she woke, but the growling urged him on. He splashed some fountain water on her wound before laying her back down onto the floor, a pang in his stomach.

He then raced down to the second floor. His pulse quickened as he witnessed the wolf-thing he had shocked earlier square off against Fentwick. The beast was trying to get past the animated suit of armor, but Fentwick was as graceful as an old dancer, giving it a firm whack on the head with his wooden sword every time it tried to get by. With each strike, the wolf-thing would yelp and stagger back, sniffing the air.

Augum remembered the lightning tearing out its pupils—the beast had to be blind!

"An unworthy attempt, sir," Fentwick said in that high nasal voice as he nimbly cuffed it on the side of the head again. The beast must have been trying to get past Fentwick for a while because its head was a bloody mess.

Augum crept forward, waiting for the right moment. When the creature took another blow from Fentwick's stick, he raised his sword and charged. The beast turned just in time for the blade to slice off its head.

"Wouldst thou care for a duel, mine lord?" Fentwick asked as Augum ran past to where Bridget and Leera waited.

"Augum—!" Leera said when she saw him, her lip quivering. "I don't think she's breathing—"

His heart squeezed as he saw how pale Bridget was. He raced to her side, stuffed an oxy shoot in her mouth, and poured some fountain water in. He handed the waterskin over to Leera and grabbed Bridget's jaw, forcing her to chew.

"Pour some of it on her wound."

Leera scrambled to unwrap Bridget's bandaged arm before pouring the water on the gash.

"Is this fountain water—?"

"Yes."

Leera gasped. "The wound! But … but healing water is the stuff of legend …!"

He could not care less how legendary or rare it was, all that mattered was that it worked. Color began to return to Bridget's face. When she stirred, they both breathed an immense sigh of relief, Augum slumping against a wall, Leera plopping into a chair.

"I'm going to go and check on the others," he said after catching his breath. "You'll be fine with Fentwick guarding."

Leera smiled. "Aug—"

"Yes —?"

"You did great."

He smiled. "Thanks," and ran upstairs to see to Mya and the others.

THE NIGHTSWORD

Stars twinkled through the arched dining room windows by the time everybody sat down to a second supper. Everybody but Sir Fostian Red that is, for Augum had been unable to rouse him.

"The bite was too severe, young man," Sir Gallows had said upon finding him kneeling beside the red-haired knight. He rested a gauntleted hand on Augum's shoulder. "There was nothing you could have done."

Augum remembered Mya, who had recovered enough to examine the fallen knight, nodding in solemn agreement, her breath labored.

That's not entirely true, Augum thought, staring at his food—he could have run faster, taken less time at the fountain, concentrated harder …

He glanced up and down the table. He and Sir Jayson Quick—the Nightsword—were the only ones not smiling. The knights had repaired the ovens and the servants certainly made use of them—broiled duck and roast chicken were the highlights, but as hungry as Augum was, he hardly noticed.

"A victory feast!" Gallows said, raising a slopping tankard. "And here's to our noble companion, Sir Fostian Red, Knight of the Royal Guard, who fell bravely in battle."

"Hear hear!"

"And now a toast to Augum Stone, Savior of Souls and Slayer of Beasts!"

"HEAR HEAR!"

Bridget and Leera beamed at him as they raised goblets of winter cider in his honor. He forced a terse smile and a quick bow of his head. Earlier, Bridget had given him the biggest hug of his life for saving them all. He had to remind her he had failed because Sir Fostian Red died.

"You're too hard on yourself, Aug," she had said. "You can't always save everybody."

"I should have run faster …"

"You did your best."

Tales of his so-called heroism began to circle the table. He pretended to eat, trying not to make eye contact, feeling the heat of both hearths on his back.

"You have no idea what you did tonight, do you?" Leera asked quietly from across the table.

"I was extremely lucky."

"You were extremely brave is what you were. I'm proud to be your friend."

That made his insides tingle, but not enough to eclipse the hollow feeling of failure. His father had taken countless lives. He had many lives to save to make up for his father's many murders.

He remembered Meli's breath leaving her body as Mr. Penderson's whip kept coming and coming. That old mule was the only thing that had gotten him through those dark days. He wondered who could no longer count on Sir Fostian

Red returning home. What kind of family did he have? Would they now go hungry?

The scars on his back began to itch, but rather than subtly scratch against the chair as he usually would, he let the gentle torment continue.

The prince, meanwhile, took the compliments directed at Augum as some kind of personal affront. He tried to get as much attention as possible, boasting how he had saved the Nightsword with an expertly timed shout of alarm.

As the Prince blathered on, Bridget rolled her eyes and Leera gave Augum a *can you believe him* look. Augum smiled half-heartedly and glanced over at the empty queen's chair, wondering when Mrs. Stone would return.

Everybody was sore and bruised, but due to the miraculous healing waters of the fountain, all were now able to attend this second supper, even the previously injured Sir Dollard Canes, who now occupied Sir Fostian Red's seat. The large pudgy-cheeked fellow with short curly-brown hair talked little. His head bobbed up and down with a forced smile as the others ribbed him about his wounds. When they toasted to his health, he merely raised a glass of water, citing an upset stomach, which of course only increased the teasing.

Despite Fostian's death, the group was in good spirits. By far the best moment was when Mya gave Augum a kiss on the cheek and thanked him for saving her life. Augum did not know what to say, but whatever his face did must have seemed very funny because both Bridget and Leera giggled into their hands.

When talk turned to the wolf-things, there were plenty of guesses as to what they were—werewolves, direwolves, or maybe even hellhounds.

Before the feast, Augum and Sir Gallows had seen to the two carcasses so that Mrs. Stone could look upon them with her own eyes. Gallows insisted Augum do the honors with him as the slayer. Augum was so tired he would have preferred to have been excused, but did not want to offend the old knight.

"It is like they are one again," Gallows had joked upon tying them together, referring to the moment he saw one beast split into two. "I had never seen anything like it before; simply disgusting. Quite strong, too, even took down the Nightsword."

"Sir, why is Sir Quick so quiet?" Augum had asked as they dragged the beasts downstairs.

"There are stories, though I doubt them true. Some say he was once a mercenary, seeking battle for coin. Others say he was a vicious masked brigand who now keeps quiet so no one will recognize his voice. One story tells of Jayson Quick eating a leg of chicken near a prisoner. The prisoner had quite the tongue, rambling on about his life, oblivious to Jayson's desire to be left in peace. When the prisoner asked one too many questions, Quick stood up, unsheathed his sword and decapitated him. He then calmly sat back down and finished his chicken leg."

"That doesn't sound very knightly."

"No it does not, but it is only a tale."

"So why is he known as the Nightsword?" Augum asked as they exited the castle.

"That is another story, and an absolutely true one. On a moonless cloudy night, back when he was a part of the town watch, Quick went on a raid against a bandit camp. He became separated from his group and found himself surrounded by ten brigands. He killed the two torchbearers and then cut down the rest—all in pitch-darkness. He took one prisoner, who happened to tell the tale. King Ridian knighted Quick for it and offered him a place on the royal guard."

Augum now peered down the table at the Nightsword, who just happened to be chewing on a leg of chicken. His pale face turned in his direction. Augum quickly looked away.

Something about the man made him nervous. He wondered if the chicken leg story was true.

"I think we can skip the sword training tonight, eh brave warrior?" Sir Castor said from beside him, taking a swig of wine.

Augum nodded. He did not want to train with a bunch of drunken sword-wielders anyway, and the sour smell of wine on Castor's breath reminded him of Mr. Penderson. He looked past and saw the Nightsword slurping his third tankard of ale. The more the man drank the more he leered at Mya. She kept her eyes on the floor, her usual delicate smile absent. It made Augum clench his fists under the table.

The crowd became rowdier with every refill.

"Let's study the blue book after supper," Bridget said amidst the loud talk, slicing up a baked potato.

"What? Aren't you tired?" Leera asked.

"Exhausted, but Mrs. Stone told me working through exhaustion makes a good warlock great."

Leera snorted. "Then we should be invincible by now." She stabbed a boiled carrot with her fork and twirled it around a bit. "Fine, but we were supposed to sword train first, so why not with Fentwick?"

"That might work," Bridget replied, salting and buttering the potato. "We'll need more wooden swords though. What do you think, Aug?"

"Huh? Oh, why not just use my sword? The prince did."

"Yes but that pea brain set Fentwick on the highest difficulty," Leera said. "At a lower difficulty your sword would chop Fentwick's in half. I'm with Bridget—let's find more practice swords."

"We can probably get them where we found Fentwick in the first place," Bridget said.

Augum speared a wrinkly mushroom as the conversation from the other end of the table caught up to them.

"Young slayer!" called one of the red-cheeked Brack brothers. "Where is that fine blade of yours? Bring it forth and let us have a gander."

"Yes, let us see the blade that pierced and beheaded the beasts," Sir Castor said, eyes shiny.

Prince Sydo quickly stood and smoothed his red hair. "No need, noble Sirs—you may gander at my fine blade." He leaned near Lord Boron. "Lord Moron, where is my sword?"

"I had it placed in Your Highness' room."

"*Well, get —it —then*," Sydo said through gritted teeth.

Lord Boron flushed and mopped his brow, eyes flicking about. "As you wish, Your Highness." He stood as gracefully as the situation allowed and strode out.

"Well then, get your sword too, Augum," Gallows said, pink from the ale. "Let us compare!"

All the knights save for one added their voices in agreement, until a chant arose. Augum finally relented just to silence them.

He passed Lord Boron in the hall. The man stood on the lowest step, idly rubbing one of his large chins.

Augum retrieved his sword from his room, but on the way back, Boron still had not moved. His heart softened. "Lord Boron, why do you let the prince speak to you like that?"

Lord Boron's face reddened. He wordlessly set off, abruptly stopping halfway up the stairs. "I swore an oath. I swore to King Ridian the Wise that I would do whatever his son asked of me. He was a good king. I am the boy's minder. It is … my duty." He sighed. "Not all of us have your courage, young man," and resumed climbing before Augum could say anything else.

"Ah, there it is—" Gallows said upon Augum's return, standing to take the blade. The moment he grasped the hilt the sword ceased shooting sparks. The knight did not notice. He stepped back and took a few practice swings. The blade hissed neatly as it sliced the air.

"Why, it is quite light, even for a short sword. Wait a moment ..." He inspected the blade, the hilt and the crossguard. "Edrian, have a gander—"

Castor stopped laughing at one of the Brack brothers' jokes and took the blade from Gallows.

Prince Sydo made a show of stretching on the throne. "It is probably cheap southern steel, Sirs. I would not give it much thought."

"I have never seen anything like it," Castor said, ignoring the prince. He took a long look at the crossguard. "It is quite impossible to forge something like this in a traditional smithy."

The brother knights leaned in for a closer look. "Castor is right, this is superb work," said one.

"I too have never laid eyes upon such a blade," said the other.

"Let me see it," said a deep voice Augum did not recognize. He looked around to find the source only to find everyone staring at the Nightsword.

"Well give it here now, stop dawdling—" the knight said, eyes gleaming. Sir Castor, wearing the same blank look as everyone else, yielded the blade. The room went silent. It was the first time Augum heard the Nightsword speak.

He turned the sword over in his hands and inspected it closely from top to bottom, then brushed his mustache with his thumb.

Gallows sat back down. "What do you think there, Jayson—?"

"A Dreadnought blade."

Gasps and murmurs circled the table. Augum looked over at Leera and Bridget, but they both shrugged. The Nightsword stood and swung the blade in a vicious arc, almost taking off one of the Brack brothers' heads.

The brother raised a hand in defense and laughed nervously. "Whoa there, Jayson, perhaps you have had too much of the drink—"

The Nightsword spun the blade with such velocity it blurred and made a sharp whistling sound. He then swung it in a figure eight to his left and right, before roaring a mighty war cry and slicing clean through one of the massive marble fireplaces, causing a shower of sparks. With hardly a pause, he then tossed the blade up, letting it cartwheel in the air three times, before gracefully catching it in his left hand—and in one smooth motion presented it hilt-first back to Augum.

For a moment, no one moved.

"What's a Dreadnought blade—?" Augum finally managed to ask, accepting the sword.

"Arcanely-forged steel from long ago, made by a lost race known as the Dreadnoughts. They forged steel using ancient arcane ways unknown to us … *ordinary* men."

"That is just legend, Jayson," Gallows said, waving dismissively. "Stop filling the boy's head with stories. Sure the blade is old, but a Dreadnought blade?"

The table plowed into animated discussion.

"What is the name of the blade?" the Nightsword asked amid the roar of conversation.

"Name? Oh, um, I don't know."

"All Dreadnought blades have names. It is unbecoming of a warrior to not know the name of such a sword." He gave Augum one last cold look before sitting back down, leaving him standing and gaping at the sword in his hand, the blade once again sparking. What *was* its name?

Lord Boron suddenly came huffing back inside, holding a jewel-encrusted long sword in a finely decorated scabbard.

"Your Highness—" he wheezed, mopping his brow, "I have your sword here—"

"Oh stuff it, Lord Moron."

THE MAP

After supper, Augum arcanely repaired the mantel the Nightsword had sliced, hoping Mya would notice, but she was too busy attending to the knights.

"Peasant showoff," Sydo muttered to Lord Boron.

Leera overheard the remark and opened her mouth to speak, but Bridget interrupted by standing. "Would everyone excuse us?"

The knights immediately stood in response. Bridget reddened like a summer apple.

"My young lady, you certainly may be excused," Gallows said, raising his glass to the trio. Augum and Leera stood and gave a kind of half-bow that generated a snort from Sydo. The trio ignored him and exited into the dark hallway, where they lit up their palms.

"So, up to Fentwick's battlement?" Bridget asked.

"Right, the practice swords," Augum said. "Let's go then."

"Wait, let me see it," Leera said. Augum handed her the sword. She examined it carefully, nodding to herself like a sage. "I see what they were on about. This is unlike any sword I've ever seen." She gave it back to him.

Bridget kept a smile at bay. "Oh please, Lee, as if *you* know anything about swords."

"What's that supposed to mean? You know that I—"

"—once wanted to be a knight," Bridget said, dropping her eyes. "I'm sorry, I forgot."

Leera pursed her lips, smiled, and punched Bridget in the shoulder. "All's forgiven, Bridgey-poo."

"Don't call me that—"

Now it was Augum's turn to keep a straight face. " 'Bridgey-poo?' "

"Oh, shut up," Bridget said, sweeping the hair from her eyes and marching up the steps to the fourth floor.

"It's what her mum used to call her," Leera said, growing somber.

He guessed what Bridget was thinking—Sparrow's Perch was still fresh in their minds, and little things like pet names were painful reminders.

"I didn't know you wanted to be a knight," he said.

"I did, but I would have started training too late. Also, mum didn't approve. Dad *did* get me a short sword though."

"I remember. You named her Careena. I didn't start young enough either, you know."

She shrugged. "I prefer arcanery anyway."

"Me too."

"Found some—!" Bridget said when they caught up. She was rummaging through a pile of wood in the southwest battlement. The structure had archer slots spread evenly around the five-foot thick stone walls. Two broken chests sat opposite each other.

"What a grim place to stand for two hundred years," Leera said. "Waiting all that time to train the next prince or princess, and none came but us …"

Bridget stopped what she was doing and glanced at Augum. "Could it be that Leera actually put herself in someone else's boots?"

"She takes after your example," he said.

"An arcanely-animated suit of armor doesn't count," Leera said, grinning. "But I'll consider that a compliment."

Bridget smiled as she passed a wooden practice sword to each of them, grabbing one extra for good measure. "Hey, while we're here, whose turn is it to repair the map?" She withdrew the wrinkled parchment from her robe.

"Mine, I think." Augum took the map from her, placed it on the ground, and concentrated. "Apreyo."

Nothing happened.

He sat there for a while and was about to give up when a piece of parchment came fluttering from behind one of the broken chests, re-attaching itself to the map. They had failed so many times the girls had not even noticed the success.

He held up the map. "You're not going to believe this, but I think we got it."

Leera almost tore the map swiping it from his hands. "I'll be damned, he did it …" She splayed it on one of the chests.

"The passage is in the cellar," Bridget said. "Southeast corner, the area we haven't explored yet."

Leera took a few steps. "Come on then, let's go!"

"Go where?" said a familiar sneering voice from the stairs.

Augum hastily shoved the map back into Bridget's hands, who promptly hid it in her robe.

Sydo smoothed his hair. "You three think you are so clever, always getting one over on the poor prince. So where are you sneaking off to this time? What, plan on opening *another* door so more beasts could try to kill me?"

Bridget straightened. "We would never—"

"Well who else would do it?" Sydo strolled forward, smirking. "My knights and servants are completely loyal to me; they would never put me in danger. It must have been one of you."

"That's nonsense," Leera said. "We were outside repairing the wall when the thing attacked us."

"You will address me as 'Your Highness'. Are you saying Lord Moron forgot to close the doors, is that right? I think it was you or that old crone—"

Augum took a step forward. "Mrs. Stone would never do such a thing—"

Sydo shrugged and held up a hand. "No need to get brutish. Very well, let us go forth on this peasant quest of yours. I am coming with you. What is it that you found again, a—"

"—swords," Bridget said. "We found practice swords, and if you're coming along you're going to need one of them." She shoved the extra wooden practice sword into Sydo's hands.

"I have a *real* one, thank you," Sydo said, holding the stick at arms' length like a filthy rag.

"We're going to go practice with Fentwick. You can either practice with one of these or go use the *real* one with the Nightsword." Bridget marched off in a dignified manner, Augum and Leera close behind.

The prince hesitated, no doubt remembering the last time he sparred with Fentwick, weighing that against sparring with a drunken Nightsword. Scowling, he decided to follow the trio.

"Ugh, does he have to drag his feet so loudly?" Leera muttered as they descended. "I swear he's doing it on purpose."

"Wouldst thou fancy a duel, mine lady?" Fentwick asked as the four arrived on the third floor.

"I certainly would," Bridget said.

"What setting dost mine lady beseech of me—defender, beginner, intermediate, advanced, or expert?"

"Beginner if you will, Fentwick."

"As mine lady wishes."

Sydo leaned on his wooden sword, trying to break it. "What a farce …"

Bridget ignored the remark and raised her sword. "On your guard."

"On ye guard," Fentwick said, crossing his wooden sword with Bridget's. She then swung at Fentwick with blow after fierce blow. Fentwick parried the first two then missed the second two, receiving two thwacks that made a gong sound.

"That's the spirit, Bridge—another dent for the collection!" Leera said, making phantom thrusting motions in the air.

"It is like watching turtles battle," Sydo muttered. "She certainly is no Speedsword …"

"Your turn, Lee," Bridget huffed after a few more rounds of swordplay.

Leera took her place and raised her sword. "Intermediate please, Fentwick."

Fentwick crossed her blade with his own. "As ye wish, mine lady."

Sydo groaned. "Oh, how *daring*."

But Leera showed a great deal more skill than Bridget—the animated suit of armor rang with hits as she flew at him like a wasp.

"Wow, Leera, you're really good," Augum said, thinking she was actually better than him.

Leera's cheeks reddened as she almost took a blow to the head.

Sydo's face showed disappointment. Soon, he was twirling his sword idly. Augum noticed that although Sydo pretended not to care, he was actually keeping a close eye on Leera's sword movements.

At last, Leera made to slash at Fentwick's legs, adjusted at the last moment, and slammed the wooden sword into the side of his helm. The animated suit of armor clanked to the ground.

Augum and Bridget clapped as Fentwick stood.

"Artfully done, mine lady."

"Your turn," Leera said, but before Augum was able to raise his wooden blade, the Nightsword staggered into the corridor. He slammed the dining room doors behind him, tankard of ale sloshing in his hand.

"Stupid wench, if you don't want to come to *my* room, maybe I should go to *yours*!" He squinted at them. "Well if it isn't the magic children ..."

Bridget primly cleared her throat. "It's *arcane*, Sir Quick."

The Nightsword bent down and tried to focus his gaze on Bridget but only succeeded in crossing his eyes. "Why, it's a talking squirrel—!"

Sydo howled with laughter and slapped his knee.

"Don't talk to her like that!" Augum said.

The Nightsword's wandering eyes tried to focus on Augum. "Come again?"

"Perhaps Sir Quick has had too much ale—" Bridget said quickly.

Quick straightened. "Where is that wretched girl! I demand service!"

"You leave her alone—" Augum began but the dining room doors flew open and Mya rushed forth.

"There you are, sweetling," the Nightsword said. "Come take me to my bed, for I fear I have become rather muddled."

"Surely Sir is able to find his room on his own," Mya said in a subdued voice, eyes low.

The Nightsword took a long swig, eyes gleaming. "Nonsense, girl, you are a royal servant. Do your royal *duty*."

Augum looked to the prince, wondering when he was planning on stepping in. This was, after all, a member of his royal guard—but Sydo only grinned.

"She can't go with you, Sir—!" Augum said.

The Nightsword thrust his face into Augum's. Ale dripped from his mustache and his breath smelled like rotten onion. "Oh? And just why not?"

Think quickly. "Because she has to come with us—"

"Where?"

"Um … to a secret passage we found!"

Leera groaned.

"I knew it—!" the prince said with a triumphant grin.

The Nightsword gulped down the rest of his ale and threw the pottery tankard behind his back. Mya winced as it smashed on the floor. He adjusted his sword belt and smoothed his mustache with his thumb. "Well then, let's make this adventure a group effort. Lead on, little worm."

"What are you doing—?" Bridget asked under her breath as they descended the stairs.

"Don't know, I'll figure something out …" He walked as slowly as he dared, but when they reached the foyer, he still had not formed a plan. His mind was racing for ideas when he felt an icy draft along with a distant thud. A moment later, the foyer doors opened and in shuffled a stooped Mrs. Stone, hood drawn over her head.

A wave of relief swept over Augum.

Bridget rushed forward. "Mrs. Stone … you're back!"

Mrs. Stone dropped her hood and adjusted her long silver ponytail. She frowned at Bridget before fixing her gaze on the Nightsword, who was swaying back and forth on the landing like a tree in a storm.

"Ah, the crone returns! And what of my companions in Antioc—any word?"

"Dead, I fear."

It took the Nightsword a few moments to register what she had said. "Indeed …?" He brought his empty hand to his lips as if to drink. It hovered there until he broke out with a ghoulish cackling that soon dissolved into a coughing fit.

When it subsided, he made a dismissive gesture. "They weren't none too skilled anyway; bunch of fools to get themselves killed, if you ask me."

Mrs. Stone pursed her lips and made an impatient motion with her hand. The familiar electric globe appeared, bathing the foyer in blue light. She then approached Mya. "Please fetch Ms. Grinds and ask her to escort Sir Quick to his quarters."

Mya gave Mrs. Stone a nervous smile, curtsied, and swiftly walked up the stairs, careful to give the Nightsword a wide berth. He leered at her as she passed.

Mrs. Stone turned to Bridget. "I have brought something back for you, child." She reached into her robe and pulled out the ornately decorated dagger Bridget had given up.

"I say, what is that?" Sydo asked.

"A piercing blade," Mrs. Stone said.

Bridget received it with both hands. "What's a piercing blade, Mrs. Stone?"

The Nightsword burped, head now resting on the marble banister. "A blade that passes through all types of armor."

Bridget unsheathed the dagger. "So that means it can pass through arcane armor too?"

"No," the Nightsword gurgled from the landing. "Just *ordinary* armor that belongs to us *ordinaries*. Only Dreadnought piercing blades can pass through arcane armor."

Augum realized what the Nightsword meant by "ordinaries"—the man lacked arcane talent.

Bridget looked up at Mrs. Stone. "So is it … is it a Dreadnought blade?"

Mrs. Stone watched her a moment before giving a slight nod.

"Well, is it or is it not?" the Nightsword asked, head lolling on the banister.

"Yes!" the prince called, shaking his head with an impatient sigh. "Give it here, let me have a gander—"

Bridget hesitated before passing it over. The prince gazed upon it with covetous eyes.

"It's name—!" The Nightsword was reeling now. "What's its name?"

"The arcaneologist declared its name to be Blackbite," Mrs. Stone replied.

"Fitting," Leera said, holding her hand out to the prince. Sydo made her wait before finally surrendering the blade. The hematite shone as she turned it over in her hands.

"Mrs. Stone, Sir Quick said my sword is also a Dreadnought blade," Augum said. "Do you happen to know its name?"

"That I do. Its name is Burden's Edge."

The Nightsword bubbled with laughter. "Burden's Edge. What a jape—" Suddenly he lost his balance and crashed to the ground.

Mrs. Stone pressed her eyes closed as if begging for patience.

Augum thought the name was indeed peculiar, but before he could ask where it came from, Mya was back with Ms. Grinds. Grinds shook her head upon laying eyes on the drunken knight sprawled at their feet.

"Come, Sir, it is time for a good sleep," Ms. Grinds said, helping him stand. The Nightsword muttered unintelligibly before placing his arm around her shoulder. The pair ascended together, Mya following, hands behind her back.

"Mrs. Stone, there was an attack while you were gone," Bridget said.

"Mercy, child, why had you not said so earlier? What manner of attack? Quickly now."

Bridget secured Blackbite to her belt and recounted what happened, starting with the child outside the walls—how she asked it to come to her, how it changed into a wolf-thing, and how it poisoned her with its bite. She went on to explain that it somehow split into two beasts, that Augum slew both, and that he used oxy and fountain water to save them all.

Augum colored from such a heroic-sounding retelling. He had to remind them he had been unable to revive Sir Fostian Red. Sydo, meanwhile, kept rolling his eyes or smacking his lips as if he had something to say.

"And how did these things find their way into the castle?" Mrs. Stone asked after Bridget finished.

"We don't know," Leera said.

"It was them!" the prince said, gesticulating at the trio, forehead redder than his hair. "They left the doors open and let those beasts in—!"

Augum, Bridget and Leera protested all at once.

"That's absurd—"

"We did no such thing—"

"Not true—"

"Silence!" Mrs. Stone barked, making them all jump. Her gaze passed over each of them in turn before she spoke again. "Bridget, when you begged the child forward you unwittingly invited it onto the grounds, thus bypassing my protective enchantments. The fault is mine, however—I should have given clear instruction on how the sanctuary enchantment works. Now, where are the corpses of these beasts?"

"But ... but ... what about the doors?" Sydo asked.

Mrs. Stone turned a sharp eye on him and Sydo withered.

"Sir Gallows and I tied them together, Mrs. Stone," Augum said. "Then we dragged them outside."

"Then I shall speak with him. Have the three of you practiced at swords?"

"A little bit with Fentwick."

Mrs. Stone frowned. "Not with the knights?"

Augum exchanged hesitant looks with Bridget and Leera. "No, they were, um—"

"—drunk," Bridget said, cheeks brightening.

"I see. And what of your studies, I gather the three of you read up on the Unconceal spell?"

The trio shifted. "No, Mrs. Stone," they said in quiet voices.

"Then *may I suggest* you begin right away. It is late, but I expect you ought to be able to study at least an hour."

"Yes, Mrs. Stone."

It did not escape Augum's notice that Sydo gave them an envious, almost regretful look. As they turned to leave, Mandy, the young servant with reddish brown hair, padded softly down the steps, curtsying at the landing.

"Begging your pardon, Mrs. Stone, but Ms. Grinds sent me to escort His Royal Highness to bed."

The prince practically shook. "But ... the doors ... the passage—!"

Mrs. Stone only raised a silver brow. Sydo's shoulders finally slumped and he dragged himself up the steps.

Augum shared a grateful look with Leera, but Mrs. Stone spotted him doing it. His stomach twisted into a knot as her eyes narrowed. Sure enough, as soon as the prince disappeared, she turned on them.

"I have taken note of late that you three seem to find pleasure in another's suffering. Shame on you."

The trio dropped their eyes.

"And Augum, you of all people ought to know how it feels to be an outsider." She paused to glare at them. "I am disappointed in the lot of you." She turned and shuffled up the steps. They watched her go in silence.

Leera rubbed her forehead. "You'd think she'd congratulate you for saving everybody, Aug. Instead, we get lectured how we should be best friends with the brat prince."

"Mrs. Stone's right," Bridget said. "Haven't made much effort, have we?"

Leera waved the idea aside. "He's a brat. That's my take."

Bridget sighed. "Come on, we have a lot of studying to do ..."

ADVENTURE

The trio spent an hour huddled around the blue book in the girls' room studying the Unconceal spell. It was tiring reading, forcing long discussions on the finer points of the spell.

"This book is massive," Bridget said, resting her back against the wall.

Leera yawned. "I'm exhausted. Have we done enough?"

"I think so," Augum said, "but before I go to bed I'm going to try that bit about adjusting your palm a certain way, see if it helps." He extended his hand and spread his fingers wide. "Un vun deo." He concentrated on feeling for the intent to conceal, then adjusted his palm in subtle ways, just like the book recommended. Unexpectedly, he began to feel a very tiny pull toward the wall of leaded-glass windows. He followed the invisible trail but, due to his tiredness, lost concentration, breaking the spell.

"There's something here behind this wall."

Bridget wandered over. "You sure?"

"Yeah, pretty sure."

Leera palmed the wall. "There's a seam here. Feel that?

Augum felt the spot. "It's well hidden."

"Wait, look at this—" Bridget clawed at something with her fingernails, raising a camouflaged handle from the stone. They pulled it and a two-foot square door rumbled open, a cloud of dust billowing forth.

"I don't believe it, a secret passage," Leera whispered, sticking her head inside.

"Careful, Lee—" Bridget said.

Leera reappeared. "It's okay, the passage travels right. It goes along the wall and behind Mrs. Stone's room."

Augum rubbed his hands together. Suddenly his bones did not ache so much. "Shall we explore?"

"But it's so late," Bridget said, "and haven't we done enough for today? Besides, what if Mrs. Stone hears us, or we can't get back?"

"Aww, come on, Bridge, where's your sense of adventure?" Leera asked. "We can leave the door open and we'll be very quiet, okay?"

Bridget gave Augum a pleading look.

He shrugged. "I say let's go."

She sighed and surrendered with a nod.

They lit their palms and crawled in one at a time, Leera first followed by Augum and Bridget. The passage was only slightly larger than the door, making it difficult to maneuver or turn around. It was roughly hewn, damp, cold and dirty, reminding him of the cellar.

Leera suddenly stopped and put a glowing finger to her lips. She extinguished her light, bidding them to do the same. Once they did so, Augum saw why—there was a very thin crack of light on the right-hand wall.

"Listen," she whispered, pressing her ear against it. Augum and Bridget followed suit.

"… amongst us," Mrs. Stone said.

"Impossible, Mrs. Stone, I picked the men myself," Sir Gallows said.

"Then perhaps one of the servants. There are means of discovery, though they take time."

"Put to the arcane question? It would be a great affront—"

"The stakes are too high, Eldric. It is possible he waits for us now."

Gallows' boots thudded as he began pacing. "What of my stranded brethren?"

"Discovered and slaughtered arcanely," Mrs. Stone said.

The pacing stopped. "I trained them myself, Mrs. Stone. They were good and loyal men. And what of their families?"

"I cannot say. The herald reports little."

He resumed pacing. "I suppose it was your grandson's work?"

"Lividius' underlings—Vion Rames, Rotus Magnavilius, Corrigus, perhaps others. I fear your men stood little chance."

"Corrigus is with Sparkstone? That man is a monster." A pause. "How much time do we have?"

"Very little, I suspect."

"Do you think he knows about the portal?"

"Perhaps."

"If he does, he would besiege the castle until we starved …"

"He may gain entry regardless, Eldric, using the scion—"

The pacing stopped again. There was a pause in which Augum imagined the two of them exchanging a dark look.

"In that event," Mrs. Stone continued, "we will have no choice but to use the portal."

"Would it even work?"

"I am not sure, it is 1500 years old."

"But he can follow us—"

"I do not believe so."

"But—"

"Enough, Eldric. Now take me to these beasts. I shall examine them myself."

There was a sigh. "Yes, Mrs. Stone."

"What portal do you suppose they're talking about?" Leera asked after Mrs. Stone and Sir Gallows left the room.

Augum thought about it. "They might mean one of the gates in the cellar."

"Maybe," Bridget said. "Anyway, I think Mrs. Stone was saying we have a traitor amongst us."

Leera scoffed. "Probably the prince."

"I don't think so. Remember that Sparkstone killed his father."

"Maybe one of the servants then?"

"Or the Nightsword," Augum added.

They fell silent for a moment.

"Let's keep going," Leera said.

They lit up their palms and crawled onward, passing by yet another secret door, this one to Augum's room. Finally, Leera came to the end of the passage.

"There's something underneath here," she whispered.

Augum squeezed his head by her shoulder and spotted a wooden trap door with an iron ring. She groaned lifting it, and leaned it up against the far wall, revealing a square black hole. A rusty iron ladder led the way down.

"Where do you suppose this goes?" Leera asked, a daring expression on her face.

Bridget glanced behind her. "I don't know about this, maybe we should go back ..."

Leera stretched her lit palm into the darkness. "It's a small room. Ceiling's only about four feet high." She climbed down.

"Don't worry, Bridge," Augum said, grabbing the ladder. "I'm sure it'll be fine."

The room had roughly hewn stone walls and a floor covered by a thick blanket of dust.

Leera slouched in the center. "Ugh ... there's nothing here!"

"It's too odd not to have anything," he said. "Let's look closer." He began groping the walls. Sure enough, he stumbled across a neatly etched oval and minaret. "Found some sort of symbol here!"

"Me too," Bridget said.

"Found one here as well!" Leera echoed.

After a bit more searching, they discovered one more. In all, there were four ovals etched into the wall, each with a different symbol next to it—a square with bars, a fountain, a tree with a small crescent moon beside it, and the minaret Augum had found.

Leera suddenly took a step back. "These must be portals ...!"

They glanced at each other.

"Then it must be some kind of emergency escape room," Bridget said. She pointed at the minaret. "This one here must go to the top of the castle." Then she pointed at the symbol with the fountain. "This one must go to the fountain room." She stepped over to the tree with the crescent moon. "This one here must go outside somewhere. And this one ..." She tapped the box with bars. "Hmm, not sure where this one goes—"

"—the cellar," Augum said. "I mean, it only makes sense, doesn't it? You have the top of the castle, the fountain room, somewhere outside ... and the cellar."

Leera raised her hands to get their attention. "Wait, these must be the portals Mrs. Stone and Sir Gallows were talking about!"

"But didn't they say 'portal' not 'portals'?" Bridget asked.

"Maybe, but doesn't it make sense? Mrs. Stone said that should they get in, 'we will have no choice but to use the portal.' "

Augum shrugged. "It does kind of make sense, Bridge."

Bridget sighed. "All right, if it *is* some sort of emergency escape room, it'd make sense that it could only be activated by residents of the castle. Therefore ..."

" 'Therefore' —?" Leera mouthed to Augum.

Bridget paced back and forth, lit hand turning in the air as if debating points with herself. She stopped midstride. "The activation word has to be on the servant plaque."

"Wouldn't that be too obvious?" he asked.

"Of course, but they're emergency portals—they're probably all over the castle! I bet it was common knowledge what the word was; and if you entered a portal, whoever's looking for you would have to correctly guess which one you'd taken *and* know the activation word. By the time they figured it out, you'd be long gone."

Leera nodded but gave Augum a sidelong look that communicated she was lost. He had to think about it himself, but Bridget's reasoning seemed sound.

"Guess there's only one way to find out for sure, isn't there?" he said.

A daring grin spread across Bridget's face. She no longer looked tired.

"All right, stop the gawking and start the walking!" Leera said in a sing-song voice, jumping onto the ladder.

The trio made their way back through the tunnel, stopping by Mrs. Stone's room to listen. It was silent.

"Wait—" Augum whispered. "Go back, let's go through my room."

"Why?" Leera asked, face bathed in the watery-blue light of her palm.

"Fentwick." Fentwick could be a bit loud at times.

She thought about it and nodded. The trio backtracked and carefully opened the secret door to his room. They piled in and quietly closed it behind them. Then he cracked open the door to the corridor, saw that there was no one in the hall, and motioned the girls to follow. Raucous laughter drifted in from the dining room—the knights were still going strong.

The trio crept down the stairs and managed to make it all the way to the foyer when the outer castle doors opened. They scampered through the nearest door just in time to hear voices. Augum realized they stood in the newly repaired servant hall, now glowing with candlelight, and should anyone step out of their room or wander through, they would have no time to hide.

"… that we cannot be sure of, but hellhounds have masters and they are usually nearby," Mrs. Stone's voice echoed.

"This is most grave," Gallows said. "Would they not have attacked us by now?"

"Perhaps they wait upon something."

"Or someone … I'll warn the others to be on their guard."

Their footsteps died as they ascended the stairs.

The trio exchanged dark looks.

"We should get back," Bridget whispered.

"We won't be gone long," Leera said. "It's only the servant plaque."

"All right, I guess …"

"What are hellhounds?" Augum asked.

The girls shook their heads—they did not know.

"Let's hurry then and hope they don't check on us," Bridget said.

They tiptoed past the servant rooms, reaching the far door to the kitchen. It was slightly ajar. The smell of roast chicken wafted from the other side, along with sounds of humming and pot scraping. Augum peeked through the crack and spotted the fiery maw of an oven, hissing away with a meal. Nearby stood the blonde servant girl Rafinda, scrubbing pots in a large washbasin over the trestle table. The stairs down to the cellar were just beyond the door and to the right. There was no way to sneak by without Rafinda noticing.

They needed a distraction.

Augum placed a finger to his lips then gestured an idea he had as best he could. Bridget and Leera nodded their readiness. He raised his arm and focused on a pot balanced on the edge of the table. It was a bit of a distance away, but he managed to give it the tiny arcane push it needed—it teetered then fell to the floor with a mighty clang. Rafinda jumped, mumbled something sharp, and marched over to where the pot lay. As soon as she turned her back, he signaled for the girls to go.

Leera scurried first, followed by Bridget and Augum. Just as he tiptoed through the doorway, Rafinda slammed the pot back onto the table. Not daring to look, he sped down the steps, joining the girls in holding his breath at the bottom. When the sound of humming and pot scraping resumed, they breathed a sigh of relief, lit their palms, and made their way to the servants' diagram.

Augum wondered if the girls would be willing to search for the secret passage now that they were down here—or would that be asking too much?

"All right, watch for an oval," Bridget said.

They scanned the diagram until Leera tapped at a spot near the middle. "Think I found it—"

They crowded for a closer look. Sure enough, there was a small oval worked into the bronze. Beside it was a symbol that looked like a shiny palm with the word "Liberai" next to it.

"That must be the activation word," Bridget said. "I'm guessing that you have to use the Shine spell, lay your palm over the symbol, and say the word."

Leera gave her a funny look. "Brilliant deduction, Bridge; a blind and daft washerwoman could have figured that out."

Bridget gave her an exasperated look and dug into her robe. "Anyway, since we're here already ..." and she unfolded the repaired map.

"Just what I was thinking," Augum said. "This might be our only chance to explore it, now that the prince knows."

Leera smirked. "No thanks to you, Loose Lips …"

"Hey now, no one else had a better idea on how to save Mya. Besides—" he made a grand gesture, "—just imagine a room full of treasure."

Leera scoffed but could not help grinning.

"So let's see here," Bridget said, perusing the map. "It should be inside this room." She led the way to the entrance of the southeast room and opened the heavy door. It screeched; the trio cringed, waiting for footsteps. When none came, they slipped inside and carefully closed the door, inspecting with lit palms.

Rows and rows of shelves stood floor to ceiling, each pierced with holes. Enormous barrel-like casks sat on the floor of the east wall, stained with dark splotches. Corks and pieces of broken glass were everywhere. The place appeared thoroughly plundered—not a single bottle remained intact. The casks all seemed drained as well, some with large puncture wounds.

"Wine cellar," Augum said, remembering Sir Westwood describing a particularly fine one he saw in some distant castle.

Leera pinched her nose. "Ugh, smells like ancient mold. So what are we looking for, anyway?"

Bridget glanced at the map. "Looks like the entrance to the tunnel should be behind the last cask, in the corner there."

Glass crunched underfoot as they walked. The light from their palms made thousands of eyes out of the shelf holes, swaying to the rhythm of their hands. Nobody spoke, though everyone constantly checked over their shoulders. Augum half expected to come across the remains of a bandit, grotesquely stuffed under a cask.

"Think it's this one," Bridget said, referencing a particularly damaged cask with the map. The metal banding lay loose and bent and there were two gaping holes in the front.

Examining it, Augum noticed there was a very narrow space between the cask and the wall. "Maybe we can get behind it—"

"—or move it," Leera said. "Telekinesis?"

"Good idea. Why don't you keep your palm lit while Bridge and I give it a try."

Leera nodded as Augum and Bridget stepped back and raised their arms. After a moment of concentration, the cask groaned but refused to budge.

"Must be stuck," he said, panting. "Hold on—" He detached Burden's Edge from his waist and climbed on top of the cask, lit his palm, and searched behind it. "That's why …"

"What do you see, Aug?" Bridget asked.

"There's a chain keeping it fixed to the wall. I'll need to break the link. Can you hand me Blackbite?"

"All right, but just *please* be careful." Bridget handed him the ornate dagger.

"Now if I can just reach it …" After a bit of trial and error, he was able to wedge the dagger between the link and the wall, then leveraged his weight onto it.

"Don't break my dagger!"

Augum grunted from the strain when the iron link suddenly split. He barely managed to avoid falling and wedging himself in.

"That should do it. All right, let's try it again." He dismounted and re-secured Burden's Edge to his waist.

Bridget snatched Blackbite back and examined it. "Look at that, not even a scratch."

"Dreadnought steel …" Leera said.

On their second attempt, the cask screeched forward just a tad.

"Leera, we'll need your help here," Bridget said, wheezing. "Thing's heavier than an anvil."

"Too bad none of us know how to chronocast," Leera said, extinguishing her palm and bathing them in darkness.

"On three now," Bridget said. "One, two, *three*—!"

The cask shrieked and rumbled, the weight of it enormous—the single toughest test of their skill thus far. It was impossible to judge how far it moved in the dark; it could very well run them over. From the terrible noise, Augum expected everyone in the castle to come down and investigate—and then lost his concentration worrying about it. The trio immediately collapsed from the effort, gasping for breath as if they had been sprinting.

Augum's head throbbed and his stomach gurgled with nausea.

"Poor Rafinda," Leera said between huffs, snorting a laugh. "Probably thinks the place is haunted."

They rested in the cool darkness, listening, hoping beyond hope that nobody heard them.

"Shyneo," Bridget said at last. Her face glistened with sweat as she surveyed their work. "We did it …"

"Now let's see what's back there," Augum said. "Shyneo." He shimmied to the rear of the cask and examined the wall closely. "Don't see anything …"

Leera climbed along the top of it. "Here, let me try Unconceal. I need the practice."

He moved aside. She jumped down, kneeled, and closed her eyes. After three deep breaths, she raised her arm and opened her palm.

"Un vun deo." Her hand stayed motionless for a while before she moved it around in circles, letting it guide her higher and higher until she found a camouflaged lever and pulled. A small portion of the wall swung inwards, expelling a plume of dust and cold air. Grinning, she made a grand gesture that said *after you, sir*.

Augum gave her a bemused look, dropped to his knees, and crawled into the tunnel. The passage was cold and stony at first but grew earthier as he went along.

"Nice job, Lee," he heard Bridget say as she dropped to her knees to follow.

After what seemed like a very long distance, the tunnel ended in a rocky door. On the right-hand side was a wooden lever. He waited until the girls caught up before giving it a pull. The door opened outward with a grinding rumble. Air swooped into the tunnel, inducing shivers.

He trundled onward, one hand on Burden's Edge, into an ancient country house with half its ceiling missing. Moonlight flooded a dirty stone floor mottled with patches of snow. The walls were mostly ruin covered with thick ropes of frozen vine.

So much for a treasure room ...

Bridget emerged. "Where are we?" she whispered, dusting her robe.

"I think it's an abandoned house outside of the castle." He wondered why it was so quiet. Sir Westwood had always cautioned to be wary of a quiet forest.

Leera stumbled out from the tunnel, clapping dirt from her robe. "Ugh, that was no fun—" When she spotted where they were, her face fell as if she had been robbed of a great prize.

Bridget was about to put a finger to her lips when a horse whinnied nearby. The trio immediately ducked. Bridget drew Blackbite, Augum Burden's Edge.

Augum prowled to the hole of a ruined window and peered over the edge. Something moved just beyond a nearby cluster of snowy trees. A horse—but where was the rider? It neighed, its breath bellowing clouds of steam.

"What is it, boy, what's the matter?" someone asked in the darkness.

"Pro'ably a 'coon, Commander," said a reedy voice.

"Keep your voice down, you fool."

"Right, sorry sir."

There was a pause, followed by, "Stay here and keep your mouth shut."

"Aye, sir."

"He's coming—" Augum mouthed, making frantic motions for the girls to get back inside the tunnel. Just as Leera reached the door though, it slammed shut. She fumbled to pry it open, but it would not budge. "No no no …"

Augum jumped to his feet, Burden's Edge in hand. Bridget was beside him, Blackbite glinting in the moonlight.

"Where is he?" she asked in a whisper. "Can't see him …"

"Of course you can't," said an amused voice from the window, the space oddly shimmering. "But I can see you just fine, younglings. O'Donnell—fetch our lord and master!"

"Me, Commander?" The reedy voice wavered. "I'm not fit to speak to *him*, sir—"

"NOW, O'Donnell! Unless you want to become a walking corpse."

"Who are you?" Augum asked.

The space within the window seemed to twist, coalescing into a person who calmly climbed over the ledge.

A chill travelled down Augum's spine as he recognized the electric eyes and the black robe with silver embroidered lightning.

"Augum Stone. What a prize," Commander Vion Rames said.

BREACHED

Augum felt dizzy. This man standing before him, besides being Mrs. Stone's former apprentice, had been the commander in charge of the column that razed Willowbrook and murdered Sir Westwood.

Commander Vion Rames' face twisted into a smile. He grasped his long night-black hair and smoothed it down his chest, something that seemed habitual, intended to maintain its perfect straightness. "I remember the first time I ever laid eyes on you, boy, quivering on the ground, clinging to a tree. I must confess, had I known you were the Lord of the Legion's own son, things would have turned out ... rather differently, you might say."

"I wasn't quivering." Augum felt sweat prickling his forehead.

"But how did you find us?" Bridget asked.

"Oh, we've kept an eye on the crown for some time. Even during King Ridian's reign, there was always someone close by whose loyalties laid … elsewhere. When Lord Sparkstone claimed the throne for himself, he wisely let the prince go so we could find any remaining insurgent holdouts. It seems the gamble paid off handsomely."

Augum exchanged looks with the girls—it had to be the Nightsword.

Rames glanced to the small door. "My pets have been sniffing for a way in, how convenient for you to give us one."

"Those hellhounds were *yours*?" Leera asked.

"Gifted to me by the Lord of the Legion. Quite remarkable beasts, aren't they? Unfortunately, it seems you have dispatched them. My heart aches, but justice shall be served." Rames' electric eyes flicked over Bridget and Leera.

"You killed Sir Westwood—" Augum said.

"Who now?"

"Sir Tobias Westwood. You murdered him—"

"Surely you don't expect me to remember every little worm I step on, do you?"

"—and you burnt down my village!"

"Oh? And which village was that, pray tell?" His voice became louder as he spoke. "I recall burning many dissenting, traitorous, insurgent-infested hovels in the service of the greatest sorcerer who has ever lived!"

For a moment, Rames just stared at them, breathing heavily, before running his fingers down the length of his hair. "There now, are we happy? I have become bothered. As it is, please allow me to infuse you with clarity." He took a step forward. The trio took one back. "You either stand *with* the Legion, or *against*." His voice quickened. "Is that in any way confusing to you? Shall I draw you a diagram, a map, ink you a book on the subject—?"

"How could she ever have trained you?" Augum asked. By the look Rames gave him, he half-expected a throttling. Instead, the man bent a knee.

"Oh, that is just a marvelous story, of which I shall only tell a tiny portion, if you will, for we have little time." He glanced over his shoulder as if expecting reinforcements to arrive at any moment. "You see, I was just like you, Augum—an ambitious, young apprentice under one of the most powerful sorceresses known. I believed every word she said. I followed every gesture. But you know what? I was not good enough for her." He paused to give the thought weight. "And I was not the only one, you see. Her very own *grandson* was not good enough either. It was he, the future Lord of the Legion—your own father—that showed me how to unlock my true potential. Under the crone, I languished and fell behind; I shriveled and withered and weakened. Under *him*, however, I could do whatever I wanted. I became strong, powerful, and learned so much more. I was … *unleashed* … as you will be when you join your father."

Rames stood up, dusting his hands. "So—want to show me how well the old crone's trained you?"

Augum tightened his grip on Burden's Edge. He knew he had to warn the others in the castle, had to save the girls—"

"All right, I shall start then," Rames said in a mock-cheery tone. He flexed and his right arm burst with ten rings of lightning, blue coils of electricity that licked the curves of his black robe. The space around the man seemed to warp as Augum felt his hair stiffen. The trio retreated another step, backs against the wall of the house, blades pointed ahead.

Augum glanced at the door at his feet. If only they could get back inside somehow, warn Mrs. Stone—

"What, no rings of your own?" Rames raised his arm. "Then you shall have no defense against this—dreadus terrablus!"

The world instantly sharpened with thousands of claws. Augum saw his poor mule, Meli, lashed again and again, her hide ripping open. Out poured more Melis, each lashed anew, each ripping open and multiplying, their stinking flesh burying and choking him.

He began shaking. His sword turned into a writhing snake with nothing but sharp edges. He let it go. It smashed against the ground. Each of the edges became a moving needle, with tiny needle feet, all running towards him. Cold sweat prickled his skin. When he glanced at his arm, each prickle was a miniature hellhound, gnawing at his flesh. He scratched at them but there was only more. Now they were on his hands—

"Augum, what's wrong!" Bridget asked, but her voice sounded demonic. She wanted to kill him—

Then he wet his pants. They knew; they saw him wet his pants! There was Mya and she saw! It shows through clothing, just as it had when he was a boy ... and there was Dap, laughing, reaching back with that ham fist that multiplied into a thousand little fists ... and the Pendersons ... each had a whip, each raised it ... everything multiplied and grew and—

He screamed.

Then, in some remote corner of his mind, he realized it could not be real. He began fighting it, until ...

His eyes flew open. He was drooling, head splitting, but at least his pants were not wet; it had been an illusion all along. Burden's Edge was on the ground and Bridget and Leera were each gripping him by an elbow.

"Aug, are you all right?" Bridget asked, voice quivering.

He could only swallow and nod.

Rames cocked his head slightly. "Fear is quite an interesting spell, is it not? Different for everyone. For some, the horror is ... indescribable. I have even witnessed people pleading to be killed. It has to be one of my favorites." He lowered his chin. "But you did shake it off. Interesting. How about this one—think you can shake this one off?" He raised his arm. "Voidus lingua!"

Augum felt his mouth go dry and his throat constrict. He tried to speak, to shout, yet nothing came. Rames studied his struggles, habitually smoothing his hair.

"Ah, I thought not. She hasn't got you that far, has she? That was always a fault of hers ... slow as a snail. Your father will get you much, much further."

Augum did the only thing he could think of—he reached for Burden's Edge.

It slid away.

Rames wagged a finger. "Mustn't make it easy now. Surely you can do better than that. Has the crone not taught you *anything*?"

Augum, realizing what he meant, stretched out his arm and willed the sword to come to him.

It flew into his hand.

"Better," Rames said with a patronizing smile. "Untrained, misguided, but not entirely without promise. Nothing a little fatherly discipline couldn't solve. Now, that old crone placed a certain powerful protective enchantment around the castle that requires an invitation. I assume I do not have to make this difficult."

Augum glared at him.

"Oh, pardon my manners. You may speak again." Rames waved his hand idly and Augum felt his throat loosen.

"Invite me. Now."

"Never."

"This is not the time to be brave, boy." He gestured at Leera and she flew to him. He sharply yanked at her hair and she screamed, tears of pain welling from her eyes.

"Invite. NOW!"

"Don't ... Aug ..." Leera managed to gurgle.

"Too slow," Rames said, withdrawing a dagger. "Say your goodbyes—" he raised it to Leera's neck. She closed her eyes and yelped.

"Wait—!" Augum said, holding out an open palm. "All right, just let her go …"

Rames threw Leera back at him. Augum caught her in his arms.

"I'm so sorry," she mumbled into his chest, sniffing and shaking.

"It's all right," he whispered, placing her behind him.

"Hurry up or I'll slice both their pretty throats."

Augum gave Rames a hard look. "Damn you. I formally invite you, Vion Rames, into the castle."

Rames smiled wickedly. "A wise decision, though you hardly had much of a choice. I would have killed them both."

They heard the gallop of approaching horses. Rames raised his brows in a smug expression. "Time to end this little charade," he said. "And now I shall have justice for my pet." He raised his arm at Bridget and Leera.

"NO—!" Augum screamed, charging at Rames who, with a quick word, became enveloped in shimmering black armor— just in time to stop Burden's Edge from piercing his gut. Rames fixed Augum with a triumphant look before his eyes flitted right. A second thrust came, this one from Bridget. Rames simply stood there, mouth puckered in a grin, confident his arcane armor would stop a paltry dagger.

The small Dreadnought piercing blade punctured the shimmering armor as if it was butter, striking flesh beneath. The armor instantly vanished along with the lightning bands around Rames' arm. He roared, his hand shooting to the wound, while Bridget and Augum jumped clear.

Rames stared at the trio, his formerly electric eyes now glassy and black. Then without removing his gaze from Augum, he gripped the dagger, winced, and yanked it out. It dropped to the snow, staining it with blood.

Rames tried to straighten. He glared at them then abruptly stumbled and fell backwards. Augum immediately retrieved his sword while Leera lunged for the dagger, shouting, "Back inside!"

Bridget was already at the stone door, desperately trying to open it with her fingernails. The sound of horses was very close now.

Rames moaned behind them. His voice slurred as if he had been drinking. "My pets ... where are my pets ... hey now ... just where ... just where do you think you are going?" He raised his arm, revealing a robe slick with blood. For a moment, Augum was afraid he would cast another spell, but nothing happened. Rames gazed at his palm, a quizzical expression on his face.

Augum turned his attention to the door. "Let me try—"

Bridget got out of the way as he raised his palm. In his mind, he saw the door open wide—and with a grinding noise, it quickly did. The three then scrambled inside, Bridget first followed by Leera and Augum. The last thing Augum saw were shadows jumping down into the house—his foot made contact with a snapping snout. There was no time to even close the door.

The trio scuttled like rats from a fire. It was pitch-black and dirt flew into Augum's eyes and mouth, yet he did not care; his only thought now was to reach the castle and raise the alarm. Something entered the passage behind, growling. The hairs on the back of his neck stood on end. He thought of Burden's Edge but it would be impossible to draw it in such a cramped space.

A green light flared to life ahead joined by a watery blue one—Bridget and Leera had made it out. At last, it was his turn to squeeze through the opening. He slammed the stone door on a furry head with red eyes. It yelped then resumed snapping its jaws. He kicked it back through the opening, slammed the door again, and bolted after the girls, who were calling for him to hurry.

Upon reaching the wine cellar door, a tremendous crumbling noise began from the tunnel, as if something very big was trying to squeeze through. Meanwhile, there was a crash and a growl inside the room.

Augum spun around. "Shyneo!" At the edge of his light padded a hellhound. It stopped and began squealing like a wounded animal, gurgling and vomiting.

The trio screamed as the pile of guts it puked out started growing into another hellhound.

"RUN—!" he yelled, pushing them to go. As soon as they were clear of the room though, he had a better idea. He turned around, raised his palm, and slammed the door shut with Telekinesis—just in time to hear two bangs from the other side.

"Won't be able to hold it long; get Mrs. Stone!" He refocused on the door.

"I'm staying, Bridge, you go!" Leera said, handing Bridget her dagger back. "GO!"

Bridget ran off while he concentrated on keeping the door shut. Every time the hellhounds slammed into it, he felt his telekinetic grip weaken. Leera was soon beside him, arm raised, sharp brows crossed with concentration.

They managed to keep the door closed for the time being, but Augum knew it could not last. Besides, something much bigger was on the way. Another idea came to him.

"Keep holding it," he said, breaking his connection and drawing his sword. He ran up beside the door. "Shyneo!" His hand crackled to life as he raised the Dreadnought blade over his head. "Ready? NOW!"

Leera dived out of the way. The door careened open and one of the beasts lunged through—only to be sliced in half in midair, the two parts flopping to the ground, dead.

"Watch for the second one, Aug!"

The other hound slunk forward through the doorway, baring black teeth and growling. Augum backed up, Burden's

Edge before him, its length glistening. Leera was just behind, edging along, one hand on his back, the other lit with glowing water.

"Steady, Aug ... keep backing up ... steady now ... almost at the stairs ..."

When they reached the steps, harsh voices began yelling from the wine cellar. Augum, however, kept his gaze locked with the remaining hellhound. The beast was at some sort of stalemate with him; it did not lunge as long as he kept his eyes on it, blade interposed between, the blood of its kin dripping from the edge.

Just as they reached the top of the stairs, they heard the sound of running from the servant hallway.

"Get ready to jump out of the way," Leera whispered into his ear. "Steady ... steady ... and ... NOW!"

Augum jumped back and away just as Sir Gallows hurled himself at the hellhound. Because Augum kept his eyes locked with the beast's, the hellhound was too late in reacting to Gallows' sword slash. Gutted, it squealed while flopping down the stairs, stopping in a silent heap at the bottom.

"More coming—" Augum blurted to Gallows while helping Leera up. "The Nightsword—traitor—"

Gallows fixed him with a grave look. His eyes were shiny with ale. "Stop jabbering, son. Upstairs and double-quick. I shall hold them off."

Augum wanted to explain but a gargantuan crimson-armored Red Guard appeared at the bottom the stairs, stepping over the hellhound without breaking its gaze. It held a flaming sword in one hand and a shield with the Legion emblem in the other. As it climbed, it stared at Augum through two horizontal slits piercing a flat helm. A prickle went up Augum's spine as he sat transfixed, unable to decide what to do. In fact, he felt possessed by hesitation.

"What are you waiting for, boy—run!"

Leera grabbed Augum's arm and pulled him through the doorway. "What are you doing, come on!"

Breaking eye contact with the Red Guard seemed to do the trick. He ran, leaving Sir Gallows behind. When they reached the foyer, moonlight filtered in through open doors. A cold draft sent a shiver through him, but there was no time to wonder why the castle was sitting open and exposed like that. They bolted up the marble stairs and almost crashed into Sir Edrian Castor and the two Brack brothers, who smelled strongly of ale, their faces anxious.

"Sir Gallows needs help below—" Leera said in a panicked voice.

"Just get to the top!" Castor said, skipping a few steps at a time with each stride.

"Damn it, they're all drunk," Leera said, watching one of the brothers stumble.

They continued racing upstairs. As they passed the third floor, Augum noted Fentwick's absence. Suddenly the door from the girls' room opened and Bridget emerged, slinging a rucksack over her shoulder.

"Bridge—? What are you doing here?" Leera asked.

"Oh thank—you're okay! I grabbed the book, just in case we leave the castle—"

"Have you seen Mrs. Stone?"

"I think she went outside—the Legion have the castle surrounded."

Frantic shouts rang up from below.

Bridget ran to the banister. "They're all waiting upstairs, come on—"

The trio made their way to the fifth floor where they stopped dead in their tracks. There at the top of the stairs stood the Nightsword and Sir Dollard Canes, their swords drawn. The Nightsword was still obviously drunk; he wavered and looked very pale. Sir Canes, however, appeared ready for battle, his curly hair bouncing. He gave Augum a surprised look upon seeing him, then stepped aside, gesturing to the prince's room.

Augum hesitated. Should he say something now? If he told Canes the Nightsword was a traitor, would he believe him in time to react?

The Nightsword adjusted the grip on his sword. Augum recalled how the man had expertly brandished Burden's Edge earlier.

"Go on then," The Nightsword croaked. "They're waiting for you."

The trio slunk by, Augum trying to use his eyes to communicate what he had learned to Canes. Canes' face changed and he seemed to give the slightest nod; but did he really understand? Augum judged it too risky to do anything else, not without more men at least.

They brushed past Fentwick, who stood guard outside the prince's room ("Wouldst thou fancy a duel—") and entered, finding a crowd of surprised faces framed in moonlight. A hastily dressed Prince Sydo stood holding his royal sword, looking too small for it. Lord Boron stood beside him, dabbing his brow with a cloth. Gertrude Grinds stood stiff as a board, frowning. More than a few loose hairs poked out from her bun. Beside her, Rafinda stood holding young Mandy in comfort. Lastly, there was Mya, who still looked as delicate and soft as a spring flower. Her almond eyes registered fear when they first entered, then relief. Augum had the overwhelming urge to go to her and say something kind and brave and—

"Where have you been—?" Ms. Grinds barked. "We have been searching all over for you—"

Augum did not know how to reply, nor did he want to tell them that he and the girls were responsible for the castle being breached. "Where's Mrs. Stone?" he asked instead.

"Why, I imagine she is outside defending the castle from the Legion."

Augum's eyes instinctively went to the window, but it was no good—an outer balcony blocked the view.

"Is … is Sparkstone out there?" He did not want to call him *Father*.

"And just how am I supposed to know *that*, child?"

Suddenly there was a commotion in the hallway. Everybody fell silent as the trio backed away from the door, Augum distinctly aware of his proximity to Mya. Had Canes made a move? Had the Nightsword?

From the other side came the sound of a gasp, then shuffling footsteps. Fentwick began to speak when the door flew open, revealing the Nightsword, face as pale as death.

This is it, he's come for us, Augum thought, raising his blade.

The Nightsword opened his mouth to speak but only blood poured out. Suddenly a wet black claw ejected from his belly. People screamed as Augum realized it was a sword. The Nightsword looked down as the blade twisted and removed itself. He gave them a stunned look, staggered, and fell forward.

Sir Dollard Canes stood in the doorway, a wild and victorious look on his face.

"Sir Canes—!" Lord Boron said. "But … what have you done!"

Canes examined his sword as if for the first time. "I do believe I have slain the famous Nightsword …"

"What is the meaning of this?" Sydo asked. "Canes—explain yourself!"

"It is *Sir Canes* to you, you little brat."

"How dare—"

"Silence—!" Canes held up a hand as he took a deep breath, eyes closed. When he opened them, they were trained on the prince. "Oh, how liberating it is to speak freely again. I have spent years pretending to be you and your father's lackey."

"You—*you're* the traitor?" Augum asked.

"The Lord of the Legion promises eternity to those deserving. Yes, I am the one who sent word of our location, and yes, I am the one that opened the doors for his hellhounds when a certain opportunity arose." His eyes fell upon Bridget, who swallowed hard.

"But your royal oath ..." the prince said in a whiny voice.

Canes laughed. "My royal oath ... I look forward to cracking your skull, you little damn—"

"Sir! Have you no shame?" Lord Boron asked, brow quivering.

Canes laughed harder. "Shame ... oh, dear me, shame ... *you* speak to me of shame, you cowardly hog."

Lord Boron's face reddened but he fell silent.

"How did they get in?" Grinds asked. "This castle was supposed to be protected by ... by magic!"

"It's *arcane*, you old wench. You should know that, even if you're as *ordinary* as I am. Yes, the crone was wise enough to restrict just who had the ability to invite strangers beyond her arcane boundary. As far as I understood it, only these three had that privilege." He nodded at the trio.

Augum felt his stomach drop to his foot. He heard Leera swallow beside him.

"That ambush on the way to this castle," Sydo said, "it has always seemed suspicious to me. You had something to do with it, did you not?"

"Indeed I had. I arranged for that little surprise as a convenient way of thinning the ranks. It was unfortunate I received an arrow wound, but I suppose it only helped conceal me. I really have you to thank though, my half-wit spoiled brat of a prince. You allowed me to report on your position all along, as well as the position of your allies. For that, you have my gratitude. As for your drunken allies, I assure you they will have all been wiped out by now."

"You traitorous dog, I shall have your head on a spike!"

Canes' eyes flashed as they drew upon the prince. "I have been waiting to carve that flesh of yours a long, long time, *Your Highness* ..." He raised his sword and took a step forward into the room.

"Fentwick, defend us from Sir Dollard Canes!" Bridget called.

Canes immediately received a thump from behind. He spun to face the enchanted suit of armor.

"Hark, knave, villain, foe!" Fentwick screeched. "Hark, for thou shalt lament thy deceitful ways!"

Augum was about to rush forward to help when he heard growling from the hallway. He raised his palm and arcanely slammed the door shut instead, cutting Fentwick and Canes off. Lord Boron, the prince and Gertrude Grinds ran over to hold it closed while Mandy whimpered in Rafinda's arms.

"Aug, over here!" Leera said amidst the chaos. She and Mya were kneeling over the floor in the corner of the room. "It's camouflaged!"

He rushed over and instantly knew what she had found—a secret hatch to an emergency escape room.

"Help me open it," Leera said. Groping about, the three of them managed to find the handle and pulled—only to have it snap clean off. They resorted to using their fingernails, but the weight of the door was too great.

"Bridge, your dagger—" Augum said over his shoulder.

Bridget drew her dagger and jammed it between the hatch and the floor. Then, using it like a wedge, lifted it just enough for them to grab hold.

"Get in!" Augum said, waving to the confused throng. Rafinda and Mandy were the first to run over, Mandy in such a crying panic she had to be helped down. Augum gestured for Bridget, Leera and Mya to go next. Lastly, he called out to Sydo and Ms. Grinds, hoping that Lord Boron could hold the door long enough for them to get down.

336

Suddenly something huge began slamming against the door. It was then Augum knew Fentwick had fallen; his heart gave a sharp pang.

With each thrust, Boron, Grinds and Sydo were sent flying back. The moment Sydo noticed the hatch, however, he abandoned the defense and scrambled down the shaft without a backward glance.

"Ms. Grinds, hurry!" Augum shouted.

"Liberai!" Bridget yelled below.

"It didn't work!" Leera said. "Try another one!"

"Do something you filthy peasant wenches!"

An even louder bang from the door drew Augum's attention.

"Go ahead, Gertrude, I think I can hold it—" Lord Boron said.

Ms. Grinds gave him a knowing look before she raced to the escape hatch. She began climbing down then spied Augum. "You too, child—come!"

"But what about Lord Bor—"

"—there's no time!" and she made a grab for him just as the door exploded. Augum covered his face to protect from flying splinters. When he looked again, Ms. Grinds was gone and Lord Boron lay still, face bloody and eyes open. Giant crimson warriors with burning swords entered the room, stepping over his body with great armored boots.

One reached out to Augum. He dodged and fell straight down the hatch. On the way, his left arm caught on the lip. He felt a sickening crack just before slamming into the ground on his side. The world shrunk to the size of an apple.

A female voice called out his name as the blur of a burning sword appeared above. "Liberai!" another voice shouted.

A vicious wind kicked up as a hand grabbed him. There was a hissing noise and a woman screamed. Someone thrashed nearby before falling still. He could not see through the blinding pain, the fire, the heat …

Another hand grabbed him, this one far stronger. There was a brief struggle between the two grips, one steel and one desperate but soft, until something ripped. His stomach rammed his throat as he fell into darkness.

ARINTHIAN

When Augum came to, he was lying face down in a thick layer of dust. It was pitch-black, his head throbbed, and there was a sharp pain in his left arm. He winced struggling to sit up. Something moved nearby.

"Who's there—?" he whispered.

"Shyneo," said a quiet voice. Leera's frightened face lit up in a weak glow. "Augum, is that you—?"

"Yeah."

"Oh, I'm so glad—I thought for sure they had you. Wait, you're hurt—"

He glanced at his limp arm, the sleeve of the robe almost shorn off. "I'm all right," he lied. Even looking at his arm, bent awkwardly like that, made him feel light-headed. The pressure and the jagged pain increased with every movement. He had to look away, peering about at what appeared to be a forest of large stone blocks.

"Where are we? Where are the others?" he asked.

"Don't know. I panicked; must have taken the wrong portal. A Red Guard jumped down and ... and ... Oh, Augum ... it killed Ms. Grinds ... and ... and then it grabbed you ... I didn't have time ... it was all I could—" She began sobbing. "This is all my fault ... if I'd only grabbed Rames' blade or something."

"No, no it's not. We had no choice. *You* had no choice." He cradled her with his good arm. She sniffed into his torn robe. "It's okay," he said soothingly. "Come on, we have to get out of here ..."

He grit his teeth as they helped each other stand. "Shyneo," he said, but the grinding pressure pain in his arm made it near impossible to concentrate; his palm refused to light. He took a closer look at the stones, noticing words carved into them. He felt a slow chill creep up his spine. "I think we're in the crypt," he whispered.

A hand shot to Leera's mouth as she froze, eyes flitting. They listened to the darkness—complete silence, as if they were in some deep cave.

She padded to a tombstone and read the inscription. " 'Tredius Arinthian ... died in combat against Edius the Great on the seventh day of the twelfth month in the 2381st year.' Augum—that's almost a thousand years ago!"

"Arinthian ... does that name sound familiar to you?"

"It does now that you mention it, but I can't remember from where ... I bet Bridget would know. Oh, Aug, I hope she's okay—"

"Me too ..."

They moved past a few more tombstones, reading them as they walked. They came in all kinds of shapes and sizes—pillars, obelisks, stone coffins and vaults. All were highly ornate and all bore the last name *Arinthian*.

They stumbled around in the dark for a while, trying to find a way out. The chamber was so vast they had yet to see a wall, though they did come across massive support columns not unlike the ones in the cellar.

Suddenly they heard wind somewhere behind them, followed by a dull thud. Leera immediately extinguished her palm and the pair froze, listening. Coughing mixed with a loud growl reverberated amongst the tombs. The cavern dispersed the sound in a strange way, making it difficult to locate exactly where it came from.

"You might as well come to me or I'll send my pet along!" Rames called, spitting with a moan. "I know you can hear me. Surrender to me now and I promise to spare her life, Augum."

"Let's run," Leera whispered, grabbing his good arm. "Maybe we can find a way out—"

"Just wait." It was difficult to think with the pain. "The hellhound will jump us from behind if we run. Let's climb one of the tombs. I'll kill it with Burden's Edge before it can get us, then at least we stand a chance against him. After all, he's injured."

She took a moment to think about it while Rames kept calling for them. "All right, but we better hurry ..."

They quietly felt around until they found a stone coffin that was the right height. They clambered on top, no easy task with a broken arm. Then they watched and waited. In the distance, about fifteen rows away, a blue light advanced in their direction, casting dagger-like shadows across the rough ceiling.

Kneeling on top of someone's grave made Augum distinctly aware of his father's pursuit of necromancy. He hoped the dead stayed dead and tried to avoid looking into the dark abyss that seemed to stretch in all directions. Suddenly he realized something.

"Leera—take my sword," he whispered. "Take it, I've only got one good arm, and you're better than me anyway."

"Oh, um, all right ..." She took the blade, her hand shaking as much as his. Augum wanted to say something brave and final, something true, but Rames was too close. He sounded like he was limping.

"You smell something girl?" Rames said only a few rows away. "Yes, they're near, aren't they?"

The hellhound growled.

Augum could almost see Rames licking his lips in satisfaction. He braced himself, Leera tensing beside him, their breathing quick and shallow now. Suddenly there was the rapid sound of four running feet even though Rames' light was still a row away.

The moment had come.

One day, you may have to perform such a spell in the din of battle, with plenty to distract you, he remembered Mrs. Stone saying. He ignored the needling pain in his arm and focused.

"SHYNEO!"

His hand lit up the jaws of a hellhound lunging right at him. He barely had enough time to raise his arm in defense when he heard the neat slice of Burden's Edge. Blood splattered on his cheek as the hellhound yelped and tumbled to the ground. There was no time to dwell on what happened as Rames' lightning palm appeared from around a pillar.

Without thinking, Augum leapt into the air, shouting some kind of garbled war cry. Rames caught him like a sack of spuds.

Augum, desperate to hold on, did the only thing he could think of—he used his electrified palm to find the wound Blackbite made earlier, and concentrated on shocking the man. Rames shook and screamed, stumbling about as if blind and on fire. He slammed Augum into a massive mausoleum. Augum cried out in pain and let go, falling to the ground, hand extinguishing.

Rames stood over him, huffing. "Vicious little brat—" He raised his palm and opened his mouth to cast a spell when a claw suddenly pierced his chest. For a brief moment, Augum saw the Nightsword before him, impaled in the same way.

Gurgling blood, Rames gave Augum an incredulous look before falling sideways through the doorway of the mausoleum. In his place stood a panting Leera, hand outstretched in midair as if she still held the sword that lay buried in Rames' back.

"Thought I was done for," Augum said, eyeing the blood on her hands. "You all right?"

Leera just stared at him a moment. "I just … I just killed someone."

"And you saved our lives doing it."

She stood frozen like that until seeing his arm; she snapped out of it and offered him a hand. "And you, you all right?"

Wincing, he let her drag him to his feet. "I think so …"

The pair just stood there, staring at the body. Augum squeezed Leera's shoulder. Before he knew it, she was in his arms, giving a tight hug, shaking like a spring leaf.

"It's all right," he whispered. "Come on." He let her go and stepped over the body into the mausoleum, where he pulled Burden's Edge from Rames' back and wiped the blade clean.

Leera still stared at the body.

"Lee?"

"Mmm?"

"You going to be all right?"

"Mmm."

"You sure?"

She glanced at him with those dark eyes. "I never killed someone before …"

"Let's hope you never have to again."

She nodded and took a deep breath before looking up. "Hey—look what's on the front of this place."

He stepped back outside and craned his neck. On the front of the mausoleum was a giant letter "A", identical to the many they saw throughout the castle.

"Let's explore it quickly," he said, and the two went back inside.

"This place is amazing," Leera whispered upon spying the ornately gilded ceiling. "Must have been someone important; and look here, there are portals." She gestured at a series of engravings on the walls, but Augum's attention was elsewhere. A large stone plaque rested above a golden sarcophagus at the end of the room. Above the plaque, gilded in bronze, was the same intricate letter "A". Augum solemnly read the inscription aloud.

Here lieth Atrius Arinthian
Borneth thy second day of thy second month in thy 1513th year

Husband to Atreya Sinthius Arinthian
Father of seven
Builder of herein Castle Arinthian
Master of thee element of lightning
First possessor of thee lightning scion
Slayer of Occulus thee Necromancer and proclaimed King of Solia in reward

Besought to renounce Sithesia for thee Ley in his 71st year
Built thy first portal to thee realm of thee Ley within these here castle walls
Chose to be the last man to lay eyes upon a living Dreadnought
Died a natural death on thy fifth day in the eighth month of thy 1849th year, aged 336
Passed in peace surrounded by thee beloved

"Thus I bequeath, with love fulfilled."
— A

"Augum, he's—"

"I know, I remember now," he said quietly, fingers tracing the raised lettering.

"That means this is Castle Arinthian—"

"—the castle of my great ancestor, yes. You know what the strangest part is?"

"What?"

"He shares my birthday."

"You were born on the same day—?"

"Yes, second day of the second month, just 1813 years later, if my arithmetic is correct." Sir Westwood always stressed how important arithmetic was.

"I just got goose bumps," Leera said. "What do you think it means that you two have the same birthday?"

"I have no idea."

After a thoughtful pause, she added, "Must have been hard …"

"You mean living back then?"

"No, I mean, watching his loving wife age and pass on …"

Augum nodded, a strange ache in his heart. They stood in respectful silence for a little while.

"This part is interesting," Leera said, pointing. " 'Built thy first portal to thee realm of thee Ley within these here castle walls.' "

"So Ley isn't just legend after all … It must be the portal Mrs. Stone and Sir Gallows were talking about. Where do you think it is?"

They searched each other's eyes.

"The note you found under the bed, what did it say again?"

He quickly dug it out of his robe. They read one particular section together.

" 'We tried everything known on the fountain, yet still it refused to yield.' "

They locked eyes before chorusing, "The fountain!"

"Of course!" Leera said. "That's what Narsus had been after—the entrance to the land of the Ley! The statue of the peaceful-looking man was a clue—the fountain *is* the portal!"

"We have to get there," he said, stuffing the note into his torn robe. "Mrs. Stone warned Sir Gallows they might have to use it if the castle was infiltrated."

"They just better not have left without us—"

They rushed over to the etchings.

"Shyneo," Leera said, lighting her palm and placing it over the oval with the fountain. "Liberai!"

A black hole appeared in the wall with a sizzle, instantly blowing wind from its gaping maw.

She waved. "You go first!"

Augum jumped. He felt his body stretch as if being pulled apart by teams of oxen. The portal spit him out onto a mossy path, nauseous and dizzy, arm throbbing. Leera landed beside him and the portal collapsed with a sucking sound. Leaves and branches calmed as the wind died away. Then there was silence, except for the quiet trickle of water.

"Did we take the wrong portal?" he whispered, pushing a thorny flower from his face.

"It's the arcane forest room."

"Oh, right."

"Shyneo." Leera's palm lit up.

"Who's there—?" said a voice from the dark.

"That you, Bridge?" Leera asked.

A dim green light flared up a short distance away. A moment later Bridget emerged, smiling broadly. Leera instantly shot forward and the two friends embraced.

"Thought for sure they got you," Bridget said, giving Augum a hug as well. He winced from the grinding pain.

Leera gently grabbed Bridget. "Careful of his arm, we think it's broken."

A deep look of concern passed over Bridget's face.

"I'm fine," he said. "Where is everybody anyway?"

Bridget nodded at the path. "They're hiding by the fountain. The portal to outside didn't work, so I opened the one next to it and ended up here. Thought you would have come much sooner. Where are Lord Boron and Ms. Grinds?"

Augum exchanged a look with Leera. "They … they didn't make it."

Bridget stiffened. "Oh. I see." She glanced at his arm and at the various bloodstains on them both. "Come have a drink of water. The others are anxious to see you're okay."

The trio made their way to the fountain where the prince, Rafinda, Mandy and Mya huddled together, looking like refugees from a tornado. After a brief welcome, Augum and Leera drank fountain water, splashed it on their cuts, and sat down, quietly recounting what happened to them while they healed. Unfortunately, the fountain did not fix broken bones.

Prince Sydo put on a brave face when they finished, though his voice cracked as he spoke. "So Lord Boron managed to get himself killed, did he?"

They averted their eyes. It was the first time Augum recalled the prince using the man's proper title.

"Poor Ms. Grinds," Mya said quietly. "She was a decent woman."

"A portal to the land of the Ley …" the blonde-haired Rafinda whispered. "How do we activate it?"

"I think Mrs. Stone knows how," Leera said.

"Why did you let them in?" Sydo blurted, pointing at the trio. "I hold you fully responsible for the death of my royal minder and my royal guard!"

"I told you, Your Highness, we didn't have a choice," Bridget said. "You would know that if you had been there."

"You speak with respect when you address me, peasant! You should have sacrificed yourselves for me! Your gutterborn lives have no purpose other than that! I am heir to the kingdom!"

"I'm too tired to argue with you," Bridget said in a resigned voice, "and that is a very hurtful thing to say."

Augum and Leera were about to jump in on her behalf when Mya spoke.

"Your Royal Highness, *please* … now is not the time."

Sydo looked like he was going to say something else, but he made a rude dismissive gesture and crossed his arms.

"Here, let me fix that for you," Leera said quietly, splaying her palms over Augum's torn sleeve. "Apreyo." They watched as the sleeve reattached itself, the fibers re-weaving and reconnecting. "There, good as new."

"Thank you."

Bridget smiled warmly. "She fusses over you like an old hen."

"Somebody has to," Leera said.

Sydo only snorted.

"We should extinguish our lights," Bridget said after a time, snuffing hers first. "Someone could walk in on us."

Leera extinguished hers too, drenching them in darkness.

"Does the crone even know where we are?" Sydo asked. When no one replied, he added, "One of you ought to search for her."

"That's far too dangerous," Bridget said. "We simply have to sit and wait. She'll come here, it's where the portal is."

"Lazy peasants …"

The castle suddenly shuddered from a series of distant muffled explosions. The group stirred.

"The castle defenses," Augum whispered, hoping he was correct. He remembered them described as "fearsome to behold" in that burned note. The castle had to be swarming with the Legion by now. It was just a matter of time before someone discovered them. The questions was, who?

He took another sip of cool fountain water and waited, listening to the distant cacophony.

A MOMENT TOO LATE

The noise subsided and for a long stretch of time, the only sound was the trickle of the fountain. Augum's exhaustion, the dull pain in his arm, and the pitch-dark all combined to make him deliriously drowsy, so much so that when he heard the squeak of rusty hinges, he believed himself back in Mrs. Stone's cave.

"We 'aven't checked this room yet, Sir," a reedy voice said from the darkness.

Augum froze—that voice did not belong!

"Give me your torch, O'Donnell," said a second voice.

"Oy then—what is this, some kind o' strange magic forest?"

"Why hasn't Commander Rames come back?"

"I don't know, Sir. He is disappeared, he is."

"Follow me."

Augum recognized the voices now—the first was the man that tended to Rames' horse, and the second was the traitor, Sir Dollard Canes.

Torchlight flickered as it fought its way through thick brush. Augum quietly drew Burden's Edge. Just as he was contemplating retreat, the door behind them opened and more torches appeared, moving quickly.

They were trapped.

The faster moving men appeared first. His throat went dry when he saw a dozen crimson-armored warriors—those were not torches he saw, but the burning swords of the Red Guard!

"Kill them all except this boy here!" said a manic voice. Augum turned to find Canes pointing a stubby finger in his face. More Red Guards stood behind the man.

"No—" Augum said, Burden's Edge limp in his hands.

Screams tore the air. He turned back to witness the Red Guardsman at the head of the line raise its burning blade and make a rasping sound. A nauseating stench filled Augum's nostrils that made his stomach spasm.

Those things were walking corpses! The realization made his blood run cold.

Augum's broken arm exploded in pain as Canes grabbed it from behind. He struggled to break free but the man was too strong, forcing him to drop Burden's Edge. Augum could only watch as a burning sword came whistling down on Mandy, the shy servant girl. She instantly fell silent, slumping to the ground.

"NO—STOP!" He thrashed in the vice-like grip.

Bridget and Leera dove to protect the girl from further strikes while Sydo scrambled to get away, pushing Mya forward in his attempt. She only wept, seemingly resigned to die.

The flaming blade rose and swooped down again, this time on the blonde servant girl, Rafinda. She too went silent.

Augum now knew madness; he flailed wildly. Suddenly one of Canes' giant hands grabbed his head and forced it to look at a Red Guard. He immediately went limp, transfixed by dark horizontal slits. He was aware of a burning sword rising into the air. Dimly, he knew Mya was next; the pretty girl with the almond-shaped eyes and that radiant smile ... He wanted to do something, but could not quite make up his mind what. A heavy feeling settled over him. It was over, she was as good as dead, then it would be Bridget and Leera ...

Time slowed to a stomach-churning crawl. Let it just end, he thought, please just let it end ...

Yet the sword did not come down for a third blow. It simply hung there, blazing quietly above Mya, who stared vacantly at Rafinda and Mandy's bodies. Strangely, the red guardsman did not move either. In fact, nothing moved—everything had become still and silent.

Was he dreaming?

Someone else entered the room, approaching from behind the column of Red Guards, someone with a bluish arm. The crimson warriors did nothing to prevent the figure from strolling past them.

"Unnameable gods, the Lord of the Legion ..." Canes whispered. "I have your son here, Great Lord!"

Augum's stomach plunged ... his father had come.

"I am honored, my lord, I was just about to—" but the words died on Canes' lips.

"I suggest you let go of my great-grandson," Mrs. Stone said, emerging from behind the foremost Red Guard, her arm a solid crackling sleeve. She stood erect, eyes smoldering.

Augum's hopes surged until he felt the touch of cold steel against his neck.

"Stay back, crone, or I'll slice his neck—" Canes tried to retreat but bumped into something.

Mrs. Stone stopped underneath the suspended burning sword, which hung over her like a flaming guillotine.

Sydo crawled to her feet, whimpering. "Save me—I am the heir!"

Mya realized who had arrived and joined Bridget and Leera in huddling over the bodies of Rafinda and Mandy, even though they were plainly beyond saving.

Mrs. Stone's steel gaze was fixed solely upon Canes. "You were the one."

"My allegiance has always been elsewhere."

She extinguished her arm and placed her hands behind her back. "What is it you think Lividius wants?"

Canes' beefy arm began to sweat. "Isn't it obvious?"

"Do enlighten me."

"The boy, the scion, and the portal."

"Ah, so he knows about the portal. I seem to have underestimated my grandson once again."

"Lord Sparkstone is more powerful than you can imagine. He found a second scion, and will soon find more. He will destroy you." Augum held his breath as the knife pressed in a little.

Mrs. Stone's face remained placid. "And it was you that brought the Legion here?"

"I proudly say yes. My reward shall be great."

"I see."

"The Lord of the Legion will come any moment now—"

"I do not think so, not any *moment* that is. I activated the castle's ancient defenses. I also found that little hole in the cellar and plugged it. I have frustrated Lividius' efforts to gain entry, and by the time he does find a way in, we shall already be gone."

Canes' breath quickened.

"And you need not bother threatening my great-grandson. We both know Lividius wants him alive. Besides, I have no intention of killing you today."

"You … you don't?"

"No. Allow me to demonstrate," and without blinking or making any apparent gesture, Canes' arms folded back and away. He cried out in pain as the knife dropped to the ground. Augum immediately escaped to stand with the others, where he watched as Canes' arms slowly went to his own neck.

"No, what are you—" His eyes widened suddenly as his hands began to squeeze. His face turned purple and the veins on his forehead popped out. "But ... you ... said ..."

Mrs. Stone raised her chin slightly and he fell to the ground, coughing.

"You are unworthy of what I offer," she said in a cool voice. "Your life in exchange for a message and a sacred vow. What say you?"

Canes stood up, still gasping, rubbing his throat. "I accept ... Mercy, I accept ..."

Her eyes narrowed slightly. "Leave the castle and inform Lividius that the hole in his heart cannot be filled with what he seeks."

He nodded. "I will do as you ask. And the vow?"

"Vow that you shall never use the title 'Sir' again. Henceforth, you shall be known as a Knight of Disgrace."

Canes blanched. "I ... I ..."

Mrs. Stone cocked her head slightly.

He hurriedly raised an arm in defense, the other still on his neck. "All right, all right! I swear I shall never use the knightly title of 'Sir' again. I shall henceforth be known as ... as a Knight of Disgrace ... a fallen knight."

"So be it, you have sworn your last knightly oath. You are henceforth a Knight of Disgrace. You may now leave; I grant you safe passage through the castle. And take your sidekick with you." She flicked her wrist and the one called O'Donnell unfroze with a start, took one look at her, and scurried away. Canes stood only a moment longer before he too turned and fled.

Sydo stood up and turned on Mrs. Stone. "Why did you let him go? He deserved nothing short of death!"

"Death comes to us all, young prince. Killing does not right wrongs, something your father understood well."

"Even my father had an executioner!"

"Ah, but his axe was rusty."

"And none of this would have happened if it was not for them!" Sydo pointed at the trio.

"Mrs. Stone," Leera began, voice trembling a little. "It was my fault the Legion got in. We went exploring through the tunnel—"

"—and my fault too, Mrs. Stone," Augum added. "If I hadn't—"

Mrs. Stone held up a hand silencing them. "Lividius planned a major attack using his scion to gain entry. It would have succeeded with far greater consequences had you not forced them to undertake it early. I consider us lucky."

Augum shared a look with Leera; they needed to tell Mrs. Stone about her former apprentice, though he feared what she might say. "Mrs. Stone … I … we … we killed Vion Rames defending ourselves."

She stared at them a moment. "So be it. Many have died today. We shall hold a memorial ceremony to honor them on the other side."

"Other side—?" Bridget asked.

"Yes, we are travelling to the land of the Ley, where we shall continue your training."

"What about all these … things?" Augum asked, pointing to the paralyzed Red Guards.

"Ah yes, Lividius' death knights." She raised her arm, flaring it into a sleeve of crackling blue light. The space around her warped and electrified, making the hairs on the back of Augum's neck stand on end. She opened her palm and an enormous bolt of lightning shot forth, plowing through the column ahead. Every death knight in the line vaporized in a sizzle of electricity, the charred crimson armor falling as empty husks. She did the same to the other column. When she finished, the air was filled with acrid smoke.

The cool darkness lasted only a moment, until Mrs. Stone cast her familiar floating globe, bathing them in blue light. She then shuffled over to Mya, who lay by Mandy and Rafinda, and placed a veined hand on her shoulder.

"Come, child, there is nothing more to be done."

Mya did not move. Mrs. Stone looked to Bridget and Leera. The two gently helped Mya move along with quiet words, leaving Mrs. Stone to stand over the bodies of the slain servant girls, face grooved with weariness.

Tears rolled down Mya's porcelain cheeks. "I shall miss you so much, my special girls ..."

Bridget and Leera gently hugged her. Augum rested a hand on her delicate shoulder and gave it the lightest squeeze.

"Let them rest in peace," Mrs. Stone said, making a graceful gesture. A pile of earth moved near the fountain, making two shallow graves. Mandy's body rose into the air and into one hole, Rafinda the other. With another gesture, the earth pulled itself over them, leaving gentle mounds.

A period of silence followed in which no one moved or spoke.

Augum, lost to his thoughts, finally became aware of Mrs. Stone arcanely healing his broken arm. She then healed everyone else's cuts and bruises. He noticed they looked to her differently now, as if she was their great-grandmother as well—except Sydo, who only wore a resentful expression on his face.

Mrs. Stone stood apart and faced them. "Before we go, there is one final task to attend to. Bridget, please come here."

Bridget gave Augum an uncertain look as she stepped forward. Mrs. Stone straightened to her full height and fixed her with a stern gaze.

"In accordance with the ancient tradition of the Founding, I, Anna Atticus Stone, having achieved mastery in the element of lightning, before these witnesses—"

Augum tensed. Could it be—?

"—hereby bestow upon you, Bridget Burns, daughter of Henry and Annette Burns, the 1st arcane degree." She raised her arm, which now shone fiercely, and touched Bridget's wrist. With an electric crackle, Mrs. Stone's arm dimmed and extinguished, channeling its light to Bridget's wrist and spiraling around it, before settling to a glowing ivy ring.

"My first stripe," Bridget whispered, inspecting her wrist. Everybody but Sydo quietly hugged and congratulated her.

"I hope you will forgive such a tranquil affair, usually this kind of event warrants a few days' celebration, but under the circumstances …"

"Oh, Mrs. Stone, of course we understand!" Bridget said. "And … thank you."

"Well earned and well done." She turned her gaze to Leera. "Please come here, child."

Leera's mouth hung open as she stepped forward. Mrs. Stone repeated the ceremony with her, naming Matilda and Oscar Jones as her parents. Leera's own arm ring was light-blue in color and shimmered like tropical water. She too received muted congratulations and hugs. Her and Bridget's eyes were moist. Augum realized they probably wished their parents were here to see them earn their very 1st degree.

Mrs. Stone stiffened and raised her chin, fixing Augum with a stern look. "Step forward, great-grandson."

He swallowed and stepped before his great-grandmother.

"In accordance with the ancient tradition of the founding, I, Anna Atticus Stone, having achieved mastery in the element of lightning, before these witnesses, hereby bestow upon you, Augum Stone, son of Lividius and Terra Titan Stone, the 1st arcane degree."

And with those words, Augum earned his first stripe, a band of lightning that crackled around his wrist. He received hugs and congratulations from the girls. Mya even gave him a teary-eyed kiss on the cheek.

Mrs. Stone let them enjoy a celebratory moment together before she cleared her throat, drawing their attention.

"The time has come to depart. I am about to summon the scion and open the portal to Ley. Once I do, the castle defenses shall cease to function. You will step through one at a time, taking your cue from me. Do I make myself clear?"

"Yes, Mrs. Stone," everyone chorused.

Mrs. Stone nodded, spread her palm, and closed her eyes. Her arm again flared into a solid electric sleeve. A moment later, the castle shook and there was a blinding flash. When Augum opened his eyes, a small crystal orb floated before them. The scion clouded with a silent storm that flashed soundless lightning. A quiet hum emanated from it though, as if a bee was trapped inside.

Mrs. Stone let it hang in the air before grasping it, turning her attention to the fountain. "Now, old friend, I ask you to open yourself to me, Anna Atticus Stone, descendant of Atrius Arinthian, possessor of the lightning scion, your one and only key."

With those words, the peaceful-looking bald figure on the fountain bowed and drew an oval in the air, which quickly enlarged to form a portal of blinding white light. Despite Augum shutting his eyes, the light seemed to penetrate his very being. Thankfully, unlike other portals, there was no wind, only a distant echo of one.

"One at a time please," Mrs. Stone said, taking Sydo by the hand and leading him up to the portal. Like leaves in a gentle breeze, it rustled softly as he stepped through. Mrs. Stone repeated this process with everybody until at last it was Augum's turn. He stopped just before the radiant portal and turned to Mrs. Stone, the pair bathed in light.

"Thank you … Nana."

Her face crinkled into a smile. She patted him on the hand. "Come, great-grandson, there is much to do," and with that, great-grandmother and great-grandson stepped through together.

FOR FANS OF THE ARINTHIAN LINE

This book is an independent work, and because honest reviews are critical to the success of an independent book nowadays, I'd be grateful if you would consider leaving one on Amazon.com and/or Goodreads.

To receive an email when the next book in the series is released, subscribe to my mailing list at severbronny.com/contact

For the latest news on *The Arinthian Line* series, swing by www.severbronny.com.

My facebook page can be found at: facebook.com/authorseverbronny

If you are on Twitter, drop by and say hello @SeverBronny. I'm also on Goodreads, where you can find me by searching for Sever Bronny.

My other passion: **Tribal Machine** www.tribalmachine.com

Need to reach me for media purposes, found a typo, or just want to say hello? Email me direct at severbronny**[at symbol]**gmail.com

Lastly, thank you, dear reader, for giving this book a chance. And thank you to my family, friends, and especially my loving wife, whose support was essential in the completion of this book.

Hope to see you again in the sequel to *Arcane*, where the adventures of Augum, Bridget and Leera continue!

All my best to you and those you love,

Sever Bronny

ABOUT THE AUTHOR

Sever Bronny is a musician and author living in Victoria, British Columbia. He has released three albums with his industrial-rock music project Tribal Machine, including the full-length concept album *The Orwellian Night*. One of his songs can be heard in the feature-length film *The Gene Generation*. *Arcane* is his first book.

71688155R00217

Made in the USA
Middletown, DE
27 April 2018